THE BLACK
AND THE RED

ELLIOT PAUL

THE BLACK AND THE RED

Elliot Paul

COACHWHIP PUBLICATIONS

Greenville, Ohio

CoachwhipBooks.com

ISBN 1-61646-395-3
ISBN-13 978-1-61646-395-3

CONTENTS

1

The Rosy-Fingered Dawn Vies with Neon Signs

WHEN THE GODDESS AURORA, harbinger of light and easy transition to activity of day-faring beasts and the less fortunate of men, took her initial peep over ancient foothills and noticed Las Vegas, Nevada, one fair Friday in November, A.D. 1954, she was more pleased than indignant. True, the neons were blazing in most of the hues and colors God overlooked in His primitive spectrum. Gamblers, prospectors, tourists, Indians, hoods, wheels, business magnates, show people, hotel folk, beauties, bums and a sprinkling of citizens (and most of those asleep in ordinary beds) but enough to supply the weird ensemble with officials, clerks, services, articles and a civic background, were tooting and convoluting in and around de-luxe palaces of chance and proletarian hangouts for the lower brackets. So in those parts, Aurora, with her tinted clouds, her scented hush and stillness, her subtle crescendo of natural light, which elsewhere served to warn the people, fauna and flora of an impending day, for better or for worse, had quite another function. Dawn, in short, was but a warning signal, scarcely noticed by the losers and not much more by the winners, or those who were even, on dead center for the moment.

That a specially selected community of sports chose to defy or ignore her did not, as we have said, offend the luscious goddess. Aurora well remembered Tyre and Sidon, Ur of the Chaldees, Babylon and Nineveh, Paris, Vienna and London in the days of Charles II. To her it seemed fitting that the U.S.A., coming into world leadership productively, politically and destructively, should, on what had been lone Nevada prairie before Brigham Young (Aurora's recent favorite), perpetuate the long tradition of prodigal spending, colossal display, and flaunt respectability as contrived by those whose purposes it served. The goddess kept her morning splendor within the bounds of good taste, for sake of contrast, and brushed the teeming hot spots with her cool benediction as she continued westward, making dark into dimness and then brightness.

If, in passing, the fair deity of mom gave fond recognition to Homer Evans and Miriam Leonard, who were saluting her calmly through the second-story windows of the View Room at the Desert Sands, let be. Homer was one of the few discerning moderns who found a world center of release and riot ideal for detachment. So, when he had realized that Montparnasse depressed him and still left him accessible to interruption and distraction, he had taken a ranch apartment within a few minutes' driving distance of the glittering Las Vegas "strip" and adapted his routine of work and recreation to the frontier confusion of America's expanding City of the Plains.

He had been writing, over a period of years, between bizarre murder cases forced on him and his volunteer contributions to Western-world defense, a sequel to Brillat-Savarin's *Physiology of Taste*, feeling it his duty and privilege to bring that old master's wisdom and philosophy up-to-date, in terms of twentieth-century science and thought. In the autumn of 1954 he had held himself aloof from other projects, however attractive, in order to finish his pet monograph. Miriam, herself a girl of the Golden West, more lovely for having grown into a woman, was thrilled. Homer, she knew, was doing what he most wanted to accomplish just then. She was studying music, to which there is no end, and giving him company and protection.

Their day, which in Montparnasse had suited the Parisian pattern, had been rearranged, as to hours—not too rigidly, of course—subject to whimsical variation, but ideal for work and relaxation. The adventurous of the epoch, sound or vulgar, urbane or anti-social, flowed through Las Vegas or stayed for periods of time. All the informed ones knew about Homer, and he recognized them, and understood them as friends or enemies to the extent he deemed convenient. Others, the barbarians, wealthy or impoverished, inquired about Homer, as a man of obvious distinction, whenever he appeared in public places. Since Miriam was so often at his side, and had earned the reputation of being the only woman bodyguard as sure a shot as Deadeye Dick and as beautiful as any Powers model, she came in for concomitant admiration or envy.

Denizens of Las Vegas expected to see them on opening nights of top-grade entertainments, and nightly in one of the gambling and feasting places from midnight until dawn. Homer slept soundly from morn until about 11 A.M., at which time Miriam awakened him in his favorite fashion, by playing, mezzo-forte, finger exercises on the Steinway grand in the music room of his apartment. Those arabesques by Czerny, mildly and insistently repetitive, or varied almost imperceptibly, crept into Homer's somnolent consciousness and eased it into readiness for awareness without irritation or shock.

Between the hour of rising until late lunchtime, in midafternoon, Homer studied and wrote, of food and evolution, civilization and philosophy, of the complexity of taste and its unfolding. Whereas in the era of the American and French revolutions, the great Savarin had dealt with the only five senses then classified, Homer took into account at least nineteen. The eighteenth-century sage had paid tribute to individual experience. Evans included the fruits of fabulous research, sometimes joint efforts of many fertile minds, and financed beyond the dreams of Midas, for mass production, even standardization.

On that particular Friday in November, 1954, Homer, at his desk and deep in gastronomy, historical and current, or prophetic, heard a light tapping on his study door. He was astonished, for an instant, indignant. His working periods were guarded, if Miriam were resting or absent, most zealously by the fiery Basque widow, Mrs. Odilla O'Brien, who rented him his spacious and sumptuous ranch apartment and had such a talent for cooking that she had held positions as chef in several of the best kitchens on the Strip.

Her obstinacy and temper, by the way, had caused her to quit each and every hot spot and very high wages, in each instance entailing much property damage and bodily injury to patrons and personnel.

Fundamentally good-natured, Homer let his curiosity assuage his irritation. He went to the door, opened it softly, and in stepped a precocious delinquent of local Basque origin, the illegitimate grandson of the terrible-tempered Mrs. O'Brien, Homer's landlady and she-chef. The Kid, unabashed by his off-beat intrusion, made a swift gesture counseling silence, and extended a cablegram which he held in his nimble hand.

"Speak up, Kid, if you've anything to say. No one'll hear us. I take it you wouldn't crash in here, while I was present and at work, unless there was a special occasion," Homer said.

The Kid's inherent viciousness and cunning were salved by Homer's tone of man to man. He relaxed. Kid Unamuno, so nick-named in derision because of his anti-social philosophy and prac-tices, looked Homer up and down, then glanced at the typewritten and longhand notes and pages on the desk.

"How'd you come out last night at craps? You usually like to play roulette," the Kid observed. "And shouldn't I stick around till you've read this cable? Maybe you want to answer?"

"Sit down, Kid. And if you must know, I switched to the crap table at the Sands last night, or this morning, as you prefer, be-cause I saw your mother was losing. I stood just ahead of her."

"I get you. So she could follow your play. Gripes, why does she gamble? She's too dumb and soft for that kind of stuff," the Kid remarked. "Is she hard up? Maybe I ought to rustle up some dough?"

Homer spoke somewhat severely, for him. "Boy," he said, "your mother is an artist, and she is not dumb. As for you, in spite of your I.Q., which almost equals mine, you'll fall flat on your face if you can't appreciate the right kind of people, your mother first of all."

"O.K. O.K. All the mummsy stuff, kiss the flag, root for law and enterprise," Kid Unamuno said impatiently.

"Beat it," Homer said. "I'll answer this by phone."

"Better read it first," replied the Kid, not budging.

"You know what's in it, I suppose," Homer said.

"Natch," answered the Kid. "So I brought it myself, and Grandma don't know, the old witch. What she knows, and plenty she don't, she yack-yacks all over town."

"Your grandmother is a gifted woman who is loyal to my interests. Again you're being stupid. Get on to yourself," Homer said. Then he opened the envelope, examined it to ascertain whether it had been sealed more than once, and read:

CANNES, FRANCE
HOMER EVANS, LAS VEGAS, U.S.

CHER MAITRE. EVENTS DEVELOPING HERE PERPLEX AND DISTURB ME. AM HOPING YOU CAN COMMUNICATE DISCREETLY.
SABIN

The Kid, contrary to his usual brash attitude, was impressed and overawed by Homer's sudden concentration. He waited, quite respectfully, in his chair, eyes studying the famous criminologist, trying hard to fathom what the vague text meant and what was going on in Evans' mind.

Homer, when he was deep in thought, waiting for a new pattern to compose itself, seemed to give off such a chill that the wicked 'teenager felt so uncomfortable that he wished to escape, and think a bit on his own account. Clearly, it was no time to ask the Big Shot questions, or try to insinuate himself into potentially profitable or intriguing affairs. Sensing how uneasy the Kid had become, Homer made a slight gesture to retain him and prolong his silence. After perhaps a full minute, Homer seemed to reach some sort of decision and relax. He took up the phone, pressed a button and began talking into the transmitter, no evidence of anxiety in his voice.

"Miriam, could you come to the study for a moment?" he asked.

Some seconds later, Miriam, arriving from her adjacent suite, entered without knocking. She saw Kid Unamuno sitting receptively, pretended not to notice, and looked inquiringly at Homer.

"Has Mrs. O'Brien gone shopping?" Homer asked.

"No. I'm sure she's in the kitchen."

Homer looked at the Kid and said, "Apparently you slip in and out of these forbidden premises at will."

"Natch," was the delinquent's pert comment. "Nearly any premises, as a matter of fact. I keep in practice to make, as Shakespeare says, 'my exits and my entrances.'"

"We'll deal with that, and you, later," Homer said. But as again the Kid seemed about to leave, Evans motioned him to "hold everything."

Miriam could not help glancing at the cablegram, and Homer extended it to her, for her to read. "Sabin," she murmured, "the famous chef at the Club des Imprevoyants, the one who makes that fish stew that tops bouillabaisse, isn't he? As I remember, he's not given to strong statements. I believe he's in trouble, or expects to be."

"I think so, too," agreed Evans. "Communicating with him discreetly, as he suggests, is impractical over the telephone, less so by cable. Maybe we should risk a short rest from the physiology of taste. Would you mind looking up planes? Commercial flights would be best. I shouldn't attract too much attention, hiring private planes, until I know more of Sabin's situation."

This off-hand acceptance of a voyage overseas was too much for the bright youth of mischievous instincts (a charitable phrase). Kid Unamuno rose, his high forehead wrinkled, his gaze incredulous.

"You mean to say you're going, just like that? Just because some Frog's perplexed?" demanded the mild philosopher, Unamuno's perverse namesake.

"I have suspected," Homer said, after an instant's consideration, "that I needed a brief respite, that my work might be in danger of going stale. Maitre Sabin, however, who signed this message you read without unsealing, or got from a leaker in the Western Union office, or of your pals and social, if not intellectual, equals, is by no means a mere Frog. If there are ten gastronomers, flavor experts, wine tasters and chefs today living, who could have matched the great Escoffier, my dear old friend Sabin is among them, near the top. His Club des Imprevoyants—Maitre Sabin's restaurant in Cannes—has maintained such a standard of excellence in the course of forty years that gourmets make pilgrimages there from all corners of our round world. A situation that would perplex him would cause one of your local gang leaders, of national or international mobs, as you call them, to bury himself in a hideout for the duration of the 'disturbance.'"

"I'll buy that, if you say so, Mr. Evans," the Kid said. "Could you do me a favor in Cannes?"

"What would it be?" Homer asked. "A ticket for their Christmas lottery?"

"No. That stuffed shirt named Jordan—Mr. Howard Scott Jordan, no less—the bookish dope and chemist I worked for here, in that crazy laboratory some rich oil man's supposed to have financed, is supposed to be in Cannes right now, with the silly old angel and a couple of dames. Give Jordan my best, with reverse English, will you? He's an expert, a scholar, and a pain in the *derriére*."

Miriam, slightly irked by the Kid's effrontery, looked at him coldly. "Mr. Evans will be too busy to bother with errands like that," she told the prodigy. But Homer was noting the name of Howard Scott Jordan.

"Jordan's oil man—who set up that mysterious lab?" Homer inquired. "Know his name?"

"Who doesn't? Clifford Orman. The old duffer's blonde's called Madeleine, the brunette, Odette. Orman has promised them a hat-and-dress shop in Paris when he kicks the pail, so they say," Kid Unamuno replied, ignoring Miriam, who, in spite of her control, was visibly disgruntled.

"Clifford Orman. Thanks," Homer said. He turned and smiled into Miriam's eyes.

"We'll enjoy the brief holiday, won't we?" he said.

Forgetting others, young or old, Miriam responded with a surge of emotion, the more intense because it was so admirably controlled.

"Excuse me. I'll check on the planes. When shall we start?"

"As soon as there's a flight to New York—or farther along the way," Homer said.

"Gee!" exclaimed the Kid, shedding for the instant his incongruous self-sufficiency and poise.

"You'd better duck now, Kid," Homer told him. "I've got to break the news to your grandmother, my excellent Mrs. O'Brien."

"She'll flip her wig," was Kid Unamuno's comment as he vanished. No lesser verb will do.

Miriam, who had not got into action with comparable dispatch, faced Homer, puzzled

"You didn't even caution that brat to keep this contretemps under his hat," Miriam reminded him.

"No use. He doesn't wear one. He's got eyes like an Indian, in spite of this desert glare and his aversion to sleeping at night," remarked Homer, a bit too casually.

"Homer Evans!" she exclaimed, catching on. "You want folks to hear about the trip and whatever's led up to it. May I ask why?" Then she realized that she had got out of bounds. "Forgive me. I'll be patient," she added.

He kissed her forehead, swiftly, and showed her to the door. "Ask Mrs. O'Brien to step in, if it's convenient," he said in parting.

Promptly the widow made her entrance.

"Well?" she demanded.

"Miss Leonard and I are flying to France, later today," Homer said with assumed nonchalance.

"For good?" growled the widow, as her face turned mauve and her blood-pressure mounted.

"For a friendly purpose, not forever. Better invite your grandson to stay here with you, to help guard my papers and the house," he suggested.

He saw the widow struggle with a volcanic urge to wreck the room and pelt him with fragments. "Is that an order?" she finally asked through clenched teeth.

"I want him on my side," Evans said. "So, you see, we *are* coming back."

2

Aurora on the French Riviera

THE PLANE TRIP from Las Vegas to New York, thence to Paris and Nice, was enjoyable but otherwise uneventful. Miriam let herself drift back to the tranquility they had shared before World War II, since Homer's state of mind was curious rather than anxious and he was the ultimate in charm and consideration. They talked of everything uncontroversial, except Las Vegas, Maitre Sabin or high gastronomy, and what Homer said on the advantages of modern transportation, as opposed to old methods, had it been recorded, would have become classic.

"A man of this epoch must accept all the implications of modernity, or become an anachronism, with the dull majority," he said. "Perhaps, two hundred years hence, the slow voyage on a freighter will again be restful and salutary. But not now. Those who emerged safely, on foot, from old Pompeii, did not have to sprint. However, their exodus was not like a stroll or a constitutional. What lay behind them impelled them forward. So it is today."

Miriam mused for a while. "A prompt response to appeals from old and trusted friends remains timeless. No?" asked Miriam.

He touched her hand and smiled.

Homer had decided to fly no nearer Cannes than Nice, where he rented a handsome "drive yourself" Rolls Royce of a size, finish and vintage not too chic or shabby as to appear conspicuous. He accomplished the drive along the Azure Coast from Nice to Cannes, by late moonlight, Saturday evening, with Miriam at his side. Soon after midnight, they checked in, without the formality of registration, at the Hotel des Anglais, where the night desk clerk was sure the proprietor, M. Hector Julian, would be glad to accommodate Evans on any terms at all. Homer and Miriam were given adjoining suites, with a view of the Mediterranean and the shore.

"Sleep late, if you wish," Homer suggested, as they said good night. "I'll catch Sabin at the market, early in the morning while shopping for provisions is most brisk."

"You prefer to meet him, unannounced?" she asked.

"Let it seem, to outsiders, by chance," was Homer's reply.

The market place in Cannes is not definitive and vast, like Les Halles in Paris. It is less compact than the Faneuil Hall district of Boston; nor is it a palace of display like the Jefferson Market in downtown New York. In the resort cities of the Riviera, peasants from the hills and native dwellers along the Mediterranean shore, inured to toil and bargaining since the days of the Phoenicians, exchange and sell sparse farm produce, imperfect sub-tropical fruits, and the rich gleaming yield of the sea which cradled our Western civilization.

Just at sun-up, when the sea, "wine-dark" at evening, was at dawn streaked with gold and amethyst, Homer started walking across the fragrant beach. As he approached the market, he was pleased to see that the buyers, vendors and roustabouts were busy and in force. He recognized the back view of a heavy-set man, Maitre Jean-Pierre Sabin, who, in the act of making his purchases for the day, was showing decision and zest. Other hotel and restaurant buyers, proprietors, chefs and managers were grouped around a slanting counter, awaiting their turn. From the edge of this group, Homer saw that M. Sabin was selecting a number of *rougets*—spiny fish with pale pink vermilion coloring, soft cream-tinted bellies, and melancholy eyes of faded blue. Without disturbing anyone, Homer advanced to Sabin's shoulder and said, in an ordinary tone:

"If you please, Monsieur Sabin, order two extra *rougets* for Miss Leonard and me. We came in late last night, and shall be with you for lunch."

Sabin, whose nature was by no means phlegmatic, faced about, alight with relief and pleasure. His colleagues and competitors joined him in overwhelming Homer with hearty salutations. Among those assembled were Monsieur La Brun, who managed the neat gambling Casino; Monsieur Gauthier, of the Hotel de France; and, of course, Monsieur Julian, of the Hotel des Anglais where Homer, unknown to the proprietor, had slept. A dozen others were well-known gastronomers, experts, gourmets and *bon vivants*.

It did not take long for Sabin to complete his purchases and to give instructions to his assistants as to how to transport and stow them at the Club des Imprevoyants.

"I, myself, shall enjoy a glass of wine with my friend, Monsieur Evans, on the *terrasse* of the Café des Mariniers. Do not disturb me, unless I am urgently needed," Sabin said. From the fish stall to the café was a short walk across the busy square, where they attracted no unusual attention beyond the pleasurable surprise the denizens of that quarter expressed on seeing that Homer was again among them. In the case of the three police officers who joined heartily in the greeting, the joy was tinged with apprehension, since every time Evans had appeared in their midst in recent years, some crime that made their life hideous had come to light.

"Does your presence mean something sinister—that is, extra duty, nerve strain, possible shock?" asked Ballangier, the senior of a pair of bicycle *flics*. The anxious officer managed to smile, but he was apprehensive. "My wife is expecting, again," he added, apologetically.

"I'm only here for a very brief rest, my parole," Evans assured him, and Sabin nodded, though with less conviction. As soon as the officers were out of earshot, the great chef looked up at Homer uneasily.

"You are not, in fact, on the track of something catastrophic—aside from my baffling but uncriminal problem?" Sabin asked.

The smile and sigh of relaxation Homer produced was comforting indeed. "Perish the thought," Evans said.

So they sat at Sabin's favorite table in his favorite café, and were attended by a waiter they both knew and trusted—in his professional capacity. The chef ordered a bottle of Chateau d'Issan, and when the soothing effect of the fine claret was perceptible in its introductory stages, Homer looked at Sabin expectantly and the latter began.

"I am desolate at having put you to such expense and trouble. What I expected was that you would write or phone me. Instead— here you are! And Miss Leonard!"

"Nothing could please us more or fit more nicely into our plans," said Homer graciously.

"You're kind to say so. Still, I have a guilty feeling."

"That your situation, whatever it is, may not prove grave enough?"

"Not that, God forbid," Sabin said, crossing himself.

"I'm still supplementing the work of Savarin," said Homer. "When my appetite began to fail me, I knew it was time for a break."

"Past time," agreed the chef, nodding his head. "But what do you eat in that wild lawless Western outpost?"

That brought a chuckle from Homer. "First, outline what perplexes you. Then I'll talk about Las Vegas," he said.

"There's a connection," Sabin said, to Homer's mild astonishment. "However, I must begin at the start."

"By all means," Evans said. As Sabin was making another, surer gambit, the waiter brought another bottle of the claret, opened it and poured.

"Feel free to confide in me," Homer urged the hesitant chef, who sighed and summoned his courage.

"I'll withhold nothing, however discreditable to me," Sabin promised, then went on: "You're aware, good friend, that in the cool seasons I place upon my menu a dessert described as 'house rum cake,' or *gâteau au Rhum, maison.*"

"Ah, the delicate cake, incomparable icing and fine liqueur from Martinique," mused Evans.

Pained, Sabin held up his palm. "Wait! Hear the worst! I had a shocking failure," said the chef, lowering his eyes.

It was Homer's turn to interrupt. "Nothing shameful about that. It was James Joyce who wisely wrote 'An artist makes no mistakes. His errors are the portals of discovery.'"

"Discovery is frequently disaster, in a roundabout way. Hear me out." Sabin's forehead was damp with sweat, despite the morning chill. "A fortnight ago, while I was preparing the icing for some rum cake, my apprentice, Monsieur Luttenschlager, who observes my work closely, spoke up, modestly. 'Maitre,' Luttenschlager said, 'I beg your pardon . . .' At that instant I realized that I had dusted, unintentionally, a little powdered pipsissewa into the frosting mix, instead of the small amount of tragacanth I customarily had used for proper consistency."

"Pipsissewa," Homer repeated. "That's not harmful. It's subtly aromatic. An evergreen *parfum*."

"Needless to say, I blushed, but I let the icing congeal, and tasted it," Sabin continued.

"That's what I would have done. And how was it?" asked Homer.

Sabin touched his fingers to his lips and blew an imaginary kiss. "Excellent! Superb!" he admitted. "My co-workers were kind enough to state, unanimously, that it was equal to if not a shade better than my traditional formula."

In the lull which followed, Homer was further at a loss to grasp why he had been drawn from overseas to protect or advise his distinguished friend. Somehow this bewilderment was conveyed without words. Sabin said, and now with a tinge of alarm unmistakable:

"The worst lies ahead. The first evening the revised house rum cake was served at dinner, we had a party of four—a certain American called Clifford Orman, who I understand is fabulously rich, from real estate and oil; his two mistresses, Madeleine and Odette, both Parisiennes about town; and a seemingly very proper young man, for an American restrained and precise in his manner, who signed my guest book as 'Howard Scott Jordan, of Cambridge, Mass.'"

At the name "Howard Scott Jordan," Homer grinned and thought of Kid Unamuno back in Las Vegas, remembering the Basque prodigy had said Jordan was a stuffed shirt, chemist and scholar who gave him "a pain in the *derrière*." However, Evans kept the ball rolling. "I take it this balanced quartette ordered rum cake for dessert," he ventured.

"The two men did," answered Sabin. "Women of that profession seldom indulge in desserts. Orman, the 'tycoon,' as you call him, although seventy or more, eats heartily of everything he shouldn't. He wolfed his rum cake and was wiping his face with a napkin before his correct young companion from Massachusetts had done more than taste the frosting. This amazing young savant— for that's what I understand Jordan is—sought me out . . ."

"You don't mean to say," interrupted Evans, now thoroughly intrigued, "that the stiff New England young man identified the flavor of your icing as pipsissewa?"

"Exactly! I was dumbfounded, as well as flattered and pleased. You are the only living American of whom I would have expected as much," Sabin replied.

"Was Jordan's taste of such keenness throughout?"

"Another mystery," exclaimed Sabin. "The answer is 'No.' Young Mr. Jordan knew nothing of wines, or how a meal should be composed."

"Mmmm. A chemist. No more," murmured Homer. But he still did not see why Sabin should be "disturbed" as well as "perplexed." The cablegram had read "Events developing here perplex and disturb me." Homer held his peace, and waited once again.

The chef was not long in getting under way.

"Other items were incongruous, concerning your compatriot, young Mr. Jordan. Outstandingly, his relationship with the aged millionaire, Orman, and the chic young beauties, Madeleine and Odette. Orman, and others like him—although most rich Americans display only one mistress at a time—have been coming to my restaurant over a period of many, many years. None of these fatuous and deteriorated old parties invite presentable young men to accompany their inflammable mistresses on train rides, auto tours, or in public for high-grade meals."

"Did Jordan appear to be attracted to one or both of Orman's girls?" Homer asked, and as he anticipated, he got a negative answer.

"I have observed and heard that Mr. Orman is fiendishly possessive and pathologically jealous. In Jordan's case he seems to have made an exception, and from my point of view, he might be right—that is, safe enough, I mean. Not that young Jordan is effeminate. On the contrary, he acts as if he were neutral. His life is of the interior—in the mind. However, his attitude posed a kind of challenge to the restless young women, who were almost blatant in their treatment of him. The wonder is that Multimillionaire Orman did not notice, and explode or take vengeance."

Homer shrugged. "Perhaps the old fox was pretending, in order to trap the girls, or Jordan, or all three, for some devious purpose of his own," he suggested. He added, though: "Surely this was not what was *disturbing* to you, *cher Maitre!*"

"Laboriously we are getting toward the crux of the situation," Sabin said. "You may recall that in 1920, for the first time, I won the international wine tasters' contest at the Ritz in Paris, with a score of 17 out of a possible 18 vintages. Since then I have never placed lower than third, and have been first many times. I seldom boast of this, and my distinguished customers take my palate for granted. Nevertheless, the day following the dinner at which young Mr. Jordan spotted the pipsissewa, I was asked, at lunch time, to sit awhile with the Oil Magnate Orman, and a type he had brought with him, an Irish American, one Monsieur Sharkey. . . ."

"Not Luke Sharkey, an agent of the Rosencrans detective outfit?" asked Evans incredulously.

"I think his given name was Luke. He handed me a calling card which, being distraught, I at once mislaid or destroyed," Sabin continued. "His proposition was so absurd that it addled my mind."

"What kind of proposition could a rich oil man and a notorious low-grade private eye, or Continental Op, such as Orman and Sharkey, offer a gastronomer of your distinction?" demanded Homer, beginning to see that there actually was smoke, if not fire, in the situation.

"They were eager, if not desperately anxious, for me to leave my restaurant in charge of my second, and go with them to Las Vegas," Sabin said, now shuddering as well as perspiring.

"You refused?" Homer asked, to observe the reaction.

"Categorically," replied Sabin, so loudly and harshly that other occupants of the Mariniers' *terrasse* were startled into spilling

wine, exclaiming involuntarily, swallowing the wrong way, and
aiming their eyes and faces toward Homer's and Sabin's table as if
they were marionettes on strings.

One of the early-morning drinkers seated near by, within earshot, was Monsieur La Brun of the gambling Casino, where the food
supplied free, or at merely token prices, was second only to Sabin's
at the latter's famous Club, where prices were commensurate with
the quality of fare. Homer realized there had been considerable
jealousy on La Brun's part, though the manager of the Casino had
preserved the amenities and shown Sabin much respect. When, at
the moment Sabin lost control of his voice, because of his emo-
tions, and cried "Categorically," Homer's sharp ears heard La Brun
say to a companion: "Two thousand a week. What madman would
not work, even on Devil's Island, for that?"

The Riviera grapevine, evidently, had been at work and someone in Sabin's own establishment must have been deplorably indiscreet.

3
Perplexing and Disturbing

IN ORDER TO GIVE HIS FRIEND, Sabin, a chance to pull himself together, Homer suggested a breakfast snack of Pharamond's tripe, which was served over a charcoal heater and meant a change of wine, from the claret of Chateau d'Issan to a sound Macon from the lower edge of the Burgundy district. Tactfully Homer reopened the subject which had worn his old friend's nerves to the raw.

"What precisely did Messrs. Orman and Sharkey suggest that you might do for them in Las Vegas? Act as chef of Orman's estate?" Evans asked.

"First they gave me to understand, and seemingly with pride or satisfaction, that in Las Vegas, all ordinary laws, either human or divine, have been suspended by common consent and with the connivance of the State and local administrations. Can that be?" Sabin began.

"To a certain extent," admitted Homer.

Sabin's nervous excitement was rising again. "Has no one in that region a sense of proportion?" the chef demanded. "Do you, who now live there, mean to tell me that instead of one modest well-policed and neatly appointed Casino as we have, there are dozens, with riotous entertainment all night and electric lights enough to illumine all of Western Europe, from here to Lapland in the north?"

"More remarkable than that, the top-flight hot spots are owned and operated, *sub rosa* more or less, by rival groups of notorious gangsters, including Murder, Incorporated, the Hudson Dusters,

23

offshoots of the old Capone mob, the Milwaukee Mooncalves, the Mafia or Syndicate . . ."

"God in Heaven! So they mow one another down with machine guns, dirks, bolos and bazookas daily, as in Chicago's prohibition days?"

Sabin's hands had begun to tremble and his teeth to rattle. Homer made haste to reassure him.

"On the contrary, the jackals lie down with the reptiles. The big wheels have declared and kept a truce. The master crooks have an understanding with the Nevada government that, in case deeds of mayhem or murder must, of necessity, be committed, the victims will be quietly transported and the acts will be committed beyond the State line, either in California, where bitter jealousy of Nevada's revenue from vice exists and increases; in nearby Arizona which prides itself on health resorts; or in Mexico, just over the border, where a crime, more or less, if it involves only Gringos, is ignored. The gang peace prevailing now in Nevada is more ominous and, in its way, spectacular to the *cognoscenti* than any of the Prohibition antics which seemed to Europeans so preposterous."

"You frighten me more than those two conspirators did," Sabin exclaimed. "But let us set aside the criminal factors, the blare and fanfare, the excesses that continue around the clock. May we consider the Orman estate?"

"By all means," Homer agreed encouragingly.

"What could be the aspect of such an estate, on a desert, bleak, scorched and flat, replete with horned toads, serpents, thorny cactus, tortured trees of Joshua, Yogi polecats who dance on their heads, lizards, nits, gnats and lice?"

"The Orman house is well designed and spacious, modern with all the old standard conveniences, I understand, and the grounds immediately surrounding the desert chateau are quite as luxurious as the hanging gardens of Babylon must have been. Undoubtedly, on the six or seven hundred acres outlying—that would be from three to three-and-a-half hundred hectares . . ."

"God have mercy! Four times the size of Fontainebleau!" interjected Sabin, frankly trembling.

"On this outer rim of waste land you will find the fauna and flora you mentioned, along with many other species less acceptable. But the desert creatures of the day and night, excepting now and then the coyote or the bob cat, seldom permit themselves to be spied or even heard. Like gangsters, they devour mostly one another," said Homer.

"Nature is malodorous," exclaimed Sabin, shrinking further into himself and away from thoughts of Nevada. "Here in France we've had time and ingenuity to subdue it, somewhat. Yet even in the heart of civilization, it is not to be trusted. I renounce it."

Homer paused again for his old friend to cool down. When the moment seemed propitious—the tripe in Caen style was proving delicious, as always—Evans slipped in a key question.

"Did either Monsieur Orman or his tricky Continental Rosencrans Op hint that the oil tycoon might be planning to build in Las Vegas another de-luxe hotel and casino, to compete with or overshadow those already in operation, and protected by the rarest crew of pirates and freebooters gangland has produced?"

When Sabin shook his head "No," Homer murmured, "I thought not." But he had another question. "Did Orman or his stooge mention a certain research laboratory the rich man had established, with young Mr. Jordan as its head?"

"Research? In what field?" asked Sabin, by his manner making it plain he had heard of no such laboratory as the one in question. The great chef's face clouded with quick anger. "If those fools think I would lend myself to debasing the art of cooking with vulgar chemicals, to pervert the public's taste in bulk . . ."

"Orman, evidently, would stop at nothing," Homer said. "Otherwise he would not consort with a licensed desperado like Luke Sharkey, or any other Rosencrans man. Still . . ." Here Evans paused wistfully, and added: "Having gone this far into this bewildering potpourri, I'd like mightily to know what Orman is up to."

Coming half out of his chair in horror, Sabin's eyes protruded, his jaw dropped and he gasped: "You wouldn't suggest that I accept?"

The reply, whatever it would have been, was cut off by the sound of a resounding pistol shot, which brought most other *terrasse*

sitters out of their chairs, caused vendors in the market stalls to
drop behind counters or sacks, buyers to face about, and gesticu-
late or cross themselves. Sabin, on the contrary, already half erect,
sank back and moaned dismally:

"It begins "

Meanwhile Homer walked deliberately toward the center of the
scene of the excitement. Two policemen, leaving their bicycles leaning against each other, preceded him, shouldering a kind of interference which enabled him to make fair time. The cops were dumbfounded, and Homer, himself, was somewhat astonished to see
Miriam, fresh as the morning and *chic* as Paris models themselves.
She was calmly indicating to another Cannes policeman, whom
Homer dimly remembered as Ballangier, and as many onlookers
as could get within earshot, a neat bullet hole in a stout vertical
timber supporting a green vegetable booth whose counter was laden
with trim pyramids of Brussels sprouts.

Officer Ballangier, the senior of the policemen then present,
took over, as best he could, while Evans watched with an encour-
aging smile.

"Mademoiselle America," the officer said reproachfully.
"Surely, even in your illogical country, well-dressed and cultured
young women do not discharge .45 automatics in a crowded market place."

"Sorry, sir," Miriam answered, with a disarming glance that
made her inquisitor somewhat dizzy. "The facts are these." Of
course, she glanced at Homer to receive his unspoken message to
tell all she thought best. "I was asleep in the secretarial bedroom
adjacent to Mr. Evans' suite in the Hotel des Anglais, we having
arrived there by auto from Nice about one o'clock this morning.
Mr. Evans had gone for a stroll along the beach, doubtless to put
his thoughts, which are frequently profound, in apple-pie order,"
she continued.

"How did you know where he had gone, when and why?" asked
Ballangier.

"I sleep well but very lightly," she explained.

"With a .45 automatic under one's pillow, one slumbers fitfully, if at all," Ballangier said. "Unless one is inured."

"I had to be heeled, day and night, as a girl in pinafores and braids. My father taught me shooting and self-defense on his Montana ranch," Miriam explained.

"And you came here, and fired into the timber support of a Brussels-sprouts booth, to attract your employer's attention?" asked Ballangier.

"Not exactly," Miriam said. "About an hour ago I became aware that an intruder had found his way into Mr. Evans' reception room and was rifling Mr. Evans' papers and correspondence. The man was a stranger to me."

"Why, may I ask, did you not plug or capture this intruder then and there?" asked one of the bicycle cops who no longer could seem to remain silent.

"I thought it best not to frighten him away, or disable him, or create a scandal in the Hotel des Anglais, *before* I could ascertain what the man was after," Miriam said, and Homer could not repress a proud approving smile, the warmth of which caused Miriam to blush becomingly.

"Can you tell us what the intruder wanted?" asked Ballangier.

"With pleasure," Miriam said. "He found and pocketed a cablegram originating in Cannes and received by Mr. Evans in Las Vegas."

By that time Sabin had edged his way to Homer's side, so Evans, receiving the chef's permission, interrupted the questioning to repeat the text of the stolen message, to Ballangier and the others assembled. As he repeated the words, their import seemed harmless enough:

CANNES, FRANCE
TO HOMER EVANS, LAS VEGAS, U.S.

CHER MAITRE. EVENTS DEVELOPING HERE
PERPLEX AND DISTURB ME. AM HOPING YOU
CAN COMMUNICATE DISCREETLY.

SABIN

"Is it not significant that Mr. X, the intruder, knew you had received a cablegram from Monsieur Sabin?" Ballangier asked Homer, then turned also to Miriam, to include her in the query.

"It was a French Government cablegram. In the P.T.T. (post, telephone and telegraph) service, all offices, large and small leak information as your fishermen's nets let water pass through," Homer said.

The officer shrugged assent. "All who work for the public in our Fourth Republic are wretchedly underpaid," Ballangier remarked. "But what man would be fool enough to break into a first-class hotel and your suite, to pick up only a trivial cable message between old friends across the sea, most probably knowing that in the next room was a young woman with a .45. Miss Leonard is a dead shot, according to her reputation, is she not?"

Before Homer could speak or anyone ask another question, Miriam whipped out her automatic, causing a near panic in the surrounding crowd.

"I shall ring the bell on the handlebars of that official bicycle on the right, without damaging the apparatus. The bullet you'll find imbedded in the post against which the bicycle leans," she said, and before the dumbfounded officer or citizen could object, she fired her gun, and the bicycle bell sent forth a clear tone, followed by tingling vibrations.

The crowd, keyed up to concert pitch, let forth a spontaneous ovation, while the officers scowled, moved over to examine the bicycle, its bell, and the bullet hole in the post. Before the flurry of awe and excitement died down, an official car with siren drove into the *place*, the Commissaire of Police of Cannes stepped out, was briefed by Homer, whom he knew of old, and Ballangier, and took over the investigation.

"Can you describe the cable-message thief, Mademoiselle? And cease to shoot on impulse, in this jurisdiction at least!" Thus the Commissaire, Monsieur Achilles Gromaire, opened his part in the puzzling, seemingly trivial, affair.

Again Homer's face was expressive of pride as Miriam set forth her description succinctly.

"The burglar of communications was conventionally dressed in blue serge," she began.

Commissaire Gromaire grunted with exasperation.

"Blue serge! The uniform of malefactors the world over. If I had my way, mesdames and messieurs, blue-serge suits with black soft felt hats, modest ties and plain well-polished shoes would be issued only by licensed respectable parties with reputations and records unstained. But go on, Mademoiselle. Other particulars may be less banal."

"Mr. X's eyes were blue-gray, cold and shrewd. His nose was long and pointed. His lips were thin and tight. He had what Shakespeare describes as 'a lean and hungry look,' the hunger for gain, not nourishment. He was 5 feet 10 inches tall, must have weighed about 165 pounds, avoirdupois. His technique of entry and search indicated he was cunning, had much practice. He may even be intelligent, in an anti-social way."

"Mademoiselle," the Commissaire said, gallantly. "Any time you wish to abandon Mr. Homer Evans and would like to teach description in our advanced classes of the Surèté, may I recommend you. Also you speak perfect French."

"Likewise Spanish, Italian, German, and American jive or vout," Homer added, for effect.

"I let Mr. X make his getaway, dressed hastily, in time to follow the man. He skirted the deserted beach, turned into this market place, and before he could lose himself in the milling throng and vanish, unmarked, I was forced to shoot, when he was in line with the Brussels-sprouts booth post, where I could nick him without endangering others. I merely grazed his elbow, what we call the 'funny bone,' believing that would not stop him, but would label him for future reference and identification." She raised her violet-blue eyes to the agate-brown ones of Gromaire and added demurely: "Did I do wrong?"

Avoiding that difficult question, the Commissaire grunted and hawed, then asked to see her passport, as a matter of form.

"The devil," he said. "Your American authorities—whoever made out this document so many hundreds of millions of sufferers would give their all to possess—have you listed, on the line with 'Profession,' as a bodyguard. Mr. Evans', of course. Commend me to Americans, when one wishes fundamentals topsy-turvy, to be read up from the bottom and from right to left. I have been in the service of my country under the Third Republic, DeGaulle, and our Fourth Republic, more years than I care to admit. You, Mademoiselle, are the first professional female bodyguard I have encountered. All my compliments and good wishes, notwithstanding."

The Commissaire turned to Homer, who was relishing the contretemps. "As for you, distinguished guest of Cannes. I must meet the morning train on which are scheduled to descend at our depot as troublesome a batch of transients as could be assembled in all Christendom. After I have noted and tabbed them, and arranged for protection of the ones important, therefore rich, and for protection against those who breed disorder and carouse, will you be kind enough to confer with me, and advise me how to apprehend our Mr. X, who stole your cable and gave Mademoiselle such stimulating practice, practically all of which was illegal, by the way?"

"Would you mind if Miss Leonard, Maitre Sabin and I go also to the depot to meet the morning Blue Train and have a look at the passengers you deplore?" Homer asked.

"On the contrary," assented the Commissaire. "Thank God most of the characters in question are quitting Cannes this evening, on the Home liner, *America* (promoted by Swedes, manned by Italians, and flying the flag of Panama) bound for Genoa, Naples, Palermo, possibly Algiers and Barcelona, then surely Gibraltar, Lisbon, Halifax, Boston and New York."

"I ought to go right back to my restaurant," Sabin objected. "Lately I find myself increasingly nervous even when I think of absenting myself during rush hours of work or those relatively tranquil."

Homer looked at his old friend meaningfully. "This particular morning, I have a strong presentiment you'll have a special interest in certain of the descending passengers," he said.

The chef's knees began to knock and he clutched at Homer's sleeve. "Call me a coward, an hysteric, if you must. I feel as if I had been injected with a virus, the effects of which, although for some days suspended, when they become active will mean disintegration or worse."

Miriam looked reproachfully to Homer. "Is it possible you've been holding out on me, that this case is not inconsequential, but momentous?" she asked, not demandingly, in fact, almost hopefully.

The Commissaire pressed his hands to both sides of his forehead and groaned. He turned to Homer with eloquent appeal in his eyes and his manner.

"Cannot you contrive, this one time, to prevent the outbreak of casualties or fatalities until the parties in question are safely out of my jurisdiction?" he pleaded. "I'm brutally short-handed and under-budgeted, as you well may understand, being such a stalwart old friend of France."

"I hope no one need be maimed or killed here," Evans assured him. "However, we must get track of Mr. X to make sure."

As many of the leading citizens of Cannes as can leave their midmorning activities for a social half hour gather on the platforms of the depot at Cannes to watch the famous Blue Train glide in. So whatever passengers get off at Cannes, seldom more than a dozen these days, pass a sort of informal inspection, civil as well as official, before they disperse to their respective lodgings. The first-class hotels, including the Hotel des Anglais, the Hotel de France, the Hotel du Casino, etc., send buses that formerly were elegant and today have more dignity than polish.

At Homer's request, Commissaire Gromaire arranged with the station master for him and Miriam to enter a private office commanding a fine view of the platform and parking space opposite the track where the prize train would stop, and Gromaire, also at Homer's suggestion, assigned a special plain-clothes man to scout the crowd of spectators for a glimpse of Mr. X, with the sore elbow and furtive manner.

The arrival of the train caused many a heart to skip a few beats, and Miriam responded quite breathlessly, remembering occasions in the days when France was herself and she and Homer had made use of the best accommodations Europe had to offer voyagers. However, her principal attention was fixed on Homer. She knew he expected some individual or group involved in whatever had "perplexed" and "disturbed" Maitre Sabin. Up to that time, she had not been enlightened as to the nature of the case, or problem. That trouble was ahead, for Sabin, for them, or, more likely, for an array of antagonists she, as yet, knew little or nothing about, she felt in her bones.

"If you'll watch the forward cars, I'll concentrate on the rear half of the train," Homer said, and thus it was that she saw, and could not repress a gasp of pleased astonishment, Homer's only close confidant and brilliant protégé as a detective, a young Irish-American named Finke McGuire, whom she, and Homer also, she believed, had assumed was in or near his office on the Hollywood Strip, back home. The gentle and helpful discipline Homer had instilled in her kept her from commenting or distracting Homer, whose gaze was fixed on the cars and platform farther back. Instead, she scrutinized the gaunt, middle-aged man with the harassed, nevertheless somewhat distinguished air, who evidently was traveling with Finke. Most likely a client, she said to herself. The closer Finke and his train companion approached the window from which Miriam was watching, the stronger her conviction grew that she had seen this man before. In a flash, the recollection came to her. Of course. At Gyro's, not two blocks from Finke's office on the Hollywood Strip. The man was the owner-manager, and, she remembered, also president of the organization which had been formed by the heads of the most exclusive Hollywood night spots, after Las Vegas had begun, by offering dazzling entertainment by the world's biggest names and talents for prices with which Hollywood, in its post-TV decline, could not hope to compete. A brisk effort brought the man's name to the surface of her active young mind. He was Talbot Forran, who, before he went into show business, through the skylight entrance, as it were, had made a sizable fortune, two or three million, at least.

Finke McGuire, seemingly unaware that curious eyes were fixed upon him, did not steer his important companion to any of the hotel buses. Instead they took a taxi, entered, waited for the driver and their porter to dispose of their luggage in the rear compartment, and rolled or bumped away. The Cannes taxis, as well as the parking lots and roads, had had no repairs or improvements since 1939. The best Miriam could do was to note the taxi number. Then, having spotted no one else of promise in her front section of the train, she glanced up at Homer and looked farther back, where he had focused his gaze. Again she gasped. In a party of six, their old friends and bottle companions from Montparnasse, Hjalmar Jansen, the roistering Norwegian painter, and Tom Jackson, star reporter of the New York *Herald* in Paris, were trailing along, both somewhat high. A portly impressive older man—he could have been any age over a well-preserved sixty—had on his arm a willowy, extremely attractive blonde, slightly on the showy side. Another young man, with rimless glasses and an expression suggesting he had just bitten into an unripe persimmon was escorting, somewhat frigidly, a young Parisienne brunette quite as striking as the blonde.

"Now isn't this convenient?" Homer said to Miriam. "The rich old party is Clifford Orman, of New York, Texas and Las Vegas; the two prize beauties are Madeleine, the blonde, and Odette, the brunette, respectively, his current mistresses. The young New Englander who has been entrusted for the moment with Odette must be Howard Scott Jordan, the chap Kid Unamuno sent his worst regards . . . Remember?"

Miriam nodded. "But what are Hjalmar Jansen and Tom Jackson doing in that kind of set-up? They must be with the party, since the baggage of all seven stands on the platform more or less together."

The porters, in fact, were just tackling the Orman contingents' luggage and the first baggage truck load was headed for the commodious station wagon of the Hotel des Anglais.

"Ah," said Homer, who was searching for a glimpse of Sabin in the crowd. Before the train had come in, Evans had urged Sabin to stand in the midst of the spectators, his townsfolk, so the passengers who descended might be observed from as many angles as possible. The Commissaire, Gromaire, of course, had his own point

of vantage, and just at that moment was taking from the train conductor a revised list containing the names of all the passengers,
and was hastily checking off those who had just got off in Cannes.
With the list, the Commissaire made haste to join Evans and
Miriam in the station master's private office.

"I know something about the lecherous old multi, Clifford
Orman, and his pair of young women. Also, the last time he was
with us, this Orman had in tow the spectacled young prude, Mr.
Howard Scott Jordan, who made no attempt to poach on the old
man's preserves. Well I recall that on other occasions—in the
course of the Druid and the Ali Baba Vases incident—you, Mr.
Evans, were assisted ably by your disciple, Mr. Finke McGuire. I
remember with more misgivings that the painter, Hjalmar Jansen,
the most preposterous drinker I ever have seen, and the No. 2 de-
stroyer of everything alcoholic, the American journalist, Mr. Tom
Jackson, have been in Cannes in your company, which was the only
thing that saved them both from deportation or worse. But first
tell me who is this Mr. Talbot Forran?"

"Mr. Forran is a Hollywood showman, one of the most prominent impresarios, head of Gyro's," Homer said.

The Commissaire looked pained. "Another millionaire, no doubt."

"I think he still has a million, at least," Homer said.

The Commissaire's eyes narrowed reproachfully. "Could you not
have told me you expected your assistant, Mr. Finke? Is it not fair
that you should give me what facts you have, in return for any I
may uncover? I have no idea what the nature of this case may turn
out to be. I have awful premonitions, nonetheless, and, with the
limited forces and means at my, disposal, am fairly sure, without
your candid help, to be disgraced."

"You can still rely on my word," Homer said sympathetically.
"When I saw Finke descend, out of the corner of my eye, since I
was concentrating mostly on Orman and Jordan, I could not have
been more astonished. I had believed he was in Hollywood, where
his practice is flourishing in spite of the motion-picture slump and
the dearth of spenders on the Strip."

"He did not greet you nor you him?" Gromaire asked, still not reassured.

"He does not suspect I am here. Until I learn more about his client, their problems and relationship, I must proceed with tact and caution," Evans said. "I don't mind admitting that in ordinary circumstances Finke would have let me know he was going abroad, even if he was not at liberty to say why or for whom or with whom. This I must make clear to you. The rivalry between impresarios on the Hollywood Strip and those at Las Vegas, mostly gangster controlled, has mounted to a dangerous level. Should Mr. Talbot Forran suspect that Clifford Orman plans to establish another palatial hotel and casino, to compete with the mobsters in Nevada and the comparatively respectable owners of night spots on the Hollywood Strip, fur would fly."

"As long as it flies outside my jurisdiction, I shall be content. But no. Such luck as that is not for me, or France," groaned the Commissaire. "I had counted on guarding Mr. Orman, when and if he returned. Now I must also protect this Forran."

"We haven't spotted Mr. X as yet," Miriam reminded the harassed Chief.

"Surely 'X' will feel obliged to contact Orman," Homer said. "I know from Maitre Sabin that the two have been in cahoots. You noticed, Gromaire, that Orman was expecting to be met by someone who failed to show up on the platform just now."

"The old chump was out of sorts, that's all I know," agreed the Commissaire. "I attributed Orman's irritability and resentment to the presence of the two famous drunks, your chums from Montparnasse, the painter and the journalist. Had I two mistresses—God forbid I should acquire even one—I would keep them as far from Jansen and Jackson as I could."

The Commissaire, without ceremony, sprinted toward the Blue Train which was just about to proceed toward Nice, braced the conductor, who seemed reluctant, and returned with six ticket stubs in his hand. His face was longer and his voice more apprehensive.

"Worse than I thought. The ticket stubs, all six, run in consecutive serial numbers. All were handed the conductor by Orman, contained in a single envelope," said Gromaire.

A rueful smile lit Homer's face an instant. "You're no more surprised than I am. The old codger must have paid for the tickets, and with some malice aforethought brought my bottle companions along. Could it be that he is trying to tempt one or both of his two sprightly girls, then denounce and abandon one or both?"

"May I hazard a guess?" asked Miriam.

"By all means," Homer said, and simultaneously the Commissaire moaned, "Most certainly, Mademoiselle."

She took a deep breath and proceeded. "Perhaps Madeleine and Odette have more of a hold on Mr. Orman than others suspect, and it is possible they work together, feeling more secure that way. Still, each one is sure to have whims, and Orman may be the sort of man to indulge them, should he see the possibility that trouble may ensue, for them; and leave them more at his mercy. Rich old men are like that."

"Amen," Homer said, and the Commissaire nodded.

"Maybe Hjalmar was introduced or recommended by someone in Paris whom Mr. Orman can use. He's a remarkable portrait painter, don't forget. Now if an American tycoon like Orman appears in Paris, the *Herald* will be bound to assign a man to cover him, and find out the purpose of his visit. Who else but Tom Jackson could qualify for that assignment?" she asked.

"I hope they'll feel free to tell us the whys and wherefores," Homer said. "We'd better get back to our hotel, which appears also to be theirs. I'll try to pump Hjalmar and Tom, and locate Finke before lunch."

"Please phone or call on me hourly," the Commissaire urged. "And if I or my men learn anything significant, I'll let you know."

As the Commissaire started to go, Homer detained him.

"You can do me a favor, if you will. I'd like to see the reservation and passenger lists for the Home liner, *America*, which touches and leaves Cannes this evening. Can that be arranged?"

"Unless the Genoa or Naples office neglects to wire one to me. In any case, the names will be hopelessly garbled," said Gromaire.

"I'll try to decipher them," Homer promised. With that he escorted Miriam to their hired car and drove back toward the Hotel des Anglais. "We'll lunch at Sabin's, of course, and so, unless I am mistaken, will Orman and his entourage. So will Finke, unless he feels obliged to avoid me."

"How could he know we are here?" asked Miriam.

"I trained him," Homer said, simply.

4

Ours Not to Reason Why

THE DEVELOPMENTS in and around the Hotel des Anglais, Miriam felt
sure, were possibly perplexing, but certainly not disturbing Homer
Evans. They reached the hotel, so well appointed for costly comfort and ideally situated at the western extremity of the matchless
crescent beach, just before the rock ledges and sub-tropically verdant promontory jutted out to sea. The desk clerk then on duty,
the experienced and competent Monsieur Truc, had served Evans
intermittently over a period of years and knew Homer could
be trusted, was on the side of the angels, and paid generously for
services rendered, particularly gems of information truthfully
divulged. More important, Truc realized that trying to lie to Mr.
Evans was more futile than reaching for the moon or diving to grasp
its reflection.

Homer, Miriam and the said Monsieur Truc soon were closeted in a snug inaccessible office marked "For Employees Only."
In his hand, the obliging clerk had the registration forms for the
past few days. They did not include the names of Luke Sharkey,
the Rosencrans Continental Op who had been stooging for Clifford
Orman; Finke McGuire, Homer's staunchest disciple; Talbot
Forran, of the Hollywood Gyro's; nor even those of Miriam Leonard
and Homer Evans, since on his arrival early that same morning,
the latter had chosen not to place himself or his priceless bodyguard on record just then.

It became clear to Homer that, since Truc did not volunteer
the information, if anyone had suspected his suite had been

38

entered by an intruder, who had been followed across the beach to the market place, the incident had not been discussed along the hotel grapevine. Truc told Homer that when Clifford Orman and his party, totaling six fantastically assorted individuals, had arrived, the millionaire oil magnate had seen to it that Hjalmar Jansen and the journalist, Tom Jackson, were assigned rooms well distant from his own suite, and on another floor. With that stipulation, Orman had gone upstairs with the two young women, leaving Jordan to prepare the registration forms, and submit them to the members of the party for signature, also upstairs.

"Did Jordan question you or examine the register as if he were trying to locate one or more parties for Orman? Or even for himself?" Homer asked.

"He did, and having failed to find the names he wanted he asked me, confidentially, if I had any idea as to the whereabouts of a certain Finke McGuire, a friend of yours, I believe, Mr. Evans. Also he inquired about a professional private detective, one Luke Sharkey, who was at this hotel with Mr. Orman on the last occasion Orman was in Cannes," said Truc.

At this point, Miriam asked and received permission to interrupt. "You saw this Mr. Sharkey while he was stopping here?" she asked Truc.

"Not only then, but several times since the war. As I understand it, Mr. Sharkey is the European representative of an important American detective agency, somewhat disreputable, but powerful, according to general belief among hotel men here."

Miriam then asked, as nonchalantly as she could:

"Does Mr. Sharkey habitually wear blue serge, with a soft felt hat and plain tie? Is he about 5 feet 10 inches tall, weighing about 165 pounds? Has he cold blue-gray eyes, a long sharp nose and lips thin and tight?"

"I can't be sure about the details of his physiognomy or attire, Mademoiselle," Truc replied. "I can say that hotel people mistrust him, on sight. For no specific or tangible reason, you understand. He is a naturally unsympathetic type and seems to cultivate antipathy, except from the kind of clients who have half the money in the world."

"Like Mr. Orman, you mean?" she asked.

"Precisely. I ought to tell you, perhaps, that Mr. Jordan, acting for Millionaire Orman, subsidized me to call key men on the staffs of each of the Cannes hotels and ascertain whether any of them could be of help in locating either Sharkey or Finke McGuire or both. Not that it seemed likely two such contrasting types would be allied, or in each other's company, except for professional reasons. Both are private detectives, after all—one a free lance, the other in a widespread organization with an international scope."

That was a long and elaborate speech for Truc, and it seemed to exhaust his reservoir of information and conjecture. But before he asked permission to go back to the desk, he added: "In spite of all I've said, and have not succeeded in doing, Cannes is not large or complex enough so that foreign transients, detectives or not, can hide for long. I happen to know that our Commissaire of Police, Monsieur Gromaire, has his dragnet out for both of the parties we have discussed."

Homer nodded and smiled. "I asked him to comb all the sanctuaries and dives," he said. "He may phone me any minute."

"I'll take the message, personally, in case you're not at hand," promised Truc, and again Homer nodded.

He led Miriam to the beach and sat beside her on a bench, pretending not to notice that farther eastward, toward the market and the Casino, Madeleine, Odette, Hjalmar and Tom Jackson were seated around a table on the sidewalk of a shore café. It was unnecessary to approach nearer in order to see that a very gay time was being had by all. In the other direction, silhouetted against the sky, sat Howard Scott Jordan on the rim of a ledge, apparently deep in thought.

Raising her eyes inquiringly, Miriam looked at Homer and waited for light and direction.

"This means," Homer said, "that Clifford Orman, as fiendishly jealous and possessive as he is, has preferred to expose his mistresses to the wiles of the two most reckless and, where roguish women are concerned, the most unscrupulous in my long list of disreputable but charming friends, in order to give Luke Sharkey a chance to contact him secretly and alone. Possibly Jordan was posted by his employer to keep an eye on the inflammable quartet, and has sunk into a brown study instead. At any rate, Orman does not want Jordan to sit in, if there is a communication from, or a conference with, Sharkey."

"You're sure, then, that Sharkey has been retained by Mr. Orman?" Miriam asked.

"No Rosencrans detective has ever been known to do something for nothing I've been told by Maitre Sabin, himself, that Sharkey, in company with and on behalf of Orman, offered our great chef $2,000 a week, with a six months' guarantee, if Sabin would work for Mr. Orman in Las Vegas," Homer said.

As soon as Miriam had recovered from her astonishment, Homer shot another item across.

"Listen well," he continued. "Young Mr. Howard Scott Jordan, whom we see perched disconsolately on yonder ledge, on his first visit to Sabin's restaurant, the Club des Imprevoyants where we have enjoyed some memorable meals, detected the subtle flavor of pipsissewa in a rum-cake frosting, a feat not a dozen men living could duplicate. To make this achievement less plausible to the nth degree, Mr. Jordan, Sabin tells me, can scarcely tell one wine from another, and cannot compose a lunch or dinner acceptably."

"You learned lots while I was stalking Mr. X," Miriam said. "Could you give me the rest, in brief, or would you prefer that I grope in the dark?"

Her tone was not petulant or resentful. Either way, she was content to be of service.

A bellhop from the Hotel des Anglais approached Homer, as the latter was finishing his disclosures to Miriam of all Sabin had said. "You're wanted on the phone, sir," said the presentable juvenile delinquent in bright uniform.

When Homer and Miriam got back to the hotel lobby, Truc dialed a familiar number hastily. "Use that soundproof booth, Mr. Evans," he said. "The Commissaire insisted on talking directly with you."

In the booth, with his ear to the receiver, Homer heard the Commissaire's voice:

"I've taken a liberty you may find unpardonable," Gromaire said. "Your erstwhile confederate and second, Monsieur McGuire, is now sitting with the Hollywood phenomenon, the one who still has a million, Mr. Talbot Forran. I had Ballangier go there, as if by chance, pass the time of day, and let it drop that you were in town, at the Hotel des Anglais, along with the oil multi-multi, Clifford Orman, two women of easy virtue, two famous Montparnasse inebriates, and a sad-eyed young Massachusetts savant, one Mr. Howard Scott Jordan."

"Excellent," said Homer, beaming into the transmitter. "And the reactions?"

"Monsieur McGuire pretended that he was aware of all that. Or was he? Talbot Forran, whose blood pressure must be high and his temper explosive, nearly had a cataleptic fit, when Orman's name was pronounced. Formerly, before Ballangier dropped his string of bombshells, both McGuire and Forran had seemed pleased with each other and themselves," said Gromaire.

"Indeed. Many thanks. We'll go to Sabin's for lunch, and sit tight."

"Patience. I'm not finished," growled the Commissaire. "Certain parties, quite a flock of them in whom you have shown some interest, have reservations on the Home liner, *America*, which is due to arrive about 8:30 this evening and sail for Genoa around midnight."

"Which parties?" asked Homer.

"Orman and his women, Jordan, the two Montparnasse roisterers, Monsieur McGuire and Mr. Talbot Forran. I shall not breathe easy until the last one of them is aboard, and the liner is well out of our harbor."

"Great snakes! This is miraculous," Evans said, but again the Commissaire cut him short.

"Another item," Gromaire said. "And this is the most sinister. Orman has arranged for two additional reservations, one first class, in a suite adjacent to his own, another in the so-called tourist class, formerly called the steerage. The names of these prospective passengers he has not yet disclosed."

"I begin to glimpse a rift in the smog which thus far has enveloped this case," Homer said, and hung up while the Commissaire was still spluttering.

In a secluded corner of the lobby, Homer made known to Miriam what he had just heard from Gromaire. Then he had the hired car brought around to the exit, and set out for Sabin's renowned club, in pleasurable anticipation both of the fare and the intriguing possibilities which might materialize. His mood was contagious, so Miriam was thrilled. However, she felt impelled to suggest softly:

"Homer, isn't this going somewhat too easily, too pat? What movie people designate as 'on the nose'?"

"Investigations which come in like a lamb, continue like wildcats or berserk rhinosauri," he said. "At least, thus far no one has committed a crime—unless Luke's misdemeanor or your gunplay in the market place could qualify."

"How lucky I marked Mr. X!" was Miriam's unabashed comment.

To Homer, that seemed the understatement of the season, so he pressed her arm and smiled. "Your presence of mind and skill enables me to construct castles of unconfirmed facts which only refutation can impossibilize," he said. "Supposing Sharkey is Mr. X. The nick on his elbow, with the consequent soreness and partial disuse of the arm, would make it imprudent for him to show himself in public, or even in private. Should he have had a professional rendezvous with Clifford Orman, he would have found it out of the question, up to now, to keep the date. What would be the effect on Orman, an egocentric to the border of madness?"

"Whatever Sharkey would be able to do for him, within ethical bounds, you, or even Finke, could do much better," suggested Miriam. "Should Orman make advances to either of you, it would be indicative that our castle of conjecture is solid. The only errand we know that Sharkey has tried to perform for Orman is the abortive attempt to lure Maitre Sabin, at astronomic wages, to Las Vegas."

Both were electrified by an indefinable noise abruptly terminated by an impact. A high caliber bullet, or missile of some kind, had passed between them, fired at an angle as they had driven by

the ambush. There was a neat hole in the windshield of semi-
unbreakable glass. As Homer braked the hired car, not so much
in the hope of catching a glimpse of the would-be assassin as in
ascertaining the point and shelter from which the shot was fired,
he sighed and said, dryly:

"What we said a while back about there being no crime is in-
valid, at long last. The question of attempted murder now poses
itself."

Silently he was thinking hard, trying to decide whether it would
be safe to inform the Commissaire of the incident which might
tempt the over-conscientious Chief to detain them in Cannes while
all prospective principals in the mysterious pickle sailed around
the Mediterranean, across the stormy Atlantic and landed in
Halifax, Boston or New York. Miriam sensed his predicament.

When shot at, from a level a few feet above the surface of the
ground, they had been passing a clump of shrubs and banana trees
between a shop and a residential building along the shore drive.
They had been heading due eastward and two blocks farther would
have turned right, to Sabin's Club in the otherwise ordinary and
undistinguished rue de la Plage. Whoever had fired could have
made an easy getaway between buildings and by now could have
been halfway or more to the Casino, eastward, or back toward the
Hotel des Anglais. More likely, he could have immersed himself in
the crowded waterfront district near the embarkation office and
the group of cheaper hotels and bistros surrounding it.

In order to find out whether the shot had been heard or the
fugitive gunman observed by any fourth party, Homer led Miriam
into the curio shop, where the proprietor, his wife, and two children were both in a rear room, at table. There he drew a satisfying
blank, without disclosing his purpose at all. He bought a gay sou-
venir of the Azure Coast for Miriam, then continued to the dwelling house on the other side of the ambush vegetation and narrow
alley of egress. When a reluctant servant woman answered the front
doorbell, Evans consulted a card in his hand and asked for a Monsieur Duval, a member of the municipal council whom he remembered lived near by.

The *bonne*, a timorous Bretonne peasant type, and her mistress, a candid and accommodating bourgeoise, showed no signs of excitement or perturbation as they collaborated in pointing out to Homer where Councillor Duval resided.

No police had put in an appearance; no one who had been driving either way along the shore road seemed to have stopped or turned back to investigate.

"I think we're in the clear, if we wish to suppress this felony for a while," Homer said, and Miriam agreed. "After all," he added, "the shot was directed against us, no one else."

"And damned close it was. Of course, it was you they were trying to get. Nobody'd be likely to risk the guillotine just to plug me," said Miriam. "However," she went on, "should you find out who the marksman was, I might feel inclined to compete with him, face to face."

"You, my dear, would not have missed," said Homer, confidently. "Let be."

The Club des Imprevoyants, at lunchtime on a Sunday, was well patronized by a faithful neighborhood and local clientele, hearty Frenchmen, a few with their families, who had relished the fine cooking and the sound French wines throughout their active lives, between tragic periods of military service. In a section set somewhat aside were the transients and tourists who were strange to the place or had not qualified. Another wing, with windows on the quiet side street, the rue de la Plage, was reserved for gourmets of repute.

When Homer made his entrance, with Miriam on his arm, Maitre Sabin came from the kitchen to welcome them in person. As Evans glanced around, he was more than satisfied. For on the edge of the section of the spacious dining room sat the foursome he had hoped to encounter, namely, Clifford Orman, Madeleine, Odette and Howard Scott Jordan. The oil man was visibly irate, Jordan was preoccupied, the lovely blonde and classic brunette seemed to be expecting the worst and counting on surviving it, one way or another. Hjalmar Jansen and Tom Jackson were in the gourmets' territory, in spite of the fact that they were consuming

Martini cocktails by the pitcher and already had ascended to Cloud Nine. When they caught sight of Homer, their greeting, had he not tactfully restrained them, somewhat, might have been too boisterous for a world-famous gastronomers' shrine. Conversely, when they learned he was entering France at about the time they were due for a stretch in the States, their lamentations would have done credit to a Job who had drunk as much as Noah. They apostrophized Fate, Miriam and all that was holy, in an effort to persuade Homer to change his plans—not having the foggiest idea what they were—when Finke McGuire, who also was in the gourmets' preserves notwithstanding that Talbot Forran, headmaster of Gyro's was with him, broke into the confused act.

The greetings which ensued, among Homer, Miriam and Finke were heartfelt, dignified and convincing. Finke extricated them from the Montparnasse jokers, steered them clear of Orman's table, where the great mogul was trying officiously to attract Homer's attention, and introduced them to the smouldering impresario from the Hollywood Strip.

"Mr. Evans," Forran began, testily, after all four were seated and armed with appetizers. "Since I'm told you understand everything, what is that insufferable fathead, Clifford Orman, doing in Europe, and was it by design that he chose the *America*, on which I have had reservations two months, for his return voyage—along with as flashy and rowdy a passel of hangers-on as could be found out of stir in any land?"

"Surely you do not include the correct young New Englander in any disorderly category," Homer said, to get Forran's mind off the craziness of the picture, *in toto*, by fixing it on a reassuring detail.

The riled impresario was not to be thus sidetracked. "The guy with the glasses and top-heavy dome? He kept the others waiting, like bugs on a skillet, and just now showed up late. For a lunch in Sabin's ritzy joint, that's as bad as wearing indecently pointed clothes, or guzzling like your lushes from Montparnasse. At least, Finke tells me they're your pals. Correct me if I'm wrong," Forran continued.

Miriam asked him softly, as if incredulous: "You say Mr. Jordan arrived late for lunch?"

"He seemed distraught, when we saw him sitting on the cliff. Remember?" Homer interposed. "Evidently Mr. Jordan was a boy prodigy, in some respects like Kid Unamuno, back in Las Vegas. Jordan has the earmarks. Such boys, and men, are always misfits, and feel it more keenly than less sensitive normals."

A waiter moved unobtrusively to Homer's side and handed him a note, at which Evans glanced.

"Must talk with you at once. Make no other commitments." The message was signed with Orman's imperative scrawl.

Homer slipped the paper in his pocket and continued as if nothing had happened, asking all sorts of polite and perfunctory questions of Finke, about his health, how was business, etc. With a smile he remarked that Finke was not an ideal correspondent. Finke did not get rattled. In fact, he made both Homer and Miriam understand that his trip with and errand for Forran were of such a nature that he was bound not to reveal them, even to his closest friend and sponsor. He did, however, by declaring he had not had a crime, inspiring or routine, to deal with since a certain Hollywood director had been murdered in the Easter Parade. Well Finke knew that Homer would deduce from that a certainty that Finke's services to Forran had to do with business and off-beat finance rather than mayhem or death. Forran, indeed, looked and acted more like a man of business than a violent criminal. He oozed resentment and disappointment, suffered from internal pains and evolutionary frustrations, and whatever he detested most seemed to be contained in, and represented by, the oil and real-estate mogul, Clifford Orman.

It was inevitable, therefore, that Orman would follow a most high-handed procedure to inflame his enemy from Hollywood. Rising unceremoniously while his luncheon guests were enjoying a Pharamond salad, Orman walked as majestically as he could to the table where Forran, Finke, Homer and Miriam were gathered. Ignoring all the others, the officious oil millionaire tried to fix Homer with a masterful eye. The gaze he got in return took starch

from his collar and wind from his sails. However, Orman had for-
mulated his opening speech on the way across the dining room and
was unable to hold it back.

"What I have to say to you can't wait, Evans," Orman said. "Shall
we go to Sabin's office for privacy?"

A slight gesture from Homer kept Forran from attacking the
oil man with the silverware. Finke was grinning; Miriam was inwardly expectant. Evans replied, coolly: "I never let business
interfere with refreshment, Mr. Orman. Be good enough to return
to your table. After lunch, if you wish, we can have a few moments
together. But I must warn you that just now I am too busy with
previous commitments to assume any new ones."

The strong necessity Orman seemed to feel for Homer's advice
kept the multi from flying off the handle. "Excuse me," he said.
"What I wish to talk about affects also a close friend of yours. That's
why I assumed you'd find it urgent, and make an exception."

In turn, Homer thawed to a certain extent. "In that case, since
Miss Leonard and I have not started our lunch, and she has stimu-
lating company, I'll relent. Sabin's office seems to be unoccupied.
I'm sure he won't mind."

With that, Homer led the jittery millionaire to the quiet room
in question, ushered Orman in, and closed the door behind them.

"I know you're hungry. You say also you're busy. So let's not
beat around the bush. I want to retain your services, at any fair
figure you care to name," Orman began.

Homer smiled with satisfaction. "To pinch hit for a detective
who seems to be lost, strayed or stolen?" he asked.

"I'd have tried for you first, had you been at hand," Orman said.

"Is it Maitre Sabin, by any chance, you had in mind as the friend
of mine affected in your pressing affair?" inquired Homer, and
added, before Orman could answer: "In that eventuality, I must
decline any offer in advance, since Maitre Sabin is a client of mine."

"Would that prevent you from persuading him to accept a position from which he would benefit hugely? Could it not be that
your interests, his and mine coincide?"

"You want to transplant him, for six months at least, to Las Vegas. For what purpose? Or, if that is too blunt a question, what exactly would he be expected to do?" asked Homer.

The ingratiating manner of Orman, at this point, testified to the fact that he had not reached the summit of success in difficult commercial fields without tact or magnetism.

"Surely you'll understand, Mr. Evans, that circumstances might obtain that would make the disclosure of the precise nature of the services I wish Monsieur Sabin to perform fatal to my tremendous project. Can't you take my word? I even could post an enormous bond, to guarantee that nothing will be asked of Sabin, while he is in my employ, that is not in his line, as an expert, or beneath his dignity, as a respectable celebrity, esteemed on all continents and revered in France. My terms are $2,000 a week, with a six months' guarantee, and an option to renew the agreement for an additional six months, if agreeable to both parties." Orman made an easy gesture. "I named $2,000 as the weekly figure only because I was sure that if I offered more, a man like Sabin might be even more reluctant to accept. If you'll help me, I'll not only let you name your fee, but Sabin's emolument."

"Did you extend the same free hand to Luke Sharkey, your Rosencrans detective?" asked Homer with mild malice.

"Not likely. I wouldn't have trusted Sharkey, even before he let me down, as far as I could kick the Cannes Casino. I had to use him, believe me, because no one else was available. If he ends by trying to blackmail me, may I count on you for support?"

"Without charge," Evans said. He rose. "I'll talk with Sabin."

Orman reacted happily, as though what Homer said was too good to be true. "You'll persuade him to accept?"

"Also without charge," Homer said, "with one proviso. The Maitre will travel to Las Vegas with Miss Leonard and me, and will be my apartment guest outside of working hours for the duration of his employment."

The oil millionaire's face fell. "But he'd tell you everything."

"Not if he pledges his word to hold in confidence whatever you say, or ask him to do, within the limits of propriety. To be frank with you, Mr. Orman, should I be over-curious as to what you are about, I'll find out for myself, and, afterward, report in detail how I got the information, provided my sources are not compromised."

Orman was truly dismayed. "Mr. Evans," he said, "I've confided my plan to no one. It is legitimate, noble in a way. A glorious climax to my career. Proof that creative work goes way beyond the limit set by that fool, Osler, and his Neo-Malthusians. I'm seventy. I'm proud, not of the years but of what life means and effort produces after the stupid Biblical dole. I don't care who knows about my pleasures. They transcend years and complement achievement. Only you, by meddling, could destroy me, in the sense of upsetting my heroic designs."

As the speech had progressed, Orman seemed to have become more and more exalted, almost to the verge of madness. Evans fixed and cooled him with his flexible voice and ready wit.

"Orman," Homer said, "after your wealth of experience you know that agreements are based on, and made valid, only by mutual trust. Size up your man, or men, and you have established your dimensions. You respect me by fearing me. Can you not go further and trust in my integrity? Thus far, up to and including this moment, I have learned or suspected nothing that would cause me to embarrass or inconvenience you in the least."

He extended his hand, which the oil multi, reassured almost to a pathetic degree, grasped and shook heartily.

"I won't take your money," Homer said. "I have all I need. With formal professional obligations on either side, you may confide in me."

Orman smiled, almost grinned, and mopped his brow.

"Well, it's happened before, but not often. I braced you, expecting defiance and a fight. Now we're . . . Damnation. We seem to be friends, at any rate, not enemies. Having money and power, as I do, Mr. Evans, makes one feel like a target for all mankind, and womankind, alas. May I shake your hand again, sir, and go back to my party, a quite different man?"

The second handshake was accomplished, Orman went back to his table, Homer detached Miriam from Forran and Finke, and they lunched. As Homer had hoped, when they reached the coffee stage, Sabin joined them, still in mufti.

"Your second, Monsieur Luttenschlager, did himself proud this morning," said Homer. "My congratulations, to him and to you."

Sabin frowned anxiously. "You divined, then, that my assistant had prepared and cooked this meal? But, of course, you have the niceties of taste. I trust the fare was different, not inferior."

"Each artist has his individual palette and touch," Homer said. "Now please take a grip on your chair "

"God above," gasped Sabin. "I saw you with that mad old agent of Satan. If you fail me, I am lost."

Briefly Homer outlined what had been said, and what he had agreed to suggest. To the stricken chef, mouth agape, eyes staring, Homer added all his blandishments. "Luttenschlager has earned a real chance. He will sustain your Club's high reputation, and thus elevate his own. You need a rest, among congenial friends. You owe it to yourself to see our American part of the world, and the fabulous Las Vegas, where the aspects of vice are largely constructive, assessed along broad lines. Also, you can do me an important favor. I believed Orman, when he sold to me the tremendousness of his mysterious plan, from his point of view. Still, as you well know, since omelettes cannot be made without breaking eggs, projects designed to shake the structure of world economy, quite possibly, will animate the organized criminal elements. Blood, sweat and tears will be the least of the by-products."

"And who is likelier than I to be scarified, flayed or skewered?"

"You hold my protection and solicitude lightly," Homer said, and Sabin was contrite. It would be impossible to say at what point the great chef yielded. The chute was gradual, though the conclusion was final enough.

"When do we leave?" Sabin said, and sighed like a weary gnu between feeding times.

"Let's decide that when the others are safely en route," suggested Homer.

"Ah," said Miriam, happily. "Then we fly."

That possibility threw Sabin into another tailspin. He had never risked his brain and body in any kind of vehicle which, should the means of propulsion fail, could not be inspected by walking or rowing around it. Miriam cited statistics to prove that more people died from housemaid's knee than were victims of airplane crashes. Again Sabin's surrender was slow and fraught with misgivings.

"I shall be a burden to you both," he objected. "How shall I adapt myself to foreign ways, in the world capital of vice and excesses? You'll have to lead me, like an infant, or I shall be toppling, bumping and caterwauling." He groaned more deeply. "At $2,000 a week! All that wealth, among a nest of gangsters who would blow their mothers to bits for a fraction of my stipend."

"I'll bank your money, and furnish you daily with a safe amount of cash," Homer promised. "And don't forget. Not a thug or hoodlum in the whole United States is as sure a shot as Miriam."

Instead of comforting Sabin, that remark set his teeth to rattling again. "Granted that Mademoiselle can shoot the eyeballs from a chromo of Whistler's mother. Are there not thousands of others in Nevada who could not miss a man of my bulk once in a lifetime?"

"Remember what I told you of the truce and peace pact. Stay away from the State borders, and you are as safe as a church."

"Unless I'm what they call 'snatched,' which, I've read, is a regional sport. Ah, well! Having no trust in myself, I must throw myself on your good offices. Is it fair to you? How can you urge it?"

Miriam touched the sweating chef's sleeve affectionately, then, with a fair extended forefinger, Homer's forehead. "Ours not to reason why," she said to Sabin, and there the matter rested, except for numb squirrel-cage revolutions in Sabin's poor head.

5
An Innocent, but Unlucky, Bystander

THE BEHAVIOR of the Home Line vessels, because its ownership and operation involved such an incongruous mixture of Nordic stolidity and Latin capriciousness, was never predictable at Cannes. The Italian officers and crewmen, nursing a rancorous dislike of the French and everything French, took little pains to make the stop at the most attractive end of the Riviera either comfortable or convenient for the passengers. So, that Sunday evening in November, word seeped around Cannes that the *America*, due to depart at midnight, was arriving about 6 P.M., instead of 9. Consequently, the bustle and confusion around the landing wharf and customs office mounted as the afternoon wore on.

Homer and Miriam drove to the adjacent square, parked the hired car (with the neat bullet hole in the windshield fairly well camouflaged with transparent scotch tape), and strolled toward the customs, where frantic refugees were milling, pleading and receiving official abuse; and the hotel agents, on behalf of the rich tourists, were hogging the useful attention, space and personnel. Commissaire Gromaire came puffing to Homer's side before the latter had got fairly settled to observe the functional hurlyburly on the dock, and just as the liner's tender, a battered raft with little shelter, was shoving off, headed for shore with a handful of passengers and shabby heaps of baggage.

"No trace of Sharkey . . . that is, Mr. X?" asked Homer.

"St. Anthony's plague on him. You know X's name? And have not told me?" Gromaire exclaimed accusingly.

"My guess is unsubstantiated by any tangible evidence. The Rosencrans Op is a possibility, that's all. Perhaps too obvious a possibility. Sharkey's an unsavory character, but not a fool," Homer said.

"I am the fool, but even my folly is not complete—one hundred percent, as you Americans like to say. My man at the private airfield just phoned."

"And?" prompted Homer expectantly. The Commissaire drew Homer and Miriam aside from some bystanders who were showing some curiosity, if not misgivings, because of Gromaire's official status and Homer's impressiveness.

"Your protégé and his client who has probably retained a million of the fortune he started with, the head of Gyro's, are double-crossing us. They have chartered a plane. I came here to find out whether they had yet cancelled their reservations on the *America*. Can you answer that?" the Commissaire said.

"It was only late this morning when Talbot Forran found that Clifford Orman, his girls, my two convivial irresponsibles from Montparnasse, and Mr. Howard Scott Jordan, had bookings on the *America*. The sight of Orman inflames Forran, for reasons I have not fathomed as yet. Finke, who is stuck with Forran as a client, respects his confidences," Homer said.

"Let's consult the superintendent of the Home Lines local office. He's no friend of mine, but he has to work with me because of my position," the Commissaire urged. Before Homer and the Commissaire started for the aforementioned office, nearby, Evans said casually, to Miriam:

"Would you mind holding the fort, right here, until I return— just to see what you can see?"

"If you think it best," she said. But she shifted the position of her handbag containing the Colt .45.

Meanwhile the *America's* unprepossessing tender approached near enough so she could scrutinize the passengers who were landing. They formed two distinct groups. A half dozen from the steerage who were bound for Cannes to hide or to work, and another half dozen conscientious tourists who had to make rubberneck tours of every port on the itinerary.

In the Home Line superintendent's office, Homer was grinning and Gromaire was fuming. Neither Finke's nor Forran's steamship passage westward had thus far been cancelled, but Clifford Orman had rescinded *his* order for tickets and accommodations for himself, for Madeleine and Odette, and Mr. Howard Scott Jordan. Also, he had notified the office that he would not need either of the two blanket reservations he had made, one in de-luxe first class, the other down belowdecks.

"That means he is abandoning the drunks—your comrades who paint and report, respectively," said the Commissaire.

"In the sense that he is sending them on a protracted sea voyage, while he remains behind with his women and his over-brained chemist who can taste pipsissewa," Homer agreed. "May I suggest . . ."

"Please do. Anything at all," groaned the Commissaire, desolate because he would not be rid of Orman and the others specified as soon as he had expected.

"Communicate with your opposite in Nice, check all airfields there, the commercial flights and planes for hire. Give them a list of names including those of Orman, his ladies, Jordan and Luke Sharkey. Ask the Nice Commissaire, as a precaution, to report the application of anyone from Cannes who wishes to go overseas, to the United States, or Canada, that is," Homer counseled.

As the two men emerged from the Home Line's office, a newsboy (aged 65 at least) offered Homer a copy of the Nice *Gazette*, which Evans bought and held in his hand, but before he could glance at the top headline, he and Gromaire heard a shot. The sound seemed to come from the direction where Miriam had been left, standing guard.

The Commissaire, trotting with Evans at his side, turned purple in the face. "If Mademoiselle has been firing again, for effect, I shall confine her in jail," he announced.

"Patience! Philosophy!" urged Evans, keeping pace with the agitated Chief.

Miriam, when they reached her, although inwardly perturbed, was standing motionless. Her handbag had not been opened. A few yards away, almost in line with the tender from which all passengers had descended, a longshoreman, clad in dungarees and sweater, with heavy boots, had slumped to the boards of the dock, and a swift examination by Homer disclosed the man had been shot from behind.

"The unlucky chap's dead," Homer said, and the Commissaire swore, assembled the waterfront cops, had one of them phone his headquarters for the homicide experts (few as they were), and in general performed his functions, resentfully and indignantly. Meanwhile, Miriam had shifted her position to one near the body, on the opposite side from that on which she had been posted and had been standing when the fatal shot was fired from behind her, from a distance of at least fifty yards.

Homer was lost in what seemed, to others except Miriam, a quandary, so distraught that Gromaire was suspicious. The dead longshoreman's papers were in his pockets and in order; his cronies who checked the identification were enraged. They had blood in their eyes. Who would want to shoot Jean Balzar from behind, or would risk it if he dared?

"Are you planning to solve this cowardly assassination of a worker of France? Or do you confine your solicitude for the upper classes?" a stevedore who knew Evans by sight asked gruffly.

"Respect yourself," growled the Commissaire and had a cop shove the inquirer away. Nevertheless, Gromaire looked hopefully at Homer.

"Let your men do the spade work, the routine investigations," Homer said, in a tone which might have implied he would help later, if he could. Miriam's eyes were flashing indignation, tempered with dismay she tried to hide, and did from all excepting Homer. He was sharing her misgivings. However, the inquiries made on the spot threw no light whatsoever on the murder of the husky, seemingly inoffensive Jean Balzar. So Homer took his leave of Gromaire, and drove the hired car, not directly to Sabin's restaurant. He stopped at the most likely garage and service station. The hopelessness of getting another windshield for a 1937 Rolls Royce almost deterred him from trying, but he got a wonderful break. A wealthy old lady of Cannes had sold her old Rolls for a pittance, the car having outlived its usefulness to her, and the garage man had bought it to make use of certain parts, in improvised jalopies. The old windshield was intact and soon had replaced the perforated one, which Homer packed and stored carefully in the baggage compartment.

Then, before reaching the Club des Imprevoyants, he parked the car near the clump of shrubs and trees that had shielded their would-be assassin of the noontide, so he and Miriam could talk. Both were in a subdued and saddened mood.

"I wouldn't have believed it, but it must have been me who was shot at this morning," she said. "That doesn't make sense."

"We must accept the facts, however bizarre," Homer said. "We can do nothing for the unfortunate Jean Balzar. I'll see his family, if any, are provided for comfortably." Then he paused and looked at Miriam tenderly. "Do you think anyone else is aware that you were exactly in line, considering the direction from which the bullet must have come?"

"Only the person who fired it," said Miriam. "I've a double score to settle with him, when we find him."

"The wretched feature about murder is that, wholesale or retail, the guilty party can only die once," Homer said. "The question before us is: had we better confide in Gromaire about the near miss this morning, which is most certainly tied up with the accidental shooting of Balzar?"

"I shifted my position, by stepping aside at the precise moment the bullet would have hit me—before I heard the report," she said miserably.

"That settles it," Homer said. "Balzar is dead, by chance. No amount of investigation will clear the situation. If I tell the whole truth, we shall be held as material witnesses, even principals and intended victims."

"Victims? Don't you mean victim?" asked Miriam.

Homer's face grew hard and his eyes narrowed.

"Whoever fired the shot this noon might conceivably have been shooting at me. This evening, it would have been much easier to pick me off, on the way to or from the Home Lines office. I was more exposed than you. The murderer well knew that your death would hurt me more than my own," he said grimly.

"Oh, Homer!" murmured Miriam. He had seldom made so open a declaration, but she knew it was true. No man of Homer's stature fears death. All sensitive souls dread bereavement.

"To business," he said, almost gruffly. "Luke Sharkey must be found."

"Are you sure that Sharkey tried to kill us? Or me?" asked Miriam.

Homer's face showed utter amazement. "Miriam. You are unstrung," he said. "Have I suggested in any way, or implied, that Sharkey is the gunman in question?"

"He could be," maintained Miriam.

"So could any other living human in this vicinity, whose whereabouts at the moments in question are unknown to us," Homer said. "I can't be positive, but I have held it so improbable that a crooked detective like Sharkey would stick his neck out as foolishly as a dope-crazed amateur that I have not tried to connect him with the actual shootings," said Homer.

"Any suspects you care to divulge?" she asked.

"Not prematurely," he replied. "And now to dinner, and a talk with Sabin. Not a word about the shooting, mind you."

"I am not a chatterbox," Miriam assured him with some nervous asperity.

It was then that Homer chanced to remember the newspaper he had bought at the dock and had in his pocket. He spread it, and by the glow of a street lamp mixed with late twilight, read the French words which translated, would mean:

"MAURICE CHEVALIER
GETS PHENOMENAL HOLLYWOOD CONTRACT"
"Weekly Pay to Exceed 5,600,000 Francs"
"U. S. Government Relents"

As Miriam watched, bewildered, a bright light of comprehension spread over Homer's face, erasing for the moment the regrets he had felt over the wanton accidental killing of the obscure Jean Balzar She suppressed her curiosity and dutifully waited. After a while, Homer spoke.

"Could the signing up of Chevalier, after assurances from Washington that neither the Revenue or Immigration or State or Justice Departments might obstruct the deal, have been Finke's commission for Talbot Forran?" he asked.

"I'm all ears," said Miriam, indicating that she had no opinion to offer, and nothing on which to base a reply.

"Surely, the animosity between Forran and Orman could have its roots in the rivalry between Las Vegas, as the new entertainment center of the West, and the Hollywood Sunset Strip, as the losing contender for that distinction, which Sunset Boulevard, between Beverly Hills and Hollywood proper, so recently monopolized," Homer said. "The newspaper and trade papers have disclosed, within the last few months, that the Thunderbird, in Las Vegas, offered Chevalier $12,000 a week, only to be topped immediately by the Sands, whose promoters were willing to go as high as $16,000, or 5,600,000 francs. Negotiations were abortive because government agents let it be known that Chevalier was in arrears for old income taxes, and was *persona non grata* for other personal reasons which do not seem to inconvenience U.S. Croesuses like Clifford Orman, for example. Chevalier lost interest, as who wouldn't who is the idol of Paris. The matter faded from the public press."

"Could Forran possibly command that kind of money, after the Hollywood slump?" Miriam demanded, incredulously.

"Finke's influence and ingenuity may be the answer to that. When I first set up Finke in his Hollywood office, I emphasized the wisdom of doing favors, gratis, for any G man, or Federal Department, any place, any time, but particularly in film-land. The movie tsars, while they have been overshadowed temporarily by TV partisans, are making a comeback with their 3-D, wide and curved screens, improved color, Cinerama, and Cinemascope. Colossal spectacles are not for a peanut-sized showing at home, condensed into an hour's time and limitations. Hollywood lately has much significant to offer that cannot be approximated in any medium other than the screen, and a very spacious screen, at that."

"That makes sense, but doesn't overload Hollywood with money for night clubs as yet," Miriam objected.

"There may be investment bankers and syndicates who suspect that the gang-ridden hot spots in Las Vegas may become mob battlefields and that prudent customers will quit Nevada forthwith. If any promoter is in a position to convince such capitalists, it would be Talbot Forran. And if any private detective, not considering me for the moment, could pave the way for a more lenient official attitude toward high-priced foreign artists, in the long view interests of law and order, who would it be other than Finke?"

Miriam shrugged. "I wasn't aware Finke, congenial and daring as he is, carried that much weight in top circles," she said. "But if he does, more power to him."

Again Homer smiled enigmatically.

They drove on to the rue de la Plage and parked on Sabin's diminutive lot. The latter, limp with forebodings, met them at the entrance and shunted them into a small private dining room, where the table was set for three.

"I must try to eat, lest hunger combine with despair to hasten my undoing," the great gastronomer said. "One dastardly event succeeds another, and I am being compelled to desert France in her hour of trial. A hoodlum ransacks a visiting notable's apartment in our best hotel, he is marked on the elbow by a gifted markswoman, and still goes free, after nearly twenty hours. Why? Because Monsieur Gromaire, my faithful client, war veteran and father of a family, is stupid? No, because France, periodically set upon by barbarians and aided far too late by allies, is short of funds and credit. Our police are a skeleton force, from lack of numbers and hearty nourishment. Milksops in our Government, having sold out the French entertainment industry, now neglect viniculture and the use of our wines. What next? A strong useful dock worker is murdered with a shot from behind his back, for no apparent reason . . ."

Here Miriam paled and winced, and Homer tried to cover her agitation.

"Maitre," he said to Sabin, "you'll return to France from Las Vegas with a wider perspective and a keener understanding, better able in all respects to shoulder your share, and more, of the burdens oppressing la belle France."

"I'm of no use to myself," the great chef sighed. "Since I'm helping Luttenschlager arrive at his just deserts, and, you insist, I'm doing you a favor, I'll proceed with this plan, however mad it seems to me. On to Las Vegas, the sooner we start the better. Let us fly, by all means. That way we shall either accomplish the journey or a graver transition. It's all the same to me. Only you must warn this wealthy crackpot who will pay me a fortune each week, for Heaven knows what, that the new environment, whether it is worse or about the same as I've been led to expect, may dull my perceptions an indefinite time."

That seemed to give Evans a welcome idea. "Excellent. Of course. That will give me time to scout around, *sub rosa*. Then, whatever occurs, we'll be better prepared," said Homer.

"Not I. Nothing could weigh harder on my mind, and make me more resigned and docile," Sabin assured his guests. "My morale is at absolute zero, or near it. That you both will be alert and near by, and may find some time for good talk, keeps me from the ultimate desolation."

There was a tap on the door, and in spite of the protests of the waiter assigned to the trio within, the Commissaire strode in, giving off black looks and assorted angry noises, all of which he mastered with an effort as he confronted Evans. The irate Gromaire was flanked by Officer Ballangier, who obviously wished he was elsewhere.

"Monsieur Evans," said the Commissaire, pointing an accusing finger within a few inches of Homer's face, "there are a few things I've uncovered that you must explain or answer for like any common culprit."

Homer nodded. "Equality before the law," he murmured. "Proceed, sir."

"You have, within the half hour, visited the Non Pareil Garage and Repair Station. No?"

"Granted. Yes," Homer admitted.

"There you bought from the head mechanic, one Alfonse Chouette, a windshield for an ancient Rolls Royce, had the same installed on your hired car from Nice, the one now on Maitre Sabin's parking lot, and the windshield you had removed from said car, you retained and placed in the rear compartment designed for honest baggage. *Pas?*"

With a sigh, Homer said: "Without a warrant, I suppose you've picked the lock of that compartment and examined the said windshield. Let's proceed from there."

"The hole in that windshield was made by a high-caliber bullet, traveling at deadly speed and shot from an angle, starting from a level of about four and a half feet. Furthermore, according to our firearms expert, the shot must have been fired at least seven hours ago, and while your hired car was moving about forty miles per hour."

Evans raised his eyebrows appreciatively. "Your expert is astute and clever," he said.

Suddenly Gromaire lost his bluster and aggressiveness.

"I would not have believed that you, after our long years of cooperation and friendship, would maliciously withhold pertinent information concerning an attempted murder," the Commissaire said. As both Miriam and Homer seemed about to reply he silenced them by raising his right hand, palm flat and bare. "Don't implicate yourselves further. Ballangier has ascertained that you halted, on your way from your hotel to this restaurant, not long before one o'clock this P.M.; stopped on the flimsiest of pretexts at a curio shop east of an alley and a clump of trees and bushes; also made pointless inquiries at the dwelling house west of said alley and natural cover for a gunman."

"Under parallel circumstances, would you not have made unobtrusive efforts to find out if such a shot had been fired by accident?" Homer asked.

"Nonsense," growled Gromaire. "I'm not an imbecile."

"Neither would you, were you less excited, assume that a stray bullet through a windshield of necessity spelled attempted murder," Homer said, calmly.

"There is more to indicate that Miss Leonard, or you, or both of you, have been in danger of assassination within the core of my jurisdiction, and have been aware of the threat. I, with my under-paid men, have had a chance to examine carefully the site of the dastardly killing of Jean Balzar. Eyewitnesses recall that Miss Leonard was standing between the killer and the victim, in direct line, until the fraction of an instant before the shot was fired on the dock. She moved just in time to be missed, so the bullet in-tended for her went into the crowd of innocent bystanders. More-over, she was careful surreptitiously to shift her position and stand on the opposite side of the corpse while I was busy with the pre-liminary survey of the tragic situation. What have you to say to that, Mademoiselle?"

Instinctively Miriam turned her large violet-blue eyes up to Homer's, which touched off the temper of the Commissaire.

"Must I interrogate you two separately? Have you lost the fa-cility of answering simple questions on your own responsibility?" Gromaire barked.

"Answer his questions. That may give Monsieur the Commis-saire time to regain his composure, and usual good sense," Homer told her. So Miriam confessed.

"Monsieur Gromaire," she began, "all you have said has some truth in it. Out of consideration for you, we did not make a moun-tain out of a molehill this noon. No man or woman, in any court or country, could be convicted of attempted murder on account of an unexplained bullet hole in a windshield. There was no other evi-dence, or indication, whatsoever. This evening at the dock, I chanced to be standing on a spot where, had I not moved just in time, would have proven fatal to me. What charge would you pre-fer when a woman, after having stood still in one position several minutes, shifts to ease her muscles? Or if she moves to get a better view, after a workman has been shot from behind, and killed?"

"I can hold you, Mademoiselle, as a material witness to the kill-ing of Jean Balzar, and both you and Monsieur Evans for having failed to report an accident involving unauthorized and wanton or careless gun play this noon," threatened the Commissaire, stubbornly holding to his own fury, as if for physical support.

"And Maitre Sabin would phone my attorney, Monsieur Ronron, who would arrange for our release on a writ of *habeas corpus* within fifteen or twenty minutes," Homer said. "Why waste effort and time when we all have so much work to do?"

"In effect," agreed Sabin, and Gromaire turned on him. "Is this your affair?" the Commissaire demanded of the chef, belligerently.

"To a greater extent than you think," Sabin replied. "Monsieur Evans has invited me to be his ranch apartment guest in Las Vegas, Nevada."

"Las Vegas! America! Nevada! The devil take them all, and all those characters who wish to go there," exclaimed the Commissaire. "I have never had to deal with such a muddle-headed congregation. Monsieur Talbot Forran and Mr. Finke McGuire, having had reservations these last two months for accommodations on the polyglot liner due to sail this night, have chartered an airplane without canceling their space on the boat. Oil Millionaire Clifford Orman has canceled princely reservations he made a day or two ago in Paris, for himself, his pair of mistresses, and a pickle-faced bespectacled young freak who, I've heard, can taste pine-nut extract when you toss it by mistake into a rum cake."

"Not pine-nut extract. Pipsissewa," correct Sabin, stiffly.

"Who cares?" demanded Gromaire. "Unless the stuff is poison." He faced about, to confront Homer. "Come along with me! Miss Leonard, too! I happen to know that the only judge who can issue the necessary papers for your release, on bail, is attending a secret meeting in Narbonne, which even I could not locate in time."

"You wouldn't dare," exclaimed Miriam, eyes shooting sparks, her hand on Homer's sleeve.

"Don't carry on, if Monsieur le Commissaire wishes to make an exhibition of himself in trying to make examples of us," Homer said nonchalantly. To Gromaire, he added: "Would it be possible for me to speak with my friends, Hjalmar Jansen and the *Herald* reporter, Tom Jackson, either in or out of jail?"

"I'll have my men round them up, and if they are drunk and disorderly, I'll incarcerate them, too," Gromaire said.

"Miss Leonard and Mr. Evans have not dined," Maitre Sabin said scornfully. "Whether you permit them or not, our friendship is at an end, Gromaire."

"Why don't we all dine, here in company? Ballangier looks famished. My appetite is brisk. Miss Leonard has had nothing since early afternoon. Sabin must fortify himself for his first airplane voyage. Not even you, Monsieur the Commissaire, can subsist on spite and spleen, or shall we be charitable and say advancing age and frustration?"

"Very well," agreed Gromaire, reluctantly. "By consenting I shall save France a few sous."

"Could you stretch a point, and include Messrs. Jansen and Jackson?" Homer asked.

"If they are in any condition to sit in chairs and behave," the Commissaire agreed grudgingly. With that, he took up the phone and issued a curt order that the Montparnasse specimens in question be contacted and brought to Sabin's place, by force if they tried to resist. Instantly, after having placed the instrument back on its cradle, Gromaire fixed Sabin with a baleful eye. "Don't try to ply me with exotic flavors," he warned. "None of your infernal pipsiss-chinoi-serie, which only effete bookworms can relish."

While appetizers were being drunk, and before Hjalmar and Tom were escorted in, there were several interruptions. An agent of police in uniform obtained admission to the private dining room, whispered something in Ballangier's ear, and the latter relayed the message to the disgruntled Commissaire.

"It seems that Messrs. Orman and Jordan have hired a sea-going private plane to accommodate four, while Messrs. Finke and Forran have canceled their lease of the plane they hired this afternoon," Ballangier said, meanwhile working havoc with the varied hors d'oeuvres.

"Watch both millionaires like hawks. Report to me half-hourly on their actions and movements, also the company they contact or keep," ordered the Commissaire, who, himself, distracted as he was, seemed to do justice to the wine and preliminary fare. Gromaire ate as if that were a detached, subconscious activity that did not interfere with speech, thought or decision.

Next a soft-footed waiter from the main dining room sashayed in, and whispered in Sabin's ear.

"Your millionaires are both at table, in this very restaurant," the chef said to Gromaire. "With Mr. Orman are Madeleine and Odette. With Mr. Forran is Mr. Finke. Only the absurd Mr. Howard Scott Jordan, who, not knowing bulk Beaujolais from 1934 Chateau Lafitte, can spot pipsissewa in the icing of a cake saturated with 110 proof Martinique, is absent, with or without leave," said Sabin, relaying the waiter's message.

All those around the table—Miriam, Homer, Gromaire, Ballangier, Sabin—were startled half out of their chairs by sounds from without, resembling the bumps, crashes and splitting noises on a baggage platform when heavy trunks and boxes are being smashed. The door was opened from outside, and six uniformed cops ushered in Hjalmar Jansen, portrait painter, and Tom Jackson, journalist They had been protesting and executing a delaying action rather than putting up the resistance of which they were capable. The moment they spied Homer and Miriam, they subsided to wait for a cue.

"Are you all right? Is this O.K.?" asked Jansen, grinning amiably.

"Quite. I asked to see you, and being under arrest, couldn't seek you out," said Homer.

The six policemen were dismissed and the waiter brought two more chairs and set two more places on an auxiliary table which was wheeled into the room on smooth casters.

"I could do with a snack," Tom Jackson said. Both he and Jansen had drunk prodigiously, but they felt a moral obligation to keep themselves in hand until Homer gave the word, one way or another. The huge Norwegian painter, however, fixed a hard, though quizzical look on Commissaire Gromaire, and another mild one, on account of his lower rank, on Officer Ballangier.

"Are these parties getting in your hair?" Hjalmar inquired of Evans.

"Fundamentally we are in accord. On certain details of procedure, we are not yet in harmony," Homer answered. "Enjoy your meal in peace, although I have some news for you that might upset a lesser philosopher."

"Don't spare us," Tom Jackson urged. "We are feeling almost too good. I should explain, if these other gentlemen will permit me, that this afternoon Hjalmar and I have launched on the tide that rises once in the affairs of men, and if not utilized to best advantage, peters out and returns not. You're familiar with the reference, and can straighten out the text."

"Damnation," growled the Commissaire. "Had I consumed in a month half as much alcohol as you tosspots have swallowed since lunch . . ."

With an owl-like somewhat injured expression the self-satisfied journalist interrupted the Chief. "No one can say we did badly before lunch, or during," he asserted.

Homer came right to the point. "May we assume that you, Hjalmar, have sold Mr. Orman and the girls on the idea of having the ladies' portraits painted?"

"In Goya style, but the old goat suspects nothing of that," Jansen replied with satyrish glee.

"And you, Tom, have received an O.K. from your paper authorizing you to follow Mr. Orman to New York and Las Vegas until you get the story your editor is after?"

"You've hit the nail right on the button," answered Jackson. "Wham!"

The wham was yelled as if a Comanche Indian had uttered it on the triumphant end of a war path, and the havoc it played with tender nerves in that closed room was shocking to behold. It was the only grave slip either of the Montparnasse revelers had made, and Homer, to quiet the raging Commissaire and reassure the swooning chef, promised that nothing like that would happen again in the course of the meal and the conference.

Homer concentrated his own attention and focused his Montparnasse cronies' still miraculously unliquefied brains before he proceeded. At last he said, bluntly:

"Evidently neither of you is aware that Clifford Orman has canceled his reservations, and those of Madeleine, Odette, and Howard Scott Jordan, on the America for the westbound voyage, and has chartered a private plane for four, leaving you both to make the long voyage home on the slow boat to America, *à deux*—among the other assorted passengers, of course."

Hjalmar was on his feet, with a wine bottle grasped in one hand. Tom Jackson had grabbed a siphon of seltzer from a side-table tray and was equally ready to set out for immediate retributive action.

"Peace, my friends," said Homer soothingly. "I have plans for you which you may find acceptable. Jackson's assignment to cover Mr. Orman's activities needs no further authorization. May I ask you both if the agreement Orman or his women made to commission the portraits of Madeleine and Odette was made in the presence of competent witnesses?"

"Two fellows and their wives whom we met on the Blue Train overheard what was said, also a couple of waiters on a shore *terrasse*, and the maitre-dee," Hjalmar insisted. "Furthermore, if that old blighter tries to renege, he knows I'd reach down his throat till I got a firm grip halfway to his feet, and turn him inside out."

"I think we can dispense with violence to Orman's person, if you're sure the girls are eager," Homer said.

Hjalmar grinned almost lasciviously. "That you can bank on, or I've never seen bimbos who were. The angle about Goya and his Duchess clinched it with them. You catch on, needless to say."

Miriam let out a silvery laugh. "And Mr. Orman doesn't."

"Naturally. Orman's slated for the role of the Duke."

Sabin shrugged, Ballangier squirmed and the Commissaire exploded. "If you amateurs of art persist in talking in code, I'll have to run you all in, before the main course comes on," Gromaire threatened.

"No chance. I can walk a chalk line, pronounce pipsissewa distinctly, and add rapidly by sevens," Hjalmar boasted, as he poured

Tom and himself another drink. Then the big painter turned to Evans disconsolately. "Just how am I going to finance the trip? I'm broke. And that old tub of the Home Line takes time enough to reach New York so that Orman could die or change his mind or his tomatoes before I worked my way to Las Vegas."

"I need your help," Homer said. "I want you to stay with me as long as I have to remain in Cannes, and make the trip with us— Miss Leonard, Jackson and me—as soon as Monsieur Gromaire gets back his senses." Turning to Gromaire, Homer said: "I shall refrain from appealing to your superiors in Paris, so your formerly well-earned reputation will not be permanently discounted."

"Duty is duty. You and your anarchistic young bodyguard stay in custody, as long as I can hold you, or until all illegal matters in question are resolved to my satisfaction," the Commissaire insisted, so stubbornly that it was plain he would not be likely to relent. He was acting, obviously, against his own better judgment, but having got on the wrong track could not back up and switch on the main line of reason again.

"It is never the duty of an official of any republic to make an ass of himself," Homer said without rancor. "Before Miss Leonard and I, your most competent allies and assistants, are placed out of commission, I'd like to ask a question. What charge, or charges, exactly, will be filed against a gunman, if you catch him in spite of your blunders, who shoots at Miss Leonard with intent to kill, and instead kills an innocent longshoreman who is exposed by the merest chance?"

The Commissaire groaned and pressed his aching forehead between both of his hands.

6

Women, Clothed, and/or Women, Nude

ABOUT NINE O'CLOCK that same Sunday evening, a trio, heartsick and
self-conscious (with the possible exception of Homer, who maintained his debonair manner), sat in the Chief's office at the Commissariat. Gromaire, his better self relenting, and his obstinate side
reinforcing itself with its own adrenalin, could neither yield nor
carry out his mission. Evans, taking advantage of those dismal
moments of the Commissaire's hesitation, reached to a shelf, took
down a law book, and read:

"Section 317, paragraph 6 (Laws of 1899). In cases of emergency, in which doubtful circumstances as to guilt or the nature of
charges to be preferred have arisen, a Commissaire may, if no authorized judges are available for consultation, fix reasonable bail
on which accused parties may be set at liberty."

"Monsieur Gromaire, Miss Leonard and I both realize your day
has been extremely trying. We are anxious and able to help you.
May I not post bail? You're aware that persons involved potentially in this affair are likely to depart this evening. Neither Mr. X
nor Luke Sharkey has been located by your men. Maitre Sabin,
whose long friendship with you cannot be dissolved with an im-
petuous word, needs comfort. For their own good, my
Montparnasse friends, Messrs. Jansen and Jackson, should be kept
within bounds of propriety and safety."

It was plain that Gromaire was thawing and that Evans had
much more to say. However, Officer Ballangier burst in without

his usual strict observance of amenities. Homer was able to arrest the officer's approach and get in one more telling barb.

"Before we hear Ballangier, who seems to have news, I should remind Monsieur the Commissaire that Miss Leonard, in the course of her association with me, has been in many jails of rather high standard. You would not wish to cast asperity on our beloved France by locking her in any of the cells of this unsanitary and insect-ridden retreat," said Evans.

"Messieurs, I beg of you," interrupted Ballangier. "I was told, among other assignments, to locate Mr. Howard Scott Jordan. I wish to report that his trail was picked up in a rather poor district southeast of the square off the docks. He had sought out, with seeming distaste and reluctance, the bereaved widow and children of the deceased Jean Balzar, and promised that he would establish a trust fund which would enable the unlucky family to live, indefinitely, in the style to which they were accustomed."

"In Clifford Orman's name, no doubt. One of his American 'public relations' maneuvers," growled the Commissaire.

"Mr. Jordan assured the Widow Balzar that he was acting purely on his own behalf and initiative. He was emphatic about that," Ballangier reported.

"Where is Jordan now?" asked Homer.

"Somehow he persuaded our experts to admit him, as an observer, to our crime laboratory, because of his scholastic credentials. In fact, he has been instrumental in establishing that the bullet which passed through Monsieur Evans' windshield this noon could have been fired from the same automatic used by the killer of Jean Balzar, who might have been aiming at Mademoiselle Leonard," continued Ballangier.

The Dr. Jekyll half of Commissaire Gromaire surged upward and asserted itself. "Your bail is 1,000 francs apiece," he said to Homer and Miriam. "Please to get busy, and justify my leniency. But" (and here Gromaire's face took on a purplish tinge again) "no more clues or details, however vague or trivial, are to be withheld. *Pas?*"

"My parole," Homer said. "And in return for your ample view of a tangled situation, I'll make a fervent suggestion. Place as careful a guard around Monsieur Luttenschlager, Sabin's assistant who'll preside at the Club in my old friend's absence, as you assign to the Master himself."

The Commissaire's forehead wrinkled and his muscles contracted and tensed. "Why Luttenschlager, in Heaven's name? All his life, at least during the twenty years in Cannes, this robust Alsatian has remained as self-effacing as a man of his bulk can be."

"Should any of our antagonists wish to make it harder for Maitre Sabin to enter the employ of Millionaire Orman, in Las Vegas, no surer way could be found than to remove Luttenschlager as a possible substitute for Sabin here in Cannes," said Homer.

The nerve-strained Commissaire gave way to lamentations.

"Why should these infernal schemers gather in Cannes? Why not Nice, or Marseilles, where crime is always epidemic?" he wailed.

"Neither Cannes nor Marseilles has its Sabin or a wine taster in his class," Homer reminded Gromaire.

"Has Orman been buying our superb wines, in vulgar quantities, and transferring them in bulk to his abominable desert? Our cinema artists and directors are lured to America and corrupted. Our perfumes prolong the second adolescence of rich middle-aged U. S. women in droves, and render possible the close attention of world gigolos. Our styles are hijacked by New York and Hollywood designers in a shameful fashion. I had formerly considered it most fortunate for us that Americans are as a rule impervious to wines, except champagne, which can be spared," the Commissaire said resentfully.

"If Orman has an extensive wine cellar on his estate, I had not heard about it," said Homer. "Still, I wouldn't put anything beyond him. Only I am sure that, if Orman has stored precious vintages, he had no guidance from Mr. Howard Scott Jordan."

Miriam, who had said little since their arrival at the Commissariat, interjected a question. "Gentlemen, if you'll allow me . . ."

"Practically anything, Mademoiselle," the two Frenchmen assured her, in effect, although somewhat absentmindedly and from force of lifelong habit.

"Could it be that Mr. Orman, having heard about Jordan's pre-cocity and amazing erudition, and having evidence that the prodigy's palate was keen and his pocketbook flat, might have hired Jordan as an all-round taste expert, only to discover what we have determined ourselves? Young Jordan can identify pipsissewa, and who knows what else, but, in general, his faculties of taste are crude in the extreme," she suggested.

"I might accept all you have suggested, except the flat purse," the Commissaire said. "Impecunious young men do not offer trust funds to bereaved widows. And don't tell me Clifford Orman is behind the gesture, and will foot the bills. Never, since I have known Orman existed, has he passed up a chance for flattering publicity. You'll see. If the oil magnate hears what his four-eyed subordinate has done, he'll be furious and jealous."

"We shall see," Homer said, as if content to wait. "Right now I'm concerned with who quits Cannes, by what means, and whither bound. Are the depot, the bus stations and all authorized air strips covered?"

The Commissaire stared hard at Ballangier. "In a manner of speaking," he finally said.

"And the landing wharf and customs office over and through which passengers destined for the *America* must pass?" Homer continued.

"Both the Home Line and the customs officials can be trusted to co-operate fully with us, unless they are distraught or are bribed," said the Commissaire.

"Those lapses could occur anywhere," sighed Homer. "Still, the parties we wish to trace and establish are conspicuous, if nothing else."

"*Et comment,*" murmured Gromaire.

A phone rang and Gromaire took up the instrument as if it was radio-active. "The Commissaire here," he said.

Voice noises issued from the receiving knob. Gromaire slammed down the phone and faced the others.

"Your Finke and his shadow, Mr. Talbot Forran, are already aboard the *America*," the Commissaire reported.

"It appears they're going to sail, after having learned that Orman and most of his entourage plan to fly. Now what may we deduce from that?" Homer said and asked.

"Two times nothing," groaned the Commissaire, and Ballangier added:

"Where affluent Americans and their assistants or bodyguards are concerned, French logic and sense of measure can rarely be applied." Swiftly, and as a matter of precaution, the officer checked by phone with the private airfield in question. He shrugged, on receiving the report, as if he had expected as much, or worse.

"The plane they leased, already paid for, has not yet been canceled by either Finke or Forran. And neither, when last I heard, have Orman and his women taken off," the officer said. "Conversely, Orman canceled four of his eight reservations, leaving two open for the Montparnasse inebriates, and the two whose occupants remain without name."

Homer tried to relieve his mind about the two anonymous places held on the liner. "The first-class one, I suspect, was for Sabin, who will travel with me. The other, in the steerage, could have been for Luke Sharkey, who, had he made the voyage with Orman, would not have let it appear he was thus attached. By donning a tuxedo evenings, or even his famous blue serge by day, he could tip practically any Italian steward living to admit him to first class, should that suit Orman's and his purposes."

The four conferees were startled by a precipitous entrance on the part of Maitre Sabin. He had a small cylindrical bottle filled with a kind of coarse beige liquid in his hand.

"What now?" demanded the Commissaire

"Pipsissewa extract," Homer exclaimed.

"Poisoned," Sabin gasped. "Luttenschlager found it hidden behind a row of books in his attic room. I immediately gathered all known pipsissewa in my establishment and placed it under lock and key, sent it post haste to the crime laboratory for analysis, and brought this, the most suspicious example, to Monsieur le Commissaire, so he would credit my story in spite of our broken relationship."

Homer sprung into action, albeit with calmness and dignity.

"With your permission, Monsieur Gromaire," he said, "I'll take a sample from this and all other containers of pipsissewa at the Club, then rush the rest to your crime lab for a fast analysis. Also, I'd like to have Miriam go out to the appropriate airstrip, contact whoever has leased his plane to Finke, and, if the vehicle has room for four passengers, I'll commandeer it (on your authority) and within two hours, at the most, will take off with Miss Leonard, Hjalmar Jansen and Tom Jackson. Tomorrow I'll get in touch with you, one way or another, and from wherever we are, to learn from you all known facts about Orman's departure, also Madeleine and Odette's, Mr. Howard Scott Jordan's, Finke McGuire's and that of Mr. Talbot Forran. Meanwhile, please find out through your Paris connections whether Maurice Chevalier actually has signed a binding contract for a Las Vegas appearance and, if possible, who was instrumental in signing him, where he will first appear on the Hollywood Strip, and which U.S. officials, if any, guaranteed him immigration clearance and nonmolestation on the part of the Internal Revenue chaps."

Sixty minutes later, Homer called at the crime lab where the local chemists, assisted by Howard Scott Jordan, who did all the actual work, were finished analyzing all of Sabin's pipsissewa extract.

"Nothing wrong with the contents of any of these bottles," Jordan assured Homer, and the French experts off-handedly agreed, the more readily because none of them ever before had heard of the evergreen flavoring in question nor witnessed any of the ultramodern tests the whiz from Massachusetts had applied.

Miriam reported success at the airfield, Hjalmar and Jackson were torn from the bistro where they had entrenched themselves, and were transported with Maitre Sabin by taxi to the hopping-off place. Before he quit Jordan at the crime lab, Homer told the strange New Englander that he and his party were flying to Rome, to study in the Eternal City, then in Florence and Assisi, the masterpieces of Italian primitive and Renaissance art. The message he sent to the Commissaire, through Ballangier, was to concentrate his main force and attention to guarding the person of

Luttenschlager, who was, because of the unexpected good fortune which had descended on him through Sabin's unforeseen absence, one of the happiest men in Cannes.

Homer's last precaution before purchasing the plane outright, so he could pilot it himself, was to get in touch by phone with the appropriate air officials in the Eastern United States, to insure that all arrivals, either in Halifax, Boston, New York, or any U.S. air terminal whatsoever, of Clifford Orman, Mr. Howard Scott Jordan, Finke McGuire, or the head of Hollywood's Gyro's, Mr. Talbot Forran.

When at last they were safely in the air, and clear of French restrictions, Miriam quoted, possibly without knowing it, Anatole France's immortal Abbé Coignard, in *La Reine Pédauque*.

"Now I feel easier," she said.

The radio apparatus of the *Peu de Souci* (Small Worry), as Homer's so recently acquired plane was named, was not effective beyond a radius of about two hundred miles, so he made straight for the Azores, where he made a neat landing about dawn. Without delay, Homer telephoned Commissaire Gromaire, who reported the following items:

(a) Clifford Orman had set out by airplane, with his mistresses and Jordan, just after midnight, having previously ascertained that Finke and Talbot Forran had sailed aboard the *America* fifteen minutes previously.

(b) Jordan, on Orman's behalf, had combed the Home liner in an unsuccessful effort to establish whether Hjalmar Jansen and Tom Jackson were or were not aboard.

(c) Gromaire, having conferred with the Home Line officials and the chief steward of the *America*, had, on his own responsibility requested that no search for stowaways be made that night, while the liner was still in French waters, and that, should any be found, particularly any tall one, with sharp gray-blue eyes, a pointed nose, and a Shakespearean conspiratorial air, he should be turned over to the police at Naples.

(d) Monsieur Luttenschlager, Maitre Sabin's second, had suffered, about one o'clock that morning, when Homer and his party
were four hundred miles distant from Cannes, a severe attack of
acute indigestion. Luttenschlager was in hospital; the contents of
his stomach, which had promptly been pumped out, were in pro-
cess of analysis, but nothing suspicious had, thus far, been established or announced.

Trying, and succeeding, not to show any detectable emotion
on receipt of any of the gems of information, Homer, in turn, promised Gromaire faithfully that he would send him irrefutable and
tangible evidence that the death of the late Jean Balzar was an
unfortunate accident. Thus, the Commissaire could close the case,
and the pious widow accept her loss, as resulting from the will of
God, operating in one of Its most mysterious ways.

"You are sure then that your Mr. X, and/or Luke Sharkey, will
show up in Las Vegas? May I ask why?" the Commissaire asked.

"No Rosencrans Op, once having browsed so near incalculable
supplies of money, has ever been known to abandon such sources,
except on pain of death or dungeon. But if Mr. X is not Sharkey,
which, from all I know now, is entirely possible, I contend that
any man who would risk coming within range of Miss Leonard's
automatic, in order to pilfer from me a used cablegram of small
importance, on the face of it, will not let the matter drop either,"
said Homer confidently.

The *America's* next port of call, after Cannes, was Genoa, and
after Genoa, Naples. Evans urged Gromaire to use what connections he had to obtain pertinent information in those Italian seaboard cities, concerning the *America* and the passengers involved
in the case. He, himself, as an extra precaution, contacted civil-
ians and officials, by wire—all men for whom Homer had done
important favors—to secure their co-operation.

While Evans was occupied as summarized above, Miriam was
nursing and reassuring Maitre Sabin, who had suffered from air
sickness and nervous demoralization because of the venture on
which he had embarked, contrary to his inclinations and sober

judgment. Hjalmar and Tom Jackson, of course, found a nearby *bodega* and laid in impressive supplies of a Spanish distillation called *cazalla*, both inside and in jugs for the air road. *Cazalla*, it should be explained, as strong fire water, bears about the same relation to raw gin as gin does to vanilla ice-cream soda. The sensation, from lips to windpipe, when one tries *cazalla* for the first time, is like that which would result from swallowing a lighted kerosene lamp. The effect is seraphic and habit-forming only to the rugged who are a match for the stuff.

After Homer had retrieved Miriam and Sabin, following his long phone call to Cannes, all four made a round of neighboring saloons and it was fifteen or twenty minutes before they caught up with Hjalmar and Tom. Emerging from the bistro with the painter and the reporter in tow, Homer and Miriam both noticed that a thin column of smoke, somewhat like the skyward wisp from an Indian signal fire, while the morning air is still, was rising from the direction of the airfield. Homer started to run toward it, and the others followed as best they could. By the time Evans had got near his plane, misnamed the *Peu de Souci*, the engine was in flames. No suitable fire-fighting apparatus was at hand. So Homer and his companions had to watch their transportation burn before their eyes.

"There's no time to be lost investigating," Homer said doggedly. "Not if we wish to be sure of spotting Orman and Jordan in New York." Sabin was all for turning back to Cannes, by water. Miriam was regretting mildly the loss of so many chic Paris clothes and accessories. Hjalmar and Tom sat down, tailor fashion, in the glow of the dawn and the embers and began punishing the *cazalla*, reminiscing and conjecturing with Olympian detachment.

It did not take Evans many minutes to get into action along constructive or positive lines. He got the superintendent of the airfield out of bed, tipped him generously, learned that a Spanish commercial plane, not too crowded, would within the hour arrive and take off promptly for Dakar, on the coast of South Central Africa, and all the trade routes. Homer arranged that all the parts of his charred engine be shipped by air express to Las Vegas, sparing no expense.

"How fortunate that I kept all our specimens of pipsissewa extract in my brief case," Homer said. Then he briefed Miriam and the others on his talk with Commissaire Gromaire back in Cannes. He told them all that Orman, Madeleine, Odette and Jordan had taken flight just after midnight, having made sure that Finke and Forran were aboard the *America*. He divulged that the Commissaire, pathetically anxious to be rid of all participants in the case, had arranged that any possible stowaways be given a chance to quit France and be dumped in Italy. Of Luttenschlager's illness, he confided only in Miriam and asked her not to trouble Sabin with the news, just yet.

"Homer," Miriam asked, "do you think someone put a gimmick in our plane, intending to murder the lot of us?"

"That's possible. And if I establish it, as a fact, what would it indicate beyond the obvious?" he asked.

"That the murderer is insane," she said. "I realize from experience that dealing with madmen, as suspects or culprits, multiplies your difficulties a hundred times. Who'd have thought, when we started on a vacation, and to resolve Maitre Sabin's perplexity, or even distress, that we should get into a hornet's nest of vicious, unpredictable crimes?"

"Had we known what was ahead, we could scarcely have done otherwise. So let's continue," Homer said. "And bear in mind that stark madness and the ultimate in intelligence, or animal cunning, approach each other, as absolute zero and infinity do in mathematics."

"Everyone known to be involved in this mess is unusual in some important respects," Miriam said, and sighed. "That is, all excepting me, and possibly Gromaire."

"Wasn't it Cleveland who said, 'We're confronted with a situation, not a theory'?" mused Evans. He glanced skyward. "Ah," he added. "Here comes our Spanish crate, headed for Dakar. In Dakar we can buy practically anything, or get any kind of a lift."

In the same way Sabin expected scalp-seeking redskins to invade the byways of Las Vegas, he believed Mau Maus slit throats on the main avenues and verandas of Dakar. However, he was in no condition to resist, and Homer persuaded him to board the

Spanish plane. Hjalmar had a harder time getting his supply of *cazalla* aboard, since the transportation of inflammables was against all rules.

Our party landed at Dakar in mid-afternoon, and within half an hour, Homer had checked with Gromaire, learned that Luttenschlager was out of danger and the experts' analysis of what he had eaten or drunk left all hands more baffled than before they began.

"Without Jordan to help them, the Commissaire's chemists are nothing to brag about," Homer said.

"Don't forget the chap who found out so much about the noon-day shot at us from ambush, with only the hole in the windshield to go on," cautioned Miriam. "Could it be that the Commissaire, in revenge for what we delayed telling him, is holding out on us about Sabin's substitute?"

"Not likely. But neither Gromaire nor his subordinates are anxious to make extra work for themselves. They figure that if Luttenschlager recovers, well and good. Let frisky dogs cavort," was Homer's observation.

Fifteen more minutes passed before Evans had purchased another suitable plane, and flashed his global and perpetual license to fly it, anywhere, any time. It was of English make, and on it was lettered "Happy Hops." He had not flown the machine five hundred miles toward Newfoundland before all aboard were aware that it dropped, dipped and fluttered in air pockets almost scandalously. Otherwise, Homer found it sound. Miriam, since Homer was content, was warm with happiness. Hjalmar and Tom were voluble and becomingly browned, if not completely fried. Sabin squatted disconsolately, like a moulting seabird with two lame legs.

"I should have followed my old father's advice and entered a seminary to train for the priesthood," he groaned. "Then the worst that could happen was that I might be drafted as a chaplain, who would most likely remain on land. Unlike our allies who pursue foreign wars, France's worst battles take place in France or her colonies."

"Wait till you see Las Vegas," said Miriam cheerfully.

Sabin winced as if a poniard had been stuck in his back, as a warning or a threat. "Gangsters, gunmen, night owls, gamblers, millionaires, courtesans, prospectors, bleached bones, *vaqueros*, reptiles, wolves," the renowned chef muttered. Just then, the "Happy Hops" thudded through an air pocket and hit bottom like the Hesperus, judging from the jar. "Welcome oblivion! Spare us, O Lord, these preliminary bumps!" was Sabin's response, as he reached for the bottle Hjalmar extended. The great gastronomer gulped incautiously and received the jolt of his life, palate-wise. Before he had stopped coughing and all but choking, he was nearer St. John's by several hundred miles, and meanwhile had worried about nothing but continued respiration. When the chef recovered, to the point where he could take a glass of water and wipe the tears from his eyes, he looked at Hjalmar and Tom as if seeing them for the first time.

"Doesn't liquor like that, even if your inner tissues are tanned and glazed to withstand it, keep you perpetually awake?" Sabin asked the lusty pair.

As a last resort, the famous wine taster determined to sustain conversation, in the hope it would make the time seem to pass less funereally.

"Friends in adversity," Sabin began, "yesterday—alas, it already seems dim in the past—you annoyed the Commissaire, for which I commend you, by touching enigmatically on matters of art. Specifically you admitted to Monsieur Evans that you had maneuvered Orman and/or his contrasting mistresses into a binding agreement that you were to paint the young women's portraits."

"You bet! In Goya style, although the old sucker knows nothing of that," Hjalmar assured Sabin, grinning quite lewdly the while.

"What should we do without Goya?" chimed in Tom Jackson.

"Having never been to Madrid, where, I assume, the Spaniards, whatever else can be said of them, have had the good sense and *amour propre* to retain their masterpieces of art within their boundaries, to a considerable extent, and never having had the leisure to read extensively about paintings or painters, I understand less than nothing on the subject. From what you said, or the suggestive way in which you said it, I had the feeling that it was your assurance to those girls that you would follow the example or style of Goya in portraying them that made them eager to obtain for you the commission. Am I far astray?" Sabin paused to ask.

"You could not be more exactly on the beam," Tom Jackson said, and he looked as gleeful in anticipation of the coming event as Hjalmar did.

Miriam, glad that Sabin had hit upon something to ease his troubled mind, took over the explanation. "You are puzzled, *cher Maitre*, by the phrase 'in Goya style,' are you not?" she began.

"Due to my ignorance," Sabin said, sadly. "I am also impressed by the fact that this rich spendthrift, Orman, tried deliberately to ditch our friends, Jansen and Jackson, by sending them on a protracted sea voyage, while he and his to-be-painted à-la-Goya mistresses flew, Mr. Evans thinks, to New York and thence to Las Vegas."

"Orman is a suspicious old bastard. He might have been afraid our influence on his women was bad—from his point of view, not theirs, you understand," Hjalmar said.

"He knew we both were without money. Could be that he expected we'd be cast ashore in Macaroni Land, and eventually be detained in quod or tardily deported. Whatever qualms we might have had, formerly, about poaching on this senile duffer's preserves, can no longer be considered valid," Tom Jackson declared.

"Right. He, himself, has declared an open season," said Hjalmar.

Miriam raised her eyebrows. "From what little I observed, Madeleine and Odette did nothing to discourage your direct approaches and blatant camaraderie," she said. "I find that stimulating."

A gasp from Sabin caused the others to look into his face, from which his eyes were bulging incredulously. "Mademoiselle, you seem not only to condone the antics of these bibulous wolves, but to encourage them in their ruthless enterprise."

"I'll admit," Miriam said, "that Mr. Evans might welcome any kind of diversion that would, when we all meet again in Las Vegas, rile Mr. Orman to the point where his jealousy and rage would render him otherwise incautious. He has a strong, tenacious and even sensitive mind, but it is not perfectly compartmentalized. A wound in his *amour impropre* might disable his other faculties."

The great chef drew himself up, resolutely if not proudly.

"The gastronomic arts and high cuisine are above vulgar intrigue, morality, good and evil, and petty considerations or reprehensible plots," Sabin declared. He relaxed, rebuked by the stiffness of his own pronouncements. "Forgive me, friends. I'll climb down from my self-erected pedestal, and laugh. Cuckoldism has been France's most fruitful source of comedy. That this brace of champion drinkers will surely seduce the oil man's blonde and brunette, respectively, or even collectively, stirs my sense of the ridiculous and at the same time of fitness."

"Now you're talking," said Hjalmar, clapping the chef on the back. Simultaneously Miriam saw Sabin's jaw drop, his eyes protrude, his gorge convulse and his breath suspend itself. For Homer, blessed with amazingly smooth weather, considering it was November over the North Atlantic, had set the automatic controls to keep "Happy Hops" on its course to St. John's. Consequently, he felt free to quit the pilot's seat for a while and join the intriguing conversation which hitherto had progressed behind his back. Sabin, unaccustomed to methods of flying or any of their details, either primitive or modern, assumed, on seeing Evans leave the tiller, that he was abandoning ship and would shout "*Sauve qui peut.*"

Any passenger in an airplane flying at an altitude of two or more miles who was given permission to "save himself" could hardly give or express his thanks. Instead, a line from Rabelais, which Panurge of yore had uttered when threatened with shipwreck, popped from the chef's blue lips.

"Happy is he who plants potatoes," was what he said, and was as much surprised as anyone.

"Don't be alarmed," Homer said, to re-establish his old friend's morale. "The automatic pilot is perfectly safe. There's no other traffic in this frigid region for miles and miles around."

"Ah, well. If one must fall ten thousand feet, most likely its less painful to plunge into fathomless water than to collide with solid ground," Sabin said.

Homer changed the subject back to the one which had interested Sabin the most. "You were asking about the painting of lovely women 'in Goya style,'" Evans began. "There's no mystery about that. Goya enjoyed, as a favorite among his many mistresses, the ardor and surrender of a Duchess whose husband, the Duke, was highly influential in court circles. The Spanish master painted this ravishing woman fully dressed, for the fatuous Duke, and the resulting canvas is now called 'La Maya Vestida,' or 'The Woman, Clothed.' But while Goya was painting the 'Maya Vestida' for frank display in court, he took time between sittings—the Duchess actually was reclining—to paint for himself 'La Maya Desnuda,' or 'The Woman, Nude.' In both instances, the pose was identical."

"Gad! What flesh tones, what soft radiance, what exquisite play of light," Hjalmar exclaimed, his face and voice both transformed by his reverence for superb painting, old or contemporary.

The high-strung chef, despite the tension of his nerves and his dismal expectations of the near or distant future, could not withhold a hearty laugh, and an eloquent shrug.

"Young men," he said to Hjalmar and Tom. "Make use of the hay or eiderdown while you still are able and inclined." And, turning to Miriam, he added: "Trust no one but yourself."

7
Near the Spreading Chestnut Tree

THE STOP AT ST. JOHN'S, NEWFOUNDLAND, was merely for refueling. Nevertheless, Sabin found much to disconcert him. The snow was from one to six feet deep, erratically drifted, and the natives either spoke a dialect of English which could have been enunciated better if they had had squid in their months, or a kind of French to be found only in discarded old books, yellowed with age.

"Monsieur Evans," the chef implored, "over the frightening desert toward which we progress, will the thermometer, at least, be moderate? Otherwise I may as well dig into a snowbank, like a discouraged Eskimo, and give up the ghost, if mine already is not depleted to a frazzle."

"The days are hot, clear and sunny; the desert nights are clear and cool. In Las Vegas one seldom sees frost on the pumpkin or icicles suspended from eaves," Homer assured him.

In a matter of minutes, Hjalmar and Tom had been torn from a bar room by Miriam, and the "Happy Hops," with all its passengers and its owner-pilot, was aloft and speeding toward the States. When they descended, three hours later, in Boston, Sabin was unstrung again.

"The skyline is all wrong," the chef insisted, under the misapprehension that they were in New York.

"We'll soon be in New York," Homer assured him. "Boston and Cambridge have only the Charles River between them. Being so near the birthplace and alma mater of Mr. Howard Scott Jordan, I would be remiss if I did not try to garner more information about that enigmatic young savant. You, Miriam, had better come along with me on my tour of inquiry. Maitre Sabin, I'd recommend that you breakfast heartily at Durgin and Park's, in the center of the Faneuil Hall market district. If you keep an open mind, you may be amazed at what Boston has to offer a true gourmet and amateur of sound provisions, wholesomely presented."

"What about us?" Hjalmar asked, indicating Tom and himself.

"Take breakfast with Maitre Sabin. In this region the morning repast is, perhaps, the most important meal of the day. Then taxi to the Bellevue bar, just east of the State House. We'll all meet here at the airport at high noon and be in New York in time for lunch," Homer suggested. "Oh, yes, I should warn you that Bostonians have a local favorite drink called a 'Ward Eight.' The color is pink and the effect varies, according to a drinker's constitution. If I were you, I should stick to old-fashioneds, with no fruit or bitters, and very little ice."

"Caesar hath spoken," agreed Tom Jackson, who had been peering around in the hope of seeing one of the traditional Boston newsboys who wore pince-nez and carried on their small talk in Latin.

With Miriam on his arm, Homer proceeded to the taxi stand and within a few minutes they descended at the Parker House, asking the chauffeur to wait.

"I'll need you most of the morning," Homer said.

"Yes, Mr. Evans," said the chauffeur, who well remembered the press reports of Homer's brilliant work in connection with the ice-pick and fireplace murder in Back Bay, and the subsequent conviction of one Edgey Gerry (or Etchegaray).

The Parker House has unusually comfortable and efficient long-distance telephone accommodations, and while Miriam glanced over the Boston *Herald*, to see if the day's crop of news items would interest Homer, he phoned

Commissaire Gromaire in Cannes. This was what he gleaned:

Nothing further had been heard from Clifford Orman, his mistresses, or Howard Scott Jordan.

Finke and Talbot Forran, having landed at Genoa, had caught a fast passenger plane for New York, which had left a few minutes before Homer's call had been put through to Gromaire.

A stowaway, answering to either the descriptions of Mr. X or Luke Sharkey, had been spotted by the Chief Steward of the *America*, who would have had him quietly deported in Genoa had not the said stowaway bribed some of the petty officers and crewmen and contrived to land, informally, on his own.

Monsieur Luttenschlager was safely on the road to recovery from his attack of acute indigestion, and the police chemists and technicians were still in the dark as to whether he might have swallowed poison or not.

A light dawned in Miriam's consciousness as Homer relayed to her the above information. "Then we'll all come together in New York . . . or don't you want it that way?" she asked.

"I'm not positive about Mr. X or Luke Sharkey. But the indications are that they are one and the same man. The steward on the *America* did not mention that his stowaway escapee had been wounded in the right arm, but quite possibly he would overlook or consider unimportant such a minor injury. Now that I'm sure that Sharkey broke into my suite at the Hotel des Anglais, just to steal Sabin's cablegram, and aware he was risking his life almost idiotically, I'm inclined to assume that the stakes in this contest are high enough to make the Rosencrans Op, possibly the whole outfit, foolhardy and reckless to the nth degree."

"You didn't hear from Commissaire Gromaire about Chevalier, whether or not he has signed up, because of Finke, or for other reasons?" Miriam inquired.

"Remind me to ask the Commissaire about the incomparable Maurice the next time I phone him," said Homer, and they made haste to re-enter their waiting taxi and proceed to Cambridge, west

of the Charles. On the Harvard campus, Evans was not at a loss as
to where to find elementary facts about one of the university's most
publicized graduates. Dean Margolis, the father of one of Homer's
Montparnasse associates nicknamed "Chowderhead," was anxious
to be of service and no door at Harvard, however private, was closed
to him. The biographical material, reduced to its essentials, was
noted by Homer, as follows:

Jordan, Howard Scott, born Cambridge, Mass., Feb. 16, 1922.
Father, Archibald Howard Jordan, of Amesbury, Mass.; mother,
Rosa Gott Birch, of Newburyport, Mass. Harvard University, class
of 1934, B.S. summa cum laude; M.S. 1936; Ph.D. 1937. At age of
13, in late 1935, Jordan was sent by parents on lecture tours, which
continued until 1942, when Jordan was twenty. From 1942 until
1947, Jordan was connected with the Army Intelligence, G-2, on
special duty, the exact nature of which is still top secret. Late in
1947, Jordan was honorably discharged from the Army and entered
the employ of the Charles E. Hires Co., of Philadelphia, in their
laboratory situated in Cambridge, Mass. He was listed as Research
Chemist, with a salary of $12,000 a year, which was gradually in-
creased to $15,000 before he quit the Hires organization to do "free
lance" work, in 1952. His last residence was listed as Las Vegas,
Nevada, where he was director of a private research laboratory
endowed by an anonymous philanthropist.

"Did you have personal contacts with the boy when he was en-
rolled here or working for his higher degrees?" Homer asked Dean
Margolis.

"Plenty. He took at least four courses, supposedly 'under' me.
Actually he was nearly always a few steps ahead of me," the Dean
said ruefully.

"Was he odd, or offensive, as some young prodigies are?" asked
Homer.

"Not exactly. The kid was disconcertingly poised and sustained
an even mood, almost uniformly. He was aware of his own almost
limitless powers, intellectually, and skeptical as to their desira-
bility. He was aghast, if not frightened, when infrequently he had
to associate with boys near his own age. Adults he treated with

aloofness and suspicion, in the case of his parents, quite well-founded. Until he was twenty, they exploited him, and must have put by a pretty penny. Since he started working for Hires, he has had no commerce with either his father or his mother, and they have complained bitterly and without too much dignity about their loss of revenue, in the press and privately."

"Excellent! Excellent!" said Homer, perversely pleased. "Can you give me their address?"

"With pleasure, if you are likely to annoy them," said the Dean. "They live in the same house, but not exactly together. For the last twenty-five years or more, since they settled in Cambridge from Essex County, they have slept apart, at different hours. Each one prepares his or her own meals, which they eat in separate rooms, alternating weekly between the use of the kitchen and dining room. Young Jordan, as far back as he can remember, and he has practically total recall, from the age of two, was obliged to eat with his mother one week and his father the next."

"By Jove," Homer said, "that may explain, in part, his vagaries of taste."

"In all his chemistry classes, where acute taste is most helpful, Jordan excelled all classmates and professors, including me," said Dean Margolis.

Homer, as if struck by an intriguing idea, rose to his feet and clapped his hands gleefully. "Could you oblige me by sending out for a bottle of Hires Root Beer?"

Dean Margolis was glad to accede to Homer's unexpected request and within five minutes the Dean's gentleman handed Homer a bottle of the soft drink in question.

"Shall I uncap it, sir?" asked the valet.

"Don't take the trouble," Homer answered. As the valet retired from the room, Homer was reading the list of ingredients set forth on the label. He smiled and chuckled happily. "The fates are with us, Miriam," he said. "May I enumerate the components of this popular beverage?"

Both Miriam and the Dean were puzzled, but anxious for him to continue. So he read, almost intoning:

"Carbonated water, sugar, dextrose, caramel, plant extractives of birch, sassafras, licorice, vanilla, spikenard, sarsaparilla . . ."

"Merciful Heaven!" exclaimed Dean Margolis, no mean gourmet himself. "Folks actually swallow that combination."

"Hear me out," begged Evans, and he continued:

"Hops, wintergreen, ginger, artificial flavor and . . ." Homer purposely kept his hearers for a moment in suspense before he climaxed his strange revelation. Then he said, triumphantly, "Pipsissewa."

With a rueful shake of his head, Dean Margolis said, "Like the proponent of Omar's great poem, as translated by Edward Fitzgerald, I seem to be coming out of this delightful and potentially instructive chat 'by the same door that in I went.' What, may I ask, is so significant about pipsissewa, whatever that may be, in a soft-drink combination?"

"Pipsissewa is an evergreen extractive, redolent of the north woods, which may be used with intriguing effect in cake frostings, icings and garnitures," explained Homer.

"In that case, pipsissewa should be proud of itself," the Dean remarked, dryly. "What has that to do with Mr. Howard Scott Jordan, or shouldn't I ask?"

"We—Miss Leonard and I—are unraveling a rather puzzling case, in which Jordan is somehow involved. In Cannes, at the leading restaurant of the Riviera, our prodigy detected the flavor of pipsissewa in the icing of pungent rum-soaked cake, and at the same time manifested indifference in choosing between ordinary table pinot and a vintage Chateau Lafitte. Furthermore, he preferred to eat his salad as a first course, which is the surest way of paralyzing taste buds and debasing discriminating appetite. . . . Well, we must be off, to call on the Jordans, *père et mère*. From what you've said, they may not prove banal."

"Bad cess to them, from me," Dean Margolis said. "And to all profiteers and exploiters of unusual genius, sprouting prematurely. Please call more often, Homer. You, too, Miss Leonard. *Au revoir!*"

The investigating couple found the Jordan residence not more than a block from Longfellow's "spreading chestnut tree" under which the blacksmith had toiled when Cambridge was a village.

Homer pressed the bell button. No response. After repeated button pushes, he knocked resoundingly, quite a while. Eventually a Judas window in the old oaken door was slid aside a mere crack and a shrill woman's voice demanded:

"Who's there?"

"Are you Mrs. A. H. Jordan?" Homer asked, as pleasantly as he could.

"Who wants to know?" Mrs. Jordan demanded.

"A friend of your son," answered Homer.

"Then you're no friend of ourn. Go away," Mrs. Jordan said, and reclosed the Judas peep slit.

A man's voice set up a hullabaloo of protest. The Judas window was opened as much as three inches, and a sharp-faced, unshaven man in advanced middle age gave Homer and particularly Miriam a suspicious once over.

"You sellin' anything?" A. H. Jordan rasped testily.

"On the contrary, I've a Thanksgiving message and present from your son, Howard. I just left him in Cannes," Homer improvised.

"All right. Come in," Mr. Jordan said.

His wife practically screamed. A. H. Jordan turned to Homer who handed him a fifty-dollar bill. "This is from Howard, for your Thanksgiving turkeys. He told me that, most likely, you'd require two of them, since you prefer to prepare them in different styles. It was the great Frenchman, Brillat-Savarin, who, after visiting America in the days of George Washington's first term, said 'The American turkey is, in a sense, a disappointing bird. It's just too big for one, and not quite big enough for two.' "

"You say Howard's in France?" Mrs. Jordan asked malignantly. "How come?"

"Last we heard, he was in Las Vegas. But for twelve years, until today, he hasn't sent us one red cent. Is that gratitude?" Mr. Jordan said bitterly.

"According to my best information, although Howard never brought up the subject, you saved enough, when he was lecturing and later, when he was in the Army, to tide you over the next hundred years," Homer said, to provoke an outburst.

"What if we did?"

"He got his brains from my side. My father was the best sing-ing master north of Boston. He could read them crazy notes as if they were print," said the touchy father, still grasping the fifty Homer had given him.

His wife made a grab for it, and would have torn it in halves had he not forcibly restrained her.

"Watch out, young lady," warned Mrs. Jordan, glaring at Miriam. "This old skinflint takes after his father, not with his brains, but his fingers."

In fact, Mr. Jordan had sidled nearer to Miriam, in the course of the colloquy. She edged away, and Homer, after saying polite good-byes and "happy holidays" to the Jordans, led her out to their waiting taxi in the quaint historical old street. The clock said 11:15, so they drove directly to the East Boston airport, where Hjalmar and Tom Jackson met them, somewhat to Homer's surprise. He was told, at once, however, that they were on time because Sabin, who was snoring in the plane, had drunk too much at the Bellevue and had had to be cared for solicitously. Among their other attrac-tive qualities, the pair of Montparnasse tosspots had the ability to come up from alcoholic depths and rally round when a friend was in need. It would be an exaggeration to say that they were as sober as judges, but they were not nearly as drunk as owls boiled in schnapps.

La Guardia Field, in New York, was only an hour away and the flight was accomplished without incident. When they landed, how-ever, Homer was approached by a couple of Federal agents who told him what he most wanted to know, namely: that Clifford Orman, with Jordan and two "secretaries" had arrived from Cannes within the hour and were resting at the Carlton House. A plane chartered by Talbot Forran at Genoa was expected soon, and had a private detective, licensed in California, aboard with him.

"What's cooking, out there on the Coast?" asked one of the ac-commodating G-men. To Easterners, generally, Las Vegas, two hundred and fifty miles inland, was considered a seaboard resort, to all practical intents and purposes.

"As matters stand at present," Homer admitted, candidly, "you know about as much as I do of the situation. Las Vegas is booming, and outwardly the set-up seems as stable as one of those old Roman structures with no mortar between stones. Clifford Orman lives there, for the time being at least, and in his head is forming some colossal design which may, or may not, transform Las Vegas' gangland truce into a sanguine free-for-all. Talbot Forran, representing the night-spot owners of the Hollywood Strip, has been in Paris on a mysterious errand, intended, I think, to improve Hollywood's position in the entertainment field and get back some of the money the Las Vegas attractions have diverted from California."

"You haven't mentioned the distinguished-looking Frenchman who still seems to be asleep in your plane," another G-man observed. "He doesn't look like an actor. Or anyone mixed up in show business."

"Just an old friend who runs a restaurant. He hasn't had a vacation in years," Homer said.

"So he hooks up with you, to visit Las Vegas. He'll have a rest, all right. Mostly likely, a permanent," the agent said dryly. "Well. Let us know if we can serve you further. Preferably by long-distance phone, from way out West. What happens on this coast piles up work for us, and since so many criminals have become climate-conscious and settled in what Californians call 'The Southland,' we've grown lazy back here."

Homer thanked his informers, wished them all the leisure in the world, and started formulating his plan. He sent Miriam, with Hjalmar and Tom, to lunch at Luchow's, while he headed for the Carlton to beard the lion in his princely suite. Mounting to the floor, far aloft, where Orman had installed himself and his entourage, Evans gained admittance and was received by the oil millionaire with misgivings.

"You followed us?" Orman asked accusingly.

"Not exactly. You preceded *me*," Homer replied. "It strikes me that all concerned, who are headed westward and have interests opposed, or in common, might just as well quit playing hide and seek. In view of modern facilities for transportation and communication, the old game, so jolly in the past, is today rather silly. Mr. Talbot Forran, with my protégé, Finke McGuire, will be at La Guardia field in a matter of minutes. I brought with me Maitre Sabin, and my Montparnasse friends, the painter and the reporter you tried to sidetrack so shabbily in Cannes, after having agreed, in the presence of competent witnesses, that Jansen should paint portraits of Madeleine and Odette."

"Be reasonable," begged Orman. "That Norwegian bruiser can't be trusted with women, young or old. You know I haven't the spare time to chaperone the girls, while they are sitting for the brute. And if I don't, I'll either suspect the worst, or be sure of it. How can a man keep his mind on a project like mine, which will reshape tens of thousands of human lives, transform maps, channel streams of currency and credit, and make my name a watchword in the annals of frenzied finance, if his young female companions are exposed to worse than death? Furthermore, that treacherous reporter, Jackson, must have been assigned to ferret out my plans, and, if he has a chance, is sure to expose them prematurely."

"Surely you're clever enough to mask your maneuvers until you're ready to strike. I confess frankly that, although you've taken considerable pains to arouse my curiosity, I haven't the foggiest notion as to what you are plotting. Neither, might I add, has Jackson—yet. Be sure you do not underrate these modest gentlemen merely because they take their daily lives more lightly than most. Hjalmar is as good a portraitist as you could engage, if you knew as much about art as I do. And Jackson, when he starts on the track of a story, seldom fails. You'd do better to treat these men considerately, and have them on your side. Hjalmar is a match for any six gangsters in the land in a battle royal. Tom Jackson responds to candor and confidence in quite a touching manner. Assure him that, when the moment is just right, you'll give him the inside track, and he'll lean over backwards to be fair with you."

"On the level?" asked Orman, impressed.

"Honor bright," Homer said. "I've known these chaps for years. And as to Finke McGuire, he's such a square-shooter with his client that he hasn't breathed a word about their pussyfoot excursions, not even to me. And I discovered him, trained him and set him up in business."

"The same doesn't go for that vicious old dyspeptic, Forran. He hates me, because I'm bigger than he is, and my town, Las Vegas, has put his on the blink," Orman declared, his own dislike of the Gyro impresario coming out like a fever or a rash.

"Should you invite him to fly west with all of us," Homer suggested, "wouldn't he eat his heart out, trying to guess why? Wouldn't he be furious, that you held his enmity so lightly? Isn't it possible that, in an outburst of temper, he might be indiscreet? You say you're a bigger man. I'm inclined to grant that. But why have scope if you're hesitant about using it?"

Orman, his eyes shining, had begun pacing the floor, chuckling and lacing and unlacing his fingers. "Evans, I must have you in my organization, which before has been a one-man show. Please, for the sake of all I represent on the summit of private enterprise, let me retain you."

"At present, as I've told you," Homer said gently, "I've a commitment to Maitre Sabin. Until I make sure that his interests do not conflict with yours, I can't take advantage of your offer. And what's more, there is the question of Luke Sharkey, and his archchief, Rosencrans. You have not formally dismissed them, as yet!"

"Damnation," roared Orman. "I'd spit in his eye if I could find him. He agreed to meet me at the train, when I returned to Cannes. Instead, so I assume, he broke into your suite, unauthorized by me, needless to say, and your Miss Leonard, instead of drilling him in a vital spot, purposely nicked his funny bone. He vanished into thin air."

"As a matter of fact, he stowed away on the *America*, was discovered by the ship's officers who had agreed with the Commissaire of Cannes, and me, to turn him over to the police at Naples," said Homer.

"Fine. Bully. That's the ticket!" said Orman, pacing and capering again. "Those boys at Naples know how to handle the likes of him."

"Not so fast. Sharkey bribed some stewards and able seamen, vanished over the side, and got clean away. In or near Naples, where crooks are as thick as maggots in overripe Brie. He may be anywhere by now. I wouldn't be surprised if he were right in this hotel," Homer said, and added: "Now isn't that another point in favor of your inviting all of us—Forran, Finke, Hjalmar, Jackson, Sabin, Miriam and me, and, of course, Jordan, Madeleine and Odette—to be your airplane guests for a westbound flight, taking off today, about sundown?"

"I must locate Sharkey, and fire him," Orman said, as if he had agreed to the rest of Homer's proposition.

"You don't have to discharge Sharkey in person, since he's deliberately avoided making himself available, after accepting your retainer. Phone Rosencrans himself, in Los Angeles. Storm, beef, protest, and insist that the Agency relieve you from all obligations to Sharkey, and vice versa. Have Rosencrans forbid Sharkey from approaching or molesting you. Say, if you like, that you're trying to retain me. Nothing will upset the whole Rosencrans outfit as much as being told that I may be entering the picture."

"I'll do as you advise," Orman said, and gave Homer free rein to charter an air transport, at no matter what cost, and with fitting accommodations for the nine passengers already specified. So Evans sped to the La Guardia airport, intercepted Finke, convinced Forran that he would lose face if he seemed afraid to accept Orman's invitation. Sabin, by twilight, had recovered from his excesses in Boston. Hjalmar and Tom had promised to let bygones be bygones and ride with the oil man without open indiscretions with his girls. Miriam bought some clothes at New York prices, to replace those lost when *Peu de Souci* burned at the airport in the Azores. Before the sun had approached the western horizon, a magnificent modern airliner, complete with pilot, assistant pilot, and stewardess, coasted down the runway at La Guardia, cleared the rooftops of Queens, and started a non-stop flight to Las Vegas.

It seemed to Homer, who had set out unencumbered, that step by step he seemed to have acquired what he least had expected or wanted, that is, a personal responsibility for the safety and the future of quite a sizable and varied assortment of his human brethren and sisters. No longer could he be the detached observer or explore the physiology of taste.

8

In Which the Impossible Becomes Probable

LAS VEGAS, heat- and dust-ridden by day, on flats shaved level when prehistoric ice receded, set between files and ranks of calico hills which once were mountains, lies inert until twilight touches stray clouds with magic. Then the nocturnal revels begin, and continue until after dawn. Nothing like Las Vegas has existed hitherto in either of the Americas. To find a true parallel, as we already have observed, one must hark back to the legendary "cities of the plain," some of which were razed in internecine strife, others by foreign conquerors, a few by the wrath of a jealous god.

It is true that Brigham Young, the Mormon sage, saint and sinner, sent a picked delegation of his toughest pioneers and their hardiest women with a wagon train, bound southwest. That wild band of adventurers, who already had made Salt Lake City too hot to contain them, were instructed to find the desert area, believed by Young to be beyond the United States borders, acquire it for token payments from the native Redskins, and start another Mormon stake. The Nevada Indians were notoriously indolent, for the most part. Troublesome braves who resisted conversion were bumped off with dispatch. Sightly young squaws who seemed willing to serve Latter-Day Saints, and contribute one-tenth of the proceeds as tithes, were "absorbed."

The braves who preferred to migrate rather than die or perform steady work were encouraged to depart. The male Mormons, Jack Mormons or Gentiles, settled all disputes about the proprietorship of amiable squaws by lot. In fact, resorting to chance on any pretext seemed to be inherent in the natives as well as the invaders. During its hundred years of history, Las Vegas has nurtured gamblers and respected them.

It was not until after World War I that what is called "big business" spread tentacles over Las Vegas. The Federal Government gave the growing gaming city a boost by building the highest irrigation dam in the world a few miles out of town, thus providing a No. 1 tourist attraction for those who did not like to proclaim that roulette, blackjack or craps had drawn them from distant and respectable places to the desert Babylon.

In a city where general abandon breeds corresponding wariness, on the part of the wise, rumors spread fast, omens are respected, alarms for one affect all, and for all seem ominous to each person. Gamblers may be gamesters first and people afterward. They are people, nevertheless, who glow when they are favored, complain when they are thwarted, cultivate friends when they can, and refrain from making enemies.

Las Vegas was subtly transformed, when the approach of Orman's chartered plane, with its mixed contingent of passengers, was heralded from the airport on the western outskirts, along the fabulous "Strip" and all the way downtown. First, a formerly distinguished welterweight who fought under the name of Gentleman Gene Delmont, and was known to boxing fans for his polished manners, correct speech and meticulously sportsmanlike conduct in and out of the ring, received a telegram from Homer Evans, requesting that rooms be reserved at the Thunderbird, a fine resort hotel and casino, where Delmont presided over the rear section of the drinking space, from 8 P.M. until 4 in the morning, for a visiting Norwegian portrait painter, resident in Paris, Hjalmar Jansen by name, and a foreign correspondent for the New York *Herald Tribune* and the Paris *Herald Tribune*, one Thomas Pantagruel Jackson.

Had not the message come to Gene Delmont, and had not other telegrams, addressed to Mrs. Odilla O'Brien and Kid Unamuno, been received, also signed by Homer Evans, at the same time, the operator who translated the dots and dashes into words might not have felt it his duty to send word to the sheriff of the county, the city editor of the Las Vegas *Bugle*, and a certain lawyer who had acted as mouthpiece for some of the most important gangsters with copies of the telegrams and a hint that something unusual might well be afoot. The superintendent of the airport let it be known that Multimillionaire Clifford Orman had chartered the plane in question and was bringing with him, among other fellow travelers, his young women companions, blonde Madeleine and olive-skinned Odette, as well as the mysterious and odd young research chemist, Mr. Howard Scott Jordan, whose functions had remained a sealed mystery to everyone in town, with the possible exceptions of Orman and the dangerous Kid Unamuno, whose brain power bore an adverse ratio to his scruples, and his malice to his years.

The Widow O'Brien had been informed that her tenant, and in a way her Nemesis, Homer Evans, was bringing with him a more or less permanent house guest, one Maitre Jean Sabin, who rated high, indeed, among French chefs. The tempestuous Basque woman had growled, erupted, chewed rugs and towels, and sworn she would have the hide of any foreigner who caused her to lose face.

Now Gentleman Gene Delmont had known and admired Homer Evans since his boxing days, during which the now famous criminologist gave the former welterweight some valuable guidance in the art of modified murder. Gene's instinct was to hasten to the Western Union office in an effort to plug any possible leaks about Homer's incipient arrival, the Chesterfieldian ex-pugilist being aware that Evans usually preferred to come or go without fanfare. Alas for Gene's good intentions, he was told all about his own telegram and those received only a few minutes previously by the city's prize juvenile delinquent and his tempestuous mother. So Gene went back to sleep. Gene's day was divided into three parts, like Caesar's Gaul. The sympathetic little scrapper worked from 8 P.M. to 4 A.M., as we have said. From 4 until 12 noon, he played poker in one of the Thunderbird's most select back rooms, with parties most of whom could afford to lose but seldom did. On that Tuesday in November, just before Thanksgiving Day, the black and the red of Gene's unwritten accounts, including receipts from his ring career and subsequent service in gambling establishments, balanced almost to the cent. His wardrobe was unusually well stocked and cared for, his word was better than his bond, and the optimism which had carried him through so many bouts of fight or frolic still held firm.

The next best thing to suppressing the spread of gossip and conjecture about the incoming "Greeley Cool" and its passengers, Gene concluded, was to meet Homer at the airport and forewarn him that practically everyone in Las Vegas was expecting him, and his known or unknown companions. With that in mind, Gene set his gold-plated alarm clock, which had been presented him on the occasion when he had stayed fifteen rounds with Mickey Walker and upset most of the bets. Mrs. O'Brien, Homer's cook, had decided also to be on hand when the private airliner landed, in order to get a fast look at the French chef she already detested. Kid Unamuno made a similar plan, to annoy his grandmother further and see what else he could see.

Ensconsed cozily in the speeding "Greeley Cool," Homer was continuing his talk to Sabin about Las Vegas, aware that his efforts, thus far, to reassure his gifted old friend, had fallen short of their mark.

"The fact that some of the most enjoyable night spots are owned and operated by characters whose past record is deplorable has been overstressed by news magazines and the daily press," Evans was saying. "True, there may be in Las Vegas, highly placed as to brackets and prospects, types representing Murder, Inc., the old Cleveland-Cincinnati backbreakers, Ward Three boys from New Jersey, the modern Syndicate which, to an extent, has developed from the sons of the aging Moustache Petes of the old Sicilian Mafia, or Black Hand."

"I beg of you, excuse me from descending. Let this plane convey me back home," implored Sabin.

"Cease worrying," Homer urged the great chef. "After a lifetime in orderly moderate France, it will rejuvenate you to enjoy a place where luck outweighs merit, the rich or poor may lose or win, and personal violence is practically taboo, as long as one is careful to stay near the middle of the State. Never forget that you have

Miss Leonard to protect you, to say nothing of our amiable giant, Hjalmar Jansen—and, for what I am worth, myself."

"Such phenomenal protection implies a need for it," reasoned Maitre Sabin. "Perhaps I should jump from a window."

"Your religion insists that self-destruction is a sin," Homer said with a smile. "My own experience in Las Vegas has not been encyclopedic, but it is extensive enough for me to have observed that abandon is contagious, and joy through risk may become epidemic. In Las Vegas, even the few who work seem to like their job and the environment. It is one of the few cities on record where nobody ever is known to have starved, although the suicide rate is lamentably high, and centers around the telegraph office, which for the tender in heart is out of bounds."

Sabin, overcome, went to the men's room to brood. Finke replaced him at Homer's side. The younger man was palpably distressed, and ordinarily almost nothing worried Finke. However, he contrived to call Homer's attention to a potentially disastrous drama affecting three of their traveling companions. Madeleine, Orman's luscious blonde, having drunk freely of the champagne the stewardess frequently served, as a matter of course, had edged into the seat with Hjalmar Jansen, who had been faithful to the *cazalla* he had brought from the Azores. Up to that time, the Norwegian painter had kept his promise to Homer, to the effect that he would make no passes at Orman's women while up in the air. The close physical contact, however, that results when a bulky man and well-rounded woman press close together in an airplane seat for two, about wide enough for one and a half, plays havoc with honorable intentions, if both parties are as susceptible as the members of the pair in question.

The covetous look that was transforming Hjalmar's all-too-expressive face was suggestive of the leer on one of the faces of an angel the old reprobate among painters, Boucher, had introduced into one of his most outrageous backgrounds. Madeleine, eyes half closed and breath coming shorter and shorter, reflected on her fair physiognomy an inner light that seemed to cry for the most disconcerting of sound effects.

So far the situation seemed inevitable, or well and good. Had not Clifford Orman, pathologically possessive, been staring at the pair, like an immobilized bird charmed by a couple of snakes, neither Homer, Finke nor anyone else would have deplored the implications of the tableau. Miriam, feeling troubled emanations from Homer's strong mind, lowered her magazine and cautiously surveyed the scene.

It was at the same instant that both Homer and Miriam, whose eyes somehow seemed to encompass an extremely wide angle, saw, with surprise, that on the signal panel above the front door of the passenger section the pilot had flashed a warning:

"No Smoking. Fasten Seat Belts."

Clifford Orman also regarded the warning signal without any visible reaction. For he was writing furiously a document which he signed, and asked the stewardess and Jordan to witness. Before the ink was fairly dry, Orman, a look of maniacal satisfaction on his face, rolled the document and placed it in an empty champagne bottle, which he re-corked after chewing down the swelled stopper to appropriate size. He then, in spite of the stewardess' protest, lowered his window and tossed the bottle out.

Simultaneously, Homer confirmed his feeling that the plane was sixty or more miles from the Las Vegas airport. Without an instant's hesitation, he went forward, careful not to walk fast enough to alarm the others, opened the door to the pilot's cabin and closed it behind him.

Both the pilot and co-pilot were too busy to explain what was wrong. The former was manipulating certain of the controls frantically, the latter was engaged in curt, emergency communication over the radio-phone.

Miriam, knowing Homer would be most useful up forward, spotted the passenger who was showing the most agitation, namely, Mr. Talbot Forran. Nothing she could do or say dissuaded the angry impresario from growling, spluttering and threatening to sue all and sundry. But he glared at Clifford Orman the while.

In turn, Orman was fixing his malicious burning eyes on Madeleine and Hjalmar, who, more recklessly pressed together, side by side, had failed to remark either the warning signal or any unusual behavior of their fellow passengers.

They had forgotten, it seemed, that they were not alone. Odette, feeling sure that Orman had made a new Last Will and Testament, cutting off Madeleine without a penny, hesitated, then reached deeply into her pool of loyalty and took the seat in front of the foolhardy pair.

"Are you both out of your minds?" the brunette whispered. "The office is watching. Beware!"

Madeleine's answer to the question about her sanity was eloquent if not audible. She allowed a more rapturous expression to pass over her face, and panted softly. Hjalmar merely grinned.

Up forward, in the pilot's compartment, Homer was in conference with the two harassed technicians. He learned that the front landing gear wheel was stuck. Apparently it had not lifted when the plane took off. It appeared to be twisted outward, at an angle of about ninety degrees. The pilot looked at Homer, soliciting advice.

"Can't we carry on until we are near the airport outside Vegas, then have an auxiliary plane come up and make a close inspection?" Homer suggested.

The pilot shrugged. "That's the best we can do, but it won't make it much easier to land. We'll be over Las Vegas in less than twenty minutes."

"You ought to have enough reserve gasoline to circle around quite a while," Homer said.

"We'll prolong the agony," the co-pilot said. "And to think I've got $1,300 to one C note, on Horsetrader Ed. Can one's heirs or assigns collect bets from bookies?"

"A moot legal question," mused Homer. "Let's hope it won't be tested, soon, in any court."

In the passenger section, another sideshow with strange psychological inspirations was in progress. Odette, who, if such things could be measured or determined, was more passionate by nature, and less cautious than Madeleine, had been stirred to an extent that dazed her by the abandoned attitudes of the blonde and the painter who was to portray them both, covered and stripped. Of the two eligibles for relief or demonstration, Finke McGuire was more than occupied keeping his client, Forran, from attacking Orman, bodily. The available candidate was the reporter, Tom Jackson, who responded in a manly way when Odette, with the imminent danger as a pretext, or perhaps a valid reason, flung herself more or less upon him, from one side, and with her gasps and palpitations, her pressures, shifts and thermal surfaces, drove all restraint and restrictions from Tom's mind.

Madeleine, meanwhile, aware that she had compromised herself in the eyes of her aged protector, tore herself from Hjalmar just as the latter was being summoned by Homer to the cockpit, sat close beside the raging Orman, who at first seemed about to throttle her, and turned on all her emergency blandishments.

"Surely you do not think I was not acting in your interests, in showing you how dangerous Mr. Jansen can be, if you're not careful," the blonde began, and she followed through with a line, and corporeal insinuations, that the confused oil magnate accepted with little resistance, having so much else on his mind. For Orman now was glaring at Odette and Tom Jackson, who were enacting a duet which Fragonard would have painted in a Louis XVI boudoir, and not a moving vehicle with its landing wheels askew.

When the multimillionaire brushed Madeleine aside and grabbed again for writing materials and his pen, Madeleine had the presence of mind to give him elbow room. She saw, from the corner of her eye, that he was writing another Last Will and Testament, which was hastily witnessed by Jordan and the stewardess. Just as the "Greeley Cool" passed over the outer runway of the Las Vegas air field for the first time, Orman again pried open his window and tossed out the document, enclosed in another bottle the bulging cork of which he had gnawed down to size. Having been so enraptured with Hjalmar that she had not known about the next to the Last Will, which had dropped to the lone prairie about sixty miles back, Madeleine's conscience began to plague her, because of her pact of solidarity with Odette, which neither girl had broken to date.

"Odette is sounding out the reporter for your sake," the blonde assured the man both girls referred to, in private, as "the office."

"If we all reach the estate, alive and able-bodied, you both shall be confined to quarters, indefinitely, where painters cannot reach you, or reporters accomplish any sounding whatsoever. Should I perish in the crash we most likely will have, and one or both of you survive, you'll rue this P.M. and your shameless exhibitions with these predatory Bohemians whom, should you consort with them when I'm in the grave, you'll surely have to support," Orman told her.

"I've a feeling we'll all survive, and you'll be more like your reasonable self, having cheated the Grim Reaper. Mr. Evans and Mr. Jansen are aiding the pilot, which means two strikes against disaster," said Madeleine, snuggling assiduously.

Homer, up with the pilots, with Hjalmar close behind him, asked them to what speed they could retard the plane, before actually touching the runway.

"About one hundred miles an hour," the first pilot said. "Hell! We've tried to right those front wheels even with the hand crank. They won't budge. To make a safe landing, we'll need a solid three points. With the front landing gear perpendicular to our line of impetus, instead of taxi-ing to a halt, this crate may turn over, split off a wing or a tank, explode—there's no telling what."

"Have you plenty of runway length?" Homer asked.

"Ordinarily. But this time the strip'll be cluttered up with fire engines, ambulances, rescue apparatus, and, most likely, assorted clergymen with last rites formulae and equipment," said the pilot in a tone far from optimistic.

"Phone the rescue chaps at the field to give you a clear runway, and park their hooks and ladders, bishops and hospital wagons well away from the edges. Then, when your tail wheels hit the concrete, Hjalmar, the co-pilot and I will pull backward on the control lever, to hold the nose off the ground," said Homer.

"Any idea what this plane weighs?" the pilot inquired, skeptically.

"I'm also figuring on our momentum," replied Homer. "With luck we could stretch the interval of coasting on the back wheels long enough so that we'll lose most of the ground speed before we have to take the final chance."

"Could be," admitted the pilot, and the co-pilot nodded.

The signal phone began clicking, and the pilot took the receiver. He began to swear most volubly. "Can you beat that?" he demanded. "The Golden Nugget's calling, from way downtown. One of their top men, Tombstone Moe, wants to know about our chances, so he can make book."

"Tell him four to five," Homer said, gravely.

"On the level?" the pilot asked, incredulously.

"That's right," Homer assured him. "Practically anything involving a human factor, according to Damon Runyon, warrants a bet at four to five."

Madeleine was still plying Orman with contact appeal and random words which were hard to return on the fly for purposes of resentment or threats. Odette and Tom Jackson were sidelocked and practically unconscious. Finke had taunted or coaxed Forran into dying like a gentleman, if die they must. So Miriam took advantage of the others' preoccupations to observe the *sang froid* of Mr. Howard Scott Jordan, whose background she had glimpsed through revelations by Dean Margolis, and the Jordans, *père et mère*, in Cambridge. The New Englander, with the phenomenal brain and disconcerting discrepancies of taste, was no physical coward. That was plain. Neither was he a dull fatalist. He was filling a sizable notebook with swift, though complicated, computations, involving, so it appeared to Miriam, higher algebra, trigonometry and both analytical and differential calculus.

"What are our chances, Mr. Jordan?" she inquired in a sympathetic most respectful tone.

The prodigy dashed off some final figures, tapped in a couple of decimal points, and said: "They seem to be, if my figures and assumptions are correct, about 3.99684624 to 5.00354311." Then he offered the notebook to Miriam for inspection. She raised the window, as the "Greeley Cool" limped rings above the airfield, and tossed out the notebook, after marking it with Jordan's full name.

"Posterity should have these, if we crash," she said. "And you should get the credit for confirming, by means of higher mathematics, what Damon Runyon established after a rich lifetime of sporting experience, namely, that all contests or crises involving human endeavor warrant odds of four to five."

"With which university was Dr. Runyon connected," Jordan inquired. "Somehow, I have not heard of him."

The plane was losing altitude so steadily that all hands in the passenger department looked down to the field as best they could. Their reactions, under the climax of suspense, were individual and characteristic. Odette, rising from the depths of fervent indiscretion, realized she had burned her principal bridge, if not utterly destroyed it. She began thinking hard, as to how to wheedle Mr. Orman back to complacency. No line of approach came readily to her mind. Nevertheless, both she and Madeleine were pathetically anxious to continue living, on any terms, and take a chance on what a future, were one granted them, could hold.

Homer asked the pilot to start dumping surplus fuel, while they were still high enough above the field so that the high octane gasoline would vaporize and disappear into the atmosphere and not a drop would reach the ground. That would lighten the load he and Hjalmar, with the somewhat slight co-pilot, would have to sustain by main force, holding up the control stick against the weight of the nose.

At this point, Forran slipped Finke's quieting influence and started bawling like a bull. Some of the others jeered or protested but Evans, having overheard, opened the door of the cockpit and said:

"Have patience with Brother Forran, I beg of you, friends! He's the only one of us who, should worse come to worst, would go to his last reward quite alone. Mr. Orman and Messrs. Jordan and Jansen have, in a manner of speaking, parts of Madeleine and Odette. I have Miriam. Jordan has his inner life. Finke is a professional. In the way that satraps of the East, when dying, took comfort in having the throats of their womenfolk slit, modern man looks upon death's mysterious moment with less misgivings if a woman he has loved is going with him," Homer said, smiled, saluted nonchalantly and again closed the connecting door.

Sabin shrugged. "Had not Monsieur Evans been pessimistic as to the outcome of this pickle, he would not have neglected to enumerate me. Or doubtless he assumed, correctly, that I had abandoned hope. My only regret is that I am not dying for liberty, equality or fraternity, that is to say, for France."

The "Greeley Cool" was by now so close to the landing field that Odette, her perceptions intensified, felt sure she could see the bottle containing Orman's Last Will which surely would cut her off, *desnuda*, by a stubby cactus grove near the edge of a runway, as the plane made its last narrow circle. She also could see, as could the other passengers, the assembled throng of firemen, physicians, nurses, deputy sheriffs, gamblers and citizens who moved nervously, like chickens crowded in a crate. Orman, so generously imbued with instincts of authority, was ultra-restless, not from fear, which his inflamed ego did not permit him, but unprecedented subordination. Homer ran the show; the pilot and crew obeyed him without question. The multi-multi, so important elsewhere, was just another possible casualty, and excess weight. However, the old oil man strode to the cockpit, opened the door and watched. Homer, Hjalmar and the game co-pilot were straining at the control stick. The frenzy of their effort transformed them, until they seemed as impersonal as materials under test. The oil magnate fidgeted, and tried to squeeze into the compartment, to lend a hand. There was no handhold left on the stick, until the exhausted co-pilot slipped and let go.

Finke, always on the alert, brushed Orman back as if he were a sack of mush, and lent his unusual strength to the pair who, on the rack, as it were, would not let themselves be stretched.

There was a blank period of suspense when no one could think, hope or brace himself.

They felt a slight jar, what seemed to be a tilt, which was instantly compensated. The rear landing wheels had hit the concrete. With tantalizing hesitation and imperceptible descent the crippled nose leveled. The cheers, sirens and pandemoniacal demonstration from the crowd assured those aboard, whose minds were too stunned for quick assimilation, that all was well.

Tom Jackson, who had to rush for a phone to send his story to New York, for relay by syndicate throughout the news world, was the first to emerge. He shook off those who would felicitate him for surviving the narrow escape and ducked into the main building.

It was Orman, majestic and unencumbered, who followed in a dignified, impressive manner, allowing himself, before giving instructions to his chauffeur, who was on hand with a limousine, to be questioned by members of the local press, and representatives of influential dailies in large distant cities who could pay for direct Las Vegas news coverage. While the oil tycoon was elaborating on the attributes of the French chef he had gone all the way to Europe to import to Nevada, Talbot Forran and Finke took advantage of the diversion to enter a taxi and start down to the Strip without disclosing their destination.

Orman was much chagrined, and could not hide his resentment, when, the instant Homer came within range, between Miriam and Maitre Sabin, all the pressmen and local dignitaries forsook the portly financier to get the lowdown from Evans.

Not aware that Orman had boasted about his having hired Sabin as a cook, Homer introduced the personable Frenchman as his ranch-house guest, and let it drop that the Master from the Azure Coast had been several times the champion of France, and the world, as a wine taster. Las Vegas extends its frankest hospitality to champions of any kind, and has entertained most living greats in no matter what field. The modest Maitre's ears were burning and he was trying to shrink into his skin when the welcoming contingent, few of whom, if any, had tasted his cuisine, lavished praises in advance and promised all possible efforts to make his stay fruitful and memorable for himself and Las Vegas.

One of the newsmen remembered that Miriam was U. S., therefore world's champion, marksman with sidearms. She was assured of a share in the publicity which would erupt like a geyser as a result of the arrival of the "Greeley Cool," the near disaster, and the influx of distinguished passengers.

While Orman, aside and disgruntled, and Homer, as acknowledged interlocuter, were focusing the general attention, Howard
Scott Jordan thought it best to maneuver the girls into Orman's
limousine, without benefit of press photography. The New England
prodigy became aware, only at that moment, that while Madeleine
was clinging to one of his arms, he seemed to have lost Odette.
Hjalmar, of course, had let all else pass in order to superintend
the transfer of his supply of *cazalla* from the baggage compartment of the "Greeley Cool" to Homer's roomy sedan, where the
Widow O'Brien sat sullenly at the wheel.

Gentleman Gene Delmont waited courteously for Homer to assuage the reporters and officials before he stepped forward to shake
hands and tell Evans the reservations for Tom and Hjalmar were
in readiness at the Thunderbird.

If the reader misses the pert Kid Unamuno, with the brain so
disconcertingly designed for mischief worthy of an otter, the stealth
of an ocelot, and the cunning of a weasel, it should be reported
here that, having sized up the incoming party from a point of vantage, the Kid had been most intrigued by the manner and movements of Odette. Not that the demon in boy's form was sex starved
or abnormal in any such obvious way. The Kid had been taught the
facts of birds and bees by a jolly district nurse when he was going
on eight. His problems were not physical. Having such unusual
intellectual equipment, he was plagued by lack of a corresponding
local outlet.

Although Kid Unamuno would not admit it to himself, and he
was little inclined toward self-deception, he was glad to see Homer
Evans safely back. Homer, the Kid knew, could talk straight sense
and did not have to be buried by a ton of falling bricks to acknowl-
edge the force of gravity. For other reasons, all perverse, the Kid
rejoiced that Jordan was slated for another stretch in Las Vegas,
where a smart boy intent on his deflation could match wits with him.
Regional rivalries are always lively between East and West, and prodigies are as jealous of one another as hunchbacks or screen actors.

By what extra sense or practice of black magic the prodigy of
Basque descent remarked Odette's perturbation the moment she

descended the steps from the "Greeley Cool," and satisfied himself that it had nothing to do with risks attending the miraculous landing, it is impossible to say. He remarked the tremulous touch of her slender and expressively gloved fingers on Jordan's coatsleeve, the tendency of her deep dark eyes to wander away from her escort and the assembled throng and dart eastward, over the prairie beyond the farthest air strip. When, so cautiously that Jordan was unaware of her maneuver, the brunette stood still and let the erudite but none-too-hep New Englander continue furtively with Madeleine, bypassing Orman and heading for his limousine that glittered blackly, Kid Unamuno made himself inconspicuous on the fringe of the press contingent and as Odette proceeded toward the main lobby and reception room, indoors, the Kid cautiously followed.

Odette, palpably nervous in spite of her becoming costume and trim natural attributes to fit it, sat on a bench between a haggard sleepy woman who must have lost money she ill could afford or explain, and Alkali Ike, a bearded self-consciously uncouth prospector from the bleak foothills to the east and south. The displaced brunette, in fact, was poised on the edge of the seat. Her lovely face showed inner concentration, unstabilized by certainty or her usual self-assurance.

Her self-appointed young "tail" knew of a nearby telephone booth where he could lurk in comparative dusk and keep her under close surveillance. The Kid had not long to wait. Odette rose and walked straight toward an exit which led toward the area on which incoming planes taxied to rest, to discharge passengers. The "Greeley Cool" was still in place, where it had scraped to a stop without disaster. Mechanics and local officials of the airport were inspecting it. There was a locker near by, in which the grease monkeys kept their clothes. Somehow, Odette was able to secrete herself inside. The Kid watched and waited. When the brunette came out, he grinned and shrugged, and watched her all the more assiduously, and with some grudging admiration. She had appropriated a man's coat, trousers and cap, put them on, over her chic costume and evidently had cached her own hat in one of the pockets. The

Kid, not given to preoccupation with non-essentials, did not try to guess where she had stashed her high-heeled shoes, which must have set Orman back at least thirty dollars. She was wearing used *alparagatos*, a kind of cloth sandal with rattan soles very popular with Las Vegas Mexicans or Spaniards.

"Fast thinking," the Kid said to himself. For, disguised as she was, Odette attracted no particular attention as she strolled toward the outer and easternmost airstrip—a little beyond it, in fact. A less brilliant lad than the Kid could have felt sure she was looking for something, in haste, and was increasingly panicky because she was absent without leave from her old multi's vicinity and his other retainers. The Kid was far enough back so Odette was not likely to spot him. He understood that whatever she had risked exposure or displeasure to find had not come within range of her eyes. She was getting more agitated, if not desperate, with each passing second.

Then the Kid's heart skipped a beat, notwithstanding his precocious *sang froid*. He saw the flash of the setting sun on something like glass, shifted his angle, and strained to identify the outlines of what seemed to be a corked champagne bottle. The brunette, who had had no such luck and dared not linger longer, had faced about and was walking back toward the locker shack. Again the Kid raised his eyebrows with perverse satisfaction.

"Amateurs can't think straight when they try to pull a fast one," he said, again to himself, reflecting how much safer it would have been if the brunette had proceeded to one of the many available telephone booths in the lobby, and shed her false outer duds there. For he had noticed that one of the plane mechanics had left the group that were fussing around the "Greeley Cool" and entered the small locker building.

Regretful that he could not be in two or more places at once, the Kid eased himself toward the corked bottle he had spotted amid the mesquite, cactus and dry cropped grass and sage fringing the outer airstrip. No one around Las Vegas would find it strange if he were seen wandering anywhere, except toward church or school. When he realized that the bottle in question contained some kind of paper, or document, he felt as the poet must have when the latter wrote "God's in His Heaven, all's right with the world."

"My hunches are still O.K.," the Kid thought. He was by that time extracting the document from the bottle. The indications that some man or animal had gnawed the swelled cork to fit the bottleneck did not escape his notice, so he slipped it into a side pocket. The paper he secreted in what the urchins call the "budge," inside the front of his shirt, near the waist. Suspecting that the harassed brunette, and possibly several other parties, might return to search for what he had found and appropriated, whatever it was, the Kid skillfully threw the empty champagne bottle clear over to the second airstrip from the edge, where it smashed to bits on the solid concrete. The breeze from the propeller of the first plane that passed that way would scatter the fragments without trace.

As the Kid made his way back to the lobby of the airport, to examine what he had found and assess it, for its nuisance or monetary value, he saw Odette emerge from the locker shack, leaning on the arm of a young mechanic and limping as if she had turned an ankle.

"That tomato has a way with men. She's given that guy some kind of a line, and he, poor sap, is playing up to her," the Kid thought. He modified his *modus operandi*, delayed his examination of that document, and cut ahead to join the agitated group around Orman's limousine. The frustrated and anxious brunette, he rightly assumed, would report to "the office" contritely, on the arm of the fatuous grease monkey she had wheedled into the mild conspiracy, and attribute her unauthorized absence to her ankle she pretended was injured. The Kid took it for granted that it was sound, fairly certain that the mechanic had not pursued Odette around the locker, like chimp after weasel, until her fair tarsus or metatarsus had gone "Pop." The financier's brunette must have developed considerable power to control male brutes, in emergencies, and exert her wiles without being bruised where it might show.

The twilight hour was yielding abundantly to the Kid's satisfaction. Without being counted as a spectator or eavesdropper he saw and heard Orman beefing, yammering, yelling and threatening, while he paced back and forth, clenched his hands, swung his arms, and generally threw his weight around most futilely. Madeleine, still faithful to her pact of solidarity with her missing opposite, was doing her best, with assorted little pats, widening of innocent blue eyes, and incoherent sounds intended to pacify the wrathful Sultan. Zachary, the round-headed, chinless, lop-eared chauffeur, who doubled as a *masseur* and stool pigeon, or informer, and who hated both his master's mistresses, was grim and stymied, since whatever the dark one did to get herself in wrong only fortified the blonde. Zachary loathed Jordan almost as much as the two girls put together, and Jordan returned the antipathy with as much force of high intelligence as the brute chauffeur had physical strength. The sulphurous aroma of murder was sharp in the air, whenever any two of Orman's entourage got together. The Kid was getting the lowdown on what became incipient when three were present and a fourth one had stolen from the reservation.

Jordan did or said nothing, aware that his aloofness and inner assumption of superiority, because he, himself, had the sense not to get involved with females, infuriated and goaded Orman beyond any spoken words. The chauffeur went as far as he dared in casting aspersions on Odette for not being handy, and Madeleine for stalling and dissembling in her confederate's behalf.

When finally Odette limped into sight, and approached, on the arm of a man, who because of his secret desires was awkward and showed what generally are mistaken for the symptoms of guilt, Orman turned russet and indigo to such an extent that all hands, including the mechanic, were afraid the old man was going to burst a blood vessel.

"The lady turned her ankle, and asked me to help her to where the gentleman was waiting," the mechanic said.

"A likely story," muttered Zachary, advancing between Orman and the grease monkey, who took on a dangerous aspect, bristling and holding every inch of his ground.

"Any baboon who calls me a liar will have to back it up," the mechanic declared, letting Odette's arm drop, and forgetting for the moment that millionaires existed.

Zachary looked at Orman, wondering how he'd react if fisti-cuffs ensued. The oil magnate was still too tightly pressed in the vise of his own rage to do anything but flap and flutter, emitting incoherent sound effects.

"Messieurs," begged Madeleine, addressing herself principally to the mechanic. "Mr. Orman must not be bothered with your feuds. He has had a trying afternoon." The blonde turned to Odette. "Are you badly hurt, dearie?" she asked.

"I tripped coming out of the Powder Room, and, in saving my-self from a fall, nearly broke my ankle," the brunette began.

A snicker from Kid Unamuno nearly gave him away as a mate-rial witness. The derisive noise, however, served only to make Orman articulate, at last.

"So you encounter types like this one" (indicating the mechanic) "in a ladies' toilet!" the oil man hollered.

"Not in, outside. Monte's been helpful and considerate. You ought to be grateful to him," Odette said. In certain situations with her protector, she knew that too much humility invited reciprocal abuse.

"Mr. Orman's had a trying afternoon," Madeleine said, aware too late that she had just used the same line. The simmering multi turned on the blonde. "Why didn't you go with Odette to the toi-let? I've told both of you, again and again, not to stray off alone. And to let me know, if you have to be absent."

Madeleine, none too tactful on instant notice, took another wrong tack. "I was so interested in what Mr. Jordan was saying, about algebra and stuff, that I didn't use my head."

The multi wheeled on Jordan. "What were you handing this woman, about algebra and stuff? Are you, at last, getting fancy ideas?"

"I don't recall having said anything at all, about mathematics or anything else, as I escorted these women from the plane to here," Jordan said. "I was thinking about the party Mr. Homer Evans designated, in Cannes, as 'Mr. X.'"

"Can nobody give out a straight story? Men called 'Monte' after a few minutes' acquaintance, educated dopes who moon about any-thing called 'X,' scheming women in whose mouths butter couldn't melt, bruisers who want to fight to show off, instead of attending to my affairs as they should."

It was then that another car (which only Kid Unamuno noted instantly was well armored and equipped with bulletproof glass and stain-resistant upholstery) drove up, came to a precarious stop with a horrid squeal of brakes and linings. Out popped a type who resembled the comic strip character known as Abie Kabibble, who rushed up to Orman, extending a plump hand.

"I'm Rosencrans," he said.

9
Descent into Oblivion

IF CLIFFORD ORMAN had been exasperated by an imaginary grievance against a woman he half-loved, when confronted by a gnome-
like physically vulnerable little man whose agency had really played
him false, his fury was proportionately violent. The oil magnate
felt so strongly, in fact, that he realized he could not trust himself
to act. As always when anything occurs around Las Vegas, at least
a half dozen strong silent deputy sheriffs more or less like William
S. Hart were near at hand.

"Officers," Orman muttered, from between clenched teeth,
"take this crook away before I destroy him."

Homer Evans and Miriam were watching developments from
the somber security of Homer's sedan, Sabin between them and
the Widow O'Brien in front, in the driver's seat. The suave criminologist and his cool bodyguard exchanged glances and smiled.
Whatever happened would be amusing as comic relief.

Now the oil multimillionaire, shrewd as he was, had not realized that the small ridiculous man before him, Ossip Rosencrans,
was one of the most dangerous and powerful individuals on the
doubtful fringe encircling all police or criminal matters anywhere.
Rosencrans, not a fighter himself, had organized a band of shady
characters and lent them enough outward show of respectability,
or legality as defined by the letter and loopholes rather than the
intent of the law.

The half circle of deputies, all with sombreros, flannel shirts,
leather windbreakers, sidearms, cartridge belts, corduroy pants and

hob-nailed boots, stepped forward at Orman's command. Before
they got within reach of Rosencrans, the latter made a peremptory,
somewhat petulant backhand gesture and immobilized them, saying:

"Take it easy, boys. This gent is upset."

The shrill cackle of laughter that issued from the Widow O'Brien
shattered the grim silence before Orman exploded. It helped, actually, to touch off the fuse.

"You poltroon! You blackguard! You shrimp! You little squirt!" the
financier roared, shaking a finger under Rosencrans' proboscis.

"Sue me," the brains of the world's most ruthless detective
organization suggested with a shrug. "You're implying, without
giving him a chance, that one of my best men has failed you."

"He left me flat in Europe. He's a common burglar, bungler
and thief, a stowaway, a fugitive," Orman replied.

"You'll learn, when you get over the fright you had from the
plane just now, that my boys come through in the end. You haven't
made a move, however slight or ill advised, without our protection," the accused *mens sana in corpore runto* declared.

That incensed Orman the more. "Your thugs have been spying,
you mean?"

"Why not let things rest till this evening? Then we can have a
quiet private talk," said Rosencrans.

"If you come near me, I'll have Zachary throw you out on your
nose," promised Orman.

Rosencrans shrugged complacently. "Zachary looks expend-
able," was his comment.

Just as Rosencrans hopped back into his car and started toward the Strip—there was no other way to go, from the Las Vegas
airport, without heading back toward California, nearly one hundred miles distant—Kid Unamuno, suspecting that his mother
would, by yelling for him, attract undue attention when he wanted
it least, absented himself, then concealed himself beyond the airstrips in a thicket of manzanita from which first he chased one
rattlesnake and two sleepy hoot owls. He made sure he had not
been observed or followed, then took out the document to read.
The further he read, the higher his satisfaction mounted.

In effect, Orman's last Last Will and Testament provided that the next to the last, dated earlier the same day, was thereby revoked and superseded. There was a list of minor beneficiaries and charities which would ensure the financier postmortem publicity and praise. Four hundred thousand dollars were to go to Madeleine de Vere, to be used for the purchase and stocking of a millinery and *haute-couture* establishment to be situated somewhere in the rue St. Honoré or the rue du Faubourg St. Honoré in Paris, between the avenue de l'Opera and the church of St. Philippe-du-Roule. Odette Monpanier was to get one dollar and whatever clothes she chanced to be wearing at the moment the testator died.

A pattern clicked in the Kid's malicious mind. "So the cagey old bloke plays one of these dames against the other. It's dollars to doughnuts the other will he wrote in the plane farther back cut off the blonde with a buck and a shift, and gave Odette the break," the Kid said to himself. And he added, to symmetrize the situation: "I ought to get the other Will, too. Then I'll have something, to trade with both those cookies."

He pondered a moment, not much longer, and a course of procedure suggested itself. Monte, the mechanic Odette had utilized, was good and sore at Orman, and had shown that whatever *gentlemen* thought about *blondes, working stiffs* would settle for *brunettes*, who, being more restless in the winter, cut down fuel bills. The Kid believed that if he could convince Monte that he was acting in Odette's best interests, the mechanic would learn and tell what he could about what occurred on the "Greeley Cool" before the passengers found out the front landing gear had gone haywire.

Monte proved already well informed and amenable to reason. He had overheard from the colloquy between the pilot, co-pilot and stewardess of the "Greeley Cool" that about sixty miles back from the Las Vegas airport, on the course the plane had followed, the oil magnate had written a Last Will, had it witnessed by the cold fish, Jordan, and Rose, the hot stewardess, had gnawed a bloated champagne cork until it could be jammed back into the neck of an empty champagne bottle, had caused a window to be raised and had dropped the corked and bottled document to the lone prairie below.

"Got a map?" asked Kid Unamuno.

A map was produced and Monte established and indicated to his juvenile inquisitor that the point at which the Will had been cast out was distant from any roadway or trail. Also, a brief talk with Rose, the stewardess, yielded the information that Orman had been goaded into changing his former Last Will because his blonde, Madeleine, had been possessed of an excruciating yen for the big Norwegian painter, Hjalmar Jansen, had wedged herself into a seat beside him, and behaved in a compromising manner before her protector's bulging eyes.

That turn of the inquiry did not please Monte, although he was rooting for Odette. He could put two and two together, and suspected strongly that if the penultimate Last Will had been provoked by the misbehavior of Madeleine, the blonde, with a big Norsky artist, the last Last Will, excluding Odette, must have had its inspiration in the brunette's attitude toward someone.

"The dark one flipped her stack on account of a reporter, Mr. Tom Jackson, the Norwegian's bottle pal," Rose said.

"And an hour or so later, she gave me the business," Monte said disconsolately. "Now how do you like that?"

"So what? Both those bimbos have ants. What more do you want? I don't mind tipping you off that Odette, the one you seem to like, just before she annexed you with the ankle routine, had been combing the flat beyond the airstrips looking for the Will the old moneybags tossed out last," the Kid said to Monte. Naturally, the Kid did not let anyone suspect that he, himself, had found and held in his possession the genuine and original Last Will, tossed off just before the "Greeley Cool" had landed. He patted Monte on the shoulder and assured him that if he stuck around and kept watch, the brunette would be back that very night.

The fact that the next to the Last Will had landed on the open desert, away from roads or trails, prompted Kid Unamuno to shed his present company and seek out Alkali Ike. Map in hand, the Kid explained to the old prospector that a corked bottle containing a document was lying on the prairie. He gave the grizzled desert rat the correct degrees of latitude and longitude where the anti-Madeleine Will should be found.

"What's in it for me, if I find this paper, and bring it in?" Alkali Ike demanded. He did not trust the Kid any more than he would a cornered bobcat.

"A case of Old Crow," was the Kid's reply.

"Where is it?" the prospector asked suspiciously.

"Never mind," the Kid said. "And don't think you're going to sample it before you bring back the document, and the cork. You'd only get a snootful, shoot off your mouth, and give the show away. If you quit stalling, hit the trail and produce what I need before tomorrow noon, I'll raise the ante. I'll guarantee you a bottle of Old Crow a day for the rest of this year, and for a week after next January first, so you won't have to sober up too fast after the holidays."

Having little or nothing to lose, the bewhiskered old prospector thought over the proposition about a minute, then set off southeastward on foot. After Ike had proceeded a few yards, he halted, faced about and yelled back:

"You got to have that cork?" he asked, puzzled.

"For teeth marks," Kid Unamuno replied.

Then a chorus of "Oh's" and "Ah's," followed by increasingly voluminous and excited demonstrations on every side, turned the Kid's attention toward the downtown section of the city, about four miles away. What he saw caused him to sprint to the parking lot where last he had seen Homer Evans' sedan. Beside the criminologist had been sitting Miriam Leonard, the newly imported French chef with the moustache and Van Dyke, and the Kid's smouldering grandmother, the Widow O'Brien. It was a forlorn hope. The sedan already was more than halfway down town. But the Kid got a lift from Monte, who drove his remodeled jalopy at eighty miles an hour.

In Homer's car, the dazed Sabin was asking no questions. If it were normal that suddenly all Las Vegas folks who could leave their posts and had transportation started converging toward a given center, why should he object? He still felt that he was living on borrowed time. Miriam, however, turned to Homer, who was absorbed in Mrs. O'Brien's hairtrigger driving and disregard of traffic signals, intersections or possible obstructions, in characteristic Basque style.

"What's burning?" asked Miriam.

Homer shook his head ruefully. "I should have foreseen this. It's the laboratory, the one an anonymous philanthropist who sports two mistresses, indoors and out, financed for Mr. Howard Scott Jordan, and which has remained closed during their absence abroad."

Unluckily for the prospects of saving anything from the raging flames, the bulk of the Las Vegas fire-fighting apparatus and the cream of its personnel, having been called to the outskirts to meet a possible emergency when the "Greeley Cool" came in, had not returned to the downtown stations. Firemen, of high or low rank, were scattered along the Strip, in saloons and halls, quenching their thirst and playing slot machines.

The doomed laboratory was on Fremont Street, down near the County Courthouse, and two blocks away from the crime laboratory supervised by the sheriff and manned by his technical experts. The crowds were dense, and not too deeply concerned with the loss of the odd institution which from the day on which building had commenced had remained a mystery to officials and citizens, and therefore a source of irritation to the uneasy top gamblers and higher-ups in the various mobs who controlled expensive night spots and hotels. The sheriff's organization and city officials, generally, abhorred any place they could not savvy or inspect. The local crime technicians, in assembling whom the city had spared no expense, took a dim view of Mr. Howard Scott Jordan, who chose Kid Unamuno, the State's most brilliant juvenile pest, for his only assistant and somehow had kept the Kid from spilling a word of useful information about what went on within those laboratory walls which now were crumbling from effects of heat and explosions, for the most part moderate in force but vivid in contrasting colors, smells and other attributes. The chemicals, salts, bases, acids, alkalis, etc., which had been collected for the purpose of still-secret tests, and had been purchased and stored in the form of liquids, gases, powders, grains, and solids, fizzed, fuzzed, rattled, whooshed, rocketed, spun, boiled and bubbled.

When Homer had seen enough to satisfy himself that destruction of the lab and its contents would be practically total, he sent Sabin to the ranch apartment, in charge of the Widow O'Brien. With Miriam he sat a while in the nearly deserted red plush bar of the Golden Nugget, to decide on a course of investigation. He did not want to apply to Sheriff Hawley of Clarke County until the situation was far enough developed so that Hawley would need his help and would be obliged to ask for it. So he got Sheriff Eugene Biscailuz, of Los Angeles County, on the long-distance phone, if in those parts a call spanning a mere three hundred miles can be classed as non-local.

"I know that Ossip Rosencrans is here in Las Vegas," Homer told Biscailuz. "I've seen him. Could you find out for me if any of his hired men have been rushed down here today, and the names of any of his regulars who represent his outfit here?"

The veteran Los Angeles County Sheriff, who had known Homer more than fifteen years (Biscailuz is over seventy, and has spent most of his life in public office), said he would do his best. Before Homer and Miriam had finished their second round of drinks Biscailuz called back. He was pleased to inform Homer that three Rosencrans detectives, all brothers, named Manny, Mo and Jack Dalton, and all great grand-nephews of *the* notorious badman, Jack Dalton, who had terrorized broad sections of the West in pioneer days, had been dispatched eastward that same morning, with Las Vegas as the first if not final stop on their itinerary. Homer was not surprised that Sheriff Biscailuz, within whose jurisdiction Rosencrans had his main office, was well posted on the bureau's internal affairs. The County kept as many spies in the Rosencrans ranks as the wily Ossip planted as deputies under Biscailuz. Evans also was aware that Biscailuz resented openly and volubly the supposedly secret deal between the Las Vegas and Nevada State authorities and the top gangsters, to the effect that no murders or conspicuous capital crimes against the persons of persons would be perpetrated within Nevada borders. The result of the nefarious pact, as already has been stated, was that many murders and beatings within an inch of the victims' lives took place in California.

A rich stretch of the Hollywood "Strip" was in Los Angeles County, and Las Vegas, as we know, was usurping the Southland's prestige.

It has been pointed out already that when the laboratory where Howard Scott Jordan (and Kid Unamuno) had worked in secrecy before Orman had suddenly taken into his head to quit Las Vegas, temporarily, for a trip to Europe, had been viewed askance by Las Vegas officials who could not get an inkling of what went on there. The mystery lab had made the top gangsters uneasy for similar reasons. One sound citizen, however, when he first spied flames issuing from the laboratory walls and licking under the eaves, reacted with such an agreeable impulse that he cut a caper in the privacy of the sheltered bin behind his well-stocked prescription counter. The citizen, one Gerald Araquistain (another Basque) was the leading druggist of Las Vegas, the man from whom Kid Unamuno counted on stealing the Old Crow he had promised Alkali Ike.

Gerald Araquistain was the only son of the peppery old lady now known as the Widow O'Brien, who ran the dude ranch called "Cottonwood Acres," where Homer Evans maintained his Las Vegas ranch apartment, and monopolized the widow's time as his cook and severest critic. As is so often the case with forceful, determined women who conceive but once, and with the aid of an adored first husband destined soon to become a memory, Odilla Araquistain y Isasi de O'Brien loved her male and only offspring as madly as she seemed to detest the rest of mankind, with a few probationary exceptions.

When mother love like Mrs. O'Brien's springs up like a tall tree, isolated on an exposed plain, lightning will strike and sear it. In the widow's case, the stroke was dire, indeed. Gerald did well as a schoolboy, in college and at pharmaceutical school. He had been manly, nice to his doting mother, shy with girls and women, and popular with he-men, with which the Las Vegas region seems almost over-supplied. Then, after his mother had set him up in business, on a corner ideally situated for a drug and liquor store, and in an appropriate and well-stocked building, with extra space for slot machines so no customer was likely to depart with any loose change, Gerald had fallen crazily in love with a torch and flamenco singer and dancer named Pilar.

No young woman, in the eyes of the frantic Widow O'Brien, would have been half good enough for her son, Gerald. Pilar, a night hawk, gambler and mother of a precocious public enemy, known as Kid Unamuno (although she never had been formally married), seemed to the outraged widow outstandingly unsuitable. In this one instance, however, Gerald showed his inherent Basque stubbornness and stood his ground. He got a marriage license, took Pilar publicly for better or for worse, and although his mother, in a frenzy, tried to foreclose the heavy mortgages she held on the drugstore property, Gerald paid off the widow in full. Gerald had been able to do this because Howard Scott Jordan, acting for some multimillionaire who preferred to remain anonymous, bought the entire stock for an experimental and research laboratory through Araquistain, and allowed the druggist a wide margin of profit.

Araquistain had helped store the various chemicals and explosives in Jordan's lab; therefore, when the druggist saw the flames he was the first to be sure that neither the building nor its contents could be saved. With the hope of restocking a new laboratory, should Jordan's backer build one on the site of the building now doomed to burn to the ground, Araquistain left his store and started driving pell mell toward the Orman estate, where he assumed Mr. Jordan would be, since neither the New England research whiz nor the cagey oil magnate seemed to be among those who were watching the fire convert the liquids and solids of and in the lab to gases, smoke and ashes.

It did not surprise Gerald Araquistain that neither Clifford Orman nor Howard Scott Jordan stayed away from the scene of the conflagration that was costing the one several hundreds of thousands of dollars, and the other a secret refuge and a stock of supplies which gave the New England savant a chance to carry on beyond the disordered dreams of the alchemists of old or the

witches in Macbeth. Orman did not want to be questioned or inter-
viewed. Jordan never did. All the hep men in Las Vegas knew that
Orman was publicity shy about his serious activities, and still felt
obliged to coddle the Press, to preserve his standing as financial
wizard and philanthropist. Jordan, more close-mouthed than the
Sphinx, had never been known to say a word of what he was about,
in or out of the lab.

Naturally, it had astonished Araquistain and put the druggist
on his guard, when Jordan had acted with outward expansiveness
and thrown so much profitable business his way. Either Jordan or
Orman would want something tangible in the way of support or
service at some future date. Araquistain counted on that, and was
disposed, when the time came, to reciprocate. Gerald had a gener-
ous nature and would share almost anything he had, excepting
Pilar, whom he loved to distraction and on whose account he suffered daily and nightly when she was performing at the various
hot spots and hotels. Pilar, when she married the infatuated druggist, thus securing a wonderful foster-father and, in her opinion, a
witch straight from hell as a foster-grandmother for her gifted and
difficult child, had conceded much, but she would not relinquish
her career. Pilar cared nothing about money, and gambled all her
pay, but she could not live without the thrill of performing, which,
incidentally, she communicated to her hearers in no ordinary way.

The reader will recall that Maitre Sabin and the irascible widow,
the latter in the driver's seat, were detached from Homer and
Miriam and left to proceed, at Evans' request, directly to Cottonwood Acres, without delaying to gape at the fire.

The renowned French chef was suffering a reaction from the
tension incident to the precarious landing. He had not feared a
possible crash, and extinction, but having prepared himself for the
worst, was having trouble in reconciling himself once more to prolonged existence in a weird foreign land better suited to the needs
of wild red men and their squaws, who, Sabin had been told, had
in primitive days worked as hard as French servant girls, or *bonnes
à tout faire*. Ordinarily, Sabin would have aroused and exerted

himself to make polite small talk. His only hesitant sallies in that direction had met with fiery disconcerting response.

"I understand from Monsieur Evans," Sabin had ventured tactfully, "that your talents as a cook ascend to realms poetic, Madame."

"Don't you dare call me Madame," the widow snapped. "And as to the cooking for that high-falutin peeper and his young woman, who spoils him, you can take over as of tonight, and welcome. With him it's always 'Shall we try a touch of this or a dash of that,' and 'I recall, Mrs. O'Brien, that in Barcelona, twenty-two years ago, at the Hostel del Sol . . .'"

At the mention of this magnificent Catalan restaurant, Sabin sighed, "Ah'd" and blew a kiss toward a clump of cactus in which were roosting a few prairie hens.

"Respect yourself," the widow said, glowering, as if the gesture had been meant for her. "I've heard how French men try to get around women, from the cradle to the grave."

They had turned south from the main highway, No. 89 which ran east, and were approaching a grove of cottonwoods from which the ranch had derived its name. In November, because of cold desert nights, one of which Sabin so soon was to sample, the leaves of the cottonwoods turn yellow and gold, in shades from gamboge to ochre. The widow, snapping her head back to the side road ahead, jammed on the brakes and brought the sedan to such an abrupt halt that she knocked most of her own wind out against the wheel, and Sabin was nearly catapulted over into the front seat from the rear.

One of the cottonwoods, as resplendent in foliage as any left standing, had fallen square across the road. The sedan came to rest as the near twigs and branches obscured the front fender, the headlights and the radiator hood.

The widow, muttering imprecations, started to open the car door at her left, then recoiled suspiciously.

"There's something fishy about this," she said.

"How piscatorial?" asked Sabin, somewhat shaken and even more bewildered.

The widow turned to glare at him scornfully. "You wouldn't notice, I suppose. There's been no high wind this P.M., and had there been, it would have come from the east. This here tree has fallen dead west. It must have been pushed, and whoever pushed it had designs on Mr. Evans. Who the heck would want to bother the likes of you or me?"

"No matter," Sabin said. "Let us walk to the ranch house, if that is what I see about two hundred meters ahead. No doubt, later, you can delegate some of your cow persons to clear the road block, saw and chop the fallen tree into fuel for the fireplaces—all ranch rooms in the American cinema seem to have fireplaces—and drive the car to the garage."

"I still don't like the layout," the widow said, and before they proceeded along the wooded road toward the ranch, opened the back compartment and armed herself with a wrench. Then she added: "A woman doesn't sweat her tripes out over a set of hot ranges and cater to a fussy detective without learning to take heed when anything queer sticks out of a picture and refuses to make sense. Unsawed trees do not fall *against* the wind."

When the widow was riled, which was most of the time, she walked fast, with aggressive jerky strides, setting her feet down with emphasis. Sabin, imbued with the Latin sense of ease and enraptured by the dappled beauty of the golden grove and its neatly paved roadway, lingered somewhat behind. Alas, he remembered somewhat later having felt, at the same instant, a silk scarf around his throat, a rope looped over his shoulders and arms that pinned them, then a drag from the roadway toward a cottonwood clump, a hand over his mouth from which he had not had the presence of mind to let a sound escape, the incisive receding footsteps of the widow proceeding alone, a sharp needle jab in one of his buttocks, then a dreamy descent into oblivion.

The widow, as she stamped her way toward the ranch buildings, was talking to herself and deeply preoccupied with whatever she was saying. Because she was overfond of Homer Evans in the guarded recesses of her heart, the incident of the tree and the sinister aspects of the road block irritated her outwardly.

"That is what comes of harboring criminologists," she mumbled. "The better they are—and this fastidious dude of mine is tops—the worse are the criminals they provoke. And do these white-gloved shamuses bear the brunt of their enemies' malice? No. It is the innocent bystander, the landlady especially, who suffers."

The widow made a few passes in the air with her wrench.

"Take that and that!" she exclaimed.

Since she had reached the nearest building, a bunkhouse for her hired help, her words were heard above the cowboys' guitar, ocarina and Jew's harp twangs and toots. Parentheses Pete (so nicknamed because of the relationship between his bow legs and other outer appurtenances) stopped wailing "Let me go, Let me go, Let me go, lariat" and asked of his co-entertainers:

"How come the widow's on foot? And fannin' herse'f with a Stillson?"

Before they could ask her, the widow had passed by and was nearing the front door of the main ranch house, the former old homestead of a famous sheriff who had died and been buried with his boots on.

Another of the cowboys, the ocarinist, looked puzzled

"She's lettin' herse'f into the front parlor door, instead of the kitchen. That ain't like her. And where is the professor's sedan? She left adrivin' it, with that grandson who should ought to a been smothered at birth," he observed.

"She'll let us know in time what's loose," a third cowboy said, and they all returned to their melancholy jam session.

Odilla Araquistain y Isasi de O'Brien, on reaching the front doorstep, which opened into Homer's suite of ranch rooms, wheeled, ready to berate the French chef, Maitre Jean Sabin, for not having spoken a word en route from car to *casa*. She choked back the ready words and blinked.

"*Now* where the hell are you?" she finally demanded, of the empty air. Not even an echo responded.

The widow looked back along the road as if she were about to rake it with bazooka fire.

She cocked a sharp old ear, and heard only the dreary moaning, twanging and plooping of the hillbilly music from the bunkhouse.

The widow loathed music. Hot-footing it back to the bunkhouse, wrench still waving, she yelled: "Stop that driveling and caterwauling, or I'll dock you. Get movin', all of you. Go back along the road a piece, snake that dod-gasted cottonwood from in front of the sedan, find a damn silly Frenchman who wears a chin-piece like a cockeyed Billy goat, and bring him *and* the car back to Mr. Evans' apartment and the No. 1 garage, respectively. Be quick about it! Chop!"

"How come a tree's across the road, ma'am? Are you positive?" asked Parentheses Pete.

The widow's face turned red and she threw the wrench for Parentheses to catch, or miss, as best he could.

"Am *I* positive?" she countered. "Are you insinuating that I don't know a tree when I see it and can't tell whether it's standing or flat?"

"No offense, ma'am," the boss cowboy assured her, and all three of them made haste to obey her orders on the double, which is none too fast in the case of a Nevada cowboy. They can move quickly, on occasion, when fighting as extras in movies. In real life, without expert direction, if they hurry, their hands and feet get ahead of their thinking and confusion is the least that may result.

The cowboys soon found the fallen tree and the blocked sedan. They were as puzzled as the widow had been. No tree could have tumbled due east, without wind pressure or artificial interference with nature's probabilities. The cottonwood in question, which had stood about forty feet high, had been utilized for purposes of deliberate and calculated obstruction of the only auto road from national Highway No. 89 to Cottonwood Acres. None of the cowboys could figure out why, when or how. Neither could they lift the sedan over the fallen tree, in order to leave evidence intact for the professor (as all the hands persisted in calling Homer Evans) to examine. All three of the widow's employees, as they contemplated the road block and made ready to clear the way, using stout chopped and trimmed branches as levers, were mildly oppressed by a feeling of guilt. The widow had forbidden them to play music during working hours, whether she was present or absent from the ranch. They had broken the rule, and while they had been absorbed in lugubrious laments and instrumental square-dance tunes, some trespasser must have pushed over that full-grown cottonwood, using an elephant or a tank, against the wind, if any, and made a getaway without leaving a trace that a Choctaw could have spotted or interpreted.

Furthermore, once the boys had pried and levered the fallen tree off the road, and started the engine of the sedan, they were discouraged from returning to the ranch proper because, in spite of their having scoured the vicinity with the practiced eyes of latter-day frontiersmen, no Frenchman, with goatee or without, had been seen or heard from.

Parentheses Pete backed the sedan into position, turned it around and drove with his two perplexed buddies all the way back to Highway No. 89. No Frenchman. After a while there seemed no alternative to driving back to the ranch.

"I dassn't face the widow," Parentheses said. "When she wants a Frenchman, a fellow's got to deliver one. You boys know that."

Eventually, however, all three cowboys walked, abreast, to the kitchen door of the homestead, knocked, were told to come in, and did so apprehensively.

"We lifted the tree off'n the road, ma'am," Parentheses said, trying to accentuate the positive.

"What did that Frog gut-robber have to say for himself? Getting himself lost on a straight clear road, first crack out of the box!" the widow demanded.

"He didn't say nothin', ma'am," the ocarinist answered truthfully. "To tell the truth, he must 'a been rootin' around the cottonwoods, somewhere, maybe lookin' for mushrooms, and after we'd passed, on the way to get the car, he could have walked back and snuck in the house unbeknownst to you or us."

"You mean to say you didn't find him, as I told you!" the widow snapped, reaching for a poker.

"If there's a Frenchman, or even a Swede or Hunyak, in them woods by the wayside, or anywhere around here, I'll give a month's pay to a temperance fund," the Jew's harpist declared with pathetic effort to convey his sincerity.

"You chowderheads lost Mr. Evans' pet chef he brought all the way from France at ruinous cost? Is that what you mean to tell me?"

"We couldn't lose nobody we never set eyes on, now could we, ma'am?" demanded Parentheses, and in spite of his inferiority feeling face to face with his shrewish employer, it occurred to him that he had hit upon a great title for a hillbilly song. There were hundreds of back country ballads about chaps losing girls they knew, and girls losing men they loved. Would it not be a step farther backward, if a singer should lose someone in advance of meeting him or her?

The widow was so mad she had to take action.

"Come with me, you numbskulls," she ordered. "We'll have a look through the apartments and see who's there or who isn't. You'll be witnesses, if anybody's fool enough to believe you."

They made, the widow and the three cow hands, an inspection of the ranch house from attic to bottom, as thorough as the search the conscience-stricken boys had made of the cottonwood groves and the road. No Frenchman. Nobody whatsoever.

"If I didn't think you might better yourselves, I'd fire the whole bunch of you," the widow said. "Now what'll I say to Mr. Evans?"

10

The Lawless Strike Too Soon and Aim Too High

WHEN MAITRE JEAN SABIN, whose life as a leading gastronomer of France and a famous restaurateur of Cannes, on the scenic Azure Coast of the Riviera, had passed so tranquilly, recovered consciousness, he found himself in a crude log shack which had been made tight, more or less, by the application of mud in the chinks. This led him to the false conclusion that he had been "snatched" by some heir of the late Abraham Lincoln. The chef was lying face up on a narrow bunk which had been built in a corner against two walls.

The dazed chef remembered the afterglow of twilight on the golden and ochre leaves of some extraordinarily beautiful trees, the charm of which had been enhanced by their location on a desert which otherwise was drab and uninviting. True, the distant foothills, he remembered, had had streaks like calico, from mineral strata, no doubt, each one of which had lured men to their death by holding out false promise of great riches involving a minimum of work. The leaves, tinted with chrome, xanthin, topaz, gamboge, cadmium, saffron and tones of egg yolk, had bolder, straighter veins and were more pointed than those of the poplars of France. The trees were more stalwart in shape, not excessively tall. Sabin made a mental note that he must ask Monsieur Evans about those strictly American trees, and in doing so was reminded of other associated happenings much less reassuring. The initial use of the chef's methodical mind, so soon after it had begun mildly to function, made Sabin aware that his arms and legs, in fact, his whole body, were wrapped and his movements confined As he examined his condition more thoughtfully, he had to admit, however improbable it seemed, that he was in a straitjacket.

He tried his voice, moderately and experimentally, found it was functioning, then protested curtly, sarcastically and soon was bellowing. No echoes responded.

There was a sore spot on his left buttock, where, he now recollected, he had been jabbed with what felt like a hypodermic needle. Thinking backward from the jab which had produced oblivion, the displaced culinary expert and renowned gastronome re-registered the sound of Widow O'Brien's sharp footsteps as she walked toward a ranch house, on a paved road; a hand which tasted of a particularly disgusting soap over his mouth; of having been dragged by the shoulders into the depths of the so-golden grove; of the tightening of a rope around his arms and shoulders, and a silk cloth wrapped around his throat. He searched his now-bewildered memories and felt sure that, while he was being thus systematically separated from the shrewish escort Homer Evans had accorded him, he had not voiced a cry or uttered a word in any language.

It did not make Maitre Sabin rest in his straitjacket, on the cot, in the crude shack, just after dusk, more resignedly when he recalled what Evans had told him about the tacit arrangements between the Las Vegas representatives of Murder, Inc., the Hudson Dusters, the Cincinnati Spine Crackers, the Milwaukee Mugs, and other criminal organizations with the state, county and city authorities of Nevada, Clarke County and Las Vegas. He had been what the North Americans called "snatched" at twilight, and it was now early evening. The question was, which evening? Had he been "out" an hour or two, or more than twenty-four? He concluded, because his mouth was not too dry and he was only normally hungry, that he had recovered consciousness soon after having relinquished it. However, he wondered if his relative, even fatuous, feeling of equanimity was not due to the aftereffects of the drug which had been shot into his bottom.

Or was he free from acute fear or anxiety because he had been following Homer Evans' instructions when he was kidnapped, and could count on Homer's perspicacity, courage and resourcefulness to rescue him?

"Sabin," he said to himself, "do not let nefarious modern drugs distort your normal objectivity. Monsieur Evans, having been lured away by a laboratory fire that obviously concerned both Mr. Orman, my employer, and that disconcerting Mr. Howard Scott Jordan, who tastes pipsissewa keenly and blunders about the grape, did not foresee that I would be riding alone with the Widow O'Brien on that side road to Cottonwood Acres."

That thought had other, more disturbing implications. Whoever had set the trap which had removed him, Sabin, from his guides and protectors, must have counted on the absence of Homer Evans from that sedan, when it was road-blocked and he, Sabin, was waylaid. Was it not, then, a fair conclusion that his kidnappers had timed the laboratory fire so that Evans, and Mademoiselle Leonard, the sharpshooter, would be drawn downtown? Very possibly.

The clearer Sabin's mind became and the more he exercised it, the hungrier he got. Having been a lifelong student of gastronomy, in all its fascinating branches, Maitre Sabin was aware that in its preliminary stages hunger sharpens the aptitude of a shrewd brain for ratiocination. Once the peak of stimulation, however, is reached and passed, the demands of the belly addle the higher intellectual apparatus and its processes. Hence the incautiousness of starved animals with regard to snares or traps, the dimmed scruples of famished men who steal foodstuffs, and the leniency of cruelty of judges just before lunch time.

Sabin's perceptions were much heightened by his predicament, in spite of the calming influence of the wonder drug he already had promised himself to identify for future use in emotional or professional emergencies. An extrasensory flash, just before a couple of shadows appeared at the shack's only window, caused him to rest immobile and reclose his eyes. His reward was to hear voices, two voices that were strangely alike, yet had discernible distinctions.

"He still out, Mo?" asked a voice behind one of the window shadows shaped somewhat like a human head, outlines softened by mellow rising moonlight from behind.

"Who's calling out names, brother?" asked the other voice re-proachfully. "This character might be playing o-tray oss-pray um-cray. And we're on certain lists. Our monikers, in brief, are not to be uttered willynilly."

"Deprive me of at least one gilded star. I'm a simpleton, tom-noddy and all wet," the first voice admitted with humility. "Why is it that once I hit Las Vegas, I get as wacky as the rest?"

"Place names are equally obnoxious. Must I report you? The super-runt's hard by," voice No. 2 admonished. "He wants results."

"It's time, then, we aroused the victim," Mo's brother said. "Let's go in."

"It was Luke who loaded that syringe. He always had a heavy hand," Mo said.

His brother was not long in catching him up. "Now who's drop-ping names?" he demanded.

Mo was inclined to defend himself as best he could. "You ad-mitted yourself this climate makes you careless. And this job is nuttier than a fruitcake."

Sabin heard a lock turn, a latch creak and felt a breath of chill desert air as Mo and his brother, associate of the heavy-handed Luke, made their way in.

"I am dealing with hoodlums who underestimate me, and have already indicated they may be associated with that scoundrel, Sharkey, and his employer, Rosencrans, whom Monsieur Evans dislikes and deplores. What could be more logical? Furthermore, had they wished to murder me, they could have done so long ago. They want information," Sabin said to himself. And it was only then he was bathed in cold sweat. For the information they were after, he did not possess. He had no more idea then than he had had in Cannes or en route why the multimillionaire, Clifford Orman, had retained him at $2,000 a week, with a six months' guarantee, and had transplanted him from his native land to wild Las Vegas. Las Vegas, he acknowledged ruefully, was living up to his expectations.

As Mo and his brother approached the cot and stood over him, Sabin opened his eyes, glanced at them noncommittally, and waited.

The brothers, somewhat nonplussed by his detachment, or lack of indignation, were caught off base. They glanced at one another hesitantly. Their uncertainty, in fact, and Sabin's increased awareness, under stimulus, that the wonder drug was lending him a provocative personality and enabling him to associate ideas and perceptions with unusual fluency, took advantage of their handicap and his own perverse inclinations.

"Messieurs," he said, "the one of you standing to my left, and consequently nearer my nose, has been handling or carrying fish, rather bulky and heavy, and with an unusually intriguing *parfum*. It must have been a fresh-water fish, most probably of the family *asipenseridae*. May I hazard a guess more specific?"

"You may," a brother said, and turning to the other he added: "Could it be we snatched the wrong gent with whiskers?"

"A sturgeon, could it be?" Sabin asked.

"By Jeepers, Manny, he's one hundred percent right," a brother said, giving Sabin the clue that the other was "Mo."

Both having made bad breaks, and having been taken aback by their victim's coolness and perspicacity, they got down to grim business.

"Look, Cap," said Mo, "we was sent here to see you got fed and since we were given to understand you were fussy about grub we were instructed to take your order and obtain your dinner at a No. 1 eating house not far distant. Tell us your pleasure, and we will return within the half hour, unless something has to be cooked to order, in which case you won't get it. We can't waste too much time."

"Messieurs," continued Sabin, in his most persuasive vein, "it has been years since I enjoyed sturgeon steaks in Madeira, and then the fish was European, not American. Could you not obtain for me the simple ingredients? Then I could cook sturgeon for all three of us which none could ever forget. If you wish, you could order the hors d'oeuvres, of course, before sturgeon black caviar is *de rigueur*, and after it endives Rossini *gratiné au four*, with cheremoya as dessert. Those items you could get in any first-class restaurant. If you would release me from this constraining apparatus I could cook the *pièce de resistance* right here on the crude stove behind you in the corner."

It was plain that Sabin's enthusiasm as he composed the sturgeon dinner had its effect on Manny and Mo. They departed from strict orders to the extent that Sabin's right hand and arm were released from the straitjacket. He was given a pad of paper and a pen that would write in air or under water. This was his list. Before he wrote it out he said, apologetically, that he needed one or two unimportant items from a drugstore, as well as the ingredients for cooking sturgeon with Madeira sauce.

The list:

Dates—Clothesline
Irish Potatoes
Madeira
Flour
Uneedas
Eggs
Noodles
~~Capers~~
Kapers
Animal Crackers
Herpicide
Salt
Thirty Olives
Butter
Bay leaves
Parsley
Dill pickle
Pepper, black
Sweet butter
Chives
Pipsissewa
Caviar
Endives
Parmesan
5 Cheremoya

Manny and Mo scanned the list. Both frowned.

"If there's anything queer about this, you'll wish you'd never been born," Manny said. "I don't mind tellin' you that after you're fed some parties are coming to acquire info. Should they suspect, in advance, you were trying any tricks, or in the course of their inquiry had reason to feel you were not being candid and co-operative, the combined agonies of every live creature you have had prepared for grilling would pale into insignificance compared with the pain you would feel."

"Come, come, messieurs," Sabin rejoined lightly. "The human nervous system, at best, can only transmit a limited load of suffering. Then—poof! The fuse is blown, the current short-circuited."

"This character's got nerve, at that," was Mo's comment.

The moment Sabin was alone again, this time with light from a railroad lantern suspended from a hook, he checked the hasty computations which had prompted the arrangement and composition of his food and drug order. Was it plausible, not too transparent? Neither Manny nor Mo seemed outstandingly bright, but if the list were submitted to Luke Sharkey, Rosencrans or any master mind before it came to the attention of Homer Evans, could it not be deciphered with ease?

It could be decoded, Sabin decided, but not with ease.

A few richly carpeted steps upward from the lobby, bar and game room of the Desert Sands is a quiet intimate drinking area with clear glass walls where discerning clients take refuge now and then from the hectic buzz and bustle sustained almost perpetually on the ground floor by the gamblers, deputies, inebriates and social consumers of alcohol and food, the new guests coming in and others going out. In one corner with opaque walls, where the view would have its foreground unromanticized by flaming joints across the main strip, rests a grand piano. The relay of pianists, tastefully chosen for mood music and soothing improvisations, evoke from this somber Steinway soft sounds that never rise above mezzo forte, and if the notes go faster than eight to the second, they have a smooth glissando effect, not calculated to irritate oversensitive nerves.

It was to that luxurious refuge that Homer had escorted Miriam, after the Orman-Jordan laboratory had been reduced to ashes and Evans had learned, from Sheriff Biscailuz of distant Los Angeles County, that Ossip Rosencrans, to supplement his own shrewd work on a still-undefined errand in Las Vegas, had sent, more or less secretly, the three unscrupulous Dalton brothers, Manny, Mo and Jack. Rosencrans, boss of the missing Luke Sharkey, had come to see Orman, either to distract the oil man's attention while Rosencrans' subordinates kept the multi-multi under surveillance or to offer some tricky proposition which might, on the surface, appear advantageous to Orman, and was sure, in its essence, to benefit Rosencrans either financially or with prestige the sharp head sleuth could later convert into cash.

As Miriam was absorbing natural and spiritual satisfaction from the early evening vista, bathed in dim light that, abetted by merciful distance, concealed the appalling nocturnal activity of reptiles, rodents, felines, canines, spined, quilled and surreptitious beasts and predatory birds and fowls, gastropods, bugs and mysterious lepidoptera. Las Vegas is about the only inhabited place on this earth where the deeds of our human brethren and sisters compare in variety and ruthlessness with those of the so-called lower animals.

Little Miriam feared neither man nor beast when Homer, in a thoughtful and inquiring state of mind, a condition approaching perfect receptivity, was close by her side.

She was not aware that Homer's ideal temper was being stirred, more than superficially, by what he was observing through the clear glass window facing northward toward the rear of the inn's spacious premises. Evans had caught the flicker of a movement which, as he reviewed it in his retentive mind's eye, indicated that a lad, in fact, Kid Unamuno, was stealthily approaching the kitchen or delivery entrance of the establishment in which he and Miriam were sitting.

Homer beckoned a Basque waiter, Jaime, whom he had known some years.

"Jaime," began Evans.

"Señor," responded the waiter with just the right degree of deference.

"Will you ask whoever might be concerned to admit Kid Unamuno, in spite of the fact that he is technically a minor, and might be classified as anti-social, in case he asks permission to enter and bring me a communication?" Homer requested.

So it was that the veteran habitués viewed with misgivings the passage of the Kid through the kitchen, the dining room, up the padded stairs and into the Twilight Room, where Homer made a place for him at his table.

"Grandma pulled a boner, or have you heard?" the Kid began. It was evident from the Kid's manner that nothing could have afforded him more undiluted satisfaction.

"I've heard nothing from or about her," said Evans. "Proceed."

"You turned her loose with that Frenchman who claims he's a chef. When she got the sedan, with the Frenchman, within a quarter of a mile of the ranch, she found the side road blocked by a fallen cottonwood. So she got out and hoofed it to the nearest bunkhouse, thinking this Sabin was following close behind her. When she hammered on the bunkhouse door—the boys, of course, were playing that corny hillbilly music—she discovered the Frenchman was nowhere in sight. She sent the hands—Parentheses Pete and a couple other saps—back to jimmy the tree off the road, drive the sedan to the garage and pick up Sabin. They got back with the sedan, but no Frenchman. He was gone. They had searched the groves, doubled back to the main highway, cased the whole vicinity, but good. That's one thing those chumps can do right."

"So Maitre Sabin has vanished, without trace," said Homer.

Miriam, who distrusted the Kid instinctively and profoundly, said to the lad: "You're holding something back. Come clean."

"Keep your shirt on, will you, miss?" retorted Kid Unamuno. "I'm not finished yet."

"Pray continue," Evans said.

"You always told me, Mr. Evans, to take note of unusual occurrences, which I did, as a matter of fact, long before I knew you or had read about your famous deductions. You know my mother's husband, Gerald Araquistain—not too bad a guy, when his mother or my mother isn't running him ragged, between them . . ."

"I know," Homer said, smiling. "Gerald's in the middle, one might say."

"With sunkist specials," agreed the Kid. "But let me tell you about my foster father. When he saw the lab burning this P.M., he dashed out to Orman's ranch to see that fathead, Jordan, on the chance that they might build another lab and order the chemicals and stuff through him, as Jordan did before."

"What kind of reception did Gerald get?" Homer asked.

"Believe it or not, O.K. Orman was huffin' and puffin' both of his women had played him in the fog with a couple of lushes you brought along from Paris. But he was mad about losing the lab and swore he'd build another, with walls as tight as an atomic pile. Gerald couldn't get a straight yes or no out of Jordan about the order for stock and equipment but he made a fair start, particularly after he reminded Jordan that somewhere in his files were stored away the old bills of lading, itemized accounts, etc."

"You mean that Jordan and Gerald have been putting something over, in the past?" asked Miriam.

The Kid looked pained at hearing any situation stated as bluntly as that. "We may consider that possibility as a factor," he said. "But I haven't got to the important part of my message yet. Gerald came back to the store from Orman's ranch. I chanced to be there, looking over the stock."

"For anything special?" Miriam asked sharply.

The Kid shrugged, sighed and appealed to Homer.

"Can't you send this tomato on an errand, so we men can talk?" he suggested. Miriam bit her lips and seemed about to swing on the Kid, when it occurred to her that Homer was not delivering the line he had used before when characters had made a similar ungallant request. The line was "I have no secrets from Miss Leonard. You may speak freely." Homer did not deliver it. So Miriam, in the interest of the case, swallowed her pride and resentment, and allowed the Kid to think he had won a skirmish in the War Between the Sexes. She rose, excused herself, and departed for the Powder Room, hoping grimly that one of the powders she might find there would have a bitter almond odor.

"What were you looking for in your stepfather's drugstore that made you so touchy?" Homer asked, and when the Kid showed no disposition to answer, he let it pass for the time.

"Do you want this info I have or not?" demanded the Kid.

"Of course," said Homer.

"It was like this. A half hour ago, a couple of strange characters—uneasy and not known around this town—came into Gerald's drugstore, with a list of things to buy. As a kid I learned to read at a distance and with the writing upside down, so I got into position and memorized this one. Only three items were in the drug or liquor line. The other stuff could be bought in any general store, or Ritzy fruit stand. I found out these two mugs had been over at the Grifty Mart, and the back seat of their car (a Buick, 47, No. 3N3892) was littered with parcels."

"The list," prompted Homer, not concealing his keen interest.

"'Twas written in a cockeyed order. But here goes: dates—clothesline, Irish potatoes, Madeira, flour, Uneedas, eggs, noodles, capers—this word was written first with a 'c,' was crossed out, then misspelled with a 'k'; animal crackers, Herpicide, salt, thirty olives . . ."

At that point Homer interrupted. "Did you say thirty olives?"

"That's what was written down. Then butter, bay leaves, parsley, dill pickle (singular), pepper (black), sweet butter, chives, and something that looked like . . ."

"May I guess?" asked Homer. The Kid assented, and was deflated somewhat when Evans said, "Pipsissewa."

"I keep forgetting you got brains, too," the Kid said grudgingly. "How come you didn't bust into print all over the country as a prodigy?"

Homer smiled. "I, like Bacchus, had a tutor, like Silenus. We both thought it better that I should lay low, and play the brain stuff close to my bib."

The Kid shrugged. "If you'd been a bastard, like me, you wouldn't have had all that protection."

"Granted," Homer said. "We can't all be bastards, Kid. You ought to see the parents Jordan drew."

"Both screwballs, I suppose," said the Kid. But Homer did not want to be further diverted just then. "Let me repeat that list, to make sure I got it straight," he said, and he recited the bizarre catalogue of provisions and articles verbatim and in order.

"Anything else to help me figure out this puzzle?" Homer asked.

"The mugs were brothers, or I'll eat my shirt. And one of them smelled of fish."

"Fresh fish?"

"Could be," the Kid agreed.

It was then that Homer drew on his reservoir of native and highly cultivated tact in dealing with the smart and young.

"I don't want to embarrass you by offering payment for a favor," he said. "On the other hand, I'm anxious that you should not think I'm unappreciative of the signal service you've rendered, at some inconvenience to yourself. Would you accept a trifling sum, without feeling that it cheapened our friendly relationship as men of intelligence?"

The Kid indicated he would take the reward in the lofty spirit with which it was tendered, and pocketed a fifty-dollar bill. As the Kid, escorted by the waiter, Jaime, started away, Homer committed the list to paper and showed it to Miriam on her return.

"That conceited little brat! Some day I'll flatten him," said Miriam, but she melted as Homer smiled and said:

"He's outdone himself this time. It's true, Sabin has been kidnapped but this list could only have originated with a true gourmet in peril and put on his mettle."

Miriam, scanning the baffling list, shrugged and sighed.

"Elucidate, master," she implored. "I'm nowhere."

So Homer began. "Let us assume that Sabin, a stranger to these parts and American customs, has been snatched within sight of Cottonwood Acres, where he looked forward to repose and good talk. Let us assume, also, that the two brothers, both mugs unknown in Las Vegas, one smelling of fresh fish, were given the list, mostly of foodstuffs, condiments, aromatics, staples, garnishings, etc., by Sabin, for a multiple purpose. Firstly, he wishes to cook a dinner for himself and his captors; secondly, he wishes to include certain items which, when asked for in drugstores, will occasion comment most likely to reach my ears, somehow. I need not say why he would list pipsissewa. While we were in New York, he bought a hair tonic called 'Herpicide' and feels sure I would remember it, and associate the word with him."

"I follow you so far," said Miriam. "The message is from Sabin, brought by confederates, at least, of his kidnappers, and intended to come to your attention. Why would the crooks be stupid enough to play thus into our hands?"

"An apt question," admitted Homer. "However, no gangster could foresee that Kid Unamuno, with his phenomenal powers of sight, upside down reading and faculties of reasoning and observation would memorize the list *in toto*."

"Most probably not," Miriam agreed.

"You've already observed that the list is headed 'dates—clothesline' and that item No. 13 designates '*thirty* olives.' That discloses much. The unfortunate Maitre has been in the company of Tom Jackson, the reporter, and those of his friends who revert now and then to newspaper lingo. So if the first item means 'dateline,' or 'beginning,' and thirteenth specifying 'thirty' may be the end of any simple code message. I started with the simplest device, using the first letters of each word, from No. 2 onward. I-M-F-U-E-N-C or K or both—A-H-S, IMFUENKCAHS means nothing in any language, nor will it divide into words or syllables. So I tried it backward, or from the bottom up. The result: SHACKNEUFMI."

"Oh, Homer. That sticks out so even I can read it. It means 'Shack nine miles.' But what about the rest of the items?"

"Correct," said Homer, pleased. "Sabin is confined in a shack he figures is about nine miles from here. Now let's have a talk with Gene Delmont."

They forsook the Desert Inn for the Thunderbird, sought out Delmont in his room just before it was time for him to start work downstairs and asked him about good fishing near Las Vegas. Lake Mead, behind the Boulder Dam, had been stocked with trout and bass and, Gene had heard, some sturgeon had come in from the Colorado River and its tributaries in the mountains.

"Could you phone the game warden at the damsite and ask to whom new licenses have recently been issued and what catches, if any, have come to his attention?" Homer asked, and within a few moments Gene had his warden on the line.

Meanwhile Homer was thinking hard. "Madeira. Madeira!" he was repeating to himself, and searching back into his gastronomic lore and experience. "I cannot quite see Sabin cooking trout or bass in Madeira."

Immediately Delmont reported that several fishing licenses had been issued within the week, and only that day, in the afternoon, to three men who gave their names as M. Dale, Aaron Deal and John Dahl, and who said they were cousins from San Francisco. One of them had had beginner's luck and caught a sturgeon which, when examined by the admiring experts at the Lake, seemed to have lost an eye.

Homer was so pleased that both Miriam and Delmont were delighted. Gene went below to oversee the rear drinking area, after urging Homer to make use of his phone, if he wished.

"The sportsmen described by the game warden as 'cousins' from Frisco are, in fact, brothers from Los Angeles. These simple-minded fellows, brave and clever as they often prove to be in other respects, resort to the most obvious switches in names and place names. Manny, Mo and Jack Dalton thus become M. Dale, Aaron (the brother of Moses or Mo) Deal, and John (for Jack) Dahl. Quick on the trigger and unpracticed with the rod and line, they shoot the noblest representative of the fresh waters of our piscatorial world instead of landing him in the approved manner. Our warden, either corrupt like many Nevada officials or careless, as the rest all are, overlooks or disregards the sporting irregularity."

"You think poor Maitre Sabin asked for Madeira wine to cook sturgeon, I take it," Miriam said.

"That becomes clear if we eliminate from his ingenious list the items included merely to form the words of his message, or to attract my special and personal attention. What ingredients are necessary for cooking fresh sturgeon steaks in Madeira sauce? Salted butter, sweet butter, bay leaves or laurel, parsley, dill pickle, salt, black pepper, flour, capers, olives, potato and chives. All the above-mentioned are on the list. Striking them out we have our date line, or beginning, our 'thirty' to indicate the end, the words 'Irish, eggs, Uneedas, noodles, Herpicide, pipsissewa, and animal (preceding crackers). Sabin needed an A, E, E, K (ingeniously inserted by misspelling 'capers') a U, and an I. Quick, sound thinking, under stress. Commend me to a Frenchman for logic."

"Did you warn that insufferable Kid not to sell this list to Rosencrans?" asked Miriam.

"On the contrary, I paid him so highly that surely it will occur to such a prodigy that the other side will pay, also, through the nose. Unless I'm mistaken, the Kid right now is with Herr Rosencrans. I wonder if Ossip and his merry men will make of the list as much as I have. I rather think not. So they'll shortchange the Kid and I'll be able to use our prodigy against them."

As if the reference to the Kid had reminded him of something, Homer took up Delmont's private phone. He called the Kid's wild gifted mother, named Pilar Araquistain, and asked her to meet him at her husband's drugstore.

11

Not Much to Go On, but Enough

FINKE MCGUIRE, with his client, Talbot Forran, the reader will remember, left the airfield purposefully, without disclosing his destination to any of his friends or even exchanging felicitations because of the narrow escape they had shared in the "Greeley Cool." Now Finke had not been gifted with tact comparable with that of Homer Evans, but the young Irish-American had been and still was an apt pupil. He had been delegated by his client the task of finding out what Clifford Orman was plotting and of determining its possible effect, if any, on the fortunes of the Hollywood Strip. He could not ask Homer, directly, not being sure that the interests of their respective clients might not conflict. He cared nothing about Orman's *affaires d'amour*, and had thought it best not to get entangled with either of Orman's attractive young women until he knew more about the game and the score.

It was becoming increasingly clear to Finke that if he were to find out anything significant for his client, he would have to persuade Forran to continue to Hollywood by the best means of prompt transportation and thus leave himself free to scout around on his own.

The mission to Paris had resulted triumphantly, up to the point Forran had learned that Orman was traveling in the vicinity and was holding his cards of purpose so close to his vest that they could not have been dealt honestly. Forran believed that if Orman was to continue to be identified with Las Vegas, the demands of his ego would require the oil man to boost the Nevada resort. If the powerful gangsters had permitted Orman's entrance and tolerated his presence, it was most likely that Orman and the arch schemers for Las Vegas supremacy, both those outside and inside the letter of the law, were allied.

Although Forran, himself, had failed to take adequate precautions to forestall premature publication of Chevalier's agreement to appear in Hollywood, the No. 1. Night Spot Tsar had begun to adjust his memory conveniently, so he could reproach Finke for the leak. Finke, aware that his client was dyspeptic and suffering from hypertension, had made no attempt to defend himself. In detective work, he had learned from Homer, the worse a duffer the client proves to be, the more he should be made to believe he is smart. His state of mind should be mixed like the batter of a cake and baked by his criminologist to a rich golden brown on the outer surfaces, while the middle stays fluffy and light. In short, Finke was obliged to devise a quick and sure way of getting his client out of the picture, and safe in Hollywood, forthwith. Conversely, Finke had to produce an equally sound reason why he, himself, should stay in Las Vegas. His fertile mind was afforded outside assistance before he had to place much strain on it.

For the full passenger list of the lucky "Greeley Cool" had been passed around among those Wheels of the underworld who were maintaining an uneasy truce while enriching themselves in America's growing Babylon. The Hudson Dusters, the Syndicate (or Mafia), the Tri-State Rippers, the Twin Cities Meat Cakes and other gangs who had found easy pickings and soft official co-operation in Nevada had received with loss of face the news concerning Maurice Chevalier, and the latter's iron-clad agreement to lend his prestige to the Hollywood Strip, which thus would get another lease on life. The more astute of the top public enemies suspected that if Hollywood nocturnal high jinks could be kept jumping, and have their place in the news long enough, during the slack period Television was imposing on the movie studios, Cinerama, 3-d, Cinema-Scope, or possibly 4-d would put the Film Capital back into the running as the playboys' Paradise.

Therefore, when Talbot Forran and his private eye, Finke, had descended from the "Greeley Cool," made for a random taxi like a shot off a shovel, and hurried past the Flamingo, the Desert Inn, the Sahara, the Sands, the Thunderbird and other hot spots, to register at the humble Clarke Hotel (only $10 and up) downtown in the gamblers' slums frequented by stray *hoi polloi* and small-time grifters who had neither made the headlines or beat spectacular raps, they were followed by perplexed tails from every important gang. And when their suspicious getaway and bizarre choice of lodgings and environment had been reported to the top gangland levels, a quick conference was held.

A conference of gangland Wheels is much like a meeting among big business men, industrialists and investment bankers. That is, each individual present has backing, an angle, and a wholesome distrust of oral, verbal, written agreements and all members of the human race. When heads were counted, one ambassador of implemented hanky-panky was missing—none other than Bolo McGurk of the Fast Roundup. The others did not bother calling themselves to order, a motion which invariably made the brightest of them laugh. So when McGurk slithered out of the rear entrance of the Clarke and dashed to his camouflaged limousine, which had been partially concealed by pyramids of ash cans, he was spotted, followed and brought before the reassembled council. What took place there is of no moment, since no lie detectors were available and neither the witness nor any of his inquisitors were straightforward. Bolo stood firmly on the Fifth Amendment, and no gangland Wheel would wish to undermine that clams' bastion, in private or in court.

The reader, however, shall know what took place. Bolo McGurk had been closeted with Forran and Finke just long enough to offer *quid pro quo*. The *quid*, as it were, was a tip that the then little-known (in the West) Eartha Kitt was on the train from New York to Los Angeles. Miss Kitt, according to Bolo, was the hottest prospect as an entertainer since Trixie Friganza had retired after the turn of the century. Eartha had signed a secret contract for ten weeks at the Fast Roundup, and would be available for Hollywood some time soon after its expiration, when she would have become the new night sensation of the continent. Now, proposed Bolo,

if Forran would give the Fast Roundup the chance to sign up Chevalier, on whom obviously the Hollywood tsar had the Indian sign,
the Fast Roundup would let Forran have Eartha Kitt for Gyro's.

"If this Miss Kitt is committed to the Roundup, why is she
going through Las Vegas to Los Angeles?" Finke asked.

"She has friends on the Coast and wishes to stop a day or two
with them before settling down to the long grind of three shows
nightly," Bolo McGurk had said.

Finke grinned. This was too good to be true for his purposes.
"Mr. Forran," he said, "let me smuggle you aboard the Los Angeles
express. You contact Miss Kitt, turn on your charm, tell her nobody else could follow Chevalier, sign her up. I'll join you right
away. If you can pull off this deal, you can write your own ticket,
and Hollywood's. Not only will you have achieved the impossible
with Chevalier, luring him again from France, but you will have
taken Eartha Kitt, Las Vegas' most sensational discovery, from
under the noses of the Nevada impresarios, after only one of them
has taken the trouble and expense to make her famous."

"What does Bolo gain by that?" demanded the cautious Forran.

"No other Las Vegas spot but his gets Eartha, until she's wowed
Hollywood," Finke replied. That clinched the arrangement. Forran
was able to board the Los Angeles train without attracting the attention of anyone except the leg men from Murder, Inc., the Black
Hand (second generation); the Milwaukee Maulers, the Buffalo
Backbreakers, the Rippers, Meat Cakes and the other ruling gangs,
who thought little or nothing of it. Forran, after all, lived in Hollywood. So why should he not be going there? And whom else, on
any train, would any man try to contact if Eartha Kitt were aboard.

First Finke tried to phone Homer at the Cottonwood Acres. The
Widow O'Brien, mad with rage because she had been tricked into
losing Maitre Sabin, gave him a short answer. Mr. Evans, she said,
had neglected to put in an appearance and everything had gone to
pot. His fool Frenchman, supposedly a cook, had got lost.

That suggested at once to Finke that he should get in touch
with Clifford Orman, who was paying Sabin two thousand a week.

If Orman knew where Sabin was, it would be indicative that the oil man was double-crossing Homer—an improbable feat. If Orman was not aware that Sabin had misplaced himself, or been lured into a trap, the great chef might well be in danger, and since Homer had Sabin's safety much at heart, Finke should, in Evans' absence, rally round. Especially, Finke thought, because an inquiry into the relationship between Orman and Sabin was vital to the interests of Finke's client, Talbot Forran, who, in order to repose peacefully, had to know why Orman had gone to Europe, secured a famous gourmet, and what the multimillionaire was planning *for* Las Vegas, therefore *against* the Hollywood Strip.

It was the work of a few moments to secure a Drive Yourself car, not the ordinary kind for tourists, but a "special" with the body of a Ford (weighted down with much lead to keep it on the road) and a powerful Rolls Royce engine capable of a speed no Nevada official could possibly match on wheels. Thus Finke reached Orman's outer Las Vegas estate just after the enterprising druggist, Gerald Araquistain, only son of the Widow O'Brien, had arrived to sound out Mr. Orman, or his aide, Mr. Howard Scott Jordan, about stocking a new laboratory for research.

As Finke drove in, he noticed that a giant-sized, bat-eared, flat-nosed, lantern-jawed plug-ugly in chauffeur's uniform looked hard at the incongruous Ford-Rolls-Royce Finke was throttling down to sixty, in order not to be conspicuous. Learning that Orman and Jordan were both in conference with a druggist, and aware that both of them were on the hypochondriac side, Finke made himself inconspicuous in a vantage point from which he could watch his Drive Yourself Special. What he saw rewarded him beyond all expectation. Zachary, Orman's vicious-looking chauffeur, while examining the pepped-up jalopy with a baleful connoisseur's eye, was joined from the shelter of an over-garage apartment by a tall thin type with a high forehead, sharp gray eyes, a pointed nose, one arm slightly stiff, a blue serge suit, a black felt hat, and patent-leather shoes.

If this lean and hungry-looking party were not Luke Sharkey, or Mr. X, who had burgled Homer's hotel room in Cannes, been nicked by Miriam in the Cannes market, stowed away on the liner

America of the Home Line only to escape and vanish in Naples, the Rosencrans Detective Agency must have employed twins.

Finke concluded that his chance discovery was of too much importance to Homer to be withheld. There were many aspects of the puzzle to be weighed and considered—whether Orman had imported Mr. X or was unaware that X was using a small corner of his premises and was in cahoots with Zachary, the villainous chauffeur—how much or how little Howard Scott Jordan knew of Sharkey's maneuvers—was Sabin strayed or snatched? But Finke now had something important to trade, and in the interest of his client, could propose that Homer and he join forces at last, if only in a limited way.

In returning to the spot where his unusual jalopy was parked, Finke made plenty of noise, so both Zachary and the Rosencrans Continental Op would have time to hide themselves. Sharkey availed himself of the warning. Zachary did not. Instead he made the mistake of confronting Finke churlishly.

"What's the idea, driving this crate on a respectable estate? And you a cheap private eye for a California saloonkeeper?" demanded Zachary, who, since his undefinitive brush with Odette's grease monkey at the airfield, had been badly out of humor. When Zachary was at his best, disposition-wise, he was far from amiable. Riled, he was poison.

Finke, who looked the bruiser up and down, asked a most unusual question, as to whether or not Zachary had ever tried to ski up a rope. Zachary reached for a pipe wrench, Finke upset him with a swift kick under the chin and while the big chauffeur was stunned and immobilized Finke ripped a redwood plank from a corral fence, rolled Zachary flat on his face, placed the stout board on an incline across his backsides, started his powerful motor and drove the right wheels of the car over the plank, so that Zachary, when he recovered full consciousness would be sore and lame, for remembrance's sake, but not crippled enough to collect disability insurance.

If Mr. X, or Luke Sharkey, witnessed Zachary's flattening and chastening, he gave no sign. Finke had hoped but not expected Luke would interfere and thus expose his presence in the vicinity.

The druggist's car was plainly marked with the name of the Araquistain Pharmacy and Liquor Mart. Finke, noting this mentally, drove straight back to the center of town and was directed to the drug and spirits store in question. He parked near by, and approached, with the intention of sounding out the druggist who had called on Clifford Orman, and using one of the battery of neat phone booths to locate Homer Evans. What Finke saw was not at all banal. In the rear of the store, and clearly visible through well-lighted windows, was the liquor department in which an extremely beautiful and shapely Basque young woman was browsing about with an unusual boy, as yet unknown to Finke as Kid Unamuno. From a shelf just too high for the boy to reach, the woman, whose every movement betrayed the grace of a practiced dancer, took down three half cases labeled Old Crow. The vacant space on the shelf they refilled with other containers of respectable liquor arranged so carefully that Finke sensed that this young woman of beauty and the boy, precocious and cynical, were in league, somehow. This conclusion of Finke's was substantiated immediately. The kid pried open a case, abstracted a quart bottle of the Crow, uncorked it skillfully, and was about to tilt it up and take a swig when his mother protested, but gently.

"Have you forgotten your manners? Ladies first," she said, and Finke was thrilled at the muffled sound of her throaty insidious voice.

The Kid shrugged. "A pointless convention, but to humor you, Mother . . ." With that the boy extended the uncorked bottle of whiskey, watched his mother swallow a copious dram, then accepted the bottle from her expressive hand and took his turn.

"Why is it, dear, that you need precisely thirty-six bottles, and that they must be of Old Crow? Me, I prefer Spanish brandy, the Fundador or Gonzalez-Byass, but of American bourbon whiskies is not I. W. Harper or Old Ripey superior to the Crow?" the indulgent mother asked.

"Please, Ma. I never make hit-or-miss decisions. Must I always explain in detail?" the boy said, and took another hearty drink. The mother reached for the bottle, smiled and drank.

"You always were a deep one," she said, touching his cheek affectionately.

Before Finke could enter the store, to make his phone call, the Kid, surprisingly strong for his age and stature, loaded the whiskey into the back of a delivery truck. Exasperatedly the boy said, "You'll have to drive, Ma. I'm still under age, and we're going all the way up the Strip."

"I'm on stage in half an hour, but maybe we can just make it," the mother replied, and took the wheel. Finke, his curiosity aroused, could not resist following. He could not explain or justify his action with logic, but he had a strong hunch. This amazing mother and son would lead him somewhere, and they must have some connection with the druggist who had called on Clifford Orman. Not much to go on, but enough.

Now Finke was a very smart young Irish-American, his wits and fibers having been tempered in one of the roughest areas in which boys may be brought up—East Boston. However, he had never tried to excel in indoor schools. Kid Unamuno, boy prodigy and brilliant malefactor of great ingenuity, intrigued him. As anthropologists love to study the roots of higher civilizations by observing primitive peoples in action, so Finke felt he could learn much about criminology by seeing it sprout in a lad of such tender years and elastic scruples. Also, Finke had been impressed with the boy's mother, Pilar, whom he spotted at once as a genuine *flamenco*, that is, natural singer and dancer of gypsy songs and numbers.

The said mother and son, observed covertly by Finke, who followed their delivery truck in his Drive Yourself, passed one hot spot after another, reached the south-western outskirts of Las Vegas proper, ignored some new motels which had recently sprung up, and kept going at a lively pace.

"Either they're headed for the airport or California," Finke said to himself. The destination proved to be the airport. Directed by the Kid, Pilar drove into a little-used delivery entrance from which a branch road led to the outer airstrips. It was an hour when no planes were departing or arriving, so Finke, without exposing himself, could stop his car at a safe distance and watch the mysterious pair. What he seemed to see was this: Pilar stopped the truck on the long airstrip the "Greeley Cool" had negotiated safely only a few hours before. The Kid swiftly got out, opened the back of the truck, took out the three half cases of Old Crow and concealed them carefully, without a second's waste of time, in a clump of mesquite and manzanita, with some sage brush and cactus so placed as to form a better screen.

With that, the Kid got back into the front seat beside his mother. They drove on, turned right to find a suitable exit, away from the principal artery of traffic, then dashed back toward the Las Vegas Strip.

That left Finke with two alternatives, either to follow them or to look around that flat beyond the airstrips and try to decide why Kid Unamuno would cache the Old Crow there. So Finke parked his car, strolled over, and on his way to the hiding place of the whiskey, noticed some broken glass on the second airstrip from the limit of the field. He stopped, picked up a number of fragments, and decided that somebody must have broken a champagne bottle. Another possibility clicked in his mind. There was enough left of the label, when he fitted certain fragments together, to indicate the brand of champagne was the same which had been served at Orman's expense aboard the "Greeley Cool." That, of course, led Finke's active brain to associate the bottle with the Will which Clifford Orman had tossed, in anger, to the prairie from the plane before the perilous landing had been made.

Those isolated and meager facts did not form a pattern, exactly, but they gave Finke a strong suspicion that Kid Unamuno might have some familiarity with that otherwise uninteresting area at the edge of the airfield. So Finke searched the vicinity most thoroughly, satisfied himself there was no longer any bottled and labeled Will near by. Therefore somebody must have found or retrieved Orman's testament which most probably, Finke thought, had cut off Odette penniless because of her impulsive lapse with Tom Jackson.

Having started out with such amorphous intentions about learning of Orman's master plan, in so far as it might affect the Hollywood entertainment Strip and Finke's client, Talbot Forran of Gyro's, the various threads of the web Finke already had traced were giving him more definite ideas. Accidentally at first, and later with conscious intent, Finke had learned many things Homer Evans might find indicative. If Finke had a few more items to trade, he might persuade Homer that it was in his interest to tell Finke what Orman was about, in order to acquire the information Finke had gleaned.

A few discreet inquiries among the porters, clerks and employees of Western Air Lines who had been on duty when the "Greeley Cool" came in yielded Finke a few more clues. First, a baggage-counter man remembered that a mild row, without fisticuffs, had taken place around the Orman limousine, involving Odette, Zachary, the rich oil man's chauffeur and masseur, an air lines mechanic named Monte, and Orman, himself. The mysterious chemist and "wise guy," Howard Scott Jordan, and the oil man's blonde mistress had witnessed the altercation without taking active parts, except that the blonde had tried to pacify the old man and Jordan had, as usual, contrived to irritate all hands.

"Did Mr. Evans know about this?" Finke asked.

He was told that Homer, Sabin and the Widow O'Brien had not been far away.

In the main waiting and ticket room, Finke found out that Kid Unamuno had had quite a talk with a cranky old prospector named Alkali Ike and that the latter, soon afterward, had started out on the desert, in a general southeasterly direction without disclosing whence he was bound or when, if ever, he would return.

"Does this Alkali Ike drink Old Crow whiskey?" Finke asked.

"When he can get it. He's been known to squeeze the wood alcohol out of canned heat when he lacked the price of a standard drink from a bar," the clerk said.

Already, Finke remembered that Orman had tossed off a Last Will cutting off Madeleine, the blonde, on the open prairie some miles before the plane had reached the landing field. Possibly, if Kid Unamuno had come upon the will disinheriting Odette, he had seen in it a reference to the previous testament pauperizing Madeleine, and had sent the old desert rat to recover it. Anyway, the situation regarding both wills needed immediate and careful investigation.

It was a ticket inspector at one of the gates who told Finke that Orman, before he departed, had been accosted and sent into a gust of sudden fury by Ossip Rosencrans, head of the notorious detective agency, who had his headquarters in the Los Angeles office. The oil magnate, according to the inspector, had upbraided and berated Rosencrans for having sent him, somewhere in Europe, an agent or operator named Sharkey. This, in view of the fact that Finke already had seen Sharkey, in the flesh, on the Orman estate, caused him to get confirmation of the report of Orman's abovementioned protest. It seemed to mean that Sharkey was at Orman's place, with the connivance of the chauffeur and ex-thug, Zachary, and unbeknown to the rich proprietor. Or was Orman carrying on a secret relationship with Sharkey, while pretending to Evans and the others that he distrusted Luke and was through with him?

Having garnered all he could at the airport, Finke set out to contact Homer.

And it was then that Fate played one of its niftiest tricks. As Finke was passing near an open window of the Thunderbird, in which hotel and casino he needs must stop a while, notwithstanding his usual habit of pursuing the course of procedure he had, after observation and consideration, determined upon. This kind of transitory call in establishments adequately equipped, such as saloons, filling stations, hostelries, privy premises, etc., has been made by every reader.

From such unliterary oaks, acorns of romance bud, develop and, the devil take the arrangement, eventually drop, if the squirrels do not get them first.

As Finke passed into the lobby, lacking time to give more than a glance at the one-arm banditti, the roulette wheels so aptly formed in essential key patterns, the key to that two-unit Maison de Flush ou Bust, the crap tables where Democratic shills and Republican suckers rubbed elbows and bones, just as he was about to skirt the show floor area, he viewed a vision and verified a voice.

Both were Pilar. In her thrifty husband's drug emporium, and at the airfield, a few moments back (they now seemed ages), Finke had been aware that something was happening to his psyche and metabolism, not to mention his circulation, pulse and pressure. Now that he saw this Gypsy Basque, wild woman and sybil in one, approach the place where she so artistically was wont periodically to preside, our junior detexuctive forgot even the insistent demands of nature and was transfixed.

Men like Finke frequently see beauty in its most dangerous form, i.e., the female of same species. Most of these women, girls or grandmas, are robed. But never before had the costume, the temperament and the allure of a pied witchy-tchornia conjelled as they jolted that P.M.

Finke would have been hard put to describe Pilar, except that she was the most wonderful animal, and he had loved animals and with them had enjoyed a mutual understanding far out, since Finke could remember. On the other hand, Finke's sainted mother had been most devout, the truly devout, those women, now fewer, who in past generations were privileged (they actually liked it) to roam in fields some feet above the city and the country levels where moth and dust do corrupt the scarlet runners also. Finke's mother had exuded a soul, and had assumed all her fellow creatures on two legs who ate cod and drank alcohol, or mated in holy wedlock with the likes of those gruff grown children who did, were likewise equipped, although in varying amplifications. Even to A.P.A.'s, the gentle Mrs. McGuire, pride of decent East Boston, granted a half-soul, not too skillfully nailed or snugly stitched.

So Finke, regarding Pilar with that inner faintness which is Fahrenheit by parties about to be booked, tentacled silently out to her, body and soul, and as her substance grew nearer he felt a chill and smelled the aroma of sanctity, compounded with all the brumes of non-calculated risk. That combination, reader, does it.

Furthermore, as with the miracle which shook Eden and its Garden preparing itself, the other half, Pilar, stop and go lamped something but mysterious, beyond all carnal or ethereal delight that churned her to quivering djello! She was not walking onward, to where she should stand for the band. The fine combination of guitar, *cor anglé*, percussion and trump were repeating and repeating the "vamp"—i.e., non-musical lout—the introductory measures accompanists play to give soloists et al. the beat, the pitch and to yell with them.

Swaying to the "vamp," Pilar raised her dark, fathomless eyes, her hands alit like birds on the film across her breasts, which had responded to some current from without and were uptilting as bodily components, prepared to brook no frustration and little delay.

What did she see? Not what photographers or friends discovered, on gazing at Finke. She gazed as through angel-blown glass, darkly, and lo, agape, there came about them all a great brightness and she beheld twin chariots whereon, Finke, he had descended from everywhere and nowhere. She beheld him, Hart, Shaffner and Marxed in the glory of that brightness, having raiment as of the sun, fair as the moon and terrible that for awe she scarce dared intercept him.

There came a voice out of ceiling, calling, "Pilar, Pilar! You who were dud are now leaving. You who were minor-mensed are now about to slip that folding ballot into a non-Australian slit and hear bump on the box."

Unnoisily Finke replied with main cry, himself. "Eureka, Excelsior, Adona, Pilar. Burn my drapes and scatter the ashes to the soft south wind, the ripping nor'easter, the whiff, the tornado, but mainzoon."

They beheld each other, that split second. He with urge compounded, she all clear of shame, bosom heaving, tossing blame on Mame. Pilar, have mercy! Save us! Finke, ben McGuire, mid clouds of angel smoke, the stiff with the mildest, ascend on the glory of that Old Frigate Fightnes. At an angle of forty-five degrees, toward the men's toilet, he halted, wheeled and spoke:

"Hello."

Pilar answered in hoarse whisper. "I must sing."

Finke: "See that you do."

And with that, risking complications of lay and laundry, he planked himself at a ringside seat, and placed palms on outspread knees like Hercules. Her voice sped over Cloud Nine, and dipped to the milltails of dell.

> "Old men give me gold
>   Young ones baloney
>   But I have embroidered on a corner of my handkerchief
>   The shape of a Corona
>   He corridás not yet—
>   The matador-detective with map of Erin
>   On his face, and halfway down his stack."

Only the Spanish-speaking hearers glanced enviously at Finke, as squarely he sat and ground his *habeas corpus*.

That was how it began.

12
Not to Be Taken Lightly, If at All

WHILE TALBOT FORRAN was on the westbound train between Las Vegas and Los Angeles:

Finke was discovering that Mr. X was Luke Sharkey and in cahoots with Zachary, Orman's chauffeur, if not, secretly, with the Multimillionaire Oilman himself;

While Sabin sagely stood pat, with his hungry kidnappers; and

Homer Evans, with Miriam Leonard at his side, was deciphering Sabin's code order for provisions with which to cook Lake Mead sturgeon in Madeira sauce;

Hjalmar Jansen, and his bottle companion, the reporter, Tom Jackson, were in the back bar area of the Thunderbird, depleting that prize hostelry's supply of Calvados (educated French apple jack aged years in the wood), with chasers of Guinness's stout.

The lives and awarenesses of Hjalmar and Tom, as well as the tranquility of our story, were at that point set a-tingle by the appearance, on the bare floor space and in spotlight, near orchestra of Pilar Araquistain, vibrant brunette *flamenca* singer, dancer who made snakes and stampers hide their heads, and woman to all intents and purposes radio-active. Pilar started singing in her throaty voice that could soar to a whisper, or be Spanishly shrill, a poignant song about a donkey who had died, a faithful unassuming donkey who in life had lugged the vinegar and, in death, was touchingly remembered and missed.

Only the Spaniards, South Americans and Mexicans present could understand the words, but tears dimmed the eyes of Hjalmar and Jackson. They summoned Gene Delmont, and the latter, with his trust in good men, judgment of sound women and inimitable tact, approached Pilar at the conclusion of her group of numbers.

"Dear Señora," Gene began, "the two gentlemen from Montparnasse, both friends of Mr. Homer Evans, have expressed a longing to purchase for you either fourteen or fifteen drinks."

Pilar, already having spotted our pair of very live ones, accepted and joined Hjalmar and Jackson at their table. That was the beginning of an explosive, fervent and parabolic friendship.

The preliminaries and much intriguing colloquy we must abbreviate for reasons of space. However, at the fourth drink, that is to say, within ten minutes after Pilar had sat down on what was only second to her voice and grace as an asset, Jackson, the more articulate if, perhaps, the less impulsive of the champion pair of tosspots, came out rather abruptly with the following question, addressed to Pilar.

"Compañera," he asked, "how do you stand with a rich old banking-stiff named Clifford Orman?"

"In that league, I'm the cellar champ," replied Pilar.

"Too bad," Jackson said, and tossed his glass and a siphon into a fireplace ten yards distant. The twenty deputy sheriffs within range, all of the W. S. Hart variety, glanced at Delmont, were reassured by Gene's gentle nod that all was well, and let the matter drop.

Now Pilar, when she liked a man, or men, could not rest day or night unless she had done him or them some favor. And she liked, already, these top-flight roisterers who depended for their standing, not on riches, but on personality, wit and capacity to give succor and absorb noble punishment.

"Should I cultivate that old slob? Please say it isn't so," begged Pilar. "But for you boys . . ." She shrugged. And when Pilar Araquistain, mother of the phenomenal Kid Unamuno, moved a shoulder, perturbations were registered on the nearest seismograph.

Hjalmar grinned, and when that Norwegian did that, one smelled the aroma of fire and brimstone straight from His Majesty, the Devil, on his genial or persuasive side.

"I'll come to the point," Hjalmar said.

Pilar glanced at the clock. "Too soon?" she murmured.

Again Hjalmar grinned, and posed his problem. He told how he had arranged to paint Old Orman's Parisian importations, both in Goya style. And Pilar, being Basque and in spite of lack of letters, knew her Goya upside down.

"My only regret," Pilar said, with that twinkle in her eye that had caused many an admirer to roll dice on a spinning roulette wheel, "is that Goya did not paint more works on ceilings."

That tickled her male companions. They both thumped so lustily on the table that couples at adjacent tables choked on their whiskey and chow mein, but ever so good-naturedly. All the Thunderbird guests had by that time tabbed a soft spot in their tolerances for Hjalmar and Tom.

However, Hjalmar had to brace his explanatory equipment in a fine brain that so long had resisted liquefaction, and try to make his pickle clear.

"Orman seems to be a jealous and suspicious man," he said, for him very gravely.

"In order to paint the blonde, Madeleine, and the brunette, Odette, *vestida* and *desnuda*, I must arrange for them to pose for me. And even if my models have clothes on, I'm too temperamental and sensitive to brook indiscriminate intrusion, or have third parties present—with only a few sympathetic exceptions."

Pilar nodded. "I am one? Of those exceptions?" she asked.

"In spades," Jackson said, and beckoned the waiter for the eighth round of drinks. "Hjalmar and I want that you should act as chaperone, while he paints, the girls pose, and I stand by to entertain the chaperone and the beauty, bare or costumed, who is not on the dais at the time."

The silvery laugh of Pilar, never sharp or startling, rose through the clubby and thick atmosphere of the drinking *platz* like clear bubbles in amber Asti.

"I've been propositioned in all styles, a million times. You boys take the cake. *Me*, a chaperone! What's wrong? just because I got legally married, to give my wonderful boy a hand-picked dad (kids need 'em, so they say, God only knows for what) have I slipped to the level where I get asked to chaperone a couple of French dolls who are only six years younger than I am?" Pilar asked, pretending to be miffed.

Both Hjalmar and Tom hastened to mollify her.

"Pilar," they said, although not in identical phrases, "we'd rather have you than all the broads in or from Paris, but for the fact that you're a friend of Homer Evans, and we, as gents of the old school, cannot make passes with our friends' women, unless we find out too little, too early, and too much, too late."

"Not with Homer's permission?" persisted Pilar.

"That remains to be seen. But don't confuse the issue just now. We've got to paint those girls, in both of Goya's styles, or lose face."

"Oh, perish that thought!" exclaimed Pilar with all her warm Basque heart as she reached for the pitcher of Calvados and another of stout. By common consent with the waiters, jiggers and bottles had been dispensed with, to give place to more spacious containers.

"But how, darling Pilar, do you propose to proceed, since on Orman's preserves you are currently less welcome than a skunk at a lawn party?" Tom Jackson asked.

Pilar smiled and smoothed her dress, with a soft rustling whispering sound. "I ask you, gentlemen. What is the use for a woman like me to chance disfigurement, endure pain, and stay puffed like a pouter for months, in order to bear a child-genius, like my darling Kid, and then have to think for myself when the thinking gets rough?"

"You mean you'll ask advice of that son of yours? We haven't met him, formally, but we understand he's slicker than the late Li Hung Chang, harder to hold than Houdini, can swap equations with Einstein, drink like a fish, drive like a demon, and beat these crap games out here whenever the deputies turn their backs. We've been told, and correct us if we're wrong, that while you make top dough performing, you squander it like water . . ."

"I do not squander water. I scarcely touch the stuff, outside the privacy of my bath," insisted Pilar.

"I express myself badly," Jackson admitted. "In dealing with a subject like you, one runs out of similes, metaphors and automatopaeia."

"Keep it pure," Pilar cautioned.

So it came about that Kid Unamuno was elected to be called into consultation, but after some delay. Pilar rose with such grace and diffusion of right perfume and musk that our tosspots could hardly stand it, and said, tilting rhythmically on her toes, not risking her heels in that fast company:

"Boys, I've got an errand in the A. and P. While there, I'll phone my Kid, bless his little heart, if the little darling really has one. He'll come up with a solution or I'll bung him back in school. Won't the school love that!"

The cynosure of all eyes as she crossed the back bar area toward the ladies' room, Pilar took her temporary leave. And before she returned, two messengers, each unaware of the other and his errand, slipped notes, respectively, to Hjalmar and Tom. The Norwegian's was delivered first. It read:

> Come save me at once, in a taxi, alone, at intersection with Highway 89 and the side road from Cottonwood Acres and the Orman Preserves. Lose no time, tell no one, if you care for my safety or XXX, plus Y and Z.
>
> > Not yet yours, but in good time,
> > > Madeleine

"Excuse me," said Hjalmar. "Tell Pilar I had to go. She'll understand. We'll get together with the Kid and her later."

Jackson had no reply, for he was thinking he would have Pilar for a while to himself, not counting the gay patrons of the Thunderbird, who mattered not at all, the way Tom was feeling.

But before Tom could consume more than six more of those Sorcerer's Apprentice Cocktails (Calvados and stout), the second messenger arrived with a note for him, to wit:

Darling Tom, my love of two miles in the air. Try me
on earth, or I perish, and what's worse, lose the
wherewithal for us to end our years, entwined and
saturated with comfort, from bottles or on beds, in
chairs, casinos, and saloons. I am hard pressed, figu-
ratively, and yearn to be pressed harder. Lose not
an instant. Meet me at the airport, in the dark. I shall
be wearing Revlon's Ruin,

To be yours, or double or nothing,

Odette

Jackson sighed, shivered, asked Gene Belmont to assure Pilar
that her new *compañeros*-till-death would be back. He then set
forth.

Since Hjalmar got started first, let us first spy on him, in that
miraculous way our Father in Heaven has granted us, I mean,
through the gift of a writer to be omnipresent, omniscient and in-
visible, and that of the reader, if he is worthy enough, to catch the
drift of prose, and supply the predicate of appreciation to the
writer's subject of inspiration. None of this is to be taken lightly,
if at all.

It was already twenty minutes of nine. Hjalmar had to think
quickly and act without delay. Somewhere near the Thunderbird's
fine taxi exit he intercepted Gene Delmont and persuaded the perplexed bar host and ex-pugilist to walk along with him.

"I've got to hire a taxi," Hjalmar said. "Not a minute to lose."

"Nothing easier. There are four right here at our stand,"
Delmont answered.

"It can't be a company taxi. This one must be privately owned
by the driver. Got any like that?"

For answer the accommodating Gene said something consol-
ing to the company taxi man at the head of the line, gestured re-
assuringly at the second as he and Hjalmar passed him by and accosted the third.

"Vince. Meet Mr. Jansen, a friend of Mr. Evans and mine. He's
staying with us," said Gene, indicating the hotel with an easy

gesture. "For some reason, he can't use a company taxi. That's why we passed up the other boys in line."

Vince was agog. "Fine. Hop in," he said to Hjalmar, and then, to Gene, "You'll square me with the other boys?"

Gene nodded, but Hjalmar hesitated. "I got to hire the taxi with no driver," he said. "Just got a message. Have to meet a party, in a taxi, *alone*."

"Look, bud," the taxi man, Vince, assured the painter. "We cart around guys and married women, or girls under age, lots of times. Nobody's ever heard a taxi man squeal, or sing, unless he's hauled into court under oath. They ought to give us boys the right to protect our clients and withhold information, like the Sky Scouts and Private Shamuses do . . . in books."

Gene used his famous tact. "This is a delicate errand. Mr. Jansen, although you may smell liquor on his breath, can be relied upon. The hotel, in fact, will be responsible."

The taxi driver, passing over his cab driver's cap to Hjalmar, got out. "If you say so, Gene, it must be all right. Only, if he's picked up for any reason, he'll have to swear he stole the car while I was having dinner."

"The hotel invites you to a very long dinner. You can catch the new show," Gene said. So Hjalmar, with appropriate thanks, got in and fished around for the starter. He was about to inquire where Highway 89 was; then he thought of Madeleine's having urged "utmost caution." So instead, he drove away, and the pair, watching the taxi anxiously, saw no signs that he had absorbed gallons of Calvados and stout.

"Some guys can drink the State dry, and still drive. For me, no such luck," the taxi driver said as he passed through a group of hotel guests at the entrance.

Vince was overheard by a gentle whimsical Ph.D. who had just tossed his Phi Beta Key into a nearby jar intended for a rubber plant. One encounters all sorts, with all ranges of I.Q.'s, in Las Vegas.

"Sir," the professor said to Vince, the now taxiless cab driver. "The rare gift to which you refer, that of limitless drinking with beneficent, not ill, effects, is known as Mithridatism."

Gentleman Gene, who reveled in rare words, inquired of the savant who had lost his sabbatical advance at roulette within the past ten minutes, "Mithridatism? Could you inform us further, Doctor?"

"Mithridates the Great was King of Pontus, and in his day the most feared and able enemy of Rome," the savant continued, nothing loath. "As a child and heir to a throne, suspecting his elders would try to poison him, little Mithridates took tiny doses of all kinds of poisons, of which alcohol seemed far the most pleasant, and, by increasing the daily dosage, gave himself the immunity which accounts for his long distinguished reign. In short, Mithridates is not only the historical patron of all amateurs of Nose-Paint, but the inventor of homeopathy and preventive medicine. All honor!"

And the group bowed their heads.

We must parallel the getaway of Hjalmar with that of his pal, Tom Jackson, accomplished a few minutes later. Jackson, also aware that he must proceed with the utmost caution, left word with the most discreet waitress, one Sally Jacobsen, that Pilar and her son could count on conferring with him and Hjalmar before the last show was over, around 2 A.M., and that their enforced absence, meanwhile, involved much worse than death, although not necessarily what Pilar might think.

Then Tom stole out through the hotel kitchens, preempted or commandeered a bicycle which had been parked near the ash-can area, and pushed pedals until within easy tiptoeing range of the airfield.

Arrived there, he started circling the outer rim of the airport, facing to windward, and it was not long before there came to his wary nostrils the faint suggestion of Revlon's Ruin, composed as it is of ambergris, synthetic peony essence, the winter fur of the late Mata Hari, and the skin effluvium of the year's most celebrated calendar model, without the corruption of soap, resurgents, detergents or pomades.

It was a matter of moments before he had seen the silhouette of Odette, accomplished the intervening distance, and had the

brunette beauty semi-swooning in his arms. As for his own sensa-
tions, they were so poignant that he did not discover until, four
minutes later, he tried to take a step backward, that he had unwit-
tingly stepped on a sharp spiny cactus. He had to use both hands
to dislodge his multiply-impaled foot, well socked and booted
though it was.

Neither one found it necessary to speak. Their palpitating silence was enough.

But intent as they were on each other, they could not help but
notice, and with perturbation, that the Orman limousine was passing by, on the nearby roadbed, and pulling into the airport parking lot. The gorilla, Zachary, was at the wheel. Clifford Orman, in
dinner clothes, with his face and shirt front skillfully scarved and
masked, and hands blackly gloved, was the only other occupant.

"We got here just in time," said Tom.

"With you, I know we can do anything. We'll beat that old lynx
to the papers. Just see if we don't!"

"You mean, find the Will he tossed down from the plane?"

"I do," said Odette.

"Darling," murmured Tom, and they clinched again, with de-
lirious results eclipsing their first kiss of the sequence.

13

Methods Inquisitorial

ON THEIR RETURN JOURNEY from their food-shopping trip in Las Vegas, Manny and Mo Dalton, legmen for the Rosencrans Detective Agency, were flagged by a sinister flashlight, dot-dashing the Rosencrans stop signal on the side-road over which they had passed, in turn, the Cottonwood Acres, presided over by the Widow O'Brien, and the Orman Preserves, or estate.

The messenger of menace turned out to be none other than their oldest brother, Jack, who had fished (with rod and heater) earlier that day in Lake Mead, under the pseudonym, John Dahl. When all three Dalton boys had been younger, and Jack still the elder, he had pushed Manny and Mo around with childish sadistic glee. Now he seemed ripe for more of the same.

"You clothhead clunks, pull over!" was his opening command.

Their company automobile, it will be remembered, was then loaded with the provender and incidentals their captive, Maitre Sabin, had listed.

"We'll be late for dinner," Mo objected, as Jack got within range, at arm's length. The answer was a left hook to Mo's chops that rattled him down to the toenails, and a surly suggestion that, if either he or Manny got any dinner, ever again, the first course would be administered rather in the breech than orally.

Jack Dalton, having greeted his youngest brother, Mo, strode around to Manny's side of the car and motioned for the latter to open the front-seat window on the right and stick out his neck. Manny, the middle brother, dared not disobey. What he got was a double-handed Judo chop on the Adam's apple which left him limp and in a state of strangulation and pain that would have been pitiful to behold had not Jack been the only qualified beholder. Mo, then being semi-conscious himself, could neither see nor hear distinctly.

After tossing his chastened brothers into the rear seat, unceremoniously, Jack took over the wheel, slammed the starter and started the car rolling. Within ten minutes he veered to the almost open prairie, along a trail which could not be seen as a road, and pulled abreast of the log cabin where Sabin, in straitjacket but not gagged, was awaiting.

The three Dalton brothers, Jack leading the way, entered the hideout without knocking. After having slapped Manny and Mo into animation again, Jack ordered them to bring the provisions from the car. He, himself, removed Sabin's straitjacket.

"Good evening, chef," Jack said, quite respectfully for him. "You will proceed with cooking and preparing the dinner. If anything happens that might ordinarily distract you, try to give it no mind. For at table we shall be five, instead of three as you had planned. You've no objection, surely, to that?"

"None at all," Sabin replied phlegmatically. His tone, in fact, was so even that Jack took heed and frowned.

"Should the sturgeon with Madeira prove defective, or below the standard of your high reputation, or contain any trace of matter injurious to the health of your guests and hosts, you will pray for death many hours before its merciful arrival sets you free," Jack Dalton added.

Sabin, unaccustomed as he was to taking insolent orders, drew himself up proudly. "I can see already that you, although self-consciously brutal, and aware that you have me at a certain advantage, are a sot and a windbag. For such cuisine as I practice, distraction or stupidity around me, is injurious, if not fatal. Cook your own sturgeon, which you shot in gangster fashion instead of hooking, like a gentleman."

The elder brother of the Rosencrans agency detachment was so amazed that he gasped. He drew out from the crude bed-table drawer, a rubber hose two feet in length, was about to make a swipe at Sabin's face, then reconsidered.

"My error, chef! I see you're a man of spirit. Pray proceed as you had intended. I'll treat you as considerately as I can. You have made me quite happy. Men of your *sang froid* hold out longer under torture, either ancient or modern. You'll be a champion subject. After having proven your own mettle as a chef and schemer, you'll afford me a chance to show you that, in my line (that of obtaining information from obstinate or reluctant parties), I am somewhere near your class, artistically."

With that Jack Dalton broke into merry song in a passable baritone voice: "Three coins in the fountain "

"Furthermore, I beg you to believe, sir," Jack resumed. "That whatever I'm obliged to administer to your person, should you not prove co-operative, will be utterly impersonal, on my end. As our Leader once said, 'What is necessary is also right.'"

Sabin glared at Jack contemptuously. "From *Mein Kampf!* I shall spit in your hors d'oeuvres, and each subsequent plate or portion," the chef said. However, he busied himself with the foodstuffs and flavorings as he readied the range. And not to be outdone, musically, he hummed the popular French nursery rhyme beginning:

"*Trois souris aveugles, regardez comme'ils courent . . .*"

By that time another silent auto had slid to the cabin door and out stepped two persons, one less than five feet tall, with a disarmingly gentle manner and a prominent proboscis, the other tall and lean, with a sharp pointed beezer.

"Monsieur Sharkey," exclaimed Sabin, in surprise, to the tall one. "I had hoped you would be here."

"You had?" demanded the short specimen, Ossip Rosencrans (for it was he), in genial astonishment. Then Ossip introduced himself thus:

"Rosencrans, the world's leading detective."

"Imagine," Sabin exclaimed with suppressed mirth. "The world's leading detective, Mr. Homer Evans, will be here in person, sooner than you think."

Then Rosencrans let a cat, if not *the* cat, out of his bag. "*Ah,* that list of yours. That very clever list. Congratulations! Had anyone but me taken a look at that list, he or she would still have been baffled. I decoded it almost at a glance."

Nothing which had been done or said had disturbed Mo and Manny as much as that mild declaration. Mo snatched at his pocket for the original. It was there, and intact.

"So help me God, boss! I gave the list to no one, and only read the grocers and that druggist their own part of it," Mo protested, and Manny confirmed Mo's statement with fervor, his teeth rattling the while.

Ossip Rosencrans smiled, while Luke Sharkey tried not to look paler. "You'll all suffer. The punishment, in my sound organization, is dealt out to fit the crime or the blunder, justly and accurately. I must explain that Mo and Manny, here, consulted your list within eyeshot of one of our local Las Vegas varmints, a child known as Kid Unamuno, who promptly read it, upside down, retained it in his precocious and phenomenal memory, and sold me the list, by dictation, item for item and in the precise order set down."

"Then Monsieur Evans did not see it or hear about it?" asked Sabin, at first apprehensively. Then he regained his confidence in Homer, which, in truth, was superb and impressed all those present. "I'll wager that Monsieur Evans has the list, also in order, and furthermore, that he paid less for it than you did, and is making better use of it right now. Or I will swear to quit cooking, if you, in case I prove to be right, will abandon your fatuous agency, turn your helpers over to the police and take up honest toil."

Impulsively Rosencrans started to shake on the bargain, then held himself back. "I am not a bad sportsman," he said. "But never having tried toil, either honest or dishonest, I cannot promise the unlikely to a gentleman of your integrity, no matter what stakes are involved."

"In short, you are afraid and rightly so," Sabin said, and began whetting an already razor-like knife, about ten inches long, not counting the handle. To make his gesture the more suggestive, he slit off the stout cork of the bottle of Madeira as cleanly and effortlessly as either of the Mayo brothers, in his prime, could have scissored off a suture or a stitch. Manny, Mo and Jack Dalton all drew their automatics, then at a peremptory nod from Rosencrans, replaced them in their hidden shoulder holsters.

This brought another smile to Sabin's Van Dyke face. He looked at Luke Sharkey, who had stood still as a stick, and snapped his fingers. "Poof. This clumsy assassin, or would-be assassin—he seldom seems to follow things through—you must have disarmed." The great chef turned back to Rosencrans. "Could it be that Sharkey, or the nicked Monsieur 'X,' who was wounded in France by a lady friend of mine who could outshoot you all, combined, has been brought here specifically to be what you call 'gone over,' in a manner befitting his blunders in Cannes?"

Little Rosencrans looked up at tall Sharkey, who turned mauve and would have begged for mercy had not Ossip cut him off.

"Maitre Sabin," Ossip confessed, "*you* have the intuition. Should you tire of gastronomy, I shall always have a place for you, at any figure, within reason, that you care to suggest. Operator Sharkey, as you know, made a hash of his assignments in Europe and since arriving here has sunk, as a detective, to still lower depths."

Ossip turned to Mo and Manny, then to Jack. "You have appropriate equipment and instruments, of course, on the premises or in the car?"

The three Dalton brothers were shivering in such apprehension that they could only grimace, flinch and whisper, "Yes, chief. Wwwwwwwwhat shall you require?"

"Only the elementary articles . . ." Rosencrans counted on his fingers as he named: "The ripsaw, the crosscut, the nutcrackers, the reinforced salt for abrasions, the strap or knout, the bamboo for bastinado . . ."

Unable to stand any longer, Luke Sharkey sunk down, *asado*, on the bed. "Not that, chief. Not the bastinado! Not the nutcrackers!"

"When next I need you, you'll be able, however painfully, to walk," the diminutive Rosencrans assured the tall one who was giddy with fright.

Sabin spoke up from the gas-stove area.

"If you, Herr Rosencrans, or any of your minions, have the intention of bruising *my* feet, I shall cut yours off with a cleaver, when Monsieur Evans, Monsieur Finke, Monsieur Hjalmar Jansen and Monsieur Tom Jackson make their appearance, which should be any minute now," the chef said.

"Don't make me laugh," said Rosencrans. "Even if Evans had the perspicacity or temerity, which evidently he lacks, to try to rescue you from me, Monsieur le Chef, he would be potted by my scouts before he turned off Highway 89."

"I can't for the life of me understand how you can have remained in business till now," Sabin retorted. "Miss Miriam could outsmart you, in her sleep, without waking Evans at all."

"I never apply strappado or the bastinado to young women, except in emergencies," said Rosencrans. "Still, if I ever do, that girl will be first in the line."

The notorious agency chief then turned to his henchmen, the Daltons. "I neglected to ask you for the ropes, the fish-line cords, the hooks, both butchers' and anglers', and the alum-stuffed sock," he said. "Sprinkle that sock on the outside with myrrh and biting black pepper. This night is a special occasion."

Groans issued from Luke: "Not the pepper, and fish hooks. Ossip! Chief! After sixteen years of service! Not those!"

The smile on little Rosencrans' countenance was something to behold.

"This night you get your service stripes, where they're least likely to show, in public," Ossip reassured the demoralized Latter Day Cassius, yclept Sharkey. "I'll be obliged to teach you how to burglarize the hotel suite of a subject like Mr. Evans, even if the latter has left the rooms, for the moment, in charge of Miss Leonard, who sleeps more lightly than an ocelot, her rod beneath her pillow. All for a cablegram I could have recited you myself, in remote Los Angeles. I'll remind you never again to forget that your Chief has contacts with all known communicating systems important enough to be chartered semipublic service corporations.

I'll save enough skin, peeled off your posterior with my newly processed knout, to fashion a tobacco pouch."

"Not that Tsarist knout," begged Luke, and slipped down to his knees. This so irked Sabin, to see a fellow human so abject before torture had even been applied, and thinking of the dead brave Frenchmen who had suffered whatever the S.S. had to offer with a sneer, and no audible cries, that the chef splashed Luke with hot water from a pot. The maneuver gave Ossip an idea. As if he needed any more!

"The Shanghai snake! Please, chef, don't waste the surplus boiling water. We shall make use of it, never fear." Rosencrans chuckled.

The mere thought of the ordeal known as Shanghai snake* reduced Luke from a limber craven to a premature pulp.

"Now, upsy daisy," admonished Ossip and kicked him. Luke drizzled blood.

The sight of blood also did something for Ossip Rosencrans, and unmistakably for Jack, the elder Dalton, although the latter was afraid that while Luke was being corrected, he, himself, might be due for a whirl. Mo and Manny had pulled themselves together, and gave promise of perishing, if need be, somewhat stolidly.

"All right, boys! Get going! Take Luke first!"

The Daltons, individually and collectively, started through a routine that gave sinister indications they had performed it before. Mo took the ripsaw and the crosscut and sawed out a parallelopipedon about twelve inches by four, as nearly equilateral as he could manage without T-square and straight edge. This aperture in the cabin wall was about six inches above the level of the floor.

---

* The Shanghai snake is a form of torture devised in 1560 by the Portuguese. A wire-bound hose is twined around and around the victim's tender torso and scalding water is funneled through, so that when the hose is removed, taking with it the affected skin, the victim is marked, for the few succeeding years, with a raw reddish snake entwining his or her body.

Sabin, now intent on his sturgeon steaks and sauce, tried to ignore the proceedings and concentrate on higher things. He succeeded, but only in part. Luke had begun to moan and whine like a poisoned lemming with asthma.

"I should have let that tomato in Cannes drill me with her Colt .45," he whimpered, as he was bound tight, first with fishline for pain, then with clothesline for strength of the bond. He was stretched tight along a one-by-twelve oak board, so he could neither sit up nor squirm. His shoes and socks were removed, so that his feet, when the Daltons lugged him outdoors, were bare.

"That Western wench shall pay for this!" Luke screamed, as his bearers tilted him to get him, trussed and boarded, through the doorway.

An involuntary laugh escaped Sabin, who, being too much of a gentleman to believe what was in store for all and sundry, caught on that Luke meant "Miriam Leonard" when he muttered the words "tomato" and "wench."

"Ho, ho, bi, bi, baw," guffawed the chef, holding his well-padded sides. "He blames Mademoiselle Montana for his present disgrace and the now impending reckoning. I wouldn't mind too much if they did whale this dunce a while."

The whaling, when it began, was something Sabin could neither condone nor ignore, puckish though his mood had become. In World War II, as chef to a fighting French General, Sabin had been captured in the original stampede and had seen the Nazis at their worst. He had never grown inured to bestiality. The bastinado, applied to Luke's feet, which were stuck from without through the hole in the cabin wall that had been sawed for that purpose by the Dalton boys, on order of their Chief, was the more cruel in the eyes and ears and on the nerves of a kind-hearted witness like Sabin because of the glee with which runt Rosencrans, himself, wielded the bamboo.

St. Lawrence on his grill, Jeanne d'Arc at the stake, might have suffered more pain, but Luke's was sharper. We have heard the piercing screams of shrill children classified in terms of rage, fear,

temper, colic, or just plain revolt. All of the above qualities of howling were combined in the tones Luke produced, with a range like
Schumann-Heink, a volume equaling Caruso's, and that indefinable scrape and squeak produced by a thumbnail plus hard chalk
on a blackboard.

Sabin bent over his range and sniffed the aromas of his delicate wine sauce to garnish the noblest of fishes.

Ossip did not interrupt the rhythm of his foot-thrashing self-
indulgence but he caught Sabin's eye and somehow, below the pitch
and dynamics of Luke's awful cries, was able to supplement his
ignoble actions with perverse remarks.

"This, honored chef, compensates one for the drudgery of an
exacting profession, does it not? Knowing, as we do, that pain is
relative, we strive to make it absolute, as great thinkers with philosophy, and scientists with mathematics. Who knew better than
your French genius, Lamarck, that mice whose tails were chewed
off would not produce offspring without rear appendages? Nevertheless, Lamarck repeated the futile experiment time and time
again, almost without number, or, at least, until he ran out of mice.
And merely to bequeath to posterity the dry statistics."

Thus provoked, up spoke Sabin in scorn.

"You, yourself, puny demon that you are," said the chef, "dis-
prove single-handedly the false theory of inherited defects resulting from injuries inflicted or accidents occurring to parents and
ancestors," Sabin retorted. "Stop maiming that fellow's feet."

Rosencrans, winded, called for Jack Dalton and let Jack carry
on with the bastinado. The horrid din from Luke, without, changed
key and reached new emphases and cadences. Dalton did not dare
demonstrate too much agility, power or relish, for if he made Ossip
envious, he, himself, would be given treatment which would make
that being suffered by Luke seem like solace from a Florence Night-
ingale. However, Jack laid on.

"I should have brought our tape recorder," Ossip said to Sabin,
who was sampling the sauce and adding a small pinch of the wonder herb, *cherveuil.*

It was then, when he returned the *cherveuil* to the closet, that Sabin got his inspiration. He knew his Balzac backward and forward, and there on a shelf before his eyes was an old-fashioned wooden powder box labeled: "DIMETHYLCARBAMIC ESTER OF 3-HYDROXYPHENYL DIMETHYLAMINE BROMIDE."*

Ossip, sniffing the miraculous dinner odors, signaled at last for the bastinado phase to terminate itself and nudged Sabin with an elbow, almost below the belt.

He turned to the Daltons. "Now the strappado, boys. Which of you shall bear Luke piggy-back? . . . You, Manny. I'm sure it's your turn for a treat."

The little Chief chuckled again, and rubbed his hands together. "Would you prefer to see the knouting on the back, or the rump, or both? As our guest of the night, I should give you your choice."

"The rump," Sabin answered. "So you won't have to stand on tiptoes to get a level view."

All the Daltons turned white, knowing that Ossip's short stature was the one attribute any reference to which stabbed Rosencrans in his most vulnerable spot. Ossip glared at Sabin and, alas, any and all present could see his keen mind working. Sabin merely shrugged. It was some moments before Ossip could recover surface affability and control his tone of voice.

"You will serve dinner after the strappado," Rosencrans said, coldly, as he would speak to a recalcitrant shoe-shine boy.

Then as Luke, his feet entirely useless, was carried back indoors and his beam end exposed for the knouting, the Chief remarked:

"We'll postpone the Shanghai snake till after we have dined."

---

* "Dimethylcarbamic ester of 3-hydroxyphenyl dimethylamine bromide" is a brusquely explosive evacuant absorbed extremely rapidly and giving such unmistakable and so short notice to the patient that he has to go that few ever make the haven of the Excusatt.

The effect of those words on Luke Sharkey can neither be described nor imagined. He could only slump and moan, and as Ossip Rosencrans snarled, everyone knew that Sabin's taunt had got under his hide.

When the shamuses all were intent, or unconscious, as Luke now seemed to be, Sabin reached for the bottle of laxative powder and committed an offense against high gastronomy no Frenchman had perpetrated since Balzac's rakish King, who at a great stag feast, the reader will recall, placed on the only seat of the single available outhouse a wax figure of the absent Queen.

Rosencrans, having paced, frowned and postured like Napoleon, halted, faced about.

"I had planned," Ossip scathingly announced, "to show Monsieur Sabin a few light examples of what he might expect, were he reticent under questioning. Then I had intended to ask him for what purpose Mr. Clifford Orman imported him from France, at $2,000 per week. Right!"

Even Luke, dimly recovering consciousness, gasped "Right!" Rosencrans continued, more ominously:

"As matters now stand, I shall try the Shanghai snake on Chef Sabin, first, following dessert, and grill him later. His time is our time and there seems to be plenty of both. Homer Evans, indeed!"

Since Manny, Mo and Jack had gathered around, softly, step by step, and stood agape, Rosencrans glared at them in turn, then barked:

"Dismissed!"

14
Sharper Than the Serpent's Tooth

HOMER AND MIRIAM had just finished dining in his ranch apartment at Cottonwood Acres, following their talk with Kid Unamuno and the decoding of Sabin's memorable list.

"Homer," she began, after sitting up firmly and bracing her sturdy although lovely shoulders as she often did when she was presuming to let even the shadow of a doubt concerning his wisdom cross her mind, "are we not leaving our dear friend Maitre Sabin in the *cirage?*" Cirage, in French means "shoe blacking, or wax" and in the French slang expression just half-Anglicized by the cool Miss Montana, she was conveying, as a French person would, that Chef Sabin was what we over here call "in the soup," or "up a certain creek in a leaky rowboat without proper means of propulsion."

The smile Homer gave her was disarming indeed.

"I'd considered his predicament," Homer admitted. "He's been snatched, evidently, by Manny, Mo and Jack, for Rosencrans. You understand why."

She nodded.

"Those thugs want to know why the Maitre was brought by Orman here from France," she volunteered.

He patted her hand. "And so do we. The difficulty is, Sabin does not, himself, know the answer to that question."

That stirred Miriam to deeper depths of concern. "That's why I'm worried. Yes, I'm worried. I've even let myself suspect . . ." Here she broke off, blushing. Homer smiled again. "That I am on a limb."

"That *he* is being *left* on a *limb* with the most murderous cut-throats licensed as private detectives busy sawing at the hunk," she exclaimed. "I shouldn't distrust you, but I've a feeling—in here."

"A little to the right, if you wish to indicate your heart, which I believed that I possessed," Homer suggested.

She blushed becomingly.

Homer lit his rare Garcia y Vegas and leaned back. That was what he often did before he offered some comforting explanation which might be the truth and nothing but the truth, but involve selected reservations.

"Try to bear with me, and my thinking," Evans said quite earnestly, for him. "Our old friend Sabin, as French as a vintage of Chateau Lafitte, came here to Las Vegas, at my suggestion, to see our modern Ninevah. He expected gangsters. Now he has them. What they will do and say he can tell to his friends and colleagues in Cannes, by firesides or after coffee, in cafés and club cars, in his twilight of well-spent years, which, let's hope, will be prolonged."

"If you ask me, they may be damned well abbreviated if we don't *do* something, *right now*," exploded Miriam.

He touched her hand again to reassure her. "I can't leave you on the anxious seat, dear," Homer said. "The moment Finke arrives, the watchword will be action."

"Finke?" she repeated, astonished. "He's on another case."

"The cases overlap," explained Homer. "I've been tipped off by Kid Unamuno, who, grace to that $50 I slipped him, plus a cue for making more out of Rosencrans, that Finke has shipped his client, Forran, to Hollywood."

"But how does Forran's absence mean Finke's presence here?" asked Miriam.

"Finke must have been anxious to contact me uninhibitedly or he would not have ditched Forran so neatly. Put yourself in his place." Even as Homer was making this impractical suggestion, the Widow O'Brien announced Mr. Finke McGuire.

Both Evans and Miriam rose. Finke looked puzzled. "Are we going somewhere?" the younger detective inquired.

"Let's," Evans said. "You may tell me what you've learned and wish to trade for my co-operation on our way."

Finke shrugged and grinned at Miriam. "For you, my info's good. Luke Sharkey is in town."

She patted her handbag with the trusty automatic. "Luke must have lost his mind, such as it was," she said. Homer was already at the door, so she added to Finke: "We mustn't keep the Master waiting. You know Sabin has been kidnapped, of course."

Finke did a double take. "The Master sits here and Sabin's in the hands of Luke and Orman's prize monkey, that Zachary?" Finke asked, loudly enough so Evans would have to overhear him.

"You might at least have granted us Tristan and Isolde," she complained, "but let it pass."

They joined Homer, the sedan was at hand, and they started out, with Evans at the wheel, Miriam at his right, in front, and Finke to cover the rear window. The farther they drove, in the general direction of California, the more bewildered was Finke—after he had told Homer the items he had acquired, for trade and co-operation between them, to wit:

That Luke Sharkey, or Mr. X, was very much at home around Orman's garage and extra pally with Orman's gorilla masseur and chauffeur, Zachary;

That Finke, in the course of his occupational hazards, had been obliged to flatten said Zachary and lame him considerably;

That Pilar, the most wonderful *unattached* woman in the world in Finke's estimation, had driven her son, one Kid Unamuno, to the airport to cache two cases of Old Crow;

That Finke had followed them and had uncovered evidence that Orman's Last Will and Testament, disinheriting the brunette, Odette, flung from the plane at the Las Vegas airstrip before the perilous landing of the "Greeley Cool," had been picked up by a party or parties unknown;

And that a prospector called Alkali Ike was hoofing it across the desert, to pick up the next to the Last Will which had been bottled and tossed out about sixty miles southeastward.

Homer, congratulating Finke and promising him every co-operation possible, remarked that Alkali Ike must be looking for the
other Will, disinheriting Madeleine, the blonde.

"Ah," sighed Homer, "for the good old days when dirty work
was confined to decent crossroads and not spattered over continents, seas and states."

Miriam had listened carefully and made the requisite mental notes,
but she was getting more anxious than she had been at Cottonwood
Acres.

"We shall *not* find poor Maitre Sabin at the airport," she announced with vehemence, risking also irrelevance.

"Most probably not," Homer agreed. "Rosencrans and/or his
muscle men, the Daltons, will not disable our gastronomer friend,
I think. They need him intact for his answers. They will make
threats, never having been able to grasp the fact that solid Frenchmen, threatened, become more cunning and less informative than
clammer-uppers of any nationality on earth. The heathen Chinese
are positively garrulous compared with the cornered exponents
of *liberté, egalité, fraternité*, America's best allies from the beginning, now and forever. The contest of wills and wits between
Sabin and Rosencrans should be on a level with Dostoyevsky's
historical duel between Raskolnikov and Pyotr Petrovitch, if the
subtle Pyotr will forgive me the comparison with sawed-off Ossip.
To make sure nothing of importance is lost to posterity, I long
ago engaged my new helper, Kid Unamuno, to find the Rosencrans
gang hideout, nine miles from Las Vegas civic center, and install a
'bug' or recording device. The recorder is a new machine, or set of
machines, and from it, or them, and their precious tapes, I expect
a rare treat."

Homer turned to Miriam. "I know you are nervous. I've kept
you in suspense. Please believe, however tardily I give you this
assurance, that should the going for my dear old friend, Sabin, get
too rugged, I shall be notified, *instanter*. Thus far, since I have
received no S.O.S., the fiesta in that hideout—not far from the
Orman Preserves, as a matter of fact—must be orderly and safe."

Miriam spoke up, relieved and most sincerely. "Since my dear father passed on, Homer," she said, "I have loved you above any man on earth, or all men put together."

"And I," said Finke, not wishing to be outdone, "have respected you, since the death of F.D.R., as the wisest, and the man of purest integrity. However, I would much rather be your prodigy or part-time assistant than your client just now."

This brought a grin from Homer. "You don't trust the Kid, to say nothing of Sharkey and Rosencrans, or the Daltons, Manny, Mo and Jack?"

"The Kid hasn't even formed behavior patterns," Finke said. "And Rosencrans! If all the 'bugs' his sharp schnozzle has spotted were placed end to end, you could trip along them halfway to the moon, like a slack wire midget with wings."

Miriam stamped her pretty foot and repeated: "Why are we going to the *airport?*"

For answer, Homer pulled his sedan into the shadow of some young bamboo, overhung with the fronds of squat palms. Within two seconds Finke, Miriam and Homer saw the great black limousine of Orman pass by. Furthermore, the wealthy Oil Tsar was, to all intents and purposes, swathed in black and masked. And at the wheel was Zachary.

Homer nearly blushed that time. "Miriam," he said, apologetically, "while we were at dinner, you recall I was summoned to the phone."

It was her turn to feel a red face hot. "I should have known that the widow would not presume to interrupt your meal unless the call was vital. Shall I ever learn?"

"The Kid phoned. He said his mother, Pilar, who, by the way, has captivated Finke and *vice versa*, had contacted *him* (the Kid) to say that our convivial friends, of the arts and letters respectively, had been with her at the Thunderbird, drinking Calvados and stout, that she had been gone on an errand to the rest room, and while she had been absent, both Hjalmar and Tom Jackson had received urgent messages. They had left verbal apologies, and rushed out into the night. Hjalmar had hired a driverless taxi and started

downtown way. Tom had pinched a bicycle and pedaled in this direction. So unless I am mistaken, we shall find at the airport, at
more or less cross purposes and without prearrangement, Orman,
Zachary, Hjalmar, Madeleine, Tom, Odette—to name a few."

This was a long speech for Homer, but it conveyed much edu-
cation. The jaunt to the airport no longer seemed futile to Finke or
procrastinational to Miriam. Let us share what occurred and de-
termine who, if anyone, was wrong or right.

Already they were near enough the airport to leave the telltale
sedan, concealed as it was in the bamboo and palm thicket, and
accomplish the remaining two hundred yards on foot circum-
spectly. By habit of long association, Miriam, sharpshooter of the
trio, walked on the right, since she preferred to shoot right-handed
and carry her handbag in her left.

First they spotted Clifford Orman, mostly because Zachary,
walking with the oil man, although perfunctorily masked, made as
much noise as a moose. Finke noted this and grinned.

"I knocked him face down, put a plank over him, and ran two
side wheels of my car over the plank. That's why he's so clumsy
and lame," explained Finke.

As soon as they were sure that Orman was headed for the area
where he had dropped the anti-Odette Will, and Kid Unamuno had
subsequently hidden two cases of Old Crow, and where, on the
neighboring concrete runway Finke had found the fragments of the
smashed champagne bottle (minus cork and document), Homer
suggested that they separate, reconnoiter and meet at the baggage
window as soon as they had had time, individually but separately,
to round the compact field and glance into its buildings.

It was on the edge of a neighboring golf course that Finke spotted Hjalmar getting out of what appeared to be a Yellow Taxi. The
huge Norwegian, jolly and expansive even in the dark, drew out
Madeleine as if she had been weightless, clasped her to his chest
until she wilted, then dropped her into one of those new motor
gadgets golfers use. The taxi had proven cumbersome, for open
prairie scouting, and Hjalmar was soon sitting with his fair model in
the golf motorized toad-hopper, consulting a map by the moonlight.

"Hjalmar," yelled Finke. "It's McGuire! Stick around."

"Aye, aye," agreed Hjalmar, who sensed there might be rough stuff.

Miriam came up with Odette and Tom Jackson, who were clasped in one of their frantic embraces, by following a trail of Revlon's Ruin. She whispered, when they relaxed: "Hold everything."

The brunette, keyed up, jumped a foot and a half and landed on all fours, like a cat. Tom bit his tongue. Then the reporter recovered and said, with relief, sotto voce: "Ah, Miriam. It's you."

"Who were you expecting?" Miriam retorted with her silvery laugh.

Odette achieved a normal posture, hand on Tom's shoulder.

"The '*office*' is here, and he's masked. That bruiser, Zach, is with him," the brunette whispered, shuddering.

"Mr. Orman and his bodyguard are being tailed by Homer, himself," Miriam said. "All's well."

Homer, at a safe distance from his quarries, and having decided where they must be going, paused and unslung his Walkie Talkie. This he tuned in, and soon the voice of Kid Unamuno, somewhat cracked in transmission, but easily discernible and informative, came over.

| Evans: | "Hello. Peninsula. Cosmo here. Over. |
| The Kid: | "Peninsula parleys. Pipsissewa safe. Requin ohne-fusses and bumbasted raw. Fre*re* Jac*que* and semblables, *Nase*-rine *nip*upping. Over. |

The above dialogue requires some explanation, to brief the reader as one should. "Peninsula" is the code word agreed between Evans and his juvenile confederate to mean "Unamuno," since the great Spanish philosopher had held that Spain's culture should be peninsular, in its essence, and not corrupted by Europe, the Orient, or the West. The use of the word "parleys" for "speaking" involves some playful alliteration, for euphony's sweet sake.

"Cosmo" was code for Cosmopolitan, Mr. Evans, himself.

"Requin" means shark, or Sharkey. "Ohne-fusses and bum-basted raw" means "De footed and rump beaten raw, or bastinadoed and strappadoed on soles and buttocks, until feet and hind-cheeks were mostly used up."

Who could "Frere Jacque and semblables" be, save Jack Dalton (Brother Jack) and his juniors, Manny and Mo?

"*Nase*-rine *nip*upping" was a master stroke for any juvenile codester. "Nase," in German means "nose" and could apply to none other than Ossip Rosencrans, whose beak or beezer was like comic-strip Abie Kabibble's.

So, in only eighteen swiftly spoken words, delivered in less than twelve seconds, Kid Unamuno had informed Homer, and Homer had grasped that at the hideout Sabin (pipsissewa) was safe, Sharkey (requin) had been brutally bastinadoed and strappadoed, and that the three Daltons were doing somersaults for Rosencrans, also present.

Going back to the exchange between the Kid and Homer:

Homer:	Peut-on rubato?
The Kid:	Linxgetty ten times. *On mange* dans l'Oncle Tom."

Decoded:

Homer:	"May I delay a while if I catch up afterward with the beat?"
The Kid:	"Twenty-five minutes. They're all eating in the cabin."

To Homer it was a rare pleasure to improvise international and interlingual codes with such a sharp lad on the long end of the air wave. "Linxgetty," the reader will readily understand, means "Lincoln's Speech at Gettysburg." This required of the Honest and Immortal Abe two and one half minutes to deliver. Ten times 2.5 make 25. "*On mange*" is plain French. "The Uncle Tom" is a cabin. So, as far as the Kid was concerned, Evans might hold off twenty-five minutes before crashing the cabinular hideout, to give all hands a chance to get deeper into dinner. After that, evidently, the Kid thought Homer should stand by.

A blood-curdling yell, not far from where Homer was standing when he was considering the Kid's terse report, prompted all the Evans party and their quarries at the airport to converge double quick to the spot ear-indicated, risking or ignoring consequences. It was a yell that important, and soon had a base drone, or *bourdon*, from the brute, Zachary, that sustained Orman's bull *canto*.

The tableau, in frantic motion but unified by space, was heart-rending to hear, and almost as frightening to behold. Both Orman and Zachary, large men in stature, were hopping, help-helping-howling and performing a grim rigadoon. Each clasped one of his ankles with both hands, and had to skip and balance on one limb. Orman circled blindly, clockwise. Zachary, narrowly missing bumping the suffering oil magnate, circled counter-clockwise, like an adjutant crane.

Homer was first on the scene. He was followed, in order, by:

> Miriam, Odette and Tom Jackson
> Finke, Hjalmer and Madeleine

"I've been bitten by a snake, a rattler," bawled Orman. "Help! Quick! The antitoxin."

Zachary was bellowing like a bishop on Atonement Day.

"I brought the wrong bottle. I've only got liquid Half-Safe."

With that the bitten pair resumed revolving, moaning, and shrieking, this time with Orman counter-clockwise and Big Zach bumbling to his left. They collided, both fell, and an ominous sound from some other snake's tail bones caused all of the company to hit the concrete runway in less than a split second. There, where they could see their hard footing by moonlight, the bitten principals sashayed on one foot, bent, hollered, raved, cursed and kicked.

"Quick! I'm dying! Bi, bah, aeiow, the needle, the serum," was Orman's refrain.

"Wrong bottle. I'm done for. Call a priest!" was Zachary's contribution, accompanied by a bearlike single shuffle, double bunt and distorted Wagnerian "Yo ho, to ho's" iced with terror ill-becoming a man of the chauffeur's past and stature.

Naturally, while Finke was having the presence of mind to dash for the Orman limousine, Homer took charge.

"We'll rush you to hospital, in plenty of time," he said. "Stand still! You're speeding your circulation! Do you want the venom to hurry to your heart?"

"Waah! Woe! Aiiiiii! Ouch! Evans. Save me, and half my fortune is yours!" This from Orman.

Then, in spite of the excruciating pain and the ghastly apprehension, the tycoon pulled himself together long enough to shake a finger in Zachary's face and roar: "You left the serum behind! You've murdered me! You're fired! I refuse categorically to cross the border of another world, no matter what it may be like, with you in my employ. Get out! Die like a rat! I wish I could throttle you myself, to atone for my sins of omission. The devil take the rest!"

Homer smiled expansively and touched the irate millionaire warmly on a shoulder. "Now that's the talk. A gentleman of spirit. You know I never lie. You'll recover, and so will this bloated scurvy fellow, if you do what I suggest," Evans said.

"God, what a man!" breathed Miriam, and she did not mean Clifford Orman, although the oil chap had gone up far in her estimation when he had, facing the Grim Reaper, as 'twere, thought only of his sins of omission (of which, incidentally, there could not have been too many in the best of catalogues).

By that time, Finke was abreast our group with the Orman limousine, the oil magnate and Zachary were dumped into the rear seat, side by side, and in a matter of split seconds, Finke was speeding hospitalward, doing ninety miles the hour, with screeching motor-sheriffed escort.

Homer then turned to Hjalmar: "Continue with fair Madeleine to recover the Will she deplores. Her 'office' has seen her in your company, after sundown, by moonlight. Not even fatuous multies need evidence much more convincing than that. You may as well be hung for goats as lambs."

To Tom Jackson, Evans said: "Abandon your search for the anti-Odette Will and Testament and expose the lady no longer to rattle-snake hazards. The serpents, more cunning with each year, already have learned that on the concrete runways, if they are careful, their pickings may outclass what they sting in the brush."

Odette, half-fainting, was carried and laid across Tom's borrowed bicycle, nothing loath.

The faint chug chug of the golfer's toad hopper seemed to indicate that Hjalmar and Madeleine were bound for the nearest motel.

That left Miriam and Homer. He took her arm, led a dual dash for the sedan, the while saying: "We've not a moment to lose. The climax at the hideout awaits."

15
Stoop to Anything and Stop at Nothing

IT WAS NOT UNTIL Homer was beside Miriam in the sedan, ready to speed to Sabin's rescue, that she learned her man had with him the improved Walkie Talkie. By ordinary road, had Homer tried to reach the hideout shack, he would have had to drive all the way back to downtown Las Vegas, from the airport, a distance of five miles or so, then take the Highway No. 89 to the junction with the side road passing Cottonwood Acres (where he lived and had dined), thence past the estate of Clifford Orman (now in throes of post-snakebite agonies), and find the hidden side trail to the log shack dubbed so aptly by Kid Unamuno, L'Oncle Tom.

So Homer contacted the Kid, with these words:

Evans:	Hello, hello. Cosmo here. Are you there, Peninsula? Cosmo calling Peninsula. Over.
The Kid:	Peninsula here, for Cosmo. Shoot. Over.
Evans:	Paderewski magnetic. Numbers *s'il vous plait*. Over.
The Kid:	Sinner, head for that old home over Jordan. Over.
Evans:	Civil victor, Sol Brody wise. Wie viel?
The Kid:	Champ won 6 straight, Diver dove 14. Seconds lousy. Dost perk? Over.
Evans:	Java java. Out.

Miriam sat straight, as Homer started the sedan, sighted on Polaris, motionlessly measured an imaginary angle north by nor'west, and hit the prairie. In spite of the hazards, such as clumps, dips and ledge juts, he seemed to be keeping a purposeful course at better than 50 miles an hour.

"Sorry if it's bumpy. There's so little time," Homer said apologetically and tenderly.

"Don't butter me," said Miriam. "I have been at your side, all but about ten minutes since twilight. You have not been alone with that impudent little monster, Kid Unamuno, more than five minutes at a stretch during that period. You have not had time to devise a foolproof all-purpose code, or teach it to a child, or an Einstein, for that matter. Yet, you and that detestable brat chatter like an ape and a bear, and pretend to understand."

Homer smiled and relented. "You know the code as well as we do. We are improvising, the Kid and I."

"Pray continue. You may improvise yourself into an off-with-the-old and on-with-the-new assistant and bodyguard. I suppose that monkey can shoot," she said frigidly.

"Darling, after our years together, you pay me the tribute of jealousy. I should adore you for your considerateness, and tact, if nothing more," he murmured, and twitched the wheel to dodge a dancing skunk, so black, white and merry in the moonlight and unaccustomed to desert traffic at that hour, in that (to a skunk) odd conveyance that he (the skunk) had let his hair down to cavort unwarily.

"What was it Bemelmans said: 'For cooking with gas all that is essential is lots of time and the best of butter'?"

"It was the ship-musical Czech, not the Deutscher, who coined that phrase," suggested Evans.

"Explain that code, or I'll jump out and walk home," said Miriam, and her fair trigger finger explored the car door lever as petulantly as ever moved nine-living tail of a cat. "What is meant by 'Paderewski magnetic'?"

Homer: Our globe's north magnetic pole.

Miriam:	And this spiritual stuff about the River Jordan.
Homer:	The home of Howard Scott Jordan, where we called in his absence not long ago, lies about 14 degrees and 6 minutes west by northwest of us. That gives me my direction, or course. Otherwise I should not be speeding at 55 miles the hour over a lone but decidedly obstructuous prairie, to save miles and urgent time, headed for the torture shack where, not Chef Sabin, but Luke Sharkey, has been scarified and flayed.

Miriam stamped her pretty feet, contracted her smooth muscles, readjusted her foundations, and finally recovered equanimity dissolved in admiration.

"All right. Use that damned Kid for brain work, and me for pecking seed from gilded donikers. That's all I'm good for, love and shooting. Ah, well. A woman's fate," muttered Miriam.

"Not many women shoot as you do," Homer remarked absentmindedly, and that time she stamped on his foot and sent the gas pedal down flat to the floor board. The peremptory speed-up nearly cracked their necks.

"Furthermore," persisted Evans, "if we must spin on like Mr. and Mrs. North, God forbid, you have not been confined, in a manner of speaking, to the birdie gilded-cageque routine. I trust you'll recover your usual ideal self-possession. What lies before us may be one of our spiciest, or more perilous, adventures, up to date. We are tangling, don't forget, with the only chap I know in the detective line who can give me decent opposition."

"That's because that Rosencrans runt will stoop to anything and stop at nothing," said Miriam, even in her mood of rebellion on the permanent *qui vive* to defend Homer and his record against all comers.

"Ossip's disregard for rules or principles is Ossip's major fault, his Achilles heel," Homer said. "Anarchists have many more accidents than their statistical share."

"I suppose you hold *yourself* up as a conformer," Miriam jibed quite sharply.

"My plans exclude brutalities which would react on my own capabilities. Nerves inured to torture, the bodily kind, I mean to say, are not secure when tuned to concert pitch for high detective work, for righting wrongs, protecting the innocent, exposing the guilty, or pandering to bodyguards who envy smart children," was Homer's last word.

He braked down the sedan, opened his door, motioned to Miriam to follow his lead, and started for the shack some yards ahead. He unslung his Walkie Talkie, so neatly packed and easy on the draw, and whispered over its directed waves, "Hello, Peninsula. Cosmo *ici*. Over."

And no air voice said anything at all, after one faint "Glub."

Homer tried again, and this time the Kid's voice came over. "Brie it," the voice began, and was cut and choked off audibly.

Homer turned to Miriam gravely. "They've got that child in there."

The windows of the shack glowed dimly, having been discreetly shaded. The desert night was silver and black. The rims of hills ringed an ominous horizon. Star patterns were in motionary place, the thermometer had sunk to 38 above zero, Fahrenheit. Relativity prevailed.

But Miriam could not hold back hot words to this effect:

"If any man raises just one finger to hurt that wonderful boy, I'll kill him. . . . I'll kill him. . . . I'll kill him," was what Homer heard, and he saw the companion of his nights and days, the woman of all women, who, with him, side by side, had passed through so much so incredibly calmly, for once on the verge of hysterics from rage.

"Pray do," was all he could enunciate.

At the Two-Armed Allway Hospital, in downtown Las Vegas, on a street one end of which was named for Lewis and the other for Clark (so that certain unfortunate patients never saw the painted and illumined names of both members of that famous team of pioneers), Finke deposited Clifford Orman and his former man, Zachary, for whom, howling and writhing with fear and pain as he was, the multimillionaire refused to be responsible, debt-wise or otherwise.

Finke waited long enough to see them both shot with super-sedatives and serum, then he sped back to the scene of the snake-bites. He figured, and oh how correctly, that this was what Homer would have asked of him, had there been space and time. Now Finke, an Easterner or tenderfoot, had, on opening his office on the West Coast, been briefed by Homer about snakes, and other lore involving the great outdoors. Finke, in fact, before he reconnoitered the spot of prairie beyond the fatal airstrip, bribed a mechanic, none other than Monte, our previous acquaintance and admirer of Odette, to pry up a number of flagstones, have the kitchen help warm them in the ovens, and wrap them in snug flannel cloths. After having equipped themselves with stout snake-proof boots (reader, never rely on those, exclusively, in rattler country), Finke and Monte the Mechanic, placed the hot flannel-swathed flat stones along the circumference of an imaginary circle, about twenty yards in diameter, and having as a center the spot marked "X" where Orman and Zach allegedly were bitten.

Finke took nothing for granted. He and Monte beat the brush in the zone beyond their warm-stoned circle, stirred up about eleven rattlesnakes they knew about, and drove them, like dogies, into the warm-stone fenced corral. The flanneled stones lay about four yards apart.

Having accomplished that preparatory work, Finke and his new buddy, Monte, repaired to the Airport Bar for six or seven good stiff drinks. After the eighth or ninth, they stole back softly, with forked sticks and gunny sacks, and found thirteen snug rattlers (*crotali confluenti*) blissfully cozy and snoozing on the stones, against the sharp chill of the prairie air. The nearby whirr and clatter of propellers and planes, or the eerie moans and wheezes of air-conditioning devices did not disturb their serpentine dreams. Snakes do not hear. Instead, they feel vibrations. But second- or third-generation rattlers around airports are conditioned to ignore these occupational noises, from the day they emerge from Mamma Rattler's neat eggs, to frisk on Mamma's scaly back.

Finke and his volunteer helper, in spite of the fact that the latter was not accustomed to Finke's hearty kind of drinking, caught all thirteen of the unwary sleeping snakes, and sacked them for tests and observation. For this purpose, they had chosen the rooms just then not being used by Hjalmar and Tom Jackson at the Thunderbird. And at that wonderful hotel and casino, the trade was so brisk and the joy and woe so unrestrained that two strange men, in dusty clothes and snake boots, could pass all the way through the lobbies with sacks of snakes slung over their sturdy shoulders and attract no attention whatsoever, except for the vigilance of the soft-voiced Gene Delmont, who, on being briefed, was tolerance and amiability personified. Gene even volunteered to be driven to the Araquistain Drug and Liquor Store for the necessary chemicals, plastic gloves, magnifying glasses, spectroscopes, etc.

Pilar, between shows, was permitted to watch, which enchanted Finke, and, if the truth must be known, Pilar, herself. She was a married woman, and had a child to think of, but not just then. In Finke's presence she mysteriously slipped into mood and mind for the true role of *flamenca*.

"Bring me an old prospector, no phony, would you mind?" Finke asked of Delmont.

"Sure. We've got three or four downstairs," agreed Gene, and suiting the action to the word, showed up a few moments later with Mercury Matt, originally from Jackson Hole.

After the introduction, and a bottle of Old Ripey had been killed, for sociability's sake, Finke asked how many rattlesnakes should be found in a circle of prairie abutting a Las Vegas airstrip, with a diameter of about one hundred yards.

"Wal," drawled Matt, spitting a stream of tobacco juice over the shoulder of the Three Graces on the mantelpiece. "Figurin' Pi to the fourth of them dulcimer places, 'twould make about 675,000 plus 2700, say . . . 677,700 square feet. . . . Rattlers in these semi-populated parts of Nevadee, they oughtta av'rage 'bout ten to the square mile. That would leave 1,405,500 in all Nevadee. Yes, siree."

Nodding as if pleased with this gem of information, Finke grinned. "Then, if we caught thirteen of these varmints right off the outer airstrip of the Las Vegas port, three-fourths of 'em could have been planted."

"Now who'd want to do a thing like that? Somebody'd be sure to get bit, if they tromped around that vicinity. Some stranger, most likely, who wouldn't know just what to do," Matt protested.

Finke gave the grand old desert rat two more bottles of whiskey, Kentucky River's finest, and had a brilliant thought.

"You know, Monte," Finke said, "Mr. Evans has tried to tell me that rattlesnake meat is better than the finest quail or abalone."

"Now you're dishing abalone," said Monte, and ducked just in time. Delmont's left, however playfully jabbed, was still fast and sharp.

The plan Finke proposed was this: "Let's phone that Wisenheimer, Jordan. He doesn't seem to get around enough, but knowing practically everything he must savvy how to fix snakes for the kitchen and the table."

So Jordan was contacted, where he was reading Kant in the original at the Orman Preserves, oblivious, seemingly, to everything around him. He readily consented, however, to join Finke in Hjalmar's room at the Thunderbird and do the needful to the thirteen succulent *crotali confluenti*, who were rattling at a rate and pitch that would have inspired a composition much livelier and more descriptive than Rimsky's dratted bumblebee. Or was it Schubert?

Far out on the prairie, halfway to the spot on which Clifford Orman had dropped Last Will and Testament No. 1 of even date, midnight not having been struck by quite a margin, Hjalmar and Madeleine were pausing for refreshments, although they had neglected to take along any solid food or liquid drink.

"Big boy," Madeleine was murmuring, "this is it! We qualify for bakers' school, and giving our all, even the ashes, to the land, which certainly did move."

"You felt it move?" asked Hjalmar, delighted.

"I know my Hemingway . . ." laughed Madeleine, and seeing the Norwegian's face seem to fall, made haste to add: "Not personally. Only his books."

Relieved, Hjalmar slapped her below the back of her belt, so briskly that six sets of sleeping magpies and assorted tree toads, respectively, flew in panic and held their peace. To the tenderfoot reader, perhaps we should mention that by night magpies sleep in pairs and tree toads make noises like slow intermittent leaks from a radiator pipe.

So it happened that, not long after, the liberated lovers (the "office" being then under heavy sedatives, though still breathing, while his money gathered interest in a thousand banks) resumed putty-puttying in the golf motor gadget across the desert, the sharp ears of old Alkali Ike, trudging steadily on and inhaling the aroma of Old Crow in his hiking reveries, caught the clatter of Hjalmar's exhaust and hid himself behind a Joshua tree. And, tenderfeet, it takes a very crooked old prospector to hide behind a Joshua, which makes a pretzel seem straight.

Old Ike was the gentle type of overland trailer who did not shoot until he saw a stranger's silhouette, although he did not always wait for the whites of his eyes. He had learned as a lad that redskins on the warpath have a way of keeping their eye whites to mere slits that can scarcely be spotted at tomahawk range.

Back at the Thunderbird, Pilar and Finke, hands frankly entwined, were watching Howard Scott Jordan de-fang thirteen rattlers, remove the poison sacs without spilling a drop, then skin them as neatly as a Huck Finn could have peeled a Mississippi eel in Mark Twain's muddiest days. The pure white meat, exposed and ranged on a Thunderbird platter (genuine Spode) donated by a certain Diggy O'Dew to the Thunderbird chef, because of the excellence of certain funeral baked meats in honor of a departed Daffy Doldstein, an ex-wheel of the third or second magnitude, seemed appetizing, even tempting.

| Finke: | Would you eat that, dark eyes (*ochi chornia*)? |
| Pilar: | I'll eat alive whatever you wish, you tantalizing Harp. Say when. |

The grin ensuing o'er-spread Finke's face from ear to ear, but something in the newly acquired familiarity between the Shamus and the Thrush so distracted Howard Scott Jordan that his sharp knife slipped and impaled itself in one of Hjalmar's picture frames the absent Norsky had brought with him, empty, for a present-day *Maja Desnuda*.

"Oh, bother," Jordan said. "I'll have to sharpen another point."

Meanwhile Finke, his arm around Pilar's waist, sidled over to the fang jar and counted thirteen sets. Of poison sacs, however, there were only twenty-two containing venom. Four poison sacs were flat and dry. He nudged Pilar, she caught on, and made no comment only after Jordan had excused himself, to go back to the Orman Preserves and his book, and Monte had beat it back to the airport to go on shift, and the newly loving pair had had a rapturous twenty-two minutes together— Then Finke started conversation intended to be understood, not merely extra-sensed.

Finke:	Darling, did you notice any discrepancy between the fangs and the sacs?
Pilar:	Two snakes had flipped their doses.
Finke:	That would make one for Orman, and one for Big Zach, *verdad? Querida?*
Pilar:	*Querido, si.* But, man, we've got to lay low. We can *querido* and *querida* to a certain extent. I've got to set a mother's example to my marvelous son.
Finke:	If you ask me, I'd say he'd got the jump on you, already, as far as eggs-sampling goes.

The talk about examples seemed to lead them to the alcove again, and for a while there was no more lucid talk.

Later, as they were kissing sadly, because Pilar had to descend and go on the show floor, to sing and dance as if that hotel had not quaked, like the earth for Hjalmar and his blonde, the dialogue ran as follows:

Finke:	Who do you think drew the biggest snake, Orman or Zach?
Pilar:	I hope you don't think I'm loose like this with every Tom, Dick and Harry.
Finke:	What I'm getting at is, that airport area was stocked with snakes, and the two without fangs could have been tossed on the ankles of their victims by the would be-murderer, if any, who previously could have shuffled the phials in Zach's bathroom cabinet, or Orman's medicine chest, or in and out of Zach's pockets.
Pilar:	Darling. Have brains and use them. I don't mind. I mothered a prodigy, most likely by some punk. What could happen if you had been the Cod?
Finke:	We should not have been together to-night. I'd have beat it, years since, as I invariably do, and neglected to leave an address.

Pilar flung herself around him and kissed him, sobbing the while, tore herself away and ran down the hall to the self-service elevator.

"I wonder," Finke murmured to himself.

16
With an Acknowledgment to Rabelais

WHEN MAITRE SABIN, at the mercy of Shamuses, spied in a kitchen cabinet, one shelf of which was used for remedies, the small bottle of Dimethylcarbamic Ester of 3-Hydroxyphenyl Dimethylamine Bromide, his heart leaped from joy. Any medicine with a name like that, he felt sure, would not only spell nature backwards but set it back at least five million years. He had, as we have remarked, read his Balzac, who had borrowed from Rabelais and lent much to Anatole France. The dark waste of his predicament was ungloomed by a slimmer of glimworm, God's original tail-lighter of the perplexial swamp.

Fascinated, the great chef, lonely, log-cabinized for drugful draining by none other than Ossip Rosencrans, repeated to himself those euphonious syllables, "Dimethylcarbamic ester of 3-hydroxyphenyl dimethylamine bromide."

"*Mais, alors!*" he exclaimed with satisfaction, half aloud.

Just at that moment, the most jittery of his warders and prospective inquisitors was Mo Dalton, whom his brother, Jack, had smote so briskly on the button a mile or more to the west. Mo had been handed by Sabin the list of groceries, drugs and sundries the Maitre had specified, if he were to cook sturgeon in Madeira sauce, and at the same time communicate, nonspecified, his plight to Homer Evans.

"What's so good you haff to laff and chuckle?" Mo asked. It had been his experience that when a victim seemed to show amusement, a spreading streak of rot transversed the state of Denmark.

"I was out—thinking," Sabin said.

"Who? Him?" asked Mo, pointing to Rosencrans. "Impossible."

"When Homer Evans next approaches him, he will catch the scent from afar . . . and I do not refer to the Woodpue your scurvy chief affects," Sabin retorted.

Ever curious, Manny and Jack had sidled within earshot. Manny said a silent prayer. Jack reacted bluffly.

"When that super-sniffer, Evans, again lamps you, male kitchen canary, he'll think you're a scarecrow against Fuller Brushmen," threatened Jack. Ossip then had stepped over, six inches at a time, and broke the news to Jack that Luke was at the foot of Abou-ben-Adhem's roll call and was slated for most of the works.

After Luke had been bastinadoed, flogged with knout, and promised, after dinner that he would suffer the Shanghai snake, the noble sturgeon, in steaks, was ready to be served in sauce de Madeira. Ossip had sent his hungry scouts to case the sage brush surrounding the shack, a precaution which had resulted in the capture of Kid Unamuno, red-handed with his modernized Walkie Talkie. It was then that Sabin took his big chance. All eyes and ears were trained on the defiant Kid, who, in truth, was proving very good in there, under Ossip's duress. Our maitre gastronome took advantage of the pitiful distraction to palm the phial of D.E. of 3-H, D.B., and dust some of the powder into the soup plate destined for Jack Dalton.

The chef figured thus. If a runt like Rosencrans has twenty-five feet, plus or minus, of intestine, middle-sized men may have more, and tall ones, like Jack and Luke, may boast of thirty feet, or even thirty-five. Now, therefore, a modern chemical preparation intended to relieve congestion, the instant it arrived, might take one dinner-course longer to reverse-geyserize tall chaps than short Ossips. Sabin had to guess, but a chef who cannot do that had better take to plumbing. So Sabin decided to give Luke and Jack their dose of D.E. of 3-H, D.B. with the soup course (the soup was clear turtle consommé with manzanilla); to put Manny and Mo's portion in the wine they would sip before the *pièce de résistance*; and to drop an extra spoonful for Ossip in the Madeira sauce which raised the steaked grilled sturgeon to gastronomic heights. Sabin had sniffed the D.E. of 3-H, D.B. powder and believed it to be odorless and tasteless, as near as powders can be.

The bright little boy, Kid Unamuno, thinking he had dotted his last "eye," never knew how lucky he had been to have been apprehended at the moment dinner was being announced. He soon caught on, however. Ossip would not use that blunt conical wooden wedge and mallet to split the Kid like tough cordwood, with the Kid's tenderest orifice as port of entry, until after all had dined. Dining, in the style to which Ossip was accustomed, would consume an hour. There was no chance to bet, but the Kid would have offered 6 to 3 that he would live until morning, and 5 to 4 that he would surpass the Biblical three-score and ten. So he accepted the place which had been set for him, and fell to with the adults, the only difference being that in his dinner was no D.E. of 3-H, D.B., or any physic whatsoever over and above the normal beneficial pungents, aromatics and condiments used by all good master chefs.

For the Kid was fairly confident that Homer Evans was without, and, most likely, was taking adequate steps.

Sabin served, the others ate. First the caviar and vodka, then the turtle consommé with manzanilla. Next, the sturgeon with Madeira was passed. The conversation was mostly confined to "Yeah-yeah" and "Nay, nay" (with more Yeahs than Nays by far), because Ossip, the five-foot Chief of Tribe Rosencrans, loved his food and liked, while eating, to clear his mind of cant, just for a change.

Let us go outside, into the desert night.

There, having ascertained that Ossip had posted no sentries, being so secretive that he had disclosed the hideout to only the selected few already named, Homer broke a stout spine from a cactus, fashioned a small peephole in a chink of plaster at eye level between Tom's cabin logs, and was surveying the banqueting scene. Miriam, when her turn came, did likewise, but with many more misgivings. She had two guns, and two fair hands. She believed she could, in a pinch, shoot two Daltons (Jack and another), also Luke and Ossip before the foe could draw a bead on her. That left a middle-sized Dalton free to drill Homer, who would be too busy to take part in active gunplay, if worse came to worst. The Kid was not heeled, and neither was Sabin. The prospect was not ideal. Then she caught a gleam in Sabin's near eye as the chef was glimpsing his array of sharp knives. The near future stabilized itself.

What was bad about the set-up was that the enemy was inside the fort, and the besiegers on a stretch of wasteland not even maudlin singing cowboys cared to be buried in. And while the brains and bodies of the Rosencrans cohorts could be dispensed with, and society the better for the lack, there was at stake the cuisinary know-how of Sabin and Kid Unamuno's remarkable brain, the only one Miriam had admitted to herself, might, if it reached maturity, approximate that of Homer, forty years the Kid's senior, and later carry on the torch. Miriam was sure that as smart a cookie as the detestable Rosencrans would have portholes camouflagedly corked. Both Miriam and Homer, it must be confessed, were wondering, without having devised a solution, how the criminals could be lured outdoors, when—how feeble are words—it happened.

The moment Sabin had hoped for arrived, according to his brilliant conjectural plan.

We go inside, again. No peephole survey is adequate for this.

The smiling chef and the unsuspecting Kid heard a concerted shout of consternation from five outraged voices, compounded with five separate sounds as if hot applesauce were being whooshed from a sizable paint gun, or five pressure hydrants had burst.

Ossip, being the most nimble, clutching his breeches frantically from behind, ran like a weasel toward the door.

Naturally, Homer got into the act. He opened the door from outside with such abruptness that all hands fell out, so closely behind the other, that Evans had to strike very skillfully, in rapid and masterly succession, each head as it passed. For that purpose, Homer had improvised a weapon designed, not to slay but to stun. It consisted of ten silver dollars secured in his knotted handkerchief. It was not a blunt instrument, within the strict meaning of the term, neither was it rigid like lead pipe wrapped in newspaper. It was right in weight, adequate in length, handy to the hand and hurtful to the head of the recipient.

Down went, flat on their faces, and piled like Jackstraws, in the order hereafter enumerated:

Ossip Rosencrans

Jack Dalton

Manny Dalton

Mo Dalton

and lastly, due to his Ossip-inflicted infirmities,

Luke Sharkey

If ever it could be said of an aggregation, "They were a mess," the Rosencrans contingent lived up, however limply, to that description. And before Homer and Miriam could say "Monsieur Sabin, I presume" to the beaming chef, Kid Unamuno, wearing an improvised gas mask, was binding all five of the bewrayed and bebopped and conskited Shamuses with fishline, for pain when they should recover consciousness, and clothesline for security.

Miriam, tingling with horror she could not help but feel with dread view of ignoble objects, was cataloguing in her tender clear mind the bloodied bastinado, the harsh-pickled strappado, or knout; the tube, wound with wire, of the dread Shanghai snake; the wedge and mallet to split little Unamuno; the nutcrackers to crush the knockers of Jack Dalton, if he had only known; and the sharpened spikes, bodkins, belayers and scrapes meant for mere Manny and Woe Mo. These torture instruments, and the others left unnamed to spare the reader's sensibilities, Ossip had planned to demonstrate, to soften Sabin, and, if need be, to use on the chef, all to find out why the great gastronomer had been lured from Cannes, France, to Las Vegas, Nevada, by the magnate, Clifford Orman, at $2,000 a week.

And still the manly Maitre could not answer that question, and the one who now could, of course, Homer Evans, thought it wiser to hold his peace—until a subsequent chapter.

17

The Plot Thickens

THE THUNDERBIRD, thanks to Gentleman Gene, stands unique in a city that puts all historical and legendary meccas of rum, cant and riot; bones, cards and slots; of ancient writ and actuality, preposterousness and celebrationism far into the shade. There the unusual may happen, and, if it seems about to sprout, the management has accommodations.

We have previously seen that when Finke wanted to take some live rattlesnakes apart, Delmont offered facilities and Howard Scott Jordan, a dude from Boston, came across with the know-how. We have noticed, I hope, that the old superstition about the number 13, one of the soundest, was not even considered when Finke and his mechanic, Monte, brought in the deadly *crotali confluenti* to the total of thirteen. Of course, two of those thirteen scaly denizens of the outskirts already had got their man, although, like the Mounted Police, there was doubt if they could make their charges stick.

Now, when for a happy conference, Homer Evans decided to hold it on the Strip, so as not to rile the Widow O'Brien, the Thunderbird opened its sumptuous Bridle Suite, reserved ordinarily for horse-players whose losses on bang-tails had exceeded the six-figure mark.

The Thunderbird's Bridle Suite was bonny and bullet-proof, with the southern and all other exposures securitied by grim deputies as non-communicative as Buckingham Guards and with costumes hardly more plausible as gents' wearing apparel than those their British cousins in peace-work were provided. Even the drinking glasses were shatterproof. They had to be melted when blasé guests wearied of them, or wished to dispose of them for ceremonial purposes.

On the walls, tastefully arranged, were horse prints, in the form of colored engravings, and a joke chair was stuffed with discarded shoes of the famous Dan Patch and of Croesus.

The rugs were from Brussels, so soft and thick one could faintly smell the ocean. On the ceiling was a fresco of plump girl angels, all flying away at close range; except a couple who, like Lot's wife, had turned back to give the revelers just one last look. Killjoys among ecclesiastics would have it that angels are sexless. They had not convinced the fresquist in question who had beautified the ceilings of the chambers of the Baba Yaga, or Thunderbird.

All in all, elegance conspired with prodigality to make this Bridle Suite unique as well as superb. Homer's conferees were as follows:

Maitre Jean-Pierre Sabin, of Cannes

Finke McGuire, of East Boston, Massachusetts

Miriam Leonard, of Three Buttes, Montana

Miguel Xavier Araquistain, known as "Kid Unamuno"

Tom Jackson, of the New York *Herald Tribune*, who had been torn from the arms of Odette, now awaiting resumption in a neighboring motel.

Sheriff Isaac Patrick Feely, of Clarke County, Las Vegas, known to his intimates as Old I.P.

The reader will doubtless wonder why the company did not include, as captives, Ossip Rosencrans (who now weighed only 90); Luke Sharkey, whose feet and beam-end were a sore sight for private eyes; Jack Dalton, who had, by grace of Evans' timely intrusion, been spared for the nonce the nutcracker suite; and the more likable younger brothers, Manny and Mo, who could feel practically nothing, they were so cruelly scared of what the future might hold.

Homer, to the astonishment, if not disappointment, of Miriam, once he had knocked senseless the above-listed badmen, by means of silver dollars wrapped in his kerchief, had left his foiled villains, bewrayed and battered as they were, to their air-rendering Fate.

When Homer's colleagues were comfortably ensconced and refreshed, with what they needed within reach, the great criminologist, with his unfailing gentility, opened by expressing a regret that the conference's loss, Hjalmar Jansen, seemed to be in the cards, but surely would be a damsel's gain.

"In *espadas, compañero*," agreed the precocious Unamuno, *sotto voce*, so as to seem as respectful of his newly accepted Caudillo as he really was.

Homer then got down to the Order of the Night.

"Our main problem has been and still remains as follows: Why did Clifford Orman hire Maitre Sabin, at $2,000 a week, to abandon Cannes for the nonce and come here to Las Vegas?"

"Homer," asked Miriam, who never had looked so fresh and lovely, or almost never, at least, not in formal costume, "you know the answer, don't you?"

"*Touché*," agreed Evans. "But I am congenitally indolent. In cases of crime, it is usually duck soup to pot the perpetrators, and takes much work to ferret out the proof, to be subsequently used as evidence that will convince a jury of the criminal's peers."

"If enough peers can be corralled in any one jurisdiction," observed Kid Unamuno, who despite his tender years was given full adult status as a conferee. The Kid turned to the sheriff. "How about it, I.P.? Could you dig up twelve peers of Ossip Rosencrans, for instance, or even three as smart as Howard Scott Jordan, the sap?"

"We have our democratic processes," the sheriff said, as if he were ducking behind a wire fence posted for miles with Fifth Amendments.

"Democratic processes apply to solid citizens, not mugs," backcracked the Kid. "However, we're interrupting the Boss Man."

Homer smiled. He was taking a fancy to the Kid, which Miriam noted with resignation and Finke with a grin. Finke liked this Kid, himself, and cared not who knew it. He could use such a minor in Hollywood, if Homer did not appropriate the little bastard.*

---

* In this instance the word "b-st-rd" is used in its literal sense, not as a complimentary or disparaging expletive.

"Here's our point, then we all can make merry," Homer said. "Ossip Rosencrans, when he recovers, will feel he has lost face. More important, he will recall with chagrin that he has failed to get the answer to our $65,000,000,000 question. He will assume, and correctly, that wild horses plus all his organization and their implements would not draw the reply from me. Who is left?"

All hands were raised, so Homer nodded to Kid Unamuno.

"Too easy," the Kid said. "Who but Orman himself? The old roué has guts, most likely. We'll hand him that. He might hold out under the introductory torture devices. But he has a pair of Achilles heels, if I mistake me not." The Kid actually turned to Miriam and apologized for having had to refer to Orman's manly appendages as bluntly as that, in presence of a lady who was champion pistol shot of both Americas.

Miriam spoke up, to show she had taken no offense. "Our colleague, Unamuno, means to convey that Orman might not crack under wonder drugs and other ordeals that left negligible marks— Ossip couldn't take the chance of leaving traces on the body of a snatchee with billions in banks. That might endanger the capitalist system, without which neither Orman nor Ossip could operate. But, as the Kid says, the nutcrackers would break Orman, with little pressure or leverage. How strange it is with us he-men and she-women. Those who excel at high finance take absurd pride in their prowess in the loose-coat skirmish. A baritone wants to brag about selling insurance. Ingres had his violin, and so has Jack Benny. Edison, although no theoretical scientist, had something on the practical side, but he boasted, not of the electric light, which, turned off or disconnected, shields so much that's shameful. He harped on an affliction we call insomnia, which a Rosencrans mere office boy might contract."

Homer beamed this time. "Miss Leonard has spoken profoundly. Ossip, once well and ambulatory, will scheme to snatch someone from his hospital bed."

Our great criminologist turned to the Sheriff. "I shall expect you, I.P., to make that easier than usual in this jurisdiction, where, I am informed, irate hotel keepers do not hesitate to kidnap and hold in captivity guests who owe them paltry sums."

"The newspapers are riding me," objected the Sheriff.

"An honor you do not yet deserve, but may possibly earn before this case is filed away," said Homer dryly.

"I'll tell the boys to lay off hospital-snatchers and put any such under round-the-clock surveillance for the duration," the Sheriff suspiciously agreed. "But I warn you. When a multibillionaire is kidnapped, the news leaks out. There'll be headlines, broadcasts . . . You see if there aren't!"

This time Homer smiled and leaned back to survey the company. "Friends," he re-began. "Out of the mouths of boobs and badgelings drops the wisdom I had expected from others among you." With this he looked hard at Finke, then the Kid.

Their faces both were red. Finke, being the older, inclined to the russet hues, while Kid Unamuno, eleven only, still stuck to vermilion and scarlet.

"O.K.," grunted Finke. "So Ossip will not snatch Orman."

"I'll explain the real play. Ossip has conspired with our murderer . . ."

"Murderer!" exclaimed all present, shocked.

At this Homer looked severe. "It is not worthy of any of you to forget that, in place of Miriam, an honest French dock worker lies mouldering in his grave Killing workers is the worst kind of murder, even if only a manslaughter charge can be made stick."

Finke interrupted to console his sponsor, who, in truth, was hard hit by what had happened only days ago, in Cannes, a mishap which had left a widow and children with no husband and father, but only dreary money to spend.

The sad note that was pianissimo shook our hearers none the less. Miriam's eyes were not dry, those which had seen butchering, torture, mayhem and whatever high criminologists have to witness without a wet wink or a wig flip. Ah, yes. She, herself, had stepped aside, and let a bullet pass, for destination in a fine young Frenchman's pulsating heart. And the heart was still, and the erect was flat, and the living was decaying, and the survivors were sorrowing as they spent.

"There's been murder," assented Finke. "So the guy—or dame—tried for Miriam, and got a working stiff by chance."

The experienced Homer never let his conferences get too far down in dumps. "Ah, the wonderful French . . ."

"Vive la France!" Sabin yelled.

Continued Homer, as earnestly as his inspired namesake of old:

"France had, for the likes of the manslaughterer in question, a resort known as Devil's Island."

"Vive l'Isle!" piped up the Kid.

"And so"—and as Homer spake, how that assembly bloomed and brightened—"our murderer . . ."

"You mean to say one bird did all this stuff you birds have been ravin' about?" demanded the Law, derisively.

"One murderer!" asserted Homer. "And *he* faces, our culprit is of the *bleaker* sex, not merely the heated squat or the Veep of all vapors, the garrot or the guillotine—all relatively merciful and quick. Our bozo will be handed to Belle France."

"Gee, Mr. Evans," murmured the Kid. "You're tops. You really got it. Can I see this joker off?"

The lapse of prodigy was boyish and touching, at the *moment juste*.

"Damn it," muttered Miriam to herself. "I shall end up by liking this pest. Thank God the end is not yet."

"Our murderer has been to France?" inquired Finke, beneficently though craftily, or provocatively. "That narrows us down."

"Nearly everyone has been to France," Homer said. "But, Finke, refrain from being coy with me. You spotted a potential murderer this very P.M. and have kept his name close to your vest."

"In our racket," Finke said, somewhat disconsolately, "potential murderers cannot be erased until after the fact. I figured I'd have to wait till some other gent or lady was bumped off, in some good old democratic way."

Sabin smiled ingratiatingly and took from his vest pocket the little phial of Dimethylcarbamic Ester of 3-Hydroxyphenyl Dimethylamine Bromide and stroked it fondly. "Vive D.E. of 3-H. D.B. I've got several doses left," he added.

The others pretended not to notice, although they reached for their drinks and tested the respective aromas, for non-remembrance's sake.

So then the company begged that Homer continue his discourse.

"What do we do? What does Ossip do?" Homer resumed. "We wait. Ossip waits! Do I make myself clear?"

"No," Miriam said, with asperity.

"If I add a slight clue, to the effect that Ossip surely bastinadoed and strappadoed Luke, not for revenge, which is too stupid even for a Rosencrans, but to give Sharkey a grievance?" was Homer's playful indication. The investigation had reached the relaxed and merry stage, which, for my money, is better than the tense hysterical and confused sort of finish.

Sabin spoke up again, and again the Frenchman roared.

"*Luke* has a grievance! O, O! Bee! Boo! I shall split my chides shlaughing! He has a pair of *pieds* I would not have wished on Goering, and a hindface that will bear the knout's tattoo long after my country finds a way to elect a stable government."

And the chef went into another spasm of Bee, boos, O Dee Mee's, and O My Spudz!

Miriam waxed stern, again. "Homer! Tell us this instant, without more stall and persiflage! We must wait. And Luke has a grievance! Agreed! But what then?"

"Orman's man, Zachary, who has no bullion in banx, *also* has a grievance. Some party not only snaked him, but, I'll wager four to one, the same cagey codger switched Zach's bottle of anti-rattler venom, which Orman always musted to be carried when he crashed snake country. That means that Orman planned purposefully to visit the airport. Zach took down the bottle of Anti-Crotali from the shelf of his jakes. But when the dual snake emergency materialized, Zach was able to produce only some lotion admittedly Half-Safe. Now surely you all grasp the plot."

As Homer sank back into comfort and ease, Miriam's eyes flashed and Finke's forehead creased itself. This time Finke took the rap.

"I am still in the smog," Finke insisted. "Pray, list us again!"

"Ossip figures," responded Homer, "that since he knows, and Orman does not, that Zachary and Luke are old pals, and that both have grievances, by rod, knout, fang and venom sac, paired respectively, during convalescence which already has started, they will flock together and brush off on each other much dirt. If Zach knows Orman's plan—and he does in very broad outline, or I lose my guess, in fact, my voluntarily and freely staked reputation—Luke will have the lowdown out of Zach.

"That, in conclusion for the evening," went on Homer, "will afford Ossip two promising human subjects from which to extract info, without fear of headlines or penalties, in Nevada or even in California. Ossip, once he has what he needs to trade with Orman, will leave no witnesses for the F.B.I. or even the A. and P. He expects to knock off Luke and Zach as soon as they have served their purposes, and knowing Ossip, as many of us do, the executions will not be speedy or quick."

"You tell Ossip that if he knocks off even a Jack rabbit in Nevada, the Law will clamp down, and the offenders, no matter which joint they own stock in, will be prosecuted. You can tell him that, from me!" the Sheriff said, looking and sounding as much like W. S. Hart in the Virginian as two M.P.'s in a quod.

Those present in the Bridle Suite arose, and Tom Jackson was out of the Thunderbird and in that fringed motel before Odette could say "Dimethylcarbamic."

18
Great Circles and Small

FAR OUT ON THE DESERT, we left Alkali Ike hiding behind a Joshua tree, to note the approach, in a golfing motor gadget, of a huge convivial Norwegian painter and a lovely blonde from Paris.

With bottle after bottle of Old Crow to think on, Alkali Ike, having really no malicious intent, decided that he could not let any Squarehead with a Frail outdo a seasoned prospector, motor or no motor, in the race for a Will. So he made a noise like the late Chief Rain-in-the-Face, and got the reckless Jansen intrigued with the prospect for a scrap with an Indian, which, with all his brawling experience, Hjalmar never had had. Old Ike led Jansen and Madeleine to motoring in ever-narrowing circles, then ditched them and plodded on his way.

Our happy pair made the best of the rotating situation, and when Aurora, the rosy-fingered goddess, made outdoor frolic somewhat disconcerting to the participants, inherently modest, Hjalmar accidentally steered his puddle jumper to a main highway, rode it back toward Las Vegas, and called it a night.

"If nobody finds those papers, you're still sitting on your share of Orman's billions," Hjalmar said, and by that time Madeleine would not have carped if he had assured her that the moon, which had served them so kindly, was made of Rochefort.

"You mean Odette will split with me?" the blonde asked.

"Who wouldn't?" was Hjalmar's reply. "There'll be enough for all."

So they stopped in at the Thunderbird to have their belated consultation with Pilar and Kid Unamuno. The latter was still around and about, the free 7 A.M. breakfast not having been served as yet. Pilar was not in evidence, which was surely just as well.

"Kid," said Hjalmar as Madeleine and Kid Unamuno gathered around a table, "Tom Jackson and I need your advice. How can we wangle it so that your mother, Pilar, can pass as chaperone while I paint this bimbo and her brunette chum in both of Goya's manners?"

"Ask me a hard one," retorted the Kid. Then he made a tentative suggestion. "The fall guy, Mr. Orman, is now in hospital. Bribe the doctors and nurses to keep the Old Skate confined with snakebite an extra week or two. By that time, we'll all know if any of this jive should be made permanent."

"Can you loan me a C-note for the purpose?" Hjalmar asked, somewhat hesitantly, never having borrowed money from children, before, in substantial amounts.

The Kid peeled off a hundred-dollar bill from his respectable roll, don't ask how it had been acquired, and they all had breakfast. Tom and Odette soon joined them. Before the sun had got far above the Nevada horizon, Hjalmar was busy, with brushes and palette, the young women in question were posing their stuff . . . and two *Majas Desnudas* were soundly in progress.

Tom, while Hjalmar painted, addressed the companions in this vein:

"The great Audubon, while in New Orleans, met one of the top women of his fruitful life, who chanced to be married to a kind of cold old bore. This woman, Solange, asked Audubon to paint her in the nude, and spare her the rest, so that her beauty, although because of scruples about violating her pledged word at the altar, must be wasted, the painting would remain, and years or decades later, passers-by would say, in some museum, 'There is Solange, the unfulfilled! God save us!'"

Hjalmar, albeit gently, was obliged to induce his eloquent pal to desist, for tears in the eyes of a model cause inspired artists to make opal stabs with brushes paint-laden, which afterwards have to be scraped off with razor blade.

P.S. Alkali Ike found the Will he was after, so that Kid Unamuno, against the day when Orman should be available for fiscal persuasion and the girls twice painted, might be ready to loosen certain strings.

The doctors and nurses at the Allway Hospital on Lewis and Clark streets accepted a fifty, apiece, and agreed to keep Orman in deep freeze, one might say, until the Kid gave the word for his pandora to be unlidded.

Zach was let go, and made a beeline for Luke, as Homer had prophesied.

Howard Scott Jordan finished his re-reading of Kant, had gone through Hegel, Sir James Jeans, Diogenes, Bertrand Russell and was wallowing in Toynbee.

The coyotes had resumed their habitual routines, the buzzards wheeled high, the roulette wheels spun, the dice rattled and rolled.

19

All Ends Against the Middle

IN HIS SUMPTUOUS LIBRARY at Cottonwood Acres, Homer Evans sat in deep contemplation of the case. His hand, as if of its own volition, at the instant when for his Crusoe he needed a girl Friday, touched the button that brought Widow O'Brien. He asked if Miss Leonard would like to join him

"Why don't you marry the girl, you overprivileged old goat?" the widow muttered for him to hear as she sidled out.

Homer glanced at the clock. Much as he adored Miriam, and esteemed her company, whenever anyone uttered the word "marry" our criminologist either looked at the ceiling or the clock, to assure himself it was not as late as we think.

The slight contretemps did not sidetrack the Occident Express of his mind, nor its dissection of the problem. For all that had occurred, since he had received Sabin's cablegram, in that self-same room, not more than three weeks previously, was of a pattern. Otherwise, reader, what in blazes would it be doing in this book?

Miriam entered palpitantly and graciously, *asseyez vooed*, crossed her legs and reposed her arms on a couple of her smoothest muscles then approximately flat, in effect, though in fact, deliciously rounded and silkily swathed.

"May I talk?" Homer asked. "This is not exactly a fishing, but an arranging expedition."

"As the Englishman said, when, in course of a bridge game he arose to twist his trousers," Miriam agreed.

She was happy enough even to be facetious, knowing Homer was at work, that he would succeed, that villains would bite the dust.

"What's that you were thinking?" interrupted Homer, with such excitement and satisfaction as she had seldom seen him display, indoors or out.

Accustomed as she was to having him read her thoughts, she shrugged with self-deprecation. "That villains would bite the dust," she repeated, this time aloud.

"How did you know?" Homer asked in amazement.

"I have my sources," Miriam said, not having the slightest notion at what he was driving.

"Amazing," Homer exclaimed "I thought I had worked it out all by myself, and still you're abreast. So, for Sabin's sake, we've got to bring this affair to its favorable conclusion. I had a word with Ossip Rosencrans today."

"You tried to pump him, I suppose," said Miriam.

"He gave the prelude to the show away," agreed Evans. "Somehow he has learned that Zach has told Luke the germ of Orman's secret. This night the torture will begin."

"Oh, dear," said Miriam, distressed. She was no broken reed, nor even bent, but the thought of such excruciating pain as would be experienced, between swoonings, by two fellow creatures, however repulsive, i.e., Zachary and Luke Sharkey, distressed Miss Montana. She did not like to think about it, even when told by her idol that the worst was about to take place; of the scraped nerves, the fiendish injections, the wedge and mallet behind, the Shanghai snake around. Nutcrackers, fingernail forceps, the blood cure (for which merciful Filipinos had formerly used water), the enema of hot apple-sauce, the odontological drill. The clubs, shillelaghs, knouts, bastinadoes, strappadoes, bamboos, hose and barbed-wire-wound hearse-horse-whips. The leverage and pressure. The pray, the puke, the fits and the loss of gore and glandular secretions.

Again Homer read what Miriam was thinking. He halted his steady pacing, then sighed again and said: "For your sake, darling, I'll try to spare them. Since Luke has had it, I was considering letting them work over Zach, to even items and balance columns, the black and the red, the debit and the credit, between those hearties. However, you outwardly cringe and inwardly shrink. I'll spare you strain, if I can, although Zach does not deserve it."

"You?" she repeated, her eyes wide. "You, Homer, were not thinking of administering, or even, by witnessing, condoning torture!"

"Not until my senses abdicate," he promised. "But, with Hjalmar, Tom, Finke, the Kid and Pilar, I may stoop to snatching the two uncouth buckoos, for a heart to punk-sack talk. I may borrow the instruments, not to intimidate those persons directly, but to remind them of things which may happen, if they refuse to listen to reason, as interpreted by me."

She beamed. "I'll be there, on the scene, and, since it is your favorite, wearing the green. When do we start?"

For answer, Homer took up the phone, contacted Pilar and asked her to send him the Kid, as soon as possible. Imagine our criminologist's gracious chagrin when, on re-cradling Bell's improved instrument, who should step before him, *instanter*, in his private and personal library he guarded so closely and well, but Kid Unamuno, with that boyish glint of mischief in his eye.

"Excuse me, Chief. I figured you'd need me today, between breakfast and lunch, and that our job might last into the night. So I told Granny in the kitchen, before I hid myself in here (natch, she knows nothing of that) to prepare box or basket lunches for seven derechos and two wrongos. Right?"

Homer was agog, not with discomfiture but admiration.

"Kid," he said, "I shall not try to influence you. I only say this. Whenever you decide to go straight, within reason, which means keeping nothing from me . . ."

"Now have a heart, Mr. Evans. Who could keep anything from you?" countered the Kid.

"You are trying," Homer said. "You have not confided in me about the shakedowns you plan to execute against Orman, Madeleine and Odette, involving those two Wills."

"Try to keep an open mind," the Kid pleaded. "Gee, what am I saying? You're the only gent alive to whom I don't have to say a thing like that. Ah, well. I'll let them all down easy, if you think best. On one condition."

"That I retain you as second assistant, in future investigations?" Evans suggested.

"Sure. She saw you first," he said, scowling at Miriam. "We'll grant her a token seniority. Cripes, how I hate that word!"

"You're on—as second V.P. in charge of monkey business," Homer agreed, and all three, if the truth be known, were happy as larks, though Miriam pretended to hold out and resent the fresh third wheel of the bike, which made it a trike, two large ones behind, a little one forward.

"You want me to assemble Hjalmar, Tom Jackson, Finke and Pilar," the Kid suggested.

"You overheard," Evans said. "So get going.'

"Where shall we find the two mugs to be snatched, and how are they watched and guarded? Surely Ossip is taking no chances that he knows about," asked Miriam.

"Zach and Luke are being bunkees in the chauffeurial suite above Orman's garage at the Preserves. Ossip stays in the main house, attended by the servants."

"You mean, with Orman's knowledge and consent?"

"Undoubtedly, although the old fox pretends he's being hoodwinked," Homer said. "Orman, in this affair, involving for him one of the most colossal financial operations and plotted monsoons ever dreamt of in any Midas's philosophy, plays all ends against the middle. He thinks he can use Ossip. He hopes he can use me. He tried his best, as you remember, to retain me, and only on the pretext that Sabin was my client, and that interests might conflict was I able, plausibly, to refuse him."

"Can you tell me, as yet, of Orman's phenomenal plan?" Miriam asked, hopefully.

"Only this. He expects to blackmail, legally, the cream of the foremost illegal super-crooks and ruthless roys in existence," Homer said.

"You mean the top gangsters, here? The wheels of the Syndicate, of Murder, Inc., the Hudson Dusters, the Milwaukee Maulers,

the Capone Alumni, the Saints Chavez, the Brooklyn Backbreakers—characters like those? *En masse?*"

"Precisely," answered Evans. "Can you help but admire Orman's
pluck? Freud calls it the Messianic obsession, or complex. We all
have it, in more wholesome moderation."

"You rate it," insisted Miriam.

"You once asked me a question I evaded," Homer said, with a
smile. "Can the Kid shoot?"

"Drat him! If he can, I'll provoke him and drill him. You see if
I don't," said Miriam, crimson now, all over, and tapping the car-
pet with a tantrum-tipping toe.

"I took him out on the range, day before yesterday," Homer
confessed.

"And?" she asked.

"Fifty times in fifty, he shot the love me love me nots from
black-eyed susans at one hundred feet, and, I have to tell you, darling, in the next test at one hundred yards, I gave up."

And, to salve her bruised vanity, he clasped Miriam in his arms.
"You have the advantage, sweetheart," he murmured. "He has to
shoot from a lower level or stance."

"Unless he can hop and not miss," she said, grinding her pretty
teeth. "So. I'm *not* the greatest."

"You always have the element of surprise in your favor," Homer
reminded her. "No one expects deadly marksmanship from a rav-
ing young beauty, well-dressed and mannered, like you."

"I suppose the cockeyed world expects it from a brat who looks as
if he's playing hooky from the sixth grade, at the highest!" she snapped,
and bit her nimble tongue, in that instance not nimble enough.

"The snatch is going to be a test between Ossip's forces and
ours," Homer said, knowing it was high time to change the subject. "I have arranged for the sheriff to remove all deputies from
within the circle of five miles centering at the Orman garage where
Luke is bedded and Zach boarded as of now."

"What about the snatch car? Our limousine's not missile
proofed and the sedan's not large enough," Miriam said, having
recovered her professional manner, and some of her composure.

"Nothing's proof against the cosmic rays, the germ sprays which can pass between the whirling molecules of atoms. Let's face it. Physics has, to the *cognescenti*, canceled itself out. Today, we combat, as did the cavemen and knights, with what we have ourselves, not properties," Homer explained

"Now you're talking with gas," she acknowledged, however backhandedly.

Homer touched his forehead. "From where come the deadliest waves? From the sun, our source of warmth? From outer space? Or was the beginning the Word, and Man, resembling his Maker, can start what no other bowers may finish, or conclude whatever Outsiders may start?"

"You give me gooseflesh when you talk like that," was Miriam's spontaneous tribute.

20
Elephants on Parade

WHILE KID UNAMUNO was rounding up Hjalmar, Tom, Finke and Pilar, Miriam left Homer in profound meditation while she repaired to her chamber to decide what she should wear for the key kidnapping (that of Luke and Zach) and do the many things fair (or unfair) women affect in order to prepare themselves for scrutinization on special occasions. The Widow O'Brien, in a huff because she did not know exactly what was coming off, had been more and more dismayed because the grandson seemed to be bettering himself. That is, he was winning the esteem, or tolerance, of Homer Evans, whom in her gnarled and tortuous heart of hearts, Odilla adored. What was good for that brat was poison to his Granny-not-by-blood. Had that child's blood been hers, she would have drained it and pan fried it in deep fat long since.

Picture the household and personnel of Cottonwood Acres, usually so strikingly efficient, diffused with talent and genius, verdant, disciplined and combinative of the fruits of all the ages—the muck from which reptiles had been retained; the fluid which had left the land some fishes; the ice which had shaved much of it flat for cultivation; the stone which had brought the romantic incredible mineral industry and helped enable Man to shoulder up no end of Bleak Hills his famous Cross of Gold, and receive an eleventh-hour reprieve—though chummy Thieves served time to left and right. The wild Indians, the Mormon pioneers, the rakes and rustlers, the tinhorns and Shanes had had their fill of Nevada and the State had made them blissfully bunco-unconscious. As a result many angels, after the great Fallen Chief, known as Lucifer, had been sorely tempted by the gullibility of those green souls newly departed from Nevada skyward.

Back to the Cottonwood Acres. Evans was deep in thought, therefore somewhat off his conque. Miriam was primping, and with what she had to pramp and all she had to prump with—her gat out of reach—she was not at her wariest and deadliest. The widow, on her way downtown for supplies, was chewing on the steering wheel, so raffled and ruffled was she by events which seemed to be piling like cumulus clouds to storm from her horizon. The cowboys were immersed in their music. Cows browsed, steers stomped, bulls rutted, in or out of season, for Nevada is against periodical deviations to confuse fall guys in spring, spring hoods in summer, or sweat indoors while outdoors the Jack frosted whiskers and made it hard, indoors or out, for the smooth ones to start their motor shavers. The gent who wrote that spring must be a dreary weather, were there nothing else but, would not dare intrude within the limits of Las Vegas, where the air-conditioning drafts and shills in top hotels inspired research scientists to find the cure for pneumonia which has kept thousands of prime suckers (born every minute, reborn, hoisted and saved every night) in Trim, with a capital "T."

When all hands around a key estate were ripe for bucking, then it was that Ossip Rosencrans, the most private of all eyes so highly organized, did his worst, which, in so many disreputable cases, had been dire enough.

Now Ossip had figured that Homer might try to pluck from their shelter both Luke Sharkey and Zach. Therefore, before the Kid had brought his hearty reinforcements, and his mother from her champion chaperonage of high art and low jinks, and thus had left Madeleine and Odette flat, and while Homer's chess-maneuvered conquest moved ahead, with Miriam making *maguillage* with the prize *margoulette*, Ossip crept in.

The tableau in Miriam's boudoir and the ensuing sequence follows:

Ossip, mounted, had passed to the center of the Acres on horseback. While high on horse, his lack of space between pratt and prairie was less reprehensible. He had unslung his guitar, which he played very well, and the genuine cowboys, in their jam, had not noticed that an extra penny ante had dropped into the pot. So Ossip was able to steal houseward, climb a vine stalk like a snail, slit a screen with a special Gillette made noiseless for nefarious purposes, squirm on his belly behind Miriam, rise to his full five feet in height and mug her with a chloroformed handkerchief. It was as simple as that.

Knowing it would not be possible to smuggle her out through exposed Cottonwood Acres in broad daylight, Ossip bethought himself of a suitable hiding place and chose the swimming pool, just aft of the suite and balcony she occupied. The clever villain, relishing his chance to match wits with Homer Evans, decided that, if he insensibilized Miriam with a suitable injection, as he promptly did, stripped her, alas, alas, and stuffed her without identifying garments under the grill of the swimming pool drain (the pool being dry) that he could bide his time till darkness, then let the pool fill slowly and, with a high-powered grenade, a brace of which he had stolen from the nearby U.S. testing base, could at any moment later bring the water to a boil in a matter of a few hundred thousandths of a second.

The most famous Madam of disorderly houses in the Casbah of Cairo had demonstrated all too successfully that young women, bare and sufficiently boiled, suffer such bloat and distortion that no Court in any land would accept their remains as an identifiable *corpus delicti*. For best results, however, girls had to be boiled alive. So Ossip drugged Miriam in a way which would leave her breathing for the ultimate boiling, and stole off the estate, guitared and remounted.

Thus, when Homer, reunited in fellowship with Hjalmar, Pilar, Tom Jackson, the Kid and Finke, tapped on Miriam's door, to say they all were ready for the snatch, not even echo answered. Homer turned the knob. The door was not locked. He entered.

So deft had Ossip proved with syringe that the lingering odor of chloroform, almost indistinguishable because of the Weil and Schiaparelli Shocking, the Ardent Illusion, Rubenstein's Pond Lily Salve from lilies, San Cyrian bath saltz, Monteuil Balm heraus

Giliad, the Spanish night betterfly, and Love's End Sashay, might have gone undetected. A nose less nice than Homer's might have snuffed only the faint whiffs.

Homer bit his lip and slapped his lap.

"Presnatching has prevailed," he said, and his eyes were truly hard and menacing. Turning to Finke, he added: "Finke, the stakes are now beyond all limit. I'll leave to you the kidnapping of Luke and Zach, with the helpers I've gathered. I, myself, will retrieve Miriam, or have the blood of every man, woman or child who e'er has darkened the doorway of Runt Rosencrans."

It was Hjalmar who, realizing to what extent Homer had been stirred and strained, placed a heavy hand upon his shoulder.

"You're upset, Chief. She wouldn't like it, in case she really were dead, to look down and see you like this. Bear up, and no more talking of butchering babes, sucklings or preserving sad tomatoes. We must all fight men, like men."

For the great hulking roaring drinking Norwegian that was a long speech, and larded with more morality than usually he let loose in year score, but it had its effect. Homer pulled himself together, then looked at the Kid.

"Kid," Homer said, "our forces now must perforce be divided. Certain ones must storm Orman's garage and bring back bums (to the number of two) we'll symbolize as bacon. I, in my moment of abject negligence, must have one Friday at my side, a brain to supplement mine, which by my loss of love has been gimped like a groaning Grenadier en route from Russia where Napoleon, napping, had been nipped by pre-Reds. Miriam, in death, will always be Miriam. Should she lead there to that far land, from which no wanderer returneth, I would be Masoch, minus, should I tarry, myself, at the crossing or bar. We need not ask who has her in his power, if he be not Almighty God!"

"Natch! Ossip!" agreed the Kid. "And if you, Mr. Evans, are beating about the bushes to get me to volunteer to stick with you, and resign, in connection with a pair of false alarms Foolish Phil could take with one hand tied behind his back, let's go. Was I or was I not appointed second Vice President, this very day?"

"Thanks, Kid," Homer said, simply, and so deeply moved were all in earshot that eyes were blurred and faces averted. So alone in disgrace and isolation, after whispered word to Finke, Homer and his remarkable young helper proceeded from that scented room.

"O.K. You guys!" snapped Finke, including Pilar in the terse salutation and command. "To the garage."

When Finke started the limousine, however, again certain parties, friends and spies, were astonished to see him turn the crested snout, not in the direction of the Orman Preserves, adjacent, but on the over-prairie roadless shortcut to town.

"May one ask where ones are going?" inquired Tom Jackson, to be doubly sure, on that day of all errors compounded, another mistake was not being made. For Tom well knew Finke's heart was sorely wrung for Homer, for Miriam, and for chagrin that he, as Junior Dick, had not foreseen such an obvious eventuality.

Finke did not bother to answer. Tom subsided. They bumped, small animals and large insects scattered for their lives, vegetation bent, and the desert dust arose. Once they hit pavements, on the outskirts of Las Vegas, those present began to believe, with real astonishment, and no company ever rode by day or night so hard to astonish as they, that they were headed for the zoo.

Once they had crashed the gates of that aromatic institution, Finke braked, broke and conferred with the Superintendent. Returning to the limousine and its bewildered occupants, he frowned and addressed them.

"Any of you know about elephants?" he barked.

No one said anything back, until at last Hjalmar swayed and growled: "Bring 'em on."

Pilar then spoke up. "I've a way with the wild. I'll take a crack at any of the males."

The Superintendent then volunteered, because Evans was in need, to send his best Swahilis (the beasts were African, not Asiatic) as elephant relations counselors and to join the expedition, himself, as interpreter.

Around the zoo bar, Finke took precious time out to explain.

"Those silly cookies on the Preserves, in the garage, will figure on a frontal attack, at ground level. So we crash the place with elephants, crash the second story, while our four-footed friends kick the foundations from under. Luke and Zach are not armed. I happen to know that Ossip is terrified of elephants and mice, and has no artillery that would even make these big fellows blink or switch a tail tassel.

"It might be easy to snatch these characters without property damage, but I want the back buildings demolished for pure sound effects. That will deter our victims from holding anything out, when they sing, each being cradled and rock-a-bye-byed in an elephant's trunk."

Pilar slapped Hjalmar, who responded in kind, till the zoo welkin fairly rang with hearty laughter and jovial josh.

"This is for the book," Pilar said. "No sheriffs for five miles around. Shanghai snakes to burn, gouges galore, and God knows all of us girls have heard so much about this flagellation jive that I, for one, am naturally curious, and want to size it up not in the breech but by the observance, first crack out of the box, at least."

"Sorry. Homer said, 'No rough stuff.' He thinks it's beneath us," Finke cautioned.

Hjalmar grinned so broadly that all four elephants the Swahilis were leading out began to trumpet and spout. "When we bust up those buildings, if a little foreign matter falls on finks (no offense), we'll be forgiven, I take it," the Norwegian said.

"So long as there's no contributory negligence. It must happen in the heat of action," Tom explained.

"In heat. So all right then," Hjalmar agreed and smacked Pilar where the bang was borderlined.

It was an odd cavalcade that set out from the Las Vegas zoo, and anywhere else would have caused comment, if not actual interference. The limousine, containing Finke and Pilar in front, and Hjalmar, with Tom Jackson and the Super in the rear seat, headed the purposeful procession. Then came Jamboree, the largest he-elephant, with the No. 1 Swahili, 'Mbergi Con Tootki, up. Carna, the largest female, followed, trunk to tail entwined. The second

Swahili, Hot Lips Ramar, rode the caparisoned Bello, a male who had it over Jamboree in weight but lacked six inches of the reach of his Leader. Turnzee Paige, another Shee, brought up a frisky rear.

As they were passing the Western Union office, where certain anxious transients of Las Vegas await, all too often vainly, for tickettang to waft them lowing home, Finke drew up to the curb. The elephants, to show they were not dumb, gave up the romp of rampaging and halted docilely in line, and as the humans pursued their mixed affairs, the beasts tried to rid their hides of the hordes of flies which had swarmed round about.

Finke, entering the Western Union office, after checking his gat in shoulder holster, aware that those near by were desperate, demanded to see the manager, who finally was produced, under much duress, by Hjalmar, from the Golden Nugget roulette two doors west.

"Have you seen any shrimp, five feet in height, with a beak like a macaw propositioning civilly any broke watchers and waiters among your customers before the counter lately?" Finke asked. For this line of inquiry he had been coached by Homer, just after Miriam had been missed.

"I see no evil and hear less than half," the manager replied.

Finke beckoned Hjalmar. "This party doesn't care to talk, and we're in a hurry," Finke said.

The Norwegian reached forward, collared the manager by his fourinhand, lifted him at arm's length and flung him at Carna, who caught him in her trunk.

"Atta girl," roared Hjalmar.

The manager was squealing so fast that no stenographer could have taken it down. It seems that Ossip Rosencrans had bribed a female derelict, who had seen better days and earned her keep with a girl's original investment while awaiting remittance from her native town, to depart with him, on unannounced assignation, and that said girl had not been seen anywhere downstairs since her exit with the Dick.

That intelligence unnerved even Finke, who said grimly to his band: "We've no time to lose."

With that the Swahili No. 1 salaamed and suggested that the elephants go first, for it is known only to Kipling and a few top elephant fanciers that these cumbersome crafty and lovable great beasts can outrun the fastest express train and, in sooth, pace a speeding limousine with a racing engine equipped for fastest beach or track. So the elephants, led by Jamboree with 'Mbergi up, streaked across the prairie, not swerving even for trees in their way, and Finke, fine driver that he was, lost ground in following. But the intelligent head Swahili had overheard much of what was to be done, so when they reached the Orman Preserves, the mammoth mates, Jamboree and Carna, Bello and Turnzee Paige, crashed the barbed wire, and butted abreast through the Orman main garage, with such effect that the first floor was demolished and the upstairs apartments were left with nothing but air, and that in swift motion, beneath them. Naturally, by force of gravity, as Finke, Hjalmar, Pilar and Tom motor-cavalryed to the fighting front, the problem was only to fish the stunned Luke and Zach from the tons of debris, an engineering task or cleanup operation.

The elephants, guided by their Swahilis, continued to the main house where Ossip Rosencrans was hiding in an Ali Baba vase.

21

A Miss Is Better Than a Mile

SINCE THE NIGHT of the Purgatorial Triumph in the prairie hideout shack now useless to the Rosencrans outfit, Sabin, the great guest gastronomer, and Howard Scott Jordan, the research chemist temporarily without lab or labor, had spent much time in each other's company, a relationship which Homer had engineered originally and had cemented covertly because, of all the avid characters then loose in Las Vegas, the pair above-featured loved best the gaming tables, wheels and boards.

The pink-fingered Aurora surprised them oft in the teeming casinos of the Strip, the Desert Inn, the Sands, the Sahara, the Flamingo, and the Thunderbird, to mention some. Now and then either one or both of the sympathetic plungers went way downtown, to the Nugget, the Rainbow, the Ramp or the secret rooms above the Western Union office where the stiffest of all games flourished while waiters for dough from home collapsed, wailed and jibbered downstairs.

Now Sabin had led a life of toil and study, so honest that it hurt, so fruitful that he had been many times champion of testers and tasters of La Belle France, for wines, distillations and samples of edibles, raw and prepared, known or experimental. We know also that young Jordan, pushed by parents for profit in his tenderest years, warped by war somewhat later, and then humiliated by subservience to lesser brains and scorned by Orman to the point his manhood was in question, had not gambled to excess until that amazing fortnight preceding the climax of our story.

The gastronome and the miracle mind, in bodies with which we have become familiar, developed new qualities hourly as the mania for risking valuables bypass, spin or flip, or even yank of One-Arm Tempter, took pathological possession of them, or so it seemed.

Like all friends and acquaintances who follow dual paths to reason's ruin known as Chance, Sabin and Jordan had devised rival systems. They never played directly against each other, but each morning, after breakfast, nobly shelled out, secretly and for no other ears, their debit or their credit balance. Since Sabin had only $2,000 a week, Jordan, in a seemingly sportsmanlike way, sheared his weekly stake to Two Grand, also, and no more.

Neither had broken any of the several waiting banks. Neither had gone broke, entirely.

On the morning Miriam was found missing from her boudoir in Cottonwood Acres, Sabin was sound asleep in his quarters on the self-same dude ranch and Homer, grief-stricken and ashamed as he was, gave orders that his guest should not be awakened.

Jordan, at nearby Orman Preserves, was getting in eight of the sweet and dreamy, with such subconscious fervor that only four huge elephants wrecking the string of garages beneath his broad bedroom windows aroused him to the point where he found it impractical to stay asleep. Instead, he sallied forth, privily, with the idea of getting away from the rough-house of the oil magnate's palatial residence to seek comfort in Homer Evans' so richly stocked library, and read against the hour when, after early cocktails, he could resume his systematic play and prove that no super-cook had the best of him in bouts against fiscality.

So, while Homer was concentrating on his personal problem, which had taken precedence over all facets of The Case, who should pop in but Howard Scott Jordan? Kid Unamuno, who had been conducting a search for Miriam, alive or dead, saw Jordan approaching and for an instant allowed his fertile young mind to stray from its vital assignment. A jealous thought precipitated the awful crystal clarity of the Kid's intelligence. Was it possible that, distrusting his (the Kid's) ability to find the lost girl from Montana, Mr. Evans had called in Jordan as consultant?

That must not be. The Kid had worked with Jordan, and knew how far to trust him, which, in comparison with the distance not to trust the New England prodigy and psycho-at-large, seemed to Kid Unamuno like the ratio between the diameter of a gnit on a gnat's gnut and the thickness of the immense galaxy of Betelgeuse.

On the other hand, the Kid dared not risk losing face with Evans, who had just begun to appreciate his abilities, by intruding when the Master was called on, no matter who had planned or failed to anticipate the occurrence. So the Kid steeled himself to continue his task, the finding of Miss Leonard. Homer would send for him if and when he wished to give further instructions. Of that the Kid was sure.

On his own, he had calculated that Ossip, having caught his fairest hostage unaware, had not been able to remove her from the immediate premises. On his own, the Kid had directed Parentheses Pete and three of his cowboy coworkers, all half-Comanches, to verify the trail followed by Ossip entering alone the dude ranch acres, and the outward-bound journey, also alone, back toward the Orman Preserves. So, while Homer thought and thought, suffering keener agonies than Jacob wrestling with an angel, pushing his prodigious powers to the ultimate his will could drive them, the Kid had divided the area in and around Miriam's now empty (of femininity's fragrant tenancy) boudoir into squares and cubes limited by his eleven-year-old arm spread and physical reach.

Each cube the Kid had searched in turn, from No. 1, in front of the boudoir make-up mirror itself, progressively outward, and clockwise. From cellar to attic loft the O'Brien ranch homestead measured about 72 feet. Indoors, therefore, figuring the outer dimensions as approximately 120 feet by 96, 72 feet in height, were 829,440 cubic feet. Dividing these by 216, the number of cubic feet in a 6 foot by 6 foot by 6 foot cube, the Kid would have to examine 3,840 cubes his own stature span high, deep and wide. When he spied Jordan approaching, the Kid was on his 184th, with 3,656 to go. Application, not deviation, was indicated. The Kid doggedly worked on, with skill, cunning and dispatch.

Meanwhile, Jordan was received by Evans in the library. Homer gave no clue to what had happened. Jordan showed no awareness of any awful or unusual eventuality. He had wished, or hoped, to talk of Sir James Jeans with Homer, but at a glance the New Englander grasped that the day had, somehow, been ill chosen. So, as best he could dissemble, Jordan asked permission to borrow a book, and when Homer had been snapped from his concentration so utterly unguarded that he had been able only to stammer, "What book?" he realized, though dimly, he had caught his caller equally off guard.

"Durant's *The Story of Philosophy*," Jordan out-blurted.

The reply from Homer was a fishy vacant stare, then he relaxed and smiled, a triumph of manners over suffering.

"You're joking," Evans said.

Again Jordan was at loss for a comeback. "I know it's superficial," he improvised. "I had a whimsical impulse to find out for myself how a book on philosophy can become a best seller."

"It isn't here," Homer said, thumbing toward the bookshelves. "But no doubt you'll find something. You'll excuse me if I continue with my own trivial speculations while you indulge your foibles or adventures of the mind. How is your system working, with roulette, may I ask?"

"Nothing definite yet," Jordan said. "It needs tightening in places. There are factors not yet integrated. It is fascinating, though."

"I understand from Sabin that you and he are horse and horse, as the expression goes," said Homer.

Jordan flushed with chagrin, and even let escape a symptom of ill temper. "Fool's luck," he muttered, then tried to pass off the slip with a nervous laugh. Homer, triumphant inwardly, concealed his satisfaction.

"Gambling makes strange bed fellows," he observed, and went to the balcony to start thinking again.

Kid Unamuno, working feverishly but efficiently, was examining imaginary cube No. 1054. This involved the removal of the grilled drain cover of the empty swimming pool adjacent to and below Miriam's former balcony. As he caught himself ruing that involuntary silent expression, her *former* balcony, as if the search already had laid bare the worst, he was so unnerved that he had to straighten his aching little back and brush sweat from his bulging Basque brow.

From his window, Homer saw the action and called out: "Please report aloft and center. I'd like to compare notes."

So the Kid left the grilled cover off the pool drain and made haste to obey, intending to return and, meanwhile, to let the cover, "X," mark the progress of his thus-far unfruitful investigation.

A desert zephyr, somehow curling downward into the drain, fanned Miriam's pale forehead and helped revive her. For Ossip, in compounding the shot he had needled into her vein, had failed to take into account her vibrant intensity and boundless resistance. He had given what he thought was a near-lethal but just un-fatal measure of that insidious wonder drug. Aware that he should have had more data, on the relationship of a given physique to the dosage administered, the weaselish proprietor of the world's crookedest agency had had to take a calculated chance.

The result, just at that phase of the affair, was that Miriam, through the open drain hole caught a glimpse of Wilde's poignant patch that prisoners call the sky, shook her aching head to clear it, wormed her way up and out to the swimming pool floor, and, as quickly as her cramped limbs and clouded wits would take her, got out of sight in a rhododendron patch.

She hoped and prayed no one had seen her escape. But Howard Scott Jordan, in trying to maneuver himself into a position where he could eavesdrop on Evans and the Kid whom Jordan so detested and feared, chanced to pass a library window commanding the pool just at the instant when Miriam, bare as a born babe, had scurried lamely for refuge in the shrubs.

Conversely, Miriam's sharp eyes, perfected by the years she had spent with her late father, on the range in northeastern Montana, caught the scholarly silhouette of the New Englander at the above-mentioned window and realized she had fewer secrets from that cold cod than devoutedly she might have wished.

Homer and the Kid, had they been overheard by Jordan, might not have given much away, for they took advantage of the opportunity, tense as the situation was, to practice their Code.

The Kid:	'lo, Cosmo. Hast cheeped for Veep?
Homer:	Alas I know not *was sol es bedeuten, dass ich solch ein Dummkopf bin.*
The Kid:	Top tomato depravity is dummheit's uncavity, old man. Upen attem! Pas?
Homer:	You've caught only gross who got los?
The Kid:	Only three months along, more or less. Squattez in tension, nix compression. My wurst to peepers creepers. Slang or slong.
Homer:	Double eero great expectations.
The Kid:	(as he returns to his search) MacDon's olde farm! If I bitch, you bugle.

Decodation:

The Kid:	Good morning, Mr. Evans. Did you summon your assistant?
Evans:	I cannot account for my lack of pertinent ideas or suggestions.
The Kid:	To lose one's best beloved tends to confuse one, old man. But courage!
Evans:	Your big ones so far all have got away, or no progress as yet?
The Kid:	I'm one third through, only. Sit tight, not cramped. My lowest regards to your caller, Mr. Howard Scott Jordan. Au revoir.
Evans:	Pip, pip.
The Kid:	E.I.E.I.O. or Cheerio. If I seem to be pulling a Snodgrass, set me right (or doing something inadvertent or erroneous).

Miriam, on her mettle and otherwise uncovered and undone, wove herself rapidly a makeshift garment of stalks and leaves, slipped cunningly as a coyote into the main house again, and regained her boudoir without being detected, not even by Jordan, who was nonplussed but thought it best to sit tight. Clothed once more, Miriam recovered her Colt .45, approached Jordan from behind as he sat reading in a nook of the library away from Homer's sight, stunned him with just the right force and eased him, bodily, into her clothes closet No. 1.

She could not be sure that Homer had noticed nothing; neither could she believe that had he seen her alive and tolerably well, even considering his phenomenal control and self-mastery, he could have remained undemonstrative, no matter how it might have helped or hurt a given case. So she had to take a chance that he had not detected her re-availability and seemingly anti-Jordan pursuits. Once she had Jordan in her fragrant clothes closet, she bound and gagged him so soundly that Houdini, with all the spirit world to aid him, could not have torn free or waxed vocal within the poetic life duration of the Old One-Hoss Shay.

Having accomplished this, she stole out of the house, by an entrance opposite the swimming pool and the busy Kid Unamuno, and crawled on her elbows through brush, sage and grasses, risking serpents and scratches, until it was prudent for her to proceed on hands and knees, and later, erect. Her destination was the Orman Preserves, and her object, one Ossip Rosencrans. Little did she surmise what had happened to him.

Back at his Cube No. 1054, Kid Unamuno had found much to disconcert, then intrigue, then thrill him. Thorough as he was he did not content himself merely with glancing down into the now empty drain. He hopped in and descended. What he sniffed was a weird combination of aromas.

He got out of that Hole and across and up to Homer in less time than it takes to type it.

"She's been there!" he announced exultantly.

"Where?"

"Down the swimming pool drain."

Evans:	Now gone?
The Kid:	Them pigeons on the grass. (Alas, alas.)

Homer hurried with the Kid to the spot in Cube No. 1054. The younger of the tense investigators could hardly breathe, so pleased he was to have unearthed, or at least, undrained, a clue.

"You see, sir," the Kid explained apologetically, "I'd just removed the grill cover and was about to case the hole when you called me in for consultation. As soon as I got back, I descended and smelled where she had been."

"You can't be sure, then, if she was or was not down there when you lifted off the cover?" asked Homer.

The Kid was so miserable from chagrin that tears stung his eyes.

"You couldn't help it. I called you. You responded," Homer said. As he spoke both he and the Kid were circling rapidly, and at the same instant spotted the telltale signs in the rhododendron patch.

"She's on her own," said Evans, and shrugging, started whistling so blithely and hieing back to the house so debonairly that Kid Unamuno could have fallen flat and banged his forehead in sheer admiration. He was learning, that young lad. He was catching on that, in high detective circles, the very loftiest mutual trust and confidence are something that have to be experienced to be believed or evaluated. "Damn it to hell," he grunted to himself, "if I start drooling about honesty as policy, I swear I'll give myself up." Still, something in his concepts was inclining toward salutary revision, not toward the right, but favoring expediency and selective co-operation. He still felt sure that of the billion and one half inhabitants of the earth, more or less, not seven were to be trusted. Of the six, he had met four or five that same A.M.

22
Anything Can, and Does, Happen

THE KID WAS PERMITTED to stick quite close to Homer through that wonderful day, and the more he saw of Evans' methods, the more thoroughly glad was the boy, for the first time, unreservedly, that he had been born as he had and still was much alive. For him, there really was a place. He felt it, now. And Homer, observing, let his own fine mind go back to certain contacts of his childhood which had helped him find himself, develop and gain the confidence which had placed him at the head of every class and the top of the highest of professions, the protection of the weak from the strong.

We must give credit to the Kid that, once he got the main idea, he offered no gush or asked no questions. Homer spent some hours closeted with the best available electricians who busied themselves around Cottonwood Acres. The great criminologist, by phone to Finke, Pilar and the great roisterers who had captured Luke and Zach and were holding them for questioning by Homer, left instructions that Ossip was to be unhampered in movements, whatever they turned out to be. This did not cause Kid Unamuno to bat an eyelash.

Around twilight, when Homer visited in turn all the top wheels of the Syndicate, the Mafia, the Dusters, Maulers, Backbreakers and De Brinx, inviting them to a mass get-together and smoker at the widow's Dude Ranch that evening, the Kid strung along, without comment aloud.

Miriam seemed to be missing. Jordan had vanished from sight. Orman was notified that he might go home from hospital, via the Clark end of Lewis Street, at 9 P.M. *environs*.

Hjalmar, Madeleine, Finke, Pilar, Tom Jackson and Odette, Alkali Ike, and others of our acquaintance, gamed and guzzled to their hearts' content, and were no worse for wear as the time for the smoker drew nearer.

Chef Sabin stuck by the head roulette table of the Thunderbird, consulting his notebook for briefing on his own system, and although chips amounting to $56,000 had passed through his hands, at cocktail time he was exactly even.

The others, the denizens and guests in Las Vegas, carried on, to keep the modern Babylon and Nineveh, Tyre and Sidon, the wild dream of all ages, a kind of sur-reality our epoch can salute and nourish, a peak of pleasure second to none which ever has erupted since the Coming of Man.

When Miriam caught sight of Ossip, as he came out of hiding on the Orman Preserves, she watched him from then on, and followed where he led.

On being notified by phone that Orman, the hitherto-disabled host, would be home that night, Ossip trotted on short fat legs to his own suite, and there broke the news to the girl he had accosted at the downtown Western Union that she must bathe and then beat it.

What followed is too terrible almost for words. For Miriam, from progressive points of vantage, saw Ossip take a curious object from under his pillow, pull from it a pin of some kind, and, after the lady had stepped into the roomy Roman bath, toss in what proved to be a grenade, then run for his life.

The explosion shook the building, the mushroom cloud arose, and Ossip, still shadowed by Miriam who now was atremble with horror such as she never had experienced, encased the ghastly boiled bloated remains, completely unrecognizable, in a cellophane sack.

The temptation to exterminate Rosencrans then and there was almost too strong for Miriam, but she knew Homer would want her to control herself. So she went on borrowed horse to a strange outlying motel and, palpitating still from incredulous disgust, mixed with pity and indignation, waited for night to fall. She had had no orders, but felt that Homer, by now, if he knew she were alive, would have sent her some word, had he wished. Her best judgment prompted her to await developments *sub rosa* and half safe.

Back in main Las Vegas, Homer was suffering another attack of chagrin. He had invited everyone but Howard Scott Jordan and by no means wished to slight his somewhat difficult and misogynistic, for New England, so talented friend. Not even the Kid could seem to find him. So plans for the party continued apace.

As darkness fell, Homer and, unknown to him, Miriam, went separately and, so each thought, secretly, to Cottonwood Acres and set up a watch. The Widow O'Brien, oblivious to everything else, was preparing huge quantities of refreshments in the kitchen wing, away from the pool. The cowboys, in their bunkhouse at some distance, were rehearsing for the gala event in which they would participate.

Just as the moon rose, Homer, from the library, and Miriam, from a downstairs nook, saw Ossip emerge from the rhododendron patch dragging a hideously bulging cellophane sack, and dump the horrid contents into the pool. He then turned on the water full force, and as the pool filled he tossed another grenade and ran as fast as his short legs would carry him.

There was the pale green flash, the thud, the mushroom cloud, and when all had cleared, and it was safe to near the pool again, there, floating on the surface, was the twice-boiled corpse of the anonymous girl who had hoped to get money from home, utterly unrecognizable as anything that ever had been humanly shaped, although such remains could have resulted from overboiling of no other kind of animal. She, or It, was in no sense a legal *corpus delicti*.

"And there, but for the grace of God, float I," said Miriam, and could not repress a shudder or last longer without a very stiff drink.

She knew that Homer had observed Operation Swimming Pool and was not aware of former Operation Bath, or so she believed. Each fiber of her being longed for his strong and comforting arms, but she held herself aloof. Seldom had she had a chance for a truly surprise entrance, when the elucidation of a complicated crime was in progress. So she was resolved to make the most of it, for Homer's sake as much as for her own.

It may seem odd to the uninitiated, that in and around Las Vegas, atomic experiments can burst into explosions and mushroom into mists without disturbing either household, municipal, social or jolly criminal routine. The nearness of the U.S. Atomic testing grounds and the assiduity of our defense officers in developing secret weapons have accustomed Las Vegas to incidents, as I hope I have demonstrated already, which elsewhere might create a stir, bring forth huzzahs, or resounding raspberries, even riot squads. When such a city is wide open, and hitting on all cylinders of enjoyable vice, under license of law, anything, reader, can and does happen. So be prepared for anything, as you arrive.

I must add, to reassure all hands, that Homer fortified and equipped himself with complete films in color of Ossip's *tour de force*, so that at the proper time and place, the dastardly deed might, if it seemed best, be exposed, in private or in public.

We dissolve now to the final meeting, for which I have prepared a list of guests, etc., as follows:

Homer Evans
Kid Unamuno
Finke McGuire and Pilar Araquistain
Clifford Orman, Madeleine de Vere, Odette Montpanier
Maitre Jean-Pierre Sabin
Luke Sharkey (in chains)
Chauffeur Zach (in chains)
Hjalmar Jansen, painter
Tom Jackson, reporter
Mr. Talbot Forran from the Hollywood Strip
Gentleman Gene Delmont
Alkali Ike, a prospector
Parentheses Pete and his musical cowboys
Manny, Mo and Jack Dalton, of the Rosencrans Agency (on parole)
Sheriff Isaac Patrick Feeley, of Clarke County, Nevada
Sheriff Eugene Biscailuz of Los Angeles County, California

Chosen and qualified representatives, to the number of one for each organization, of the principal gangs owning and operating Las Vegas hotels or establishments.

The directors of the Las Vegas Chamber of Commerce.

An emissary from the Governor of Nevada, another from the State Supreme Court, another from the State cossacks, who are no worse in that state than anywhere else, and no better, either.

The above list covers the principals when the meeting, presided by Evans, was thrown open and he made the opening address, substantially as follows:

23
The Tangled Web Unwoven

"WHAT SEEMS, MY FRIENDS, a tangled web of skulduggery constituting what we call our 'Case' is best unified, perhaps, if I relate it from a personal angle, for my own interest in the related matters lends it a plausible pattern and welds it into a whole," Homer Evans began.

"I was working in my library, some weeks ago, trying to bring up to date the *Physiology of Taste* by the great Brillat-Savarin, when Kid Unamuno, who, today, I wish publicly to announce, did me the honor to accept a loose vice presidency in my informal group who seek truth, brought me a cablegram. It was from my old friend, Maitre Jean-Pierre Sabin, indicating that conditions prevailing or developing in Cannes, on the Azure Coast of France, perplexed or troubled him."

At the mention of the modest great chef's name, Homer urged him to rise and take a bow, for identification and purposes of emphasis, there being in the assembly men who, whatever else their gifts and accomplishments, would not know putty from *pâté de foie gras.*

"Naturally, I set aside my monograph, flew with my colleague and bodyguard, Miss Miriam Leonard, to those Mediterranean shores which cradled our civilization and maintain it today, under stress and misunderstandings. Vive la France!"

A scattering of cheers, although the house had not yet warmed up. In a gathering like that, where so many have a past, the audience response starts sluggishly.

"Before I had had a chance to contact Maitre Sabin to ascertain what bothered him, I was, in my absence, paid an illegal call by the chief Continental Op of the Rosencrans Detective Agency, Mr. Luke Sharkey, who pinched the copy of my cablegram already mentioned, was caught in the act but not denounced by Miss Leonard, and fled, but not far," continued Evans.

All eyes turned toward Luke, whose face grew as red as his unhealed behind and the swatted soles of both feet.

"Orders," muttered Luke, and, like the others, craned and swiveled their necks to spot Ossip Rosencrans. So Homer, always thoughtful of his guests, gave the word that Rosencrans be driven in, and prodded by two deputy sheriffs with drawn jack-knives eight inches long, Ossip made his appearance, a somewhat sorry sight. However, the Rosencrans Chief made an impressive effort to regain his dignity.

"I had my reasons for those orders," Ossip squeaked. "I wanted to provoke Miss Leonard to shoot this string-bean and get herself in quod."

Evans indulged in a good-natured shrug. "Roundabout methods, not strictly ethical," he observed. "But let those pass."

"Miss Leonard," Homer went on, "who is unavoidably absent from our midst (for a reason or reasons concerning which your guess, the least pretentious of this company, is as good as mine), having no chance to consult me, marked Luke for future reference by shooting off the tip of his crazy bone in Cannes' busy market place."

Rosencrans got back a little of his own by remarking, loudly: "'Methods, ethics,' the man says."

"I must be brief," continued Homer. "Maitre Sabin informed me that a certain American oil magnate, Mr. Clifford Orman, had been in the city of Cannes lately, in company of Mr. Howard Scott Jordan, a research chemist and former boy prodigy of Cambridge, Mass. It was then the master of gastronomy confided in me the item which marked this case as a weird and rare one, indeed. For Mr. Jordan, on tasting the frosting of a rum cake in Maitre Sabin's famous restaurant had detected the flavor of the evergreen 'pipsissewa.'"

The effect Homer had hoped to get by this announcement fell flat. The mugs and wheels frowned and moved uneasily, like fowl in a crate, the others with pretensions to learning or culture seemed as far in the fog, to the point that Gentleman Gene Delmont, next to Homer the most considerate gentleman extant, arose to a point of information.

"You, sir," Delmont said to the Chair, "know all, see all and say the damnedest things. What, pray, is pipsissewa?"

"Thanks for the question. It will make clear much of this elucidation," responded Evans. "Pipsissewa, friends, is an evergreen herb of the ericaceous genus Chimaphila, the leaves of which have tonic, diuretic and moderately astringent properties. Now do not chide me with introducing fantastic or unfamiliar elements into my explanations. For what numbers of American boys or girls, when young, and how many of them, on arriving at adult estate, have enjoyed a popular beverage called Hires Root Beer without the common curiosity to read the ingredients. Among them, those herbs, roots and savory preventers, quenchers and provokers of thirst, is 'pipsissewa.' Maitre Sabin, an expert on flavors, had the extract in his superbly stocked kitchen and dusted some of this magic powder into a batch of frosting, instead, we must admit, of tragacanth. As Joyce so aptly said, the artists' errors are the portals of discovery.

"Of what practical use are such trifling bits of food lore, or general information? You well may ask that, not being, for the most part, professional criminologists or advanced students of mankind. In this case let me come down to earth and illustrate. The fact that young Mr. Jordan, who also seems to be absent tonight, I regret, could taste 'pipsissewa' led me to the Hires Company, a former employer, and helped me unravel his whole amazing past, throw telling sidelights on his employment by Mr. Orman, define certain of his limitations, and give him status as a prime factor in this remarkable case. For Mr. Jordan, with taste so keen he could spot 'pipsissewa' over the pungency of martinique black rum in the frosting of a cake, made an abject exhibition of himself selecting wines and discriminating between them. What did that indicate?

That Jordan had special training enabling him to taste 'pipsissewa' and not much else, and suffered gaps in his unusual background which had kept him off gourmandization."

Homer saw his audience was getting restless. "Peace, folks. I'll get down to brass tacks. Sabin told me also that Clifford Orman, not through his employee, Jordan, but the agency of Luke Sharkey, a Rosencrans Continental Op, had offered the great chef $2,000 a week, or practically any figure, if he would quit Cannes at least six months and come here to Las Vegas.

"Now the secret of my moderate success in investigations, ladies and gentlemen, lies in my passion for simplicity and directness. What, I asked myself, would a smart business man who had amassed a huge fortune want with a champion taster of wines and food, if not to taste things for him. Since Clifford Orman—I'm sure Mr. Orman will not mind my saying so in public—while he is a wizard at finance and the collection of ravishing women about him, is a mere dunce or tomnoddy concerning edibles and fancy drink. What then would he pay high salary to great chef to taste?

"The question posed itself at the very start of this inquiry and I knew the answer within one-tenth of a second. At the risk of making my finish anticlimactical, I shall tell you all. No longer does modern enterprising man have to drill and delve at enormous risk and expense to establish points on ground surfaces beneath which oil gushers, if properly prepared, are sure to spout."

If the tone of the audience and the meeting had been blasé before, the mention of oil, or petroleum, electrified all hands, so that strong men trembled, blinked, scratched and gesticulated, while fair women counted beads of diamonds toward a cross of platinum. "Oil! How? Where? When?" was the roaring exclamation, in essence. It was only the chief wheels of Murder, Inc., the Syndicate, the Mafia, the Dusters, De Brinx, Maulers and their competitors and social equals who blanched and quivered like jelly with St. Vitus dance. To see those powerful enemies of the public and one another glance this way and that, shift their eyes, bang their fists, growl like jungle cats, and scream soundlessly, like birds behind soundproof plate glass, was enough to give the bravest pause.

Sabin, himself, was the most amazed in the hall. For, until that moment, he had had not the remotest idea what Orman had wanted of him.

"Let me deal first with stratagems and plots, and later summarize briefly the criminal considerations and overt acts," Homer suggested. "I'll begin with Orman's master plan which, in the public interest and that of Las Vegas, the city I have come to love, I shall logically expose to wreak its ruin. Now Mr. Orman and I have become friends, with mutual respect, and will remain so. His brain is vast enough to concoct other plans even more nefarious, if possible, than this one which crumbles tonight, as I let in the light."

Homer turned to the high gangster section. "You, gentlemen, who have invested so much of gold, blood, sweat, tears and credit in this wonderful community—and honor to you for it—having indulged in blackmail with mastery over periods of years, were to be fall guys, yourself."

The wheels of the powerful gangs could scarcely credit the testimony of their hairy ears, so neatly trimmed by the land's best barbers, often more than once each day. In fact, they laughed and their incredulous mirth, at first sinister, became comradely and human in the extreme. In advance they had forgiven the supreme chump who dared beard them in their own home precinct, known as blackmail, high shakedown and bold-barefaced racketage, or racketismo, for just plain American racket.

"Unbeknown to all real-estate owners, Mr. Orman had obtained earth samples from the surface of all large Las Vegas properties, and had assumed, because young Mr. Jordan had keen taste, that said taste was catholic and universally to be applied. As soon as Orman found that Jordan, as earth taster, could not tell oil top soil from uranium or guana, if we can brook a disgusting comparison, he decided to go to Europe, contact the champion tasters there, bring one back alive and kicking, and get evidence where oil was, or was not.

"Orman believed that not even gangland menace could hold off an oil stampede if the presence of petroleum in prodigious quantities was proved to underlie Las Vegas, especially the Strip."

"Tell us it isn't true," implored Bolo McGurk, for the gangster chiefs who stood to lose their pastimes.

"It is there, all right. I've tasted Orman's hidden samples, without his knowledge or consent, myself," Evans admitted. "But there is no trace of oil. Secrets about atomic defenses have leaked out sufficiently so that our public enemies today, with help from scientists of good will like myself, need fear no mass invasion. These miscreants and super-thugs have done better than they knew, have given us Las Vegas. They shall have it, intact, as long as the spirit of game and gamble lives in Americans."

The discomfiture of Orman was mollified by the general relief and wave of human fellowship which swept over the gathering.

"Now, for a counter plot, then we'll talk about incidental crime and punishment," resumed Homer.

"As all of you know, the Hollywood night spots have suffered cruelly from competition by Las Vegas and its Strip. Mr. Talbot Forran, as a desperate move, retained my protégé, Mr. Finke McGuire, to induce Maurice Chevalier, at $25,000 per week, to perform in Hollywood and help bring back filmland's night prestige. Forran, not in the best of health, has developed a dislike for and jealousy of our own Mr. Orman, and worried himself into a new set of ulcers in the mistaken belief that Orman, who was plotting the ruin of Las Vegas as a pleasure resort unless he was paid billions and billions of hush money by men most unaccustomed to being held up, was intending to boom and boost Las Vegas, at Hollywood's expense. Forran knows better now, and he realizes, also, that the world leadership of Las Vegas in the entertainment field has come to stay for many generations. Hollywood will thrive on the overflow, and royally. So let us end the futile inter-state and city strife."

The response indicated that all Homer's hearers were agreed and reconciled on this important point.

"The solution of the crimes has been so simple that I am almost ashamed to dwell on it as a criminologist. Only one man among all involved can be placed on the scene, or had opportunity most surely to be there, when Miss Leonard and I were shot at with intent to kill in Cannes, by daylight; when, in an attempt to shoot Miss Leonard in a crowd at the Cannes dock, an innocent bystander was manslaughtered, a working man, at that; when Sabin's assistant, Monsieur Luttenschlager was poisoned with drugged pipsissewa in an attempt to discourage Sabin from quitting Cannes for the nonce; when my chartered airplane, the *Peu de Souci*, was rigged with a time bomb in Cannes and burned later on the Canaries; when, here in Las Vegas, Mr. Orman and his chauffeur, Zach, were assaulted with attempt to kill with rattlesnake venom—need I go on. Unfortunately, as I have said, the culprit has made himself scarce, and cannot be produced tonight, if ever."

The sweet ringing voice of Miriam, entering with her rod in Howard Scott Jordan's back, thrilled the assembly.

"Oh, yes, Homer! He is herewith and *thoroughly* produced, and me, myself, for better or for worse—if you'll pardon the unfortunate phrase which I did not use with predatory or blackmailing intentions, Lord perish the thought!" Those were Miriam's words.

Thinking back on the case, those, like Finke, familiar with details from the start, began kicking themselves.

"Mr. Jordan," Homer explained to all and sundry, "a former boy prodigy at Harvard, is a psychological curiosity and cripple. He resented Mr. Orman's wealth, which a thinking man would not wish on his worst enemy. He was jealous of Sabin, who made him a monkey in matters of taste. He hated all women, and most men, and tonight feels surer than ever that this viperous animosity is sound. Now because Jordan killed, by malicious accident, a workman in France, I have arranged that he shall be turned over to the French authorities, in pursuance of a promise I made to the Commissaire of Police in Cannes. He will be shipped for life to Devil's Island, and, ladies and gentlemen, I am happy to express the opinion that there he has a sporting chance, since a man of his comparative youth and unexampled hatred and cunning may influence Devil's Island as much as that resort does him."

Homer then turned to Rosencrans, who tried to shrink smaller than he was.

"This specimen," Homer said, pointing an accusing finger, "has had the temerity to challenge me, in the realm of the mind and my calling, criminology. Merely in order to complicate a murder he planned of my Miriam, he took the life this day, by instantaneous boiling, of an unfortunate girl of Mary Magdalene's profession, as casually as one would step on a spider. I, my friends, would not knowingly perpetrate insecticide. We have much to learn from spiders, which the patient Bruce overlooked.

"I am turning Mr. Rosencrans over to the Clarke County sheriff, who already has guaranteed me that Ossip's license as a detective-bureau head will be suspended, for this heartless murder of a lady known as Lou, at least thirty days. More than that, to paraphrase the words of the late Mary Baker Eddy, 'we cannot ask.'"

"Why not?" demanded Miriam. "He wanted to boil me. I can testify that he did boil that sad girl. What kind of justice deals out a sentence of life on an island for manslaughter, and thirty days' suspension of a trade license for the foulest murder I've ever seen, first hand?"

"Ours not to reason why," Homer said, soothingly. "Western justice has always been, in substance, pure anarchy, and the natives like it that way. We must be democratic. We mustn't show zeal or the missionary spirit. In short, we must live and be glad."

About The Author
(From the 1956 Edition)

ELLIOT PAUL, author of *The Black and the Red* and twenty-seven other books, was born in Malden, Massachusetts, on February 11, 1891. His boyhood was spent in the bosom of his conservative New England family, but an unappeasable wanderlust carried him all over the world. He joined his older brother as a timekeeper and surveyor on an irrigation project in Idaho and Wyoming, and after several jobs in construction camps in the Northwest, he enlisted in the AEF. He decided to remain in France after the Armistice. Off and on he lived on the rue de la Huchette, that street so lovingly celebrated in *The Last Time I Saw Paris*, for eighteen years. With Eugene Jolas he founded *Transition*, the startling avant-garde magazine of the Parisian expatriates. In 1931 Elliot Paul went to live in Santa Eulalia, Ibizia, in the Balearic Islands. The story of an idyllic life wantonly destroyed was told in *The Life and Death of a Spanish Town*.

The outbreak of World War II brought the novelist back to New York, where he scored an immediate success with his first detective story, *The Mysterious Mickey Finn*. There followed eight accounts, including *The Black and the Red*, of the prodigious exploits of his debonair detective, Homer Evans.

Now living in California, Elliot Paul makes frequent incursions into the neighboring state of Nevada, to try his fortune in Las Vegas.

COACHWHIP PUBLICATIONS

COACHWHIPBOOKS.COM

The Mysterious Mickey Finn

Elliot Paul

The Mysterious Mickey Finn
ISBN 1-61646-293-0

COACHWHIP PUBLICATIONS

ALSO AVAILABLE

Hugger Mugger in the Louvre

Elliot Paul

Hugger Mugger in the Louvre
ISBN 1-61646-294-9

COACHWHIP PUBLICATIONS

COACHWHIPBOOKS.COM

Mayhem in B-Flat

Elliot Paul

Mayhem in B-Flat
ISBN 1-61646-295-7

COACHWHIP PUBLICATIONS
ALSO AVAILABLE

Fracas in the Foothills
Elliot Paul

Fracas in the Foothills
ISBN 1-61646-296-5

COACHWHIP PUBLICATIONS

COACHWHIPBOOKS.COM

I'll Hate Myself in the Morning

Murder on the Left Bank

Elliot Paul

Murder on the Left Bank
ISBN 1-61646-312-0

COACHWHIP PUBLICATIONS

ALSO AVAILABLE

The Black Gardenia
Elliot Paul

The Black Gardenia
ISBN 1-61646-313-9

COACHWHIP PUBLICATIONS

COACHWHIPBOOKS.COM

Waylaid in Boston

Elliot Paul

Waylaid in Boston
ISBN 1-61646-342-2

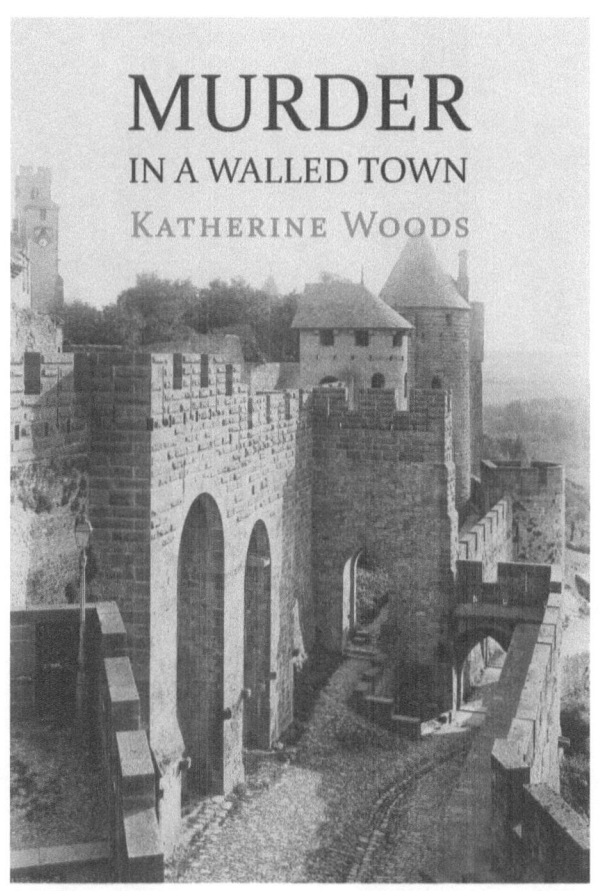